The Caliph's Heirs

Brothers at War: the Fall of Baghdad

Novels of Islamic History in Translation Series

Written by Jurji Zaidan and published by the Zaidan Foundation.
(in historical chronological order)

The Conquest of Andalusia
translated with an Afterword and Study Guide by Roger Allen

The Battle of Poitiers
Charles Martel and 'Abd al-Rahman
translated with a Study Guide by William Granara

The Caliph's Sister
Harun al-Rashid and the Fall of the Persians
translated by Issa J. Boullata with a Study Guide

The Caliph's Heirs
Brothers at War: The Fall of Baghdad
translated with an Afterword and Study Guide by Michael Cooperson

Saladin and the Assassins
translated by Paul Starkey with a Study Guide

The Caliph's Heirs
Brothers at War: the Fall of Baghdad

A historical novel in which al-Amin and al-Ma'mun quarrel after the
death of their father al-Rashid and the Persians rally around al-Ma'mun,
capture Baghdad, and kill al-Amin, restoring the caliphate to al-Ma'mun,
'their sister's son'; interspersed with an account of political machinations
by the Arabs and Persians, and descriptions of such manners, morals,
and customs as follow upon the telling of the tale

Jurji Zaidan

translated from the Arabic
with an Afterword and Study Guide by

Michael Cooperson

With an Introduction by the Zaidan Foundation

The Zaidan Foundation
For Enhancing Intercultural Understanding, Inc

7007 Longwood Drive
Bethesda, MD 20817
Email: george@zaidanfoundation.org
Website www.zaidanfoundation.org
Tel: (301) 469-8131
Fax: (301) 469-8132

Table of Contents

The Caliph's Heirs
Brothers at War: the Fall of Baghdad

Introduction

About the Novel[1]

This historical novel[2] is one of four novels by Jurji Zaidan whose story is set amid what the author imagined to be the military and political intrigues and conflicts between Persians and Arabs at the zenith of 'Abbasid imperial power during the eighth and ninth centuries. The Caliph al-Mansur had relied on the critical support of Abu Muslim from Khurasan, to found the 'Abbasid dynasty in 745 AD but had executed Abu Muslim after his accession.[3] But not long thereafter the Barmakid family was to assume a position of unparalleled influence as Yahia the Barmaki was instrumental in helping Harun al-Rashid become Caliph. His son, Ja'far, was to become the Caliph's vizier. But Harun executed Ja'far in 803 AD and within a day of Ja'far's death, he ordered the imprisonment of his father, brother and all his children and removed all other Barmakids from any authority or influence in the affairs of state.

The present novel, *The Caliph's Heirs—Brothers at War: the Fall of Baghdad*, opens very shortly before Harun al-Rashid's death in 809 AD following the recounting of the events leading to Ja'far's execution and the fall of the Barmakids in the previous novel, *The Caliph's Sister—Harun al-Rashid and the Fall of the Persians*[4]. The historical context is the war of succession

---

1 I am grateful to Michael Cooperson for his comments on this Introduction.

2 First published in 1907 in *Arabic as Al-Amin wa'l-Ma'mun.*

3 These events provide the background for Jurji Zaidan's novel, *Abu Muslim al-Khurasani,* which was first published in Arabic in 1905 and immediately precedes *The Caliph's Sister.* It has not been translated into English.

4 First published in Arabic in 1906 as *Al-'Abbasa ukht al-Rashid.*

between al-Rashid's two sons—al-Amin and al-Ma'mun. Zubayda, Harun's favorite Hashemite wife was the mother of al-Amin. Al-Ma'mun, the son of a Persian slave girl and al-Amin's rival, had been raised by Ja'far. Harun admired al-Ma'mun's gifts and at the prodding of his Persian advisors[5] and to Zubayda's dismay decreed that his son al-Amin would succeed him first but that his heir apparent would be al-Ma'mun. Both sons swore to this agreement which was hung from the ceiling of the Ka'aba. After Ja'far's execution and their demise, the Persians lay low, ever so vigilant to exploit any opportunity that might arise for them to reassert themselves and recapture their authority and return to run the affairs of state and more. Al-Fadl Ibn Sahl, a very ambitious Persian who was to become al-Ma'mun's vizier, had been assigned by Ja'far to raise al-Ma'mun. But after al-Rashid's death, al-Amin made his own sons his heirs and removed al-Ma'mun from the succession reneging on what he had sworn to his father. The Persians saw in this turn of events an opportunity to support al-Ma'mun and work towards removing al-Amin.

This novel weaves parallel love stories, political intrigue and machinations, nobility and treachery, spies and counterspies all against the backdrop of the historical events surrounding the war between al-Amin and al-Ma'mun. Behzad is a famous doctor with an agenda all his own who lives outside Baghdad and whose comings and goings are not easily traceable. He and Maymuna are both members of well-known Persian families persecuted by earlier 'Abbasid caliphs and are deeply in love; but the son of al-Amin's Hashemite vizier is also enamored with Maymuna and wants to marry her. Behzad's and Maymuna's love unfolds as part of the narrative of political intrigue that shows how the Persians helped al-Ma'mun, with inferior forces, to prevail and conquer Baghdad. A parallel love story develops between Buran, the niece of al-Ma'mun's Persian vizier, and Salman, a "servant" of Behzad; but Buran's family has promised to marry her to no less than the Caliph al-Ma'mun himself. How do all these lovers make out? Who wins and who perishes? The fast-paced action and suspense leave us guessing to the very end. At the nexus of all these relationships is al-Amin's mysterious Chief Astrologer, whose true identity and loyalties remain unknown to al-Amin and his court. He not only presumes to divine the future

5 The label 'Persian,' and the casting of this conflict in ethnic terms, was characteristic of historians in the early twentieth century; this is how Jurji Zaidan reconstructed and depicted the historical events in the novel. But subsequent research qualified and questioned in several important respects this version of events as detailed in Michael Cooperson's Afterword at the end of the novel.

but also wants to shape it. And he sets out to influence the outcome of all these love affairs; to shape the battle between the two brothers; and then to influence al-Ma'mun's succession.

By the end of the ninth century the 'Abbasids were unable to exercise real religious or political authority. The territories they controlled fell apart, as independent states arose in regions previously under 'Abbasid rule, although they were always honored to the end of the 'Abbasid caliphate as symbols of the unity of Sunni Islam. The war between al-Amin and al-Ma'mun was a turning point in this respect and led inexorably to the decline of 'Abbasid control and the disintegration of the empire. After al-Ma'mun, temporal authority became fragmented and devolved to various regions including Khurasan, Syria, Egypt, the Maghreb, etc.[6] who were all able to exercise directly their own authority in independent states while paying lip service to the sovereignty of the caliph.

Jurji Zaidan—The Historical Novelist

Jurji Zaidan (1861–1914) was a prolific writer who at the dawn of the twentieth century sought to inform and educate his Arab contemporaries about the modern world and the heritage of the Arabs. He is considered one of the most prominent intellectual leaders who laid the foundation for a pan-Arab secular national identity. Pioneering new forms of literature and style in Arabic, he founded in 1892 one of the first—and to this day most successful—monthly journals, *al-Hilal* a magazine that is still popular today in its 120th year. The *Dar al-Hilal* publishing house in Cairo is one of the largest in the Arab world. It is a fitting tribute to Zaidan's legacy that new studies reassessing his contributions, and translations of many of his novels—this one among them—are being published one hundred years after his death.

Zaidan was one of the pioneers in the composition of historical novels within the modern Arabic literary tradition and in their serialization in magazines. New editions of the entire series of the novels are still

---

6 *The Bride of Ferghana*, the last of Jurji Zaidan's novels set in the 'Abbasid period takes place mainly in non-Arab countries of Central Asia. Ferghana is now the capital of a Province in eastern Uzbekistan, at the southern edge of the Ferghana Valley in southern Central Asia, cutting across the borders of Kyrgyzstan, Tajikistan, and Uzbekistan. These countries lie outside or at the frontiers of the 'Abbasid Empire. When the empire started to decline, the eighth 'Abbasid Caliph (al M'utasim) had to depend on Turks, Circassian, Tajiks and other Central Asian mercenaries to man his armies to defend the eastern part of his Empire, centered in Baghdad, while the western part broke away into autonomous states.

being published almost every decade and widely distributed throughout the Arab world – a testament to their lasting popularity. Zaidan's novels were not just for entertainment; national education was his primary goal. The twenty two historical novels he wrote cover an extensive period of Arab history, from the rise of Islam in the seventh century until the decline of the Ottoman Empire in the nineteenth. The stories depicted in these novels are grounded in the major historical events of various epochs. The particular manners, lifestyles, beliefs and social mores of those periods, as well as political events, provided the context into which Zaidan weaved adventure and romance, deception and excitement. They were therefore as much "historical" as "novels" reminiscent of the historical novels of Alexandre Dumas in France and Sir Walter Scott in Britain, though Jurji Zaidan's novels more closely reflect actual historical events and developments as understood by historians of his time.

Over the last hundred years, Zaidan's historical novels have been translated into many languages; every novel has been translated at least once; many into four or more languages. To our knowledge there are about one hundred translations of individual novels in more than ten different languages—most in Persian, Turkish/Ottoman, Javanese, Uighur (in China), Azeri, and Urdu—but several also in French, Spanish, German and Russian. What is noticeable, however, is that not a single one has been translated into English until the present time.

The Zaidan Foundation has so far commissioned the translation into English of five of Jurji Zaidan's historical novels and more are being planned. The present novel, *The Caliph's Heirs* was first published in 1907. Since then there have been five translations of this novel, all in Persian. In addition to a second novel (*The Caliph's Sister*) also set in the period immediately preceding the historical events of this novel, the Foundation has commissioned the translation of two novels set in Spain—*The Conquest of Andalusia* (*Fath-al Andalus*, 1903) as well as *The Battle of Poitiers* (*Sharl wa 'Abd al-Rahman*, 1904). The fifth novel, *Saladin and the Assassins* (*Salah ad-Din al-Ayyubi*, 1913) takes place at the time of the Crusades.

The Zaidan Foundation[7].

The Zaidan Foundation, Inc was established in 2009. Its mission is to enhance understanding between cultures. To this end the Foundation's

---

7 More information about the Zaidan Foundation and its activities can be found on the Foundation's website at www.zaidanfoundation.org.

principal objective is the international dissemination of the secular and progressive view of the Arab and Islamic heritage. Its first program is the study and translation of the works of Jurji Zaidan. Our audience is the broader English speaking world: the United States, England and Canada to be sure, but also English-speaking Muslim populations with little or no knowledge of Arabic such as in Bangladesh, India and Pakistan. To achieve its objectives, the Foundation supports directly or through educational or other institutions, the translation of historical, literary and other works, research, scholarships, conferences, seminars, student exchanges, documentaries, films and other activities.

Acknowledgements and Thanks

The Zaidan Foundation was fortunate to have Professor Michael Cooperson undertake the translation of this novel. He is professor of Arabic language and literature, Near Eastern Languages and Culture at the University of California, Los Angeles and a noted scholar and specialist of the cultural history of the early 'Abbasid period. Professor Cooperson is a graduate of Harvard University and of the Center for Arabic Study Abroad (CASA) at the American University in Cairo. His publications include *Classical Arabic Biography* (2000) and *Al Ma'mun* (2005). He has translated Abdelfattah Kilito's *L'Auteur et ses Doubles* (*The Author and His Doubles*, 2001) and Khairy Shalaby's *Rihalat al-Turshagi al-Halwagi* (*The Time Travels of the Man Who Sold Pickles and Sweets*, 2010). He is co-author, with the RRAALL group, of *Interpreting the Self: Autobiography in the Arabic literary tradition* (2001); and co-editor, with Shawkat Toorawa, of *The Dictionary of Literary Biography: Arabic Literary Culture, 500-915* (2005).

Many people have generously contributed their time and energy to the Zaidan Foundation, helping to craft our mission and goals, designing and advising on the implementation of our programs and reviewing studies and translations. Foremost among these are Ambassador Hussein A. Hassouna, ambassador of the Arab League to the United States, Ambassador Clovis F. Maksoud, Professor of International Relations and director of the Center of the Global South at American University, as well as Edmond Asfour and Bassem Abdallah – all members of the Foundation's Advisory Council. Professor Thomas Philipp was instrumental in helping launch the Jurji Zaidan project following our fortuitous meeting after several decades. Last but not least my greatest debt is to my wife Hada Zaidan and our son George S. Zaidan for their support of all aspects of this project. The original idea of the Jurji Zaidan program came from Hada who had more than a marital interest in this project as her grandfather, Jabr Dumit, was one of Jurji Zaidan's closest friends. In addition to their general and unstinting support, both she and George Jr helped design the program and made detailed reviews and many suggestions on the products sponsored by the Foundation.

George C Zaidan
President
The Zaidan Foundation

Washington DC
March 2012

Dramatis Personae [*]

AL-AMIN[8]   son to the Caliph al-Rashid
AL-MA'MUN[9]   son to the Caliph al-Rashid
IBN AL-RABI[10]   vizier to al-Amin
IBN AL-FADL[11]   son of al-Amin's vizier
IBN SAHL[12]   vizier to al-Ma'mun
ZUBAYDA[13]   wife to al-Rashid
ZAYNAB (Umm Habiba)[14] daughter to al-Ma'mun
DANANIR[15]   nurse to Zaynab
'ABBADA (Umm Ja'far)[16] mother to Ja'far of the Barmakid family

* Footnotes in this and the following section (numbers 8 to 30) are those of the translator

---

8 Al-Amin: Muhammad al-Amin, sixth 'Abbasid caliph (r. 809-813 AD).

9 Al-Ma'mun: Abd Allah al-Ma'mun, seventh 'Abbasid caliph (d. 813-833 AD).

10 Ibn al-Rabi: a historical figure (d. between 822 and 824 AD). He was vizier (chief administrator and advisor) to the fifth caliph, Harun al-Rashid (r. 786-809 AD), and his successor al-Amin. His full name is al-Fadl ibn al-Rabi', with the stress on the second syllable of al-Rabi'. Zaidan usually refers to him as al-Fadl, but he is here called Ibn al-Rabi to distinguish him from al-Fadl ibn Sahl, vizier to al-Ma'mun; and al-Fadl ibn Yahya, another vizier who is mentioned in the novel.

11 Ibn al-Fadl: in the novel, the son of Ibn al-Rabi, but apparently not based on any real historical figure. His name does not appear in the original list of characters.

12 Ibn Sahl: a historical figure (d. 818 AD). He was advisor to al-Ma'mun (see above) and held the title of 'Dual Vizier' signaling his authority in civil and military matters alike. His full name is al-Fadl ibn Sahl. Zaidan usually refers to him as al-Fadl, but he is here called Ibn Sahl to distinguish him from other people named al-Fadl (see the note on Ibn al-Rabi above). His brother al-Hasan ibn Sahl also served under al-Ma'mun; he appears briefly in the novel and is called al-Hasan in the translation.

13 Zubayda: a historical figure (d. 831 or 832 AD). She was the most famous wife of the 'Abbasid caliph Harun al-Rashid (r. 786-809 AD). Zaidan, following the Arabic chronicles, often calls her Umm Ja'far, 'mother of Ja'far,' an honorific title apparently based on the name of her father Ja'far, son of the caliph al-Mansur. She is here called Zubayda to distinguish her from 'Abbada, Ja'far's biological mother, on whom see below.

14 Zaynab: the daughter of al-Ma'mun (see above). A daughter of this name is mentioned in the Arabic chronicles, though her adventures in the novel are the invention of the author.

15 Dananir: literally 'silver coins,' the sort of name typically given to slaves. Apparently an invented character, though there was (as the novel notes) a famous singer by this name.

16 'Abbada: a historical figure. She was the mother of Ja'far the Barmaki, the vizier executed by Harun al-Rashid in 803 AD. Also called Umm Ja'far ('mother of Ja'far') in the novel.

Dramatis Personae [continued]

MAYMUNA[17]   daughter to Ja'far of the Barmakid family
BEHZAD[18]   grandson to Abu Muslim of Khurasan
SALMAN[19]   servant to Behzad
TAHIR IBN AL-HUSAYN[20] general to al-Ma'mun

---

17 Maymuna: an invented character. One famous woman of the early 'Abbasid period did claim to be the daughter of Ja'far the Barmaki, but she was a singer and her name was 'Arib.

18 Behzad: an invented character. He is described as the grandson of a real figure, Abu Muslim, who led the uprising that overthrew the Umayyad dynasty and brought the 'Abbasids to power in 750 AD.

19 Salman: an invented figure. He does not appear in the original list of characters. This is a surprising omission given his important role in the story.

20 Tahir ibn al-Husayn: a historical figure, d. 822 AD. As al-Ma'mun's field commander, he played a critical role in the overthrow of al-Amin. Even so, he appears only incidentally in the novel.

Sources[21]

Works used by the author as a basis for the events depicted in the novel:

The History of Islamic Civilization, by Jurji Zaidan[22]

The Matchless Necklace[23]

Ibn al-Athir's *History*[24]

Abul-Fida[25]

Tales of the Kings[26]

Yaqut's *Dictionary*[27]

Ya'qubi's *Book of Countries*[28]

Abul-Faraj's *Book of Songs*[29]

Mas'udi's *History*[30]

---

21 Zaidan lists his sources as translated here: that is, in abbreviated form. I have added brief identifications in the notes. Further information on works and authors may be found in the *Encyclopaedia of Islam, Second Edition*, ed. P. Bearman et al, and *Encyclopaedia of Islam, Three*, ed. G. Krämer et al. (both online at http://www.brillonline.nl).

22 This is Zaidan's pioneering five-volume history, published in Cairo between 1901 and 1906.

23 An anthology of historical and literary anecdotes compiled by the Andalusian Ibn 'Abd Rabbih (d. 940 AD).

24 A chronicle of events from the creation of the earth down to 1230-31 AD, by Izz al-Din Ibn al-Athir of Mosul (d. 1233 AD).

25 A prince of the Ayyubid dynasty of Syria and the author of *al-Mukhtasr fi akhbar al-bashar* ("A short history of mankind"). Translated into Latin in 1754, this work long served as a major source for European accounts of Islamic history. Extracts, not including the parts Zaidan uses here, have been translated into French and English.

26 Probably *Khulasat al-dhahab al-masbuk fi siyar al-muluk*, an abridgement by Abd al-Rahman al-Irbili (d. 1317) of a historical work by the Baghdad preacher, Hadith-scholar, and biographer Ibn al-Jawzi (d. 1201 AD). The abridgement was published in Beirut in 1885.

27 A biographical dictionary of literary men, by Yáqút al-Rumi (d. 1229 AD). It has been translated into English by D. S. Margoliouth as *The Irshád al-aríb ma'rifat al-adíb; or, Dictionary of learned men of Yáqút* (London, 1923-31).

28 A work of geography by al-Ya'qubi (d. after 905 AD?). It has been translated into French by Gaston Wiet as *Les pays* (Cairo, 1937).

29 An enormous work on poets, singers, and musicians, compiled by Abu al-Faraj al-Isfahani (d. 972 or 973 AD?).

30 A supplement, by the traveler and chronicler al-Mas'udi (d. 956 AD), to his now-lost works of geography and universal history. The whole work is available in French as *Les prairies d'or*, tr. by Barbier de Menard et Pavet de Courteille, revised by Charles Pellat (Paris, 1962-1971).The section on the 'Abbasids is available in English as *The Meadows of Gold: The 'Abbasids*, tr. Paul Lunde and Caroline Stone (London, 1989).

Chapter 1

At Simon's Tavern

In 145 AH (762 AD), the Caliph al-Mansur built the Round City to house his capital, his troops, and his officials. In the center he built a palace called the Palace of Gold and beside it a mosque known as the Mosque of Al-Mansur. The remaining space was given over to state offices and accommodations for his retainers. Around the city the caliph built a triple wall with four gates, each named for the region it faced. To the northeast was Khurasan Gate; to the northwest, Syria Gate; to the southeast, Basra Gate; and to the southwest, Kufa Gate. The land around the capital he divided into allotments for his men, who built homes for themselves and gave their names to the districts where they settled. New neighborhoods, of which the most famous were Harbiyya to the north and Karkh to the south, soon grew up around the capital. On the east bank of the Tigris new buildings rose as well, and quarters such as Rusafa, Shammasiyya, and Mukharrim were born.

Outside Khurasan Gate the caliph built a palace called Eternity. Between Eternity and the gate was a great square, from which the road to Khurasan veered towards the northeast. After crossing the Tigris at the Middle Bridge, it turned north and then east along the border between Rusafa and Mukharrim. These were districts full of mansions, gardens, and canals branching away from the Tigris in all directions. One of these canals—the one named for Umm Ja'far—flowed eastward through Rusafa and Shammasiyya. Along the banks beyond Rusafa were orchards thick with trees and plantings, interspersed with the occasional building.

In one of the orchards that lay between the Khurasan Road and the canal, an Aramean Christian wineseller from the fertile plain of Iraq had set up an inn for travelers on their way to Baghdad. From a house along the road, he sold wines and served food to locals and out-of-towners alike.

Distant from the city but located along a main road, the wine-shop beckoned those in search of rest and refreshment. It also attracted members of the lower orders who liked their wine cheap and plentiful, as well as some upper-class personages who, fearful of scandal, preferred to drink in a place where they were unlikely to be recognized.

The owner of this establishment was a man of some sixty years of age. A lifetime of toil and trouble had softened his heart to the point that he seemed to radiate kindness and good will. He had seen the reigns of three caliphs—al-Mahdi, al-Hadi, and al-Rashid—and witnessed his share of horrors, most recently the fall of the Barmakid family six years earlier. For three of those years, he had seen the corpse of Ja'far displayed on the Baghdad Bridge.

Forced to spend their time among drinkers and revelers and to accommodate themselves to the vagaries of their clientele, tavern keepers acquire a mildness of disposition that allows them to shrug off insult and abuse as the price of doing business. They are gentle, long-suffering men well acquainted with human foibles and careful not to reveal the secrets that come to light when men are in their cups. For this reason, their trade was monopolized by the 'protected peoples', the abased and impoverished Jews or the native Aramean Christians—not to mention the fact that Muslims could not trade in a commodity forbidden to them.[31]

The Aramean's tavern consisted of a single room of the building. The floor was strewn with reed mats and cushions of burlap stuffed with straw. Along the walls were alcoves stocked with casks of wine made from grapes, dates, apples, and other fruits. Above the alcoves were shelves lined with bottles, carafes, and cups of glass or wood used to measure out wine in pints, half-pints, and gills. Hanging at the back of the room were Persian and Arab lutes and a tambourine, placed there to encourage patrons to enjoy themselves. Many tavern keepers could sing and play some or all of these instruments, though in Baghdad, one was more likely to drink to airs sung by attractive women with melodious voices.

---

31 In the early caliphate, Jews, Christians, and (without Qur'anic support, and less consistently) Zoroastrians lived under the 'protection' (*dhimmah*) of the Muslims. This meant that they were allowed to practice their respective religions, though they were subject to a special tax and to various other penalties and restrictions. *Translator's Note*

Chapter 2

The Ruffian and the Soldier

One day in 193 AH (809 AD), the tavern, being some distance from the city, had seen no customers. The tavern keeper made most of his profits from people traveling along the road.

He naturally preferred out-of-towners: they were unfamiliar with how much things cost and unsure of how to bargain, and he could overcharge them, asking five dirhams for a pint of date wine worth only two.[32] As the day was coming to an end and no customers were in sight, he lit a fire in a corner of the orchard to grill a fish he had prepared for his dinner. Sitting up straight, rolling up his caftan, and tucking the ends into his *zunnar*,[33] he blew on the coals, sending up a cloud of smoke that rose to his face, curled through his beard, and settled on his turban. Then he heard a voice calling him from the tavern door: "Master Simon!" Rushing over in anticipation, he saw a Ruffian—probably an idler who lived by vice and plunder, of the sort then common in Baghdad—with a companion. Seeing the Ruffian, Simon backed away and appealed silently to God. But knowing that if he did not play along he might bring some misfortune on himself, and accustomed to feigning cordiality in such situations, he gathered his courage and went forward to receive them as cheerfully as he could.

The Ruffian was wearing a helmet made of palm fronds and a jacket of tanned leather decorated with colored paint. His arms were bare. Over his right shoulder he had slung a bag full of rubble that rested on his left hip. He wore knee breeches of rough burlap. Dangling from his elbow was a slingshot, the weapon of his kind. He was barelegged and shoeless. In one

---

32 A dirham was a common silver coin, in this period ideally weighing 2.97 grams or 0.104 ounces. *Translator's Note*

33 A caftan is a long, full-sleeved cloak of cotton or silk, buttoned down the front. The *zunnar* was a characteristic waist-band worn by the 'protected peoples.' *Translator's Note*

hand he carried a heavy stick and in the other a half-eaten loaf of bread, which he was still chewing on as he called on Simon to give them something to drink.

With a word of welcome, the tavern keeper poured date wine into a pint glass and handed it over. Then he looked at the other man, who wore the clothes of a soldier—a tunic with the slogan of the ruling dynasty painted on the back:

God shall protect you against them; He is the All-Hearing and
All-Knowing

On his head was a tall cap made of cloth stretched over a wooden frame. His sword hung from a belt worn over a black coat with long sleeves. The sight of him reassured the tavern keeper: once they received their pay, soldiers paid for what they ordered. He was motioning for a pint, and Simon hastened to comply. The soldier drank his wine standing up, then belched and began walking with a swaggering gait. The Ruffian, meanwhile, took his glass, raised it to his lips, and said, "Bless you, Master Simon! When I become a captain or a major, I'll take you into my service!"

Chuckling, the soldier came forward and put a hand on Simon's shoulder. Speaking with the Persian accent that betrayed his descent from the Ferghani fighters brought to Iraq by the Caliph al-Mansur, he said: "I promise you: soon enough, when this regime is overthrown and we get what's coming to us, I'll pay you for these drinks and more besides. I think I owe you for my last visit, too. But there's nothing I can do about it now, so you'll have to wait a little longer."

"You're crying poverty?" exclaimed the Ruffian. "You lot get paid, don't you?"

"We do, my friend," said the soldier. "But we don't make enough to satisfy our wives and children. The only way a soldier can make a living is by taking spoils in battle, or else..."

As if suddenly realizing that someone might overhear him, he dropped his voice to a whisper. But the Ruffian finished the thought for him: "Or else, when something happens at the palace and a dynasty is overthrown. Then you collect your pay many times over, not to mention a bonus for your oath of allegiance. Don't worry: you'll be getting that bonus any day now!"

Hoping to forestall another scandalous outburst, the soldier put his hand over the Ruffian's mouth. But Simon, though he had been listening to their little argument, was interested in only one thing: the prospect of being paid. Seeing them shush each other as they approached the door, he stepped forward and invited them in, motioning toward the mats on the floor.

As soon as he and the soldier had entered the room, the Ruffian reached for the Persian lute hanging on the wall and took it down. He handed it to Simon and took a seat. "I hear you're a good singer and lute player," he said, "all because you're related to Barsoma the lutenist. So play for us!"

Simon took the instrument and began tuning it. "I wish I were related to Barsoma," he mumbled. "He's a favorite of our master, the Commander of the Faithful, and collects a salary, and gifts besides."

"If you were good at playing the flute," said the soldier, "you'd be as well-off as Barsoma, or Ibrahim of Mosul and that lot. But be grateful to God that you're not: being close to the court can be life-threatening. No one was more favored than the Barmakid family, and you know what happened to *them*."

"You talk like a philosopher or an ascetic," interjected the Ruffian. "Put me in the Palace of Eternity and let me sing or play or recite poetry for the caliph, and I won't care what happens to me after that! Or put me in the army, at least, where they pay you for doing nothing. And if you do fight, you come back with spoils and plunder and beautiful women captives..."

"That's if you make it back alive," the soldier retorted.

"So why," said the Ruffian, finishing his thought, "didn't you join the caliph when he left to fight Rafi' ibn Layth in Samarkand a few months ago? Didn't you think he was going to win?"

"Only God knows what the future holds for us," answered the soldier. "We don't choose where we're sent; the commanders do that for us. Not to mention that al-Rashid was ill when he set out and left al-Amin to rule in his place. You know what al-Amin's like: he's an easygoing young man who doesn't intimidate people the way his father does. The situation seems to be working out well for you, too. Your chief, al-Hasan Harch, is so close to the court he might as well be a minister of state."

"So it seems," said the Ruffian. "But we won't get everything we're hoping for unless..." He glanced around and lowered his voice. "Unless al-Amin becomes caliph. If that happens, you'll envy us Ruffians the way we envy you soldiers now." Turning suddenly toward the orchard, he cried: "I smell fish cooking!"

During this conversation the tavern keeper had been absorbed in tuning the lute. Night had fallen and the glow of the fire was clearly visible, with smoke rising into the air. Suddenly he dropped the lute. "I left the fish on the fire!" he exclaimed. Finding that he needed some light, he made his way over to a clay lamp that stood on a stand attached to the wall. After adjusting the wick with his forefinger, he produced flint, steel, and a wad of cotton and set about lighting the lamp. First he ignited the cotton by placing it beside the flint and striking the flint with the steel. Then he put a stick tipped with sulfur near the end of the burning cloth. When the sulfur blazed up, the stick caught the flame. He touched the flame to the wick and the lamp began to glow.

While Simon busied himself with the lamp, the Ruffian seized his chance. Hurrying over to the fire, he snatched up the fish with his bare hands, not caring whether he burned himself. Then he rushed back and put the fish down on a flat loaf that lay before the soldier. "Bring us two cups of Qatrabbul!" he shouted to Simon.[34]

"I don't have any Qatrabbul," said the tavern keeper, "but I'll give you some date wine with grape syrup and honey."

Still playing the gracious host, he poured his guests a strong drink, praying all the while that they would leave him in peace, but they continued laughing heedlessly, and he forced himself to join in their carousal.

---

34 Qatrabbul was a region outside Baghdad famous for its fine vintages. *Translator's Note*

Chapter 3

Malfan Sa'dun and Harch

Amid the revelry, they suddenly heard a man calling in the road outside, "Fresh fish! Two pounds for a dirham from Bitar Hayyan!" Such was the cry of the fishmongers in that day and age. The Ruffian leapt to his feet. "Master Simon!" he cried, "here's a chance to pay you back!" Taking a chunk of rubble from his bag, he put it into his slingshot and went outside, telling Simon to come along and pick up the fish that would soon be on the ground.

Seeing that the Ruffian planned to use the slingshot against the un-lucky fishmonger, Simon, moved by concern for the fellow, laid his hand on the Ruffian's arm to stop him from shooting. Then he took a closer look at the fishmonger, who was almost invisible in the darkness. He was a poor man, bare armed and bare legged, wearing only a ragged garment and a turban, on top of which was a straw pallet piled with fish.

"Let me pay for your fish with two of those," said the Ruffian, pulling free.

"I'm afraid you'll kill him," said Simon. "I don't need any more fish."

"Don't worry," laughed the Ruffian. "I'll hit his catch without touching him or his pallet. Watch!"

So saying, he let fly. The piece of rubble struck the top of the pile and some of the fish fell to the ground. The fishmonger walked on, having noticed nothing: such was the skill of the Ruffians with their slingshots. The fishmonger was carrying a loaf of bread, too, and the Ruffian offered to knock it free as well. This time the victim overheard him and turned around. When he spotted the Ruffian, he threw the loaf to the ground in a panic. "Here's the bread," he cried, running off. "Take it and leave me alone!"

Laughing, the Ruffian rushed back with the loaf and two fish and handed them to Simon. Marveling at the man's skill, Simon went inside to cook the fish, imploring God to deliver him from his predicament.

God Almighty must have heard his plea. A moment later, Simon heard the sound of hoofbeats and the jingling of a bridle as a rider approached the garden gate. The drinkers suddenly ceased making a racket and a welcome silence fell. Simon, his eyes smarting, turned toward the gate. Through the smoke he saw a tall, slightly stooped man who carried himself with dignified authority. He wore a large black turban, a honey-colored robe, and a long cloak clinched with a sash, in the manner of the protected non-Muslims at that time. Tucked into his sash was a silver pen-case. His face was handsome but so thin that the cheekbones stood out and seemed to be stretching his skin tightly over his bones. His black eyes sparkled with intelligence. His nose was large and slightly hooked, his sideburns thick, and his beard dense, long, and streaked with white strands. He came through the gate holding his staff with his right hand and clutching something to his side with his left.

Simon realized that the visitor was a Sabean—a high official perhaps, or a scholar—but could not guess what he wanted, as persons of that class did not patronize taverns.[35] The Ruffian and the soldier scuttled out of his way. Simon came forward and bowed, as if to ask what he wanted.

"This is Master Simon's establishment, I presume?" asked the man in a quiet, rasping voice.

Pleased to find himself well known to prominent members of society, Simon replied that it was.

"Is there a comfortable place to sit in the garden?"

"Yes, my lord," said Simon. "Come in!"

He hurried toward the garden and the man followed, saying, "If Harch, the chief of the Ruffians, should ask you where Malfan Sa'dun is tonight," he said, "tell him I'm waiting for him here." 'Malfan' was a title for Sabean scholars, corresponding to "doctor" in our day.[36]

---

35 The Sabeans were members of a Syriac-speaking religious community from the region of Harran in what is now southeastern Turkey. Reportedly, they studied Greek philosophy and worshiped the ancient astral gods. One Sabean of this period, Thabit b. Qurra (d. 901), was a prolific translator of Greek scientific texts and a renowned mathematician and astronomer. *Translator's Note*

36 *Malfan* is a Syriac word meaning 'teacher.' *Translator's Note*

The Ruffian and the soldier had risen to their feet to look at the new-comer. Hearing him mention Harch, the Ruffian remembered with a start that he had noticed the two together more than once. Deciding that it would be wise of him to clear off before his chief arrived, the Ruffian turned and went out. The soldier, on the other hand, wanted to stay and see what this meeting, the likes of which rarely took place outside the city, might be about. Choosing a spot along the wall that enclosed the garden, he sat down on a mat and cushion with his sword in his lap.

For his part, the tavern keeper was delighted by the arrival of the Sabean and the expected arrival of Harch. If they ate dinner, or drank, they might spend enough to make up for his losses that evening. He made haste to lead Sa'dun into the garden. The Sabean was so tall that he had to stoop for fear that his turban would get entangled in the branches overhead. They reached a little platform, covered with a mat and two cushions, that stood in the shelter of a large tree overlooking the Umm Ja'far canal. Simon in-vited the visitor to sit and then hurried back to the tavern for the lamp. Placing it on the stump of a nearby tree he had cut down a few days earlier, he asked his guest if he wanted anything to eat or drink. "No," said Sa'dun, leaning back on one of the cushions. Laying his staff to one side, he reached into his sleeve, pulled out a little pouch, and set it down in front of him. So Simon left him there running his fingers through his beard and listening to the sound of a waterwheel turning in a nearby orchard.

Returning to the tavern, Simon found another lamp and lit it. Seeing the soldier sitting alone, he asked him what had happened to the Ruffian.

"He was afraid to see his chief so he ran away," said the soldier. "So what do you make of the Sabean? With him here, you might earn back what you've lost on us."

"God willing!" replied Simon.

"Something big must be happening. Why else would that Sabean be meeting with Harch here?"

"I hope it *is* something big," said Simon. "The Sabeans know magic and astrology, and there's no keeping a secret from them. Maybe this is the Sabean who helps Harch uncover all those secrets he's so famous for knowing."

The soldier nodded and fell silent, suddenly fearful that Sa'dun would use his magic to hear what he had been saying and harm him in some way.

Meanwhile the tavern keeper had busied himself with cleaning up the remains of food and drink on the ground and preparing for the arrival of Harch.

Moments later, they heard the Sabean's horse, which was tethered by the side of the road under the eye of a servant boy, neighing loudly. From a distance came an answering neigh. The tavern keeper was delighted: persons of rank were evidently converging on his establishment. The neighing grew louder and there was a sound of approaching hoof beats. Presently a horseman, along with a page dressed in the manner of the Ruffians, appeared at the gate and called for Master Simon.

Hastening to receive the new arrival, the tavern keeper noticed his sumptuous clothes: a short cap and turban, short trousers, a sword, and leather leggings that fell to the heel and draped over the shoes.

"Has Malfan Sa'dun arrived?" asked the page. Simon replied that he was in the garden.

The newcomer was clearly Harch the Ruffian chief. Simon came forward, took the horse's bridle, and held the stirrups while he dismounted. Harch was short, stocky, and surprisingly strong and nimble for a middle-aged man. He walked with a swagger. His lips were thick and his beard and sideburns sparse and graying. On his forehead was a deep scar, the souvenir of a youthful battle that had almost killed him; it still served as a point of pride in his rivalry with his fellows. His eyes were always red, as if he had just awoken from a deep sleep. His character was as one would expect of a bandit prince. He and his men lived by robbery, assault, and the like. Unable to rein them in, the government frequently enough resorted to employing them. When they were loyal, the Ruffians, being well equipped to track down prostitutes and robbers, did a great deal of good. One group of thieves had even sworn off crime and taken the title of 'the Penitents.' The government paid them to investigate robberies,[37] but they usually proved fickle and switched sides. Such corruption proliferates only under despotic regimes: when a ruler is weak, his men begin looking for ways to enrich themselves. Then integrity vanishes and people begin bearing witness against each other.

---

37 *History of Islamic Civilization*, IV.

Chapter 4

Alchemy

Leaving the page boy at the bend in the road to mind the horse, Harch went into the garden. Simon hurried after him and led him to the bench under the tree. Malfan Sa'dun rose to greet him and Harch, grinning broadly, sat beside him and signaled to the tavern keeper that he need not bring them anything. Understanding that the two wanted to speak in private, Simon went back to where the soldier was sitting and gestured for him to leave so as not to arouse suspicion. Reluctantly, the soldier departed.

Meanwhile, Harch was asking Sa'dun with a smile whether he had been waiting long.

"Not at all," said Sa'dun.

"I've been keen to see you," said Harch. "If I weren't, I would never have come here—especially now that al-Rashid, the Commander of the Faithful, has left Baghdad."

"Isn't his son al-Amin ruling in his place?"

"He is, but—as you know better than I do—he's a boy, and he lacks his father's touch when it comes to politics. All he's interested in is women, boys, and drink. I don't leave the house much, so the police chief comes to me time and again with questions about things they want to know, as if I were the great Malfan Sa'dun, the Sabean of Harran, who can divine the future and read the secrets of the stars!" This he said with a laugh, hoping that by changing the subject he might get to the point that had brought him here.

Sa'dun saw what Harch was getting at but pretended not to. "Not at all, sir: it is you whose feats none can match. Whatever I know, I've learned using books and calculations; but what you know, you've acquired through your bravery and your understanding of human nature."

Flattered, Harch replied: "You may think I know everything, but I don't know where to find you. I've hardly ever been able to find you unless you agree to meet me."

"That's no failure on your part, only my bad luck," rejoined Sa'dun. "To practice alchemy, divination, and astrology, I need my solitude. That's why I left my family in Harran: so they wouldn't distract me from my work. I've been gone so long now that they no longer know anything about me. If you asked them where I was, they wouldn't know."

Harch was glad that alchemy had come up: it gave him a chance to ask about the chunk of brass he had given him some days ago to be converted into gold. "I suppose you've forgotten about me and my…"

"Not at all," interrupted Sa'dun. "I'd never forget the chief's orders. I've got good news: your fortune is in the ascendant. I've found a most unusual process for transforming your brass into gold."

Harch had given Malfan Sa'dun a big chunk of brass. If the process worked, he would give him more, and that way become rich. Thrilled by the prospect of sudden wealth, he could not resist asking how the process had turned out.

With a smile, Sa'dun reached for the pouch, untied it, and took out an ingot of pure gold.

"Here's the piece I tested the process on. When the rest is ready I'll return it to you." Handing over the gold, he continued in a whisper: "I'm sure I don't have to remind you not to tell anyone about this. You know my reasons."

Harch took the ingot and held it close to the flame of the lamp. Without a doubt, it was gold. Even so, he suspected a trick. In that age of bad faith and mutual suspicion, he had grown accustomed to finding trickery and flattery everywhere. Of all the citizens of Baghdad, he was the slowest to trust, given all the secrets a man in his position came to learn. He lifted his hand to test the weight of the ingot. Seeing what he was doing, Sa'dun offered a mild reproach.

"Have no fear, my lord," he said with quiet dignity. "If you sell it in the goldsmiths' market tomorrow, you'll see I'm telling you the truth. Not that I blame you for having your doubts: people aren't used to honesty and they haven't seen enough alchemy to trust it entirely. Too many alchemists who know the secret of the process keep the gold for themselves."

Embarrassed by this polite reproach, Harch felt renewed respect for Malfan Saʻdun. Reassured, he hastened to apologize. "Far be it from me to doubt your honesty," he said. "I've known you for a long time, and you've revealed no end of secrets and mysteries to me. You're as dear to me as a brother—even more so."

"What? You, a Muslim, willing to have a Sabean for a brother?" laughed Saʻdun. Meanwhile he had taken the codex that he had been turning over in his hands during their conversation, rolled it up, and put it into the pouch where the ingot had come from.

Knowing that Saʻdun was joking, Harch replied, "If all Sabeans are like Malfan Saʻdun, I'll take them all as brothers. What a fine thing, to know the secrets of the stars…" Suddenly he stopped. "I think I hear a courier coming."

The Sabean had already tied up his bundle and put it under his arm. "That's the courier from Khurasan,"[38] he said, "with something important to tell us. Didn't you see I was about to get up?"

Again amazed by Saʻdun's abilities, Harch wondered what news the rider would be bringing from Khurasan. Rising, he adjusted his tall cap, hung his sword from his sash, and said: "Whoever said that the jingling of the courier's bridle commands respect was right. I'm going out to meet him and see if I can get some information out of him. It sounds as if he'll be here any moment."

He hurried away, with Saʻdun following at a more leisurely pace. Even before they reached the tavern door they saw the courier's mule standing at the gate. Astride the mule was a rider swathed in a muffler and girded with a broad sash. The mule was gasping with exhaustion, sweat pouring down his chest and foam welling up around his bridle.

"Simon!" called the rider. "Give me a drink!"

---

38 In early Islamic times, Khurasan was the name of a vast region that included what is today northeastern Iran as well as Afghanistan, Turkmenistan, Uzbekistan, and Tajikistan, as far as Sind, in what is today Pakistan. It was the Arab and Muslim Persian military elite of Khurasan that overthrew the Umayyad dynasty in 750, and the province continued to play an important role in power politics. *Translator's Note*

Chapter 5

Important News

The tavern keeper quickly found a cup, filled it with water, and held it out. In the meantime Harch had reached the gate. When the courier spotted him, he dismounted without drinking and moved as if to kiss his hand, but the Ruffian chief gestured for him to go ahead and drink. Handing the cup back to the tavern keeper, the courier went up to Harch and said something in his ear. The two fell to whispering. Sa'dun, meanwhile, was still standing at the threshold of the tavern near the garden, too far away to hear anything. But he could tell from Harch's reaction that something was afoot. Moments later, the whispering came to an end. Excusing himself, the courier mounted his mule and raced off. Judging by the man's haste, Sa'dun felt even more certain that the news was important: otherwise the courier would have tarried longer with the Ruffian chief.

The Sabean entered the tavern to find Harch coming toward him. The Ruffian chief, looking both perturbed and relieved, was smiling tightly. Sa'dun assumed that the news concerned al-Rashid, who had traveled to Khurasan despite his illness. From private sources he had learned that the Caliph's condition had worsened and there was no hope that he might recover. Thus it was that when he heard the jingling of the courier's bridle, he had thought it likely that the news was of al-Rashid's death. As Harch approached, he shook his head and said with a smile, "My condolences!"

Startled by this exclamation, which seemed like a prophecy, Harch took Sa'dun by the hand and led him a short way off.

"You know the Caliph died?" he whispered. "How?"

"May God have mercy on him!" said Sa'dun. "He perished far from home. But I expected no less since the day he left on the campaign. I knew it from his horoscope. And I can see that you're pleased. As well you might be: all the commanders and soldiers will receive a bonus, and you'll receive a bigger share when al-Amin becomes caliph and makes you a favorite." He cleared his throat and then interrupted himself with a fit of coughing.

"That courier may trust me and want to win me over," said Harch. "But he still wouldn't tell me the other piece of news he was carrying, except to say that it was critical and I would hear it soon enough."

"Of course you'll hear it," said Sa'dun, "but only when the whole world does. If I had my divination book with me, I could tell you what it is right now." Calling for his groom to bring his horse, he rose to go, as if rushing off to perform the divination ceremony. Harch held him back.

"You're disappearing just when I need you!"

"I'm at your service, of course. But I want to divine the other piece of news."

"We agreed to meet here but we've hardly had time to talk. 'Ali ibn Isa ibn Mahan, the chief of police, wants to meet you. I've told him all about you and your miracles."

"I hope you haven't said anything about alchemy!"

"Not at all," laughed Harch, busying himself with his sword-belt. "But I did tell him how good you are at astrology and divination, and he told me to bring you to see him. He's a good man to know: he's the police chief of Baghdad and he has a lot of influence, especially now, since al-Amin likes him and trusts him. Introducing you is my chance to repay you for all you've done for me."

Sa'dun stood silent for a moment, head bowed, scratching at his beard and poking at the earth with his staff.

"Let me go now," he said, "and I'll bring you the news tonight."

"As long as you find me later," said Harch, "then I suppose it's all right for you to leave now. Even if you come in the middle of the night, you can find me at the Ruffians' hall in Harbiyyah. You know where I mean. As soon as you arrive, we'll go together to the police chief's house. He'll be awake. I don't think anyone will sleep tonight—not after they hear about al-Rashid. His death means some big changes: changes I hope you and I can profit from."

He extended a hand toward Sa'dun as if to salute him. Then he called for his page boy, who appeared carrying a box, a staff, and a cloak of the sort one might use on the road. He gestured for the page to give some money to the tavern keeper, who took it gratefully and would have kissed the Ruffian's hand if the latter had not prevented him.

"Have I been here tonight?" asked Harch.

Understanding what he was driving at, Simon replied: "No Master, nor Malfan Sa'dun either. You can be certain of that."

Laughing, Harch turned to Sa'dun, who asked him to ride out first. "That way no one will know that we met."

"Why so worried, my friend?" asked Harch. "We've got nothing to hide. There was no need to come all the way out here for a meeting."

"The only thing I worry about," said Sa'dun in a low voice, "is people finding out about my alchemy. I imagine ears on every wall and tongues in every corner. Forgive me!"

"As you like!" said Harch, mounting his horse. Accompanied by his page boy, he rode off along the Khurasan Road, heading west toward the bridge and then south toward Harbiyyah.

When he was certain they had disappeared, Sa'dun mounted his horse and turned its muzzle south, then east, toward Mukharrim and the Palace of Al-Ma'mun.

Chapter 6

Al-Ma'mun's Palace

At the time of these events, al-Ma'mun's residence lay in the southwest part of Baghdad, beyond the palace of al-Amin. The building had a long history. In former times it had been known as the Palace of Ja'far, after Ja'far of the Barmakid family, vizier to al-Rashid. Ja'far was passionately devoted to wine and song, as recounted in the novel *The Caliph's Sister—Harun al-Rashid and the Fall of the Persians.*[39] His father Yahya, a man known for his dignity and good judgment, feared that his son's excesses might have unpleasant consequences. He forbade him to indulge himself in the pleasures of life, but to no avail. He then enjoined him to practice his vices in secret, as an Islamic tradition advised, but his son refused. At wit's end, Yahya finally said, "If you won't be discreet, then build a palace for yourself on the east side of Baghdad." At that time, the east side was still sparsely populated. "That way, you can gather your drinking companions and courtesans where no one can see you and disapprove."

Taking his father's advice, Ja'far built a lavish palace on the east bank. When it was finished, he and a group of companions, including a particularly wise and loyal friend named Mu'nis Ibn Imran, went to see it. As they toured the palace, all of them gaped in admiration and lavished extravagant praises on everything they saw. All, that is, but one: Mu'nis remained silent.

"Why so quiet?" asked Ja'far. "Won't you join the conversation?"

"There's nothing left to say," he replied.

Ja'far saw that his friend was holding something back and demanded to know what it was.

---

39 This is the title of the new translation into English. Zaidan's original Arabic title is *'Abbasa, Sister of al-Rashid; or, the Catastrophe that Befell the Barmakids. Translator's Note*

"If you insist on knowing," said Mu'nis, "let it be your responsibility, not mine."

"Agreed. Out with it!"

"If you visited a friend's house," said Mu'nis, "and found it finer than your own, what would you do?"

Here Mu'nis was alluding to al-Rashid's resentment of Ja'far's growing wealth and influence.

"I see what you mean," said Ja'far. "So what do I do now?"

"Present yourself to the Commander of the Faithful. When he asks where you've been, tell him that you've been building a palace—for our master al-Ma'mun."

Ja'far was pleased with this suggestion. After spending the rest of the day at the new residence, he went to the Palace of Eternity to present himself to al-Rashid, who had already learned from his spies that Ja'far was building a mansion more splendid than any that belonged to the ruling house.

"Where have you been all this time?" he asked Ja'far.

"At the palace I've built for my master al-Ma'mun on the east bank of the Tigris."

"You built it for al-Ma'mun?" asked al-Rashid.

"Yes, Commander of the Faithful. The night he was born, I held him in my lap before you held him in yours, and my father placed me in his service. For that reason, I've built a palace for him on the east bank, where I'm told the air is healthier; and I hope it will balance his humors and help his mind grow strong. I've also written to craftsmen trained in making the appropriate furnishings. But there are still some things that need to be done, and I was hoping that the treasury of the Commander of the Faithful might cover the expense, either as a gift or as a loan."

This speech struck the right note and defused al-Rashid's anger and suspicion. Brightening, he quickly replied that he would give the money as a gift. "God forbid that you be denied credit for your efforts, or that anyone find reason to impugn your conduct. By God, no one will live there but you, and whatever furnishings are still missing will come from our treasuries." With the Caliph reassured, Ja'far won his palace back at no cost to himself. During what remained of his days of wine and roses, he was constantly there, and the place came to be known as "Ja'far's Palace."

In 187 AH (803 AD), al-Rashid removed the Barmakid family from power and plundered their houses and holdings. Ja'far's palace became the property of al-Ma'mun, who was next in line after al-Amin to succeed to the caliphate.

Al-Ma'mun, then in the first vigor of youth, came to love the place more than any other. He expanded it on the landward side, adding a plot of land that served as a field for equestrian exercises, a racetrack, and a polo ground. On the outskirts of the compound he built paddocks for wild animals. To the east he added a gateway that faced landward and an opening to channel the waters of the Mu'alla Canal. Nearby he constructed residences for his intimate friends and associates. The whole complex was dubbed al-Ma'mun's palace, and the area around it came to be known as al-Ma'muniya. In later times, a road by the same name became a Baghdad landmark.[40]

---

40 Ya'qut, *Dictionary*, I: 806.

Chapter 7

Ibn Sahl

During the time he resided in Baghdad as heir apparent, which lasted until 193 AH, al-Ma'mun brought al-Fadl Ibn Sahl and his brother al-Hasan to live there. Both would play important roles in his career. Ibn Sahl was an ambitious Persian from Sarakhs who enjoyed al-Ma'mun's trust and esteem.[41] Like all Persians, he bore a grudge against al-Rashid for deceitfully executing Ja'far the Barmaki. Having agreed to work together to avenge themselves, the Persians pinned their hopes on al-Ma'mun because his mother was one of them. Moreover, he had been raised by Ja'far to feel sympathy for the Shi'a of 'Ali, the movement that united them. Ibn Sahl had been chosen by Ja'far's father Yahya to serve al-Ma'mun. As part of the plan to further the interests of the Persians, he asked al-Ma'mun to sponsor his conversion from Zoroastrianism to Islam.[42]

In 192 AH (808 AD), al-Rashid resolved to lead an expedition to Khurasan to fight a rebel named Rafi' ibn Layth. Rafi' had risen against the caliphate in the lands beyond the Oxus and defeated all the governors and commanders sent against him. Before setting out, al-Rashid named his son al-Amin governor of Baghdad and ordered al-Ma'mun to remain in the city as well. It was understood that if al-Rashid died during the campaign,

---

41 Sarakhs is a town located near what is today the Iranian border with Turkmenistan. Despite what Zaidan says here, a person from Sarakhs would not necessarily have been a Persian, at least not according to early 'Abbasid usage. See Afterword. *Translator's Note*

42 Zoroastrianism was the official faith of the Sasanian Empire. Its followers represented themselves as taking the side of Ahura Mazda, the god of goodness and light, against Ahriman, the god of darkness and evil. They worshiped Ahura Mazda by venerating sacred fires and adhering to strict codes of purity. Under Islamic rule, Zoroastrians were sometimes tolerated and sometimes persecuted. Almost all eventually embraced Islam, though communities of Zoroastrians still exist in Iran, India, and elsewhere. *Translator's Note*

he would be succeeded by al-Amin, and then by al-Ma'mun, who in the meantime was to assume the governorship of Khurasan.

When Ibn Sahl learned that al-Ma'mun had been asked to remain in Baghdad, he realized that if al-Rashid died then al-Amin would succeed him and the plan to bring al-Ma'mun to power would fail. So he appealed to al-Ma'mun. "Khurasan is promised to you," he said, "but anything may happen to the Caliph. Al-Amin is first heir apparent, and I'm afraid he'll remove you from the succession. Remember that he's the son of Zubayda, who has no end of money; and his maternal uncles belong to the clan of Hashim.[43] So ask the Commander of the Faithful to let you join him on his expedition."

Al-Ma'mun duly asked his father for permission to come along. Al-Rashid at first refused but finally relented.

When the Caliph's party left for Khurasan, Ibn Sahl and his brother al-Hasan came along as well.

As for his palace, al-Ma'mun left it in the care of certain members of his family, along with servants, slaves, and overseers to look after his property and landholdings. The palace lay on the east bank of the Tigris, facing the river, and had balconies and skylights. The rooms were carpeted with gold-threaded rugs and cushions imported from distant lands. The doorways were adorned with curtains and the storerooms crammed with luxury goods. The palace was staffed by slave men and women and by eunuchs, who in those times were considered an indispensable part of the household.

Along the river was a marble wharf where boats were moored. From the boats one climbed up to the wharf on broad marble steps with handrails on both sides. The posts, evidently salvaged from an ancient royal palace, were decorated with Persian designs. The wharf itself extended from the water's edge to the western wall of the palace. There, by the gate, was a spacious sitting room where velvet rugs and chairs were often placed along the walls for those who wanted to watch the boats passing to and fro upon the Tigris.

Among those left in residence at the palace when al-Ma'mun departed for Khurasan was his daughter Zaynab, also known as Umm Habiba. She was still young—not yet twelve years old. Like her father, she was perceptive

---

43 The clan of Hashim, also called the House of Hashim, is the kin group to which the Prophet's tribe of Quraysh belonged. The 'Abbasids belonged to the clan inasmuch as they traced their lineage back to al-'Abbas, the Prophet's paternal uncle. Several present-day rulers, including the kings of Saudi Arabia and Jordan, describe themselves as Hashimites as well. *Translator's Note*

and clever, and a free-thinker as well. Like her grandfather al-Rashid, she was a fierce partisan of her clan, the House of Hashim. Despite her youth, she was willful and imperious. Realizing this, and worried about the consequences, her father, who was eager to win over the Persians, placed her in the care of the same slave who had raised him: a woman named Dananir, who had belonged to the Barmakid family at the peak of its glory. When Ja'far had been given custody of al-Ma'mun he had asked Dananir to take charge of the boy, giving her to understand that she should raise him to love the Persians. Placed in her care from infancy, al-Ma'mun regarded Dananir with special deference and respect. When he grew older, he took her into his cohort of slaves. When his own daughter Zaynab was born, he entrusted her to Dananir, asking her to instill in her a love for the Persians and a capacity for independent thought. Dananir did her best to carry out this responsibility. Al-Rashid, for his part, was smitten with his granddaughter: it was he who named her Zaynab and gave her the nickname Umm Habiba. Whenever he had time, he would send for her, play with her, and give her necklaces and bracelets. She was often present during his conversations with his wife Zubayda, who frequently boasted of her Hashimite lineage. Overhearing their conversations, Zaynab came effortlessly to acquire the same pride in her clan, despite Dananir's efforts to root out any such chauvinism. Even so, Zaynab loved and respected her nurse, and felt so comfortable with her that she would tell her whatever was on her mind.

Chapter 8

Zaynab and Dananir

Physically and mentally, Zaynab was a precocious child. Though not yet twelve, she looked nearly sixteen. She had striking features: black flashing eyes, a small nose, thin lips, and a jutting chin. The set of her mouth indicated firmness, composure, and strength of will; and her eyes shone with intelligence and wit. Dananir had raised her to live simply and instilled in her an aversion to the strutting finery of the age. Thus it was that she spent the day in nothing but a simple gown, with her hair bound in a single braid hanging down her back.

As for Dananir, she was a woman of fair complexion and a firm cast of mind. She was originally the property of a man from Basra who had trained her in the arts and graces and taught her poetry. While still a girl, she had come into the possession of Yahya ibn Khalid of the Barmakid family, who raised her in his household. Although she had the same name as the singer Dananir, who was famous for her voice and her memory for verse, her interests lay in the rational sciences. Her masters, the Barmakids, were responsible for the revival of learning in the 'Abbasid period, and hardly a day passed without a scientific debate or literary discussion taking place at the house of Yahya or one of his relatives. When Yahya assembled a group of scholars to translate the *Almagest* into Arabic, Dananir found ways to engage them in conversation.[44] As the savants debated the astronomical and astrological problems that arose in the course of their work, she could often be found listening in, prompting the other slave women to laugh scornfully at her fascination with the seemingly mysterious symbols indecipherable

---

44 The Almagest is a Greek work on mathematical geography by the Alexandrian scholar Claudius Ptolemy (fl. second-century AD). It was translated into Arabic several times during the early 'Abbasid period. Its premise that the earth stood at the center of the cosmos was questioned by at least two medieval Muslim astronomers, but it was not definitively overthrown until the sixteenth century. *Translotor's Note*

to all but the *dhimmi* experts.[45] At the time, the ancient sciences were just becoming known in Arabic: the only books available were some on astronomy and a few on medicine that had been translated during the reigns of al-Mansur, al-Mahdi, and al-Rashid. Nevertheless, Dananir—thanks to the conversations among Yahya's guests—learned about these subjects even before the books had been translated. She became famous among the women of the Barmakid household for her love of learning and rational inquiry. After Ja'far placed al-Ma'mun in her care, she would never take him out to play in the garden without bringing sheets of parchment or paper containing the star charts and medical treatises she enjoyed puzzling over. When al-Ma'mun reached the age of understanding, she was able to supply a reasoned answer to every one of his questions. Then she began to teach him whatever elements of science he was able to understand. This she did, not because she had planned to instruct him, but only because she enjoyed doing so. Nothing gives an inquiring mind more pleasure than to acquire and spread knowledge.

By the time al-Ma'mun was old enough to be sent to the tutors, he had acquired an interest in the problem of causation and a passion for finding rational proofs for everything. It was this interest that led him to explore the Mu'tazili doctrine,[46] Shi'ism,[47] science, and philosophy, and to sponsor the translation of ancient books into Arabic.

Al-Ma'mun had grown to respect Dananir as a son respects his mother, and had often passed his leisure hours discussing one or another problem with her and taking pleasure in the workings of her mind. When his daughter Zaynab was born, he placed her in the hands of Dananir, confident that she would raise her as he wished. Like her father, Zaynab was an inquisitive

---

45 The 'protected peoples'; see notes to Chapter 1. Many of the translators of scientific works were Christians. The eastern churches had long been engaged in translating from Greek into Syriac; under Islamic rule, they extended their work into Arabic. *Translator's Note*

46 The Mu'tazili school of thought took a skeptical position on Hadith (reports of what the Prophet had said and done), preferring to settle matters of faith by appeal to reason. They argued, among other things, that God could not break his own promises. Their belief that the Qur'an was not God's living speech but rather a created thing became a point of contention between al-Ma'mun and the early Sunni movement. *Translator's Note*

47 As will be evident, Zaidan here has in mind the Shi'ism familiar to him, which held that 'Ali Ibn Abi Talib (d. 661 AD) and certain of his descendants had privileged insight into matters of faith and practice and should therefore serve as guides to the entire Muslim community. In reality, al-Ma'mun appears to have been an 'Abbasid Shi'ite: that is, he thought that members of his own family, most notably himself, could serve as guides as well. *Translator's Note*

child, and Dananir made every effort to shape her intellect. Having lost her real mother, Zaynab grew up calling Dananir 'Mama.' She may even have loved her more than she loved her father, who was preoccupied with his own affairs. In those days, parents rarely lived with their children, preferring to place them in the care of slave women. So it was that Zaynab was raised to be a philosopher, indifferent to all but the facts of the case, and scornful of the frolicking and merriment that captivated her peers. In those days, the palaces of the caliphs, including al-Ma'mun, offered the women and servants of the household every kind of diversion, but Zaynab did not join them in their revelry or mix with any of the servants except for her governess, whom she followed like a shadow: to the gardens to pick flowers, or to the menagerie to watch the keepers offering chunks of meat to the lions. When she needed a diversion she played chess, which had been introduced to the court by al-Rashid. Zaynab played well and could sometimes draw Dananir into a game. Other times she would accompany her to the wharf by the western gate, where they would sit in a window seat or on a balcony and look through the curtains at the boats sailing down the Tigris. Such sessions could be quite entertaining, as many of the passengers were revelers who had brought singers and lute players on board with them.

Chapter 9

The Doctor from Khurasan

One day, it so happened that Zaynab and her governess were sitting on a balcony above the wharf and looking out over the Tigris. Zaynab was wearing a pink gown and a string of pearls given to her by her grandfather al-Rashid before his departure. They were discussing a problem involving the relationship between human dispositions and the signs of the zodiac. It proved too complex even for Dananir, who said, "What a difficult question! When our physician comes, we'll ask him about it."

"Do doctors understand astronomy too?" asked Zaynab.

"Many of them, especially the Persians, understand all the sciences. Our doctor in particular is a great philosopher and a genius among physicians."

Zaynab laughed in the manner of one whose experience of the world had been confined to its delightful aspects. "You mean he knows more than you?" she asked in surprise. She had always assumed, as one always assumes of one's parents and teachers, that her governess was the most knowledgeable person in the world. Children imagine their parents to be perfect, and their teachers—even the ignoramuses—to be great thinkers, and they invoke their authority and parrot their words with enormous reverence. If the teacher is so limited in his experience as to believe what his pupils say about him, he foolishly comes to think of himself as a giant among scholars, even if his learning is limited to the rudiments of grammar. Dananir, however, knew her place, and smiled at Zaynab's praise.

"I know nothing, Mistress," she said. "All I've done is to pick up a bit of learning from the scholars I've overheard. Our doctor studied medicine and philosophy at the famous academy of Jundishapur, where Ibn Bakhtishu, physician to the Commander of the Faithful, completed his studies. But he knows about many other things, especially alchemy and astronomy. Otherwise Ibn Sahl would never have recommended him to my master al-Ma'mun."

"Ibn Sahl recommended him?" interjected Zaynab. "When was that? Isn't Ibn Sahl with my father in Khurasan?"

"Yes, they're both there. But the doctor came to us some years ago, when Ibn Sahl told us that he was the greatest physician and scientist in Khurasan—so much so that you can even see it in his face."

"Why doesn't he live here with us?" asked Zaynab. "Doesn't my father let him?"

"It's not that," said Dananir. "On the day he arrived, he explained to my master al-Ma'mun that he had his own reasons for not being able to stay here."

"Where does he live, then?"

"I've heard he lives in Ctesiphon because he likes being close to the Palace of Chosroes, who was the greatest and most just of the Persian kings.[48] You see, our doctor is a Persian."

"I knew he was a Persian from his accent: he still can't pronounce Arabic properly. If he lived here, the people of Baghdad would teach him how to speak!"

"Ctesiphon isn't so far. It's only a few hours south of here."

"He should have moved here after my father left and we moved out here, so far from the city, so we'd have someone to take care of us. He's a giant: remember how big he is? Even though he's been here often, he still frightens me whenever he takes my hand to feel my pulse."

"You're right," said Dananir, "he is tall, and his long robes make him look taller. But he's well-spoken and polite, and he's easy to trust. Though he does sometimes disappear for days and if we need him we can't find him. There are plenty of doctors, but he seems more knowledgeable than the rest."

Putting her hands affectionately on Dananir's shoulders, Zaynab broke in with: "Mama, tell him to come and live in one of the residences here."

48 Ctesiphon was the capital of the Sasanian dynasty (224-651 AD), and Chosroes is Khosrow I Anoshiravan (r. 531-79 AD), famed in Arabic literature for his justice and wisdom. *Translator's Note*

"When he comes, I'll ask him, and he may even agree. There's a boat coming up the river now. Perhaps it's him."

Throughout the conversation, Zaynab had been watching the river and staring at the opposite shore, where the palm trees stood like giant idols. Between their trunks, a landscape rich with trees and greenery was visible all the way to the horizon. Buildings lay scattered like gemstones on a bolt of green silk brocade. Cast by the lengthening rays of the afternoon sun, the shadows of the palms lay long on the water, creating the appearance of trees rooted on the bank with their crowns growing downward into the river and their trunks rippling on the surface as if made up of unconnected but overlapping parts. The twisting shadows seemed alive, as if on the verge of pulling their roots free from the shore and swimming away. They looked like snakes trying to wriggle free of someone who had seized their tails.

Zaynab, who had been distracted by this sight until roused by Dananir's remark, glanced around and asked: "Does he come by river or by land? Every time we see him he's on a horse."

"There's two ways to come here from Ctesiphon," said Dananir. "One by river and one by land."

Chapter 10

The Old Woman and the Girl

They had continued to peer at the boat through the curtain, but still could not tell who was sailing in it. When a bend in the river took the boat out of sight, they forgot about it for a time. But when Zaynab, weary of sitting so long, rose to go, she heard a splash and a flapping of sails nearby. Turning around, she saw a boat coming alongside the wharf, its two crewmen busily untying the rigging. In the middle of the craft were two women. One was wearing an old, faded cloak and a headcloth, and seemed well advanced in years. The other wore a black gown and veil draped across her face to conceal everything but her eyes. Within moments the sailors had made the boat fast to a ring on the wharf and put down a gangplank between the wharf and the boat. The two women rose and, leaning on one another, made their way across to the base of the stairs, the older one looking up at the palace as if casting about for someone to speak to. One of the sailors said: "This is al-Ma'mun's palace, lady."

Leaping to her feet, Dananir went to the door and looked out at the boat, trying to guess who the women were. Zaynab stayed where she was, waiting to see what would happen next. To her surprise, she saw Dananir hurry down the stairs to the old woman, embrace her, and shower her hands with kisses. Then she was helping her up the stairs, with the girl behind them. Zaynab waited for Dananir to say something that would reveal the visitors' identity. But she gave nothing away. Walking beside the old woman, who was leaning on a cane, she leaned forward and said softly, "Come with us, Mistress."

Zaynab jumped up to join them. The party passed through a reception room that lay between the western gate and the palace proper and reached a large salon. Dananir dismissed the slave women who were there and invited the old woman and the girl to enter. After removing their shoes and leaving them by the door, the visitors went in and Dananir invited them to sit on the velveteen spread.

Taking a cushion for herself, Zaynab scrutinized her visitors, who had removed their headcoverings, revealing, in the old woman's case, a head full of white hair. Her companion, on the other hand, was in the first bloom of youth and looked like an angel in human form. She was slender and attractive, with golden-brown skin and regular features. Her appearance suggested noble parentage while her simple clothing betrayed a poverty that only made her beauty all the more striking. Hers was a youthful radiance that shone through the mournful expression, the black gown, and the tears that glimmered in her eyes. Coming in, she had kept her eyes down, as if hiding her thoughts. Now seated, she raised her head, revealing deep-black eyes full of enchantment. Her glance fell on Zaynab, who was staring at her eagerly. When their eyes met, Zaynab felt an attraction to her of a kind she had felt with no one else, even though the visitor was a girl just like her. She seemed to remember having seen her before.

The old woman, though she bore the marks of sorrow and humiliation, seemed still to exude pride and dignity. After they had settled into their seats, Dananir pointed to her and asked Zaynab if she recognized her. Zaynab signaled that she did not. Shaking her head in sorrow, Dananir said: "This is my lady Umm Ja'far: the mother of Ja'far."

At first Zaynab thought that she meant Zubayda, the wife of al-Rashid, who had the same title.[49] She was surprised that their aged visitor lacked that youthfulness that Zubayda still possessed, not to mention the difference between their features. Knowing why the girl was confused, Dananir went on: "I mean my lady the mother of Ja'far the Barmaki, al-Rashid's vizier: that is, 'Abbada, daughter of Muhammad, daughter of Husayn, daughter of Qahtaba."[50]

Zaynab had learned that her grandfather al-Rashid had executed his vizier Ja'far and confiscated his estates. She had never heard anything about the vizier's mother, and had assumed that she was dead. Overcome by her

---

49 Zubayda was called 'Mother of Ja'far' in commemoration of her father Ja'far, son of the caliph al-Mansur. 'Abbada, on the other hand, was given the title for the more usual reason that her son (the deposed vizier) was named Ja'far. *Translator's Note*

50 Though 'Abbada is supposed to be a Persian, her genealogy consists of Arab names, indicating that her family had been Muslim for generations. Typically, converts to Islam would take an Arabic name. *Translator's Note*

feeling of partisanship for the House of Hashim, Zaynab felt herself shrinking from her visitors. But Dananir quickly pointed out that 'Abbada had a special connection to al-Ma'mun, whom she had carried in her lap, served, and adored. "Al-Ma'mun always respected her, and after what happened to her son, he often mentioned her, saying that he hoped to see her so that he might pay his respects. If he knew that she was alive he would certainly summon her, treat her fittingly, and offer his condolences in her bereavement."

During this speech 'Abbada dabbed at her eyes, making an effort not to weep. For her part, Zaynab, when she heard what her governess said and saw the old woman on the verge of tears, felt a surge of pity and nearly wept as well, though her toughness of mind and her aversion to the Barmakids held her back. Knowing what Zaynab was thinking, and hoping to arouse her sympathy as much as she could, Dananir said: "Even our master al-Rashid, the Commander of the Faithful, respects Umm Ja'far, despite what happened between him and her son. He holds her in high esteem because she nursed him and raised him after his own mother died when he was still a baby. He would always ask her advice, treat her with honor, and consider her approval a good omen. I remember how often he used to call her 'mother of al-Rashid'!"

Hearing this, Zaynab asked: "So she's my grandmother?"

"Your handmaid, rather, Mistress!" interjected 'Abbada. "The Commander of the Faithful honored me with that name out of kindness. What happened to us after that was only by decree of the Almighty," she said with a sob.

"Poor Umm Ja'far!" said Zaynab, moved. "But why didn't my grandfather pardon your son for your sake?"

"Our master al-Rashid did what he did because my son's enemies envied and slandered him. They convinced al-Rashid that killing him was the right thing to do. And once al-Rashid—may God preserve him—resolves to do something, he carries it out, without being swayed by pleas or appeals. In all things, his command is binding upon us and we accept it." Turning to Dananir, she continued: "Our enemies also managed to turn al-Rashid against my husband Yahya and my son al-Fadl. He had them taken and put in prison. I appealed to him by my right as his nurse to forgive them and release them, or one of them at least; but in vain."

"What did you do?" asked Dananir.

Chapter 11

'Abbada and al-Rashid

'Abbada reached into her sleeve and pulled out a jewelry box carved from a single emerald. She opened it with a gold key and looked at Dananir. "I made my appeal with the items in this box," she said.

From the box she removed a lock of hair and several teeth. A smell of musk filled the air. "This is al-Rashid's hair, and these are his baby teeth. I've kept them since he was a child. But he refused my appeal."

"What happened, my lady?" asked Dananir.

Looking aggrieved, 'Abbada sat up haughtily in her seat. "When I learned what had happened to my poor son Ja'far," she said, "and that al-Rashid had arrested Yahya, I decided to go to al-Rashid and intercede for my husband. Al-Rashid had always treated me with respect and never refused my requests when I intervened on behalf of others. When I think of all the prisoners of war I set free and all the cells I opened..."

She swallowed, then recovered her composure and continued her tale. "I went to al-Rashid. I had always been admitted to his presence without being stopped, but this time they stopped me. I tried and tried, but was never allowed to see him. Finally I appeared at the gate on foot, barefoot, and without a veil. When the chamberlain saw me in that state, he went in and told al-Rashid that his former wet-nurse was at the door, in a state to move even her rivals to pity. The chamberlain described the state I was in and I heard al-Rashid exclaim: 'She came here on foot?' 'Yes,' he replied, 'and barefoot too!' 'Admit her, then, damn you!' he said. 'Many were the times that she comforted the bereaved, succored the afflicted, and shielded noble reputations from disgrace.'

"When I heard him say that, I began to think he might grant me my request. The chamberlain came back and ushered me in. Al-Rashid stood and welcomed me, coming so far as to meet me between the pillars in the hall, and then kissing my head and breast and seating me beside him."[51]

"'How,' I asked, 'can fate turn against me, your fearful retainers scorn me, and lies be spread against me, when it is I who nursed you, and by that right can call you my protector?'

"He asked me what I wanted. 'I am here for Yahya, your second father,' I said. 'In his defense I need not remind you that he supported you, counseled you, and risked his life for you when your brother al-Hadi was caliph.'

"He frowned and said, 'Mother, what God's wrath has decreed cannot be undone.'

"'God effaces what He wills,' I recited, 'and retains what he wills; with him is the original of the Book.'[52]

"'True,' he said, 'but this is a decree that God has not effaced.'

"'Not even prophets know the mind of God.'

"He hung his head for a moment, then recited:

Once he unsheathes his bloody claw
No amulet can Death forestall[53]

"'It's not I who can protect him,' I responded immediately. 'Rather, it's as the poet says:

There's no better treasure in days of woe
Than a store of good deeds done here below.[54]

"'Or better yet, as the Qur'an says: 'Those who restrain their fury and pardon others; God loves those who do good.'[55]

---

51 The ensuing dialogue is in genuine classical Arabic, borrowed from Zaidan's source, Ibn 'Abd Rabbih. The classical style places value on Qur'anic references, apt citation of poems and proverbs, and spontaneous verbal cleverness. In this (doubtless invented) anecdote, both 'Abbada and al-Rashid prove themselves experts at it. The passage differs from Zaidan's usual style, which is relatively straightforward. *Translator's Note*

52 Qur'an 13:39. *Translator's Note*

53 A line by Abu Dhu'ayb al-Hudhali (d. 649 AD?) *Translator's Note*

54 A line by al-Akhtal (d. before 710 AD). *Translator's Note*

55 Qur'an 3:134. *Translator's Note*

"He stared for a moment at a staff he was holding, then said: 'Mother:

Should my soul recoil from a certain act
Never while I live will it turn back.[56]

"Seeing that he would not relent, I said:

If you sever me, your own right hand
Another such you'll never find.[57]

"He replied: 'I accept the consequences of my choice.'

"'Give him to me, Commander of the Faithful,' I said. 'The Prophet of God, may God bless and save him, said that whoever gives a thing up for the sake of God never loses it.'[58]

"He bowed his head for a moment, then said: 'All things done and undone are in the hands of God.'[59]

"'On that day,' I recited, 'the believers will rejoice in the triumph of God, who aids whom He wills; He is the Mighty and Merciful One.[60] Do you remember, Commander of the Faithful, your promise to me that you would pardon anyone I interceded for?'

"'And do you remember, Mother,' he said, 'that I refused to intercede for wrongdoers?'

"Seeing that he had no intention of granting my request, I took this little box from my sleeve, unlocked it, took out the baby hair and the teeth, and said, 'Commander of the Faithful, I implore you, and call on God as my witness, and call on these relics of your noble person, to allow your servant to live.'

---

56 A line by Ma'n Ibn Aws al-Muzani (d. after 684 AD?). *Translator's Note*

57 A line from the same poem as above. *Translator's Note*

58 A Hadith (account of a statement or action by the Prophet) known in various forms. *Translator's Note*

59 Qur'an 30:4. *Translator's Note*

60 'Abbada completes his verse and cites the next one (Qur'an 30:5). *Translator's Note*

"He took the box from me and kissed it. Then tears came to his eyes and he sobbed. All those present wept as well. Then I was sure that he would do as I asked. But when he recovered, he put the box down and said, 'How well you have kept your trust!'

"'And could you not reward me, Commander of the Faithful?'

"He fell silent. Then he closed the box, handed it back to me, then recited: 'God commands you to return items entrusted to you to their rightful owners.'[61]

"I replied from the same verse: 'I command you, when judging among people, to do so justly.'

"He recited another: 'Fulfill the compacts you have made with God.'[62]

"He looked at me. Accustomed as I was to guessing his intentions, I could see from his expression that he wanted me to tell him what I wanted.

"'Didn't you always swear to grant me access to you and never to humiliate me?'

"Remembering his promise, he said, 'Umm Ja'far, I want you to buy him back at a price I empower you to name.'

"I said: 'Judge fairly, Commander of the Faithful, since I won't allow you to back out of the sale once you've agreed to it.'

"'What are you offering in exchange?' he asked.

"'Your satisfaction with the loyalty of those who have kept your favor,' I replied.

"Irritated, he said: 'Umm Ja'far, don't I have the same rights as they do?'

"'Of course,' I replied. 'I respect you most, but I love them more.'

"Stirring in his seat, he said: 'I would consider any offer but the one you've made.'

"When I saw that he would never agree to do as I wanted, I rose, saying, 'I give him to you, and declare you free to do as you like with him.'

"I left, dried my tears, and put my grief aside. Today you've seen me sob, but on that day my eyes stayed dry."[63]

---

61 Qur'an 4:58. *Translator's Note*

62 Qur'an 16:91. *Translator's Note*

63 *The Matchless Necklace*, III: 23.

Chapter 12

Ja'far's Corpse

Having finished her story, 'Abbada put the tokens back in the little box and closed it before returning it to her sleeve.

"I have no one left to plead for," she said. "The one I hoped al-Rashid would pardon escaped the misery of this life by dying in Raqqa prison. And yesterday, my son al-Fadl followed him."[64]

She sat silent for a moment, dabbing at her eyes. Then, eyes averted, she said: "I feel certain that my son's death is the sign of dire events to come. He always used to say that al-Rashid's life was bound up with his.[65] But I pray that God will grant long life to the Commander of the Faithful."

Zaynab was suddenly afraid for her grandfather, and her heart beat faster. But she admired how 'Abbada had overcome her emotions and asked God to grant al-Rashid a long life. Then she found herself marveling once again at the old woman's story.

Watching intently as 'Abbada told her tale with heartbroken eloquence, her eyes fixed on the old woman's lips, Zaynab had more than once felt deeply moved, and nearly wept. By the end of the tale, her pity had given way to admiration for the old woman's indomitability. Softening towards her, she could sense the pain of her bereavement and defeat. Even though she had no experience of heartbreak, she was a perceptive, big-hearted girl who understood more than one might think given her age.

Absorbed in the story, Zaynab had forgotten her curiosity about 'Abbada's companion. Now that the tale was over, she turned her eyes back

---

64 Al-Fadl was another member of the Barmakid family of viziers, not to be confused with al-Fadl ibn al-Rabi and al-Fadl ibn Sahl, viziers to al-Amin and al-Ma'mun respectively. Raqqa is a town on the Euphrates in what is today Syria. *Translator's Note*

65 Ibn al-Athir, *History*, VI: 84.

43

to the visitor and, restrained by her sense of propriety from asking her a direct question, scrutinized her intently.

Her interest was shared by Dananir, who if anything was even more curious. As she listened to the story, she had stolen many inquisitive glances at the newcomer. Unable to guess who she was, she forced herself to sit patiently until the tale was over. Now, noticing that dusk was falling, she ordered the servants to light the candles that stood along the walls. They were enormous candles, expertly crafted, and mixed with aloes, so that they perfumed the air as they burned. Then she went back to wondering why 'Abbada had emerged from seclusion. Hoping to elicit an answer, she said, "What an astonishing story, my lady! And even more astonishing is how you were able to remain hidden from us for so long without anyone knowing where you were. Where have you been living?"

'Abbada sighed. "I went into hiding, though being buried alive would have been better. If only I had died ten years ago and been spared the misery of disgrace! You of all people, Dananir, know how well I lived in the house of Ja'far." She swallowed and dropped her gaze.

Dananir intervened to finish the thought, saying to Zaynab, "It's true, Mistress. I know better than anyone how Umm Ja'far lived in the days of her glory. I remember one year, on the Feast of Sacrifice, when she received visitors at the house of her son, the vizier, with four hundred slave women in attendance!"

"And I still thought my son was ungrateful," broke in Umm Ja'far. "But since the hard times began, I've had days where I couldn't find one sheepskin to throw on the ground and another to use as a blanket.[66] But none of that matters. What matters is the reason I came here tonight. But I don't want to impose on my mistress Zaynab."

By that time, Zaynab had come to feel affection and respect for 'Abbada, and forgotten that the old woman was dressed in threadbare garments. People often judge new acquaintances by their appearance only to change their impression when they get to know their talents and abilities. So it was with Zaynab, who said to her respectfully: "Not at all, my lady! You are a welcome guest, and anything you require is yours." Turning to Dananir, she said: "Mama, give her everything she needs!"

---

66 Mas'udi's *History*, II: 802.

Rising, 'Abbada kissed Zaynab's head and said, "Thank you for your kindness, my lady! But the matter that brings me here is more important than my needs—not that I am worthy of any of your favors at all."

"Speak!" urged Dananir. "Anything you ask for is yours, as our mistress has commanded."

"You asked me," said the old woman, "why I stayed away from Baghdad for all those years. How could I live in a city where I could see my son's corpse hanging from the bridges, after they cut him in two, crucified half his body on one bridge and the other half on another, and hung his head from a third, for everyone walking by to see it, day and night? Didn't the body stay up there for over two years, until al-Rashid came back from Rey in 189 AH (805 AD) and ordered it cremated? It seems that he himself realized how horrible it was: that very day, he left Baghdad, moved to Raqqa,[67] and stayed there until this year, when he left for Khurasan. And even if I had wanted to stay, how could I, with spies everywhere, and strict orders from the Caliph to punish anyone who said anything good about the Barmakids? How, if they were to find me, could they do any less than cut me to pieces? Not that I'm afraid of death: it would be the least of my troubles. But I wanted to live—for the sake of this young woman." She pointed to her companion, who suddenly became the center of attention.

67 Ibn al-Athir, *History*, VI: 77 and 78.

Chapter 13

The Young Woman

Embarrassed, the young woman blushed and they could see tears in her dark eyes even though she kept her head bent nearly to her lap. Seizing her chance, Dananir said, "I've been looking at this lovely young lady ever since you arrived, but I can't see a resemblance to anyone I know."

"She is the daughter of hardship and the child of woe," said 'Abbada. "In all Baghdad, none but I know who she is. I've kept her secret for fear of endangering her life. She's the only reason I have for remaining alive. I have never before told anyone her name. Is it safe for me to reveal it to you?"

"There's no need to be afraid," said Dananir, "now that my mistress has proclaimed her affection for you. Who could hear your tale and not be moved? Speak without fear! Any service we can render is yours for the asking."

'Abbada sighed, adjusted her veil, and said, "This girl is the step-child of misery. She is the daughter of my son Ja'far, the late vizier!"

Startled, Dananir looked at the young woman again as if trying to remember her. "I don't think I recognize her," she said.

"You wouldn't, since she was born after you left to enter the household of our master al-Ma'mun. You were lucky to leave when you did: the house that once drew so many visitors and petitioners and seekers of refuge became the blight of all who lived there and their names a curse on all those near and dear."

She succumbed to tears, then regained her composure. "This grand-daughter of mine," she went on, "was born after you left. She was still young when her father met with his misfortune. It so happened that, on that day, one of the slaves had taken her to an estate of ours outside Baghdad. When al-Rashid ordered our property confiscated, the slave escaped with the girl

47

to a distant village where no one would have thought of searching for them, and there they stayed. When I learned what had happened, I collected the girl and ran as far from Baghdad as I could. We ended up in Ctesiphon, with people who did not know who we were but gave us shelter as an act of charity. We stayed with them for several years and were never denounced. Then God sent us a man, a stranger, who became like a father or a brother to us. We met him several years ago, as he lived next to the house where we were staying in Ctesiphon. We knew nothing about where he came from or who he was, but some unseen Providence must have guided him to us. He would look after us and tend to our needs without asking for money or even thanks in return. During all those years, he supported us without telling us anything about himself. We thought of him as a messenger from Heaven, sent by God as a favor to two creatures who hardly deserved it."

While 'Abbada was talking, Dananir kept glancing at the young woman and marveling at her beauty. When her grandmother mentioned the man who had helped them, the young woman suddenly became preoccupied with rearranging her face-veil to conceal the blush that appeared on her cheeks. Had Dananir noticed the blushing, she would have realized that the young woman was trying to hide an involuntary reaction. But she was too absorbed in 'Abbada's story to notice.

At the mention of the strange benefactor, Dananir exclaimed that the world still had some good men in it. "I've heard stories of how charitable the Barmakid family was, but I've never heard of anyone else being so kind. Did you ever find out who the good man was?"

"We never have. We think he's a Persian by origin, and that he's been in Ctesiphon for a few years. He never talks about himself, and when he goes into his house he locks the door and stays inside for days at a time. People have started to talk about him. They say he practices alchemy; he's a sorcerer; he's enormously rich because he discovered a treasure in his house. The house, you see, is built over the ruins of Sabur's palace, where the Caliph al-Mansur lived before he built Baghdad."

"What's his name?" asked Dananir.

"They call him Behzad of Jundishapur."

Zaynab thought back to their Persian physician, who as she recalled also lived in Ctesiphon. "Maybe our doctor knows him," she said. "He's always going to Ctesiphon. When he comes tonight we'll ask him."

"I doubt anyone knows who he is," said 'Abbada. "But, whoever he is, he deserves all our gratitude. I pray God gives us the power to reward him someday. But Fortune favors no one for long. Indeed, Fortune has made a point of hounding us. No sooner do we catch our breath than some new calamity befalls us."

"What do you mean?" asked Dananir.

"Just when we thought they'd forgotten all about us, we found out that certain people are planning to inflict more misery on our family."

"What do you mean?" asked Dananir.

Chapter 14

The Secret

'Abbada turned to her granddaughter and then looked away, and the young woman blushed. Realizing that the granddaughter was somehow involved, Dananir suspected that 'Abbada preferred not to speak openly in front of her. To divert the young woman's attention, Dananir said, "It seems we've neglected to serve you any supper! Will my mistress give us permission to send for a meal?"

Understanding what Dananir had in mind, 'Abbada said, "I'm not hungry, but I think Maymuna should have something."

Understanding what was going on, the young woman, respecting her grandmother's wish to speak about her in confidence, signaled with her silence her assent to this suggestion. Rising, Dananir said to Zaynab, "Mistress, would you allow our noble guest to join you at the table?"

Zaynab, who customarily did as her governess bid her, complied with her suggestion for the same reason as Maymuna had, and the two girls rose to eat. Maymuna already felt comfortable in the presence of al-Ma'mun's daughter, whom she admired for her beauty and intelligence. In any case, Zaynab's kindness alone would have been enough to inspire Maymuna's affection, kindness being the best way—as the saying goes—to sway a heart.

Dananir escorted the two girls out, ordered the servants to prepare a meal, and returned to her guest eager to hear the rest of the story.

'Abbada was waiting, head bowed. Dananir came in, shut the door behind her, and sat down, smiling and repeating her words of welcome. She was happy to offer her former mistress whatever help and consolation she could, not only because of the pitiful spectacle of fallen glory she presented, but also because she felt indebted to her. Among the virtuous, it is a pleasure to express gratitude and acknowledge debts. Persons of depraved character, on the other hand, deny receiving help from anyone and wax so proud as to repay kindness with harm. In particular, those lifted out of poverty and want by some turn of fortune may even succumb to their basest instincts and murder their benefactors. But Dananir was a generous, open-hearted woman, and it gave her pleasure to serve her mistress as a token of her gratitude. Seeing, furthermore, that 'Abbada set great store by what she was going to tell her, Dananir gave her all her attention.

When the two women were alone, 'Abbada sighed deeply and gazed at Dananir with tears glistening in her eyes.

"Oh, Dananir!" she said. "Seeing you again reminds me of the good old days. I'm grateful to you for showing me such kindness when even those closest to us have forgotten about us, or pretend to. But this world is nothing but shifting fortunes, and there's no point in worrying about people of that sort. In any case what matters now is the danger that brought me here tonight. If it weren't so important, I wouldn't have put you to all this trouble."

Putting her hands on her companion's shoulders, Dananir came to the point with a smile. "Tell me what you have to say, my lady. I am yours to command."

'Abbada sighed. "You know who al-Fadl Ibn al-Rabi is, don't you?"

Hearing the name, Dananir realized that the problem was serious. Ibn al-Rabi was the one who had turned al-Rashid against Ja'far and taken his place as vizier after his death.

"Yes, my lady, I know who he is. How can he do anything worse than what he's already done?"

"It's not him this time, it's his son."

"What's he done?"

"I don't know how he found out about Maymuna," said 'Abbada, "or how he was able to look at her closely enough to be taken with her beauty—or perhaps he isn't really taken with her at all, and only wants some excuse to torment us. But a few weeks ago, he sent the forewoman of his father's household to ask for her hand in marriage. The woman spoke kindly enough and promised that things would turn out well if we accepted the offer. I put her off, hoping that Ibn al-Rabi's son, Ibn al-Fadl, would drop the idea on his own. Also, I was afraid that a direct refusal would provoke him into hurting us. But he persisted, with more kindness and more promises that he would treat us well for Maymuna's sake, since he was smitten with her. The forewoman assured us that he was madly in love and wanted only the best for us if we accepted his proposal. I made one excuse after another. I even asked the forewoman to help me by discouraging him. She promised to try, and then stayed away for a few days. Thinking she had succeeded, I was reassured. But then last night I received some news that made me give up hope altogether." She sobbed and fell silent, dabbing at her eyes.

Craning her neck to catch every word, Dananir saw the tears and tried to comfort her. "What happened?" she asked.

"The forewoman came back, this time to threaten that if I didn't accept the proposal, we would suffer for it. She said that Ibn al-Fadl had reported us to 'Ali Ibn Mahan, the chief of police, who was now acting as his representative and would keep after us until we accepted al-Fadl's proposal and the gifts he had offered. Otherwise, something terrible would happen to me and Maymuna. I promised the woman that I would think about it and give her an answer. But you know how we feel about that family, especially about Ibn al-Rabi, who was the one behind my son's death. How can I let my granddaughter marry his son when I can't even bear the sound of his name?"

With that, she gave free rein to her tears. Dananir ached for her, knowing as she did that the danger to 'Abbada and her granddaughter was real: they were dealing with people who would carry out whatever threats they made. Head bowed, she thought for a time, then said, "I can't argue with my lady's aversion to that man and his son, but still…" She shrugged, frowned, and fell silent.

"I cannot accept a marriage between Ibn al-Rabi's son and Ja'far's daughter," declared 'Abbada. "And even if I could, do you think Maymuna would consent, knowing as she does that Ibn al-Rabi is the source of all our sorrows? Never!"

"If you feel you must refuse," said Dananir, "then I'm at your service, and so is everyone else at the palace. If you wish to stay here please do: I don't think anyone would dare force you out. I'm happy to see how Zaynab warmed to you, and you know how much influence she has over the Commander of the Faithful. When he returns we'll ask her to put in a good word with him. He never refuses her anything."

'Abbada sighed, sat quietly for a moment, then said: "Dananir, I'm afraid that if we stay here we'll bring disaster down upon you. Bad luck follows us everywhere and I don't want it to strike you as well."

Moved by these words, Dananir said whatever she could to reassure her.

Chapter 15

The Arrival of the Khurasani Doctor

At that moment, they heard the sound of hurrying footsteps in the ante-room. Dananir rose and opened the door to find a page standing outside. "My lady, the doctor has arrived."

Brightening, she exclaimed: "The doctor! What took him so long? Have him come in!" Then she turned back to 'Abbada. "Our Khurasani physician is here," she said, smiling. "He's the one who goes back and forth to Ctesiphon. He might be able to tell us who your benefactor is." Cheered by this prospect, 'Abbada said she was eager to see the visitor.

A few minutes later, the sound of footsteps reached their ears. Dananir went back to the door to welcome the newcomer. As he approached, she said, "It's been so long since we've seen you, Doctor! I hope nothing was wrong."

Adjusting her veil, 'Abbada fixed her eyes on the door. "It was an urgent matter that kept me from coming," she heard the doctor say. "Did you have any need of me?" He spoke with an accent. Her heart beat faster: he sounded like their neighbor Behzad. The physician entered the room, and she saw that it was indeed he. For his part, as soon as he saw her he removed his shoes, hastened to her, shook her hand, greeted her graciously, and asked: "Is it you, my lady?"

"Yes, my lord," she said. "I've come to visit Dananir."

Startled, Dananir asked her: "So Behzad your benefactor is our physician? What a coincidence!" Pointing to a chair, she invited him to sit.

Behzad strode forward and took a seat. He was tall and broad-shouldered, with a massive head, a wide brow, and black, piercing, deep-set eyes.

His beard was thin and his mustache small. He was about twenty-five years old. He was wrapped in a black cloak and wore a short cap with no turban. He was so tall and broad-shouldered that he walked as if working his way down a hill. When he turned to face you, you felt as if you were meeting a giant. In his eyes you could see a tenderness and a penetration that bespoke a strong will and a sincere heart. He was always solemn but never cold or harsh. He was thoughtful, speaking little and laughing only rarely. In company, his presence exerted a kind of dominance; one felt comfortable with him but not over-familiar.

He had hardly taken his seat when Dananir said, "We were talking about you this evening, and then you came up again during our conversation with my lady Umm Ja'far. I never suspected that you were the Behzad she was talking about, since we know you by another name. But I thank God that you are the one who has been so kind to her!"

Glancing furtively at 'Abbada, Dananir saw her raise her eyebrows and bite her lip as if to say 'Don't mention my real name!'

Dananir immediately understood what she was driving at. Behzad, who had noticed nothing, said: "In Ctesiphon I'm known only as Behzad, which is the name the people gave me when they saw I was a Persian. But my name is Abdallah, as you know."

Turning to 'Abbada with affectionate respect, he said: "My lady, I've done nothing to merit any sort of acknowledgement."

Then, turning back to Dananir, he asked whether Zaynab was keeping well.

"She's well," said Dananir. "She's eating dinner with a guest in the dining room. I was going to send her to bed as usual."

Appearing not to notice what she had said, and concealing his uneasiness by busying himself with the adjustment of the scabbard-loop on his belt, Behzad asked whether his servant Salman had arrived.

"No, sir; I've heard nothing of him. Was he supposed to meet you here?"

"Yes, I was expecting him to arrive at dusk. I wasn't able to come here any sooner, and I thought I would find him waiting for me." So saying, he rose with his eye on the door.

"Is there something we can do for you?" asked Dananir.

"Nothing, thank you," he said. "But I'd like to make sure that Salman is here. He may have arrived and gone to the pages' quarters."

"Please have a seat," said Dananir, making for the door. "I'll go look for him."

She had not yet reached the door when she heard a commotion in the anteroom. Zaynab was coming back, laughing at something her companion had said. Smiling in turn, Dananir peered out into the anteroom and said, "Is that you? Haven't you gone to sleep yet? Shall I come and tuck you in bed?"

Before she had finished speaking, Zaynab had dashed up next to her, dragging Maymuna along by a corner of her gown and pulling her playfully toward the door. Maymuna for her part was submitting cheerfully to her antics.

"What's so funny, dear?" Dananir asked Zaynab.

Looking over her shoulder in mock horror, Zaynab shouted, "It's the doctor's page. Come and look at him!"

She pointed into the anteroom. There Dananir saw a man whose dress and appearance were nothing like Salman's. But then she realized that it was indeed he, albeit disguised in a large turban, long sideburns, a wide beard streaked with gray, and a wide-sleeved, open cloak like the ones worn by rabbis. Unable to control herself, she laughed and asked what on earth had happened to him.

Chapter 16

Maymuna

Salman vanished into a corner of the room and then reappeared looking like himself again in his long-sleeved cloak, trousers, and skullcap. The sideburns were gone; his beard was now trimmed and there was no grey in it. Even more surprised at this second transformation, Dananir returned to the sitting room to tell the doctor what she had seen and to let him know that his servant had arrived. But the doctor, having overheard the conversation, had already risen and was hurrying out towards them. He had hardly reached the door when he saw Zaynab come in, trailing Maymuna in her wake and laughing. Zaynab had not known the doctor was there, and when she noticed him, she straightened, averted her eyes in embarrassment, and tried to hide behind her friend.

Seeing her abashed, the doctor smiled, bowed, and asked, "How are you, Umm Habiba?" He reached for her hand. Still overcome by shyness, Zaynab backed away and disappeared completely behind Maymuna. The latter, for her part, had been startled at the sight of the physician and had blushed, though for a reason different than Zaynab's. Uncertain whether to look away modestly or greet her protector and benefactor, she stammered, knees trembling. Seeing how flustered she was, the physician greeted her as if nothing was amiss, and then turned back to Zaynab, trying his best to cajole her into returning his greeting.

'Abbada noticed her granddaughter's consternation but attributed it to the surprise of seeing Behzad so unexpectedly. She knew nothing of Maymuna's innermost thoughts and had never noticed that her feelings for Behzad had gone beyond mere gratitude. Rising immediately, she approached Maymuna, saying, "This is our lord and benefactor! Why ever don't you greet him, Lamya?"

59

Hearing 'Abbada call her granddaughter Lamya, Dananir realized that she was trying to keep the young woman's identity a secret from the doctor. As for Maymuna, when her grandmother asked her to greet him, she plucked up her courage and held out her hand. When he took it, he felt her shiver. He could guess what was going on, but pretended not to notice. Smiling at her as usual in his courteous and deferential manner, he said: "So you're here too, are you, Lamya?" Then he turned back to teasing Zaynab.

Blushing, Maymuna looked away. If she had raised her head, Behzad would have seen her eyes flash and felt the force of her gaze. But he was making a point of paying no attention to her. He turned his gaze on Dananir and noticed that she was watching Maymuna. Observant and experienced as she was, Dananir noticed that the young woman was flustered for reasons that went beyond propriety. She was also surprised to see the doctor so composed, as if he had no idea of what was going on in the young woman's mind. Uncertain of what was happening, she hoped an opportunity would arise to confirm her suspicions. Thus preoccupied, Dananir heard the doctor say, "Where's Salman? I heard you talking about him."

Pointing to the anteroom, Dananir said, "He's here. Shall I call him?"

"No, I'll find him myself," said the doctor, then shouted: "Salman!" He marched out, leaving the company in various states of bewilderment, some surprised, some abashed, and others flummoxed.

"At your service, master," came the reply. "Are you here?"

"You were supposed to be here some time ago," said the doctor, putting on his shoes. "I was worried about you." Walking away, he said to Dananir, "I'll be back shortly." She understood that he was going out to the house—one of the many in the great complex—where he usually stayed during his visits to al-Ma'mun's palace. He met Salman halfway, and then the two men left the anteroom and crossed the grounds to their quarters.

Salman hurried along behind the doctor, who was pacing along with his head bowed. Though he too was tall, he could not match his master's measured but still enormous strides. When they reached the house, he stepped forward and opened the door. He and the doctor removed their shoes and went in. Going to the lamp stand, Salman lit the lamp and shut the door behind him. He remained standing until the doctor had taken a seat on a cushion at the far end of the room and bade him to sit as well. When they had settled themselves comfortably, the doctor asked, "What have you to tell me, Malfan Sa'dun?"

"Even you call me Malfan now?" said Salman, laughing.

"You'll be Malfan until we finish the job we came to do in this part of the world. So what do you have to tell me?"

"I've come with news that no one in the city has heard yet," said Salman. "When it breaks, people will be in shock, either with joy or fear."

The doctor cleared his throat and gave him a sharp look that seemed to penetrate his innermost thoughts and read the secrets in his heart. "Besides the news of al-Rashid's death, what do you have to tell me?"

"You know?" Salman exclaimed, taken aback. "But how on earth? The news just arrived, and no one but the courier knew what it was. If I hadn't seen the copper badge hanging around his neck,[68] I wouldn't have believed he was a courier and his report could be trusted. How did you find out?"

"I found out without seeing a badge or checking up on the honesty of the courier. Al-Rashid is dead. So, Salman: any other news?"

"What could be more important? I thought I was bringing you intelligence you would envy me for! I learned of it by chance, though it did cost me a gold ingot. But all my efforts were in vain. I'm still no good to you."

"On the contrary," said the doctor. "Your energy and sagacity are indispensable. If nothing else, you keep us abreast of the words and hopes of the lower orders, and of how to deal with the Ruffians."

"What good does any of that do?" asked Salman. "You seem to be able to glimpse the Unseen. So tell me: what could be more momentous than al-Rashid's death?"

"What his entourage has done: they've removed al-Ma'mun from the line of succession by repudiating their oaths of allegiance to him. For them, the consequences will be terrible—as you'll see."

"Repudiated their oaths?" asked Salman, astonished. "Traitors! But who was it who did that?"

"Ibn al-Rabi."

"Ibn al-Rabi?" asked Salman, horrorstruck. "Al-Rashid's vizier—the one who accompanied him on his campaign?"

---

68 *Subh al-a'sha* 1: 71.

"That's the one," said the physician, his eyes flashing angrily. "He's embarked on a course that will bring this dynasty to ruin, as he did when he brought about the execution of poor innocent Ja'far. Either deed by itself would be enough to topple a dynasty, and he's committed both!"

"How did this happen, master?" asked Salman, shocked into timidity by his master's anger.

Chapter 17

A Reliable Report

"As you know," said Behzad, "when al-Rashid left he took al-Ma'mun along and bid all the generals, commanders, and officers in his camp to swear allegiance to him. He also named him as heir to all the property and possessions he had brought with him on the expedition. For that we can thank Ibn Sahl, ambitious man that he is."

"Right," said Salman.

"Al-Rashid appointed al-Amin, who is still here in Baghdad, to succeed him as caliph. Al-Ma'mun he named governor of Khurasan and heir apparent to al-Amin. So al-Ma'mun joined the expedition expecting to stay in Khurasan. The day they left, as you know, al-Rashid was ill but concealed his illness. Sabah Tabari—who is close to the Caliph, as you know—went to see him off on the day he left Baghdad. He told me that al-Rashid said, 'I don't think you'll see me again.'

"When Sabah protested and told him there was nothing to worry about, al-Rashid said, 'My illness is worse than you think.'

"'I had no idea,' said Sabah.

"Al-Rashid then turned off the path toward the shade of a tree and dismissed his retinue. Alone with Sabah, he bared his belly. It was wrapped in a silken bandage. 'I'm not telling anyone what's wrong with me,' he said. 'Each of my sons has a spy working for him: al-Ma'mun has Masrur, and al-Amin has Jibril ibn Bakhtyashu.[69] They're all watching and waiting for me to die. If you don't believe me, watch what happens when I call for a mount: they'll bring me a lean, slow-stepping beast, to make my ailment worse. But keep all this to yourself!'

---

69 Masrur served as executioner under al-Rashid, and Jibril was one of the Caliph's physicians.

"Sabah said a prayer for the Caliph's health. Then the Caliph called for a mount. When it came, it was a lean, slow-stepping beast. With a glance at Sabah, al-Rashid mounted and rode off.[70] Sabah returned and told me what had happened."

Salman was astonished at his master's ability to discover such a secret, not to mention his silence on the matter up to that point. Curious about Ibn al-Rabi, he asked what the vizier had done.

"He left Baghdad along with al-Rashid," the physician said. "Along the way, he sent messages back—different than the ones he was sending by official courier—keeping al-Amin abreast of what was going on. When word came that al-Rashid had fallen gravely ill, al-Amin prepared letters and had them placed inside the legs of storage chests for the kitchen. He had the legs hollowed out and then covered with leather, and entrusted one of his retinue, Bakr ibn Mu'tamir, with the task of delivering the chests. He ordered him not to let al-Rashid, or anyone else, see the letters before the time was right. 'Wait until you hear that the Commander of the Faithful has died, then deliver each one to its addressee.'

"When Bakr reached Tus, where al-Rashid was lying ill, his arrival was reported to the Caliph, who summoned him and asked him why he had come. Bakr replied that his master al-Amin had sent him to bring back news. 'Have you any letters?' asked al-Rashid.

"'No,' said Bakr.

"But al-Rashid, who knew that they were plotting and scheming and hoping for his demise, did not believe him; and so ordered his men to search his possessions. They found nothing, but al-Rashid was not satisfied. He ordered them to beat him until he confessed. They did so, inflicting great pain, but he confessed to nothing, and so they nearly killed him.

"Finally, fearing for his life, Bakr asked Ibn al-Rabi to give him some more time, and he would tell them something of significance. But al-Rashid, who was still afraid of what Bakr might be carrying, ordered him executed. Then, as Bakr's luck would have it, the Caliph lost consciousness and everyone stopped what they were doing to gather around him. Soon afterwards, al-Rashid died. Ibn al-Rabi sent someone to inform Bakr, who finally handed over the letters. They turned out to include a message from al-Amin to his brother al-Ma'mun, who was already in Marv, advising him to lay aside his grief and summon the people to swear allegiance to the two

70 Ibn al-Athir VI: 83.

of them. There was also a message to another brother, Salih, ordering him to put the army on the march, and telling him and his men to follow the advice of Ibn al-Rabi. There was also a message to Ibn al-Rabi ordering him to keep close watch on the property in his care. The other letters confirmed the appointments of all present.

"When they had read these messages, the Caliph's men deliberated with the generals about whether they should uphold the oaths they had sworn to al-Ma'mun and follow him to Khurasan, or go back to al-Amin in Baghdad. It was Ibn al-Rabi's idea that they should rejoin al-Amin. 'I shall not renounce a living kingdom,' he said, 'for one that may never come to be.' Therewith he ordered the company to return to Baghdad.

"Now that they've renounced their allegiance to al-Ma'mun," continued Behzad, "I expect them to arrive within a few days. The only reason they broke their oath is that al-Ma'mun's mother is Persian, and they claim to be defending the Arabs. But the only thing they're fighting for is their own ambitions. Soon enough they'll have al-Ma'mun's maternal uncles to deal with!" As he made this speech, Behzad waxed ever more furious, and Salman, though he had known him for a long time and was familiar with his temperament, still found him frightening. He then thought of saying something, but the physician was already rising and saying, "No need to fear for our cousin, though. He's in Khurasan with his kinsmen, including Ibn Sahl."

Rising as well, Salman asked, "What do we do now, master?"

"I've suddenly remembered that I have an urgent errand to run," said Behzad, bowing his head and rubbing his brow between thumb and forefinger.

"Shall I come with you?"

"No, it's best for me to go alone, for reasons you'll learn soon enough."

Shaking his head in perplexity, Salman said, "I'm amazed at the secrets you keep, and the ones you reveal—as if you had the jinn at your command!"

"There's nothing supernatural about it at all," said the physician, adjusting his headgear and sword-belt in preparation for his departure.

"If you don't need me," Salman said quickly, "I'll go and finish the errand I began at sunset. If I hadn't been in such a hurry to tell you about al-Rashid, I would have completed it; but how was I to know that you have second sight?"

"Second sight has nothing to do with it," said Behzad. "As you'll learn, it's all quite natural. But I've learned never to say anything unless I'm sure it's true. Only rash, impulsive people blurt out everything they know. But all their babbling and chattering comes to nothing. As far as I'm concerned, to reveal your decisions is to subvert your aims. That's why you'll hear me make definite statements only under exceptional circumstances. How apt is the saying: 'To achieve your ends, act in secret.'"

Salman, who had been listening carefully, said, "Good advice, certainly! And I'll take it: I'm going now to finish the mission I started, and when it's done I'll tell you about it. I hope you'll be pleased, and won't have already taken care of it yourself!"

"Go, and may God watch over you," said the physician, putting on his shoes. "We'll meet here tomorrow. But if I'm late, don't worry." So saying, he departed, leaving Salman to lock up the house, and headed back to the hall they had come from.

Chapter 18

Does She Love Him?

After the doctor had left, Dananir tucked Zaynab into bed. She asked Maymuna if she wanted to go to sleep as well, but the young woman replied that she preferred to stay up with her grandmother and Dananir. Dananir ordered the servants to prepare some food for herself and 'Abbada. As they ate, they spoke of nothing but Behzad, each telling the others about the strange things they had seen him do. 'Abbada, in particular, praised his brave, generous heart, his noble bearing, and his fine manners, adding that the people of Ctesiphon thought of him as some kind of saint and marveled at his secretiveness, which only made him seem all the more intimidating. Just as one fears the unknown until it is revealed, so too does silence make a man seem more imposing while verbosity undermines his dignity. Forced to guess what someone else is thinking you might imagine it to be something impressive, but when you finally hear it, it turns out to be trivial. Similarly, an incisive remark is all the more impressive when it comes from someone who otherwise has little to say. A wise man, rather than saying the first thing that comes to his mind, knows how to keep his thoughts to himself until the opportune moment.

Listening to her companions talk about Behzad, Maymuna felt her heart leap with emotion. She had known the young man for over a year, during which he had treated her with the kindness of a benefactor and the protectiveness of a close relative. She had come to respect and admire him. Eventually she had grown accustomed to seeing him at regular intervals. When he stayed away, she became fretful. The only thing that reassured her was to see him, even if only for the moment it took him to pass by on the street. Her grandmother's constant praise of his fine qualities made her all the more well-disposed toward him. Seeing him, or hearing his voice, began to make her heart beat faster. When he spoke to her, the blood would rush to her face and shyness would overcome her. After that she would feel her heart thumping at the mention of his name, and she began to take pleasure in talking about him. Should anyone criticize him or find fault with anything he did, she would take this as a personal affront, and rush to defend him with passionate outrage. All this she did without realizing that she loved him. Had she been asked whether she loved him, she would have found the question odd and disturbing—not out of hypocrisy or deceptiveness, but because she was truly unaware of her feelings—all the more so because she had never heard him say anything to suggest that he might be in love with her. When he came home, he would talk to her grandmother about things she needed. Whenever he came across her, he would greet her while looking elsewhere. Occasionally he would ask her how she was, but in a casual, indifferent manner. None of this prevented her from falling ever more deeply in love with him, since it never occurred to her to wonder whether he cared for her. Had she wondered, she would have avoided any kind of involvement, since she could sense no interest on his part.

And so matters stood until she encountered him unexpectedly that night and saw him teasing Zaynab. Though she knew that he was only being kind, she felt a pang of jealousy, as if an arrow had been shot into her heart. Taking a step back, she tried to persuade herself that there was no reason for her to be jealous. Rationally, she knew that that should be so; but her heart remained in turmoil. From that moment on, she began to question her feelings. Now, left to herself—as her grandmother and Dananir were busy eating and talking—she asked herself why she felt as she did. Whenever she thought about whether she loved him, she was overcome with shame and decided that she did not, since she could see nothing in his actions to justify her feelings. So she explained to herself that she loved him because he had been so kind and generous to her.

But then she recognized that that argument made no sense. Her feelings towards him were not at all like those she had for her grandmother, the person who had been the kindest of all to her. It was then that she realized that she felt more than gratitude toward him. Yet she shrank from this realization because she had noticed nothing more than simple kindness from him. Casting her mind back, she thought about all she had seen him say and do, and could find no sign that her feelings were reciprocated. Even so, she thought that perhaps his silence was the result of his penchant for secrecy.

'Abbada and Dananir continued eating and talking, leaving Maymuna lost in thought. When the meal was over, Dananir said, "It's the middle of the night. Would you two like to retire?"

"I don't feel sleepy," said 'Abbada, "but Maymuna should go to bed."

Hearing her grandmother's words, Maymuna recalled that Behzad had promised to return before too long. Since he had left her feeling so bewildered, she felt the desire to see him, especially now that she had begun to suspect that she loved him. Perhaps he would comfort her with some word or sign that would let her believe that he had feelings for her as well. When her grandmother spoke to her, she resented having to obey her—when normally she would comply without a second thought. For the first time in her life she wished she could disobey her, but hardly dared to express her wish aloud. Her dilemma was not lost on Dananir. Unlike 'Abbada, who knew nothing of what her granddaughter was feeling and fully expected her to go off to bed, Dananir understood the reason for the young woman's distress. "What's the point of going to bed now?" Maymuna heard her say. "Let Maymuna stay with us! This is one of the most important nights of my life. That's how happy I am that both of you are here." Reaching out and clasping the young woman to her breast, she continued: "I'm especially delighted to have found my dear Maymuna. Let me have the pleasure of seeing her."

Maymuna's happiness at this welcome intervention is best left to the imagination. She brightened and, laughing with uncontrollable joy, responded to Dananir's embrace with warm kisses of her own.

Chapter 19

An Awkward Moment

'Abbada thanked Dananir for her kindness. Hardly had they resettled themselves when the doctor's footsteps reached their ears. Maymuna's heart began to pound, but she forced herself to remain calm. Rising to receive him, Dananir saw that he was still dressed for the outdoors. He had also wrapped a scarf around his head with the ends trailing, as if embarking on a journey. Before he could say anything Dananir asked him where he was going.

"I need to go and take care of some important business. Otherwise I would have preferred to stay here. But I'll be back tomorrow, God willing."

'Abbada had risen to receive him, and Maymuna with her. After he had spoken, 'Abbada came forward and met him at the door. "Go and God be with you, my son," she said. "I pray you return quickly, and that you not forget us."

Coming forward, the doctor took her hand respectfully. "God forbid I should forget you!" Turning to Dananir, he said, "I would ask you to take good care of my lady 'Abbada, but seeing how kind you are to her, I know I need not ask."

Maymuna, meanwhile, was standing there tongue-tied and weak-kneed. She had prepared something to say by way of a farewell, but no sooner had she seen him than she forgot every word and lost the power of speech.

For his part, the doctor, after bidding farewell to 'Abbada, turned to Maymuna, put out his hand, and took hers. Her hand was cold, and it trembled; so he gave it a covert squeeze while addressing himself to Dananir. "May I ask you to take care of Lamya? I should have asked Umm Habiba, but the two of them get along so well that there's no need. Actually, I should be asking Lamya to put in a good word for me with her mistress." Then, pressing Maymuna's hand, he addressed himself to her, as both their hands trembled: "Will you do that? I saw how quickly you won her over. She feels as comfortable with you as she would with someone she's known for years."

He smiled, and his eyes shone so brightly that they seemed on the verge of revealing what was in his heart. Maymuna became acutely conscious of his sudden kindness, and, finding in his words all the proof she needed of his feelings for her, felt herself pulled in different directions by embarrassment, gratitude, and joy, leaving her in a state best left to the imagination. She fell silent and looked away, thus giving the most eloquent reply available to a young woman in such a circumstance; but even so she could not help smiling and letting her happiness show. As if catching himself and regretting his effusion, Behzad let go of her hand and assumed his usual cryptic countenance. Turning to Dananir, he saluted her quickly and bid the company farewell until the morrow. Then he hurried out.

Dananir had noticed the doctor's interest in Maymuna, and was happy to see it, especially after finding his seeming indifference to her unbecoming. But, pretending not to have noticed anything, she returned his farewell and went back to her guests, saying, "How busy the doctor is! He hardly sits down before he goes off again on some errand or another. I don't understand him at all."

"He's been that way since we've known him," 'Abbada broke in. "As kind as he's always been to us, I can't recall a time when he sat down with us for more than a short time. He always looks preoccupied. This is the first time I've seen him smile, but as you saw it didn't last long."

As for Maymuna, she dwelt happily for a time on the memory of what she had glimpsed in Behzad during their conversation, but then, thinking of the moment when he had let go of her hand and suddenly resumed his usual distant expression, again fell prey to unhappy thoughts. To distract herself from her misgivings, she threw herself into the conversation. Before long, Dananir repeated her expressions of welcome, then invited them to retire; and they went to bed.

Chapter 20

The Ruffians' Hall

As for Salman, recall that he had assumed the identity of Malfan Sa'dun to mix with the common people and befriend the Ruffian chief in order to further the cause of his master Behzad. He had taken his leave of Harch that evening with the promise to meet him that night, no matter how late the hour, at the Ruffians' hall. We have also seen Salman hurrying to the palace to inform the physician of the death of al-Rashid. Discovering that his master knew more than he did about the oath of allegiance and the events that followed, Salman decided to go meet Harch. If the Ruffian then took him along to the police chief, he could break the news to them and thereby persuade them of his soothsaying powers.

After seeing his master off, Salman changed back into his turban, gown, beard, and sideburns, hastened to his mule, and rode toward the Ruffians' hall. It was already midnight. The houses were locked and patrolmen walked the streets, calling out to each other and stopping any strangers they saw. Thanks to his dress and countenance, Sa'dun was able to pass unmolested as far as the Baghdad bridge. The bridge, guarded at both ends, provided the only passage to the west bank and the Ruffians' hall in Harbiyya. He crossed it without incident. On the west bank stood the original Baghdad and the Citadel of Al-Mansur. It was surrounded by the old allotments, where lamps hung over the entries of narrow passageways guarded by sentries armed with truncheons. Sa'dun was afraid of them, but he called one of them over and asked him to walk ahead of him as far as the Ruffians' hall.

Hearing Salman's imperious tone and seeing his attire, the sentry decided he must be a *dhimmi* whose skill in doctoring or astrology had won the Caliph's favor. So he marched on ahead of him as far as the splendid building on the edge of Harbiyya whose gate was manned by two Ruffians dressed in loincloths and palm-fiber helmets. Recognizing Malfan Sa'dun, they came forward and helped him off his mule, saying, "Our master Harch hasn't gone far. He'll be back soon. He told us to welcome you and ask you to wait for him in the hall."

Salman dismounted and, tapping with his cane, followed the Ruffian through a reception room into a courtyard and then into a great hall illuminated by lamps that hung from the ceiling like chandeliers. The floor was covered by figured carpets, cushions, and chairs. At the Ruffian's invitation, he took a chair on the right side of the room.

This was the first time he had seen the Ruffians' hall. The sumptuous furnishings did not impress him, but the weapons and equipment hanging on the walls did. There were swords, bows, and lances, as well as slingshots made of leather, twisted hair, and silk, each with its bag of projectiles. Here and there he could see the long sticks of ashwood that the Ruffians would clamber on to cross the canals, and hanging next to them were rope ladders, called 'scaling coils,' with hooks at the ends, used to climb onto roofs. There were also devices used to set ablaze the rags soaked in naphtha that were launched from catapults. He could see only one catapult, of the small type used to fire flaming rags or bolts, not the large type used to launch boulders. Hanging across the room were the "pins," that is, the truncheons, studded with nails, most of them iron but some of silver and gold. These "pins" were carried only by commanders; some were made entirely of iron. On a shelf he saw the lead projectiles that the Ruffians would fling at their enemies, killing several at a time. There were many other items too: weapons, tools for breaking and drilling, various sorts of rope, and other equipment needed by the Ruffians.

Chapter 21

The Chief of Police

Salman waited for a half-hour that seemed much longer as he anxiously reviewed the singular events he had already witnessed that night. Then, hearing noises from the direction of the doorway, he guessed that Harch had arrived. Adjusting his costume, he roused himself to meet him. A moment later Harch hurried into the hall. Behind him was a handsome young man wearing a cloak, trousers, and a tall cap, with the first growth of beard showing on his cheeks. Because of his fair complexion, he looked like a white slave. The young man stopped at the door but Harch made his way quickly to Salman, who had risen to his feet. Harch greeted him first and said, "I didn't mean to be late. But Hamid"—here he pointed to the youth—"has a request to make of the chief of police and insists that I go with him. Can you join us?"

"I'm here," said Sa'dun, "only because you insisted that I come and see you again, even though it's the middle of the night. If you'd rather I didn't go with you I can come back later."

"Nothing of the kind," exclaimed Harch. "I very much want you to come, even though the night is almost over. Let's be on our way: the animals are ready." Turning to the youth, he said, "We're going with Malfan Sa'dun to see the police chief. When we get there, I'm going to ask him to enroll you in the Shakiriyya. That's better than being a Ruffian."

Salman realized that Harch had promised Hamid a posting to the Shakiriyya corps. Looking at the young man more closely, he could see that he was not only handsome but also proud and alert. None of this surprised him: among the slaves brought to Baghdad, or born there, were some of the most beautiful and intelligent creatures in God's creation. Most were enrolled in the militia or the guards, or in the Shakiriyya corps, which was in charge of delivering messages within the palace.

75

Taking Salman's hand as a gesture of welcome, Harch led the way out-side. Uppermost in his mind was the desire to ask him what news he had brought, but he would not allow himself to rush into unseemly questions.

They came out of the hall. Salman mounted his mule and Harch his horse, and they set out accompanied by two of the Ruffians, with the young man riding behind them on a donkey and marveling at the special treat-ment the Sabean was receiving from Harch. Hamid himself had only one concern: that Harch would be able to secure him entry to the Shakiriyya. He had been preparing himself to join the regiment of Ruffians, but he could hardly ignore the wishes of his master, who had raised him and who was the only guardian he had ever known. Harch had shown him kindness, treated him with paternal affection, and—in a manner unusual among the Ruffians—seen to his education, thus earning his unswerving loyalty.

The police chief's residence was not far from the Ruffians' hall, and the party reached it quickly enough. They dismounted before a gate manned by two sleepy sentries who, when they heard the creaking of the bridles, straightened up, saw Harch, and made way. Harch entered without asking permission, and Sa'dun followed, leaning on his staff. A guardsman carry-ing a lamp led them along a long colonnade to a hall concealed by a drawn curtain. Harch cleared his throat loudly. A chamberlain appeared and reached out to shake his hand, but Harch cut him off by asking whether his master was in.

"He must be waiting for you," came the reply, "as I've never known him to stay up this late before—not since he's gotten old."

Ignoring this remark, Harch stepped forward, lifted the curtain, and motioned for Malfan Sa'dun to go in. With a gesture, he asked Hamid to wait in the colonnade until he was summoned.

"Harch is here, master," declared the chamberlain.

After removing his shoes and placing his staff by the door, Salman, dressed in his Sabean costume, entered the hall. There, sitting on a cush-ion, was Ibn Mahan. Beside him were two men. One of them was leaning over him as if reporting something important. Salman recognized him as Sallam, chief of the courier service, and guessed that it was to the news of al-Rashid's death that the astonished Ibn Mahan was listening so intently.

The second man was a youth of some twenty-five years of age, of comely appearance and goodly dress. His face was pink and his eyes shone with youthful vigor. He was wearing a costly gown and a brocade turban wrapped around a conical cap. The hall was redolent of his perfume. He was listening to the Chief Courier's news no less intently than Ibn Mahan. Salman recognized him as Ibn al-Fadl, the son of Ibn al-Rabi. He himself was known to none of the men as Malfan Sa'dun except insofar as Harch may have described him to them.

Ibn Mahan was an old man whose ambition had not been diminished by the passage of time. He wore a broad beard dyed with henna. His brow was lined and his face betrayed his age, but pride and self-importance were evident in his way of sitting, moving, and speaking. He was especially proud of his closeness to the ruling elite, a closeness he had earned by serving them since the days of al-Mansur. When the latter had died in 158 AH (775 AD), 'Isa ibn Musa had refused to swear allegiance to his son al-Mahdi; but Ibn Mahan had put his hand on the pommel of his sword and shouted, "Swear, or I'll behead you!" 'Isa complied. From that time on, Ibn Mahan had enjoyed the confidence of the 'Abbasid caliphs. He had witnessed the accession of four caliphs, of whom the last was al-Rashid. Jealous of the Barmakids, he had joined forces with Ibn al-Rabi against the Persians and their allies. It was for this reason that al-Amin had promoted him to chief of police. Ibn Mahan's foremost concern was now to shore up al-Amin's power.

Apprehensive about the fate of the caliphate after al-Rashid's departure, Ibn Mahan had shared his misgivings with Harch, who had informed him of Malfan Sa'dun's power to foretell the future and promised to bring the two together that night. Ibn Mahan had awaited the appointment on tenterhooks. Meanwhile, the Chief Courier had arrived to report the death of al-Rashid, and the two sat discussing what would happen next. As for Ibn al-Fadl, the son of Ibn al-Rabi, he was a frequent caller on familiar terms—thanks to his father's position—with Ibn Mahan, and thus joined in listening to the Chief Courier's report. Hearing the chamberlain announce Harch's arrival, Ibn Mahan turned toward the door to welcome him and Malfan Sa'dun with a forced smile of the sort affected by conceited men when they make a pretense of humility.

Salman, or Malfan Sa'dun, unswayed by Ibn Mahan's smile, entered the room and offered a greeting.

"This," said Harch, "is Malfan Sa'dun. He's come along with me."

Without stirring from his seat, Ibn Mahan ran his fingers through his beard, smiled, and said, "Welcome to the learned astrologer!" He motioned for his visitors to take a seat. Then he turned to the Chief Courier. "I was worried," he said, "about the event you've just reported to me, and I sought the help of this astrologer to help me learn what happened. But there's no need for that now." Sitting up, he continued, "But I'm glad to have met him. Perhaps I'll require him on some other occasion."

Harch realized that the police chief thought that the courier's report was a secret to them as well. He shot a glance at Malfan Sa'dun, who understood what it meant, and was sure that he himself was carrying a secret unknown to any in Baghdad. He gave Harch a shrewd glance in return, and shrugged his shoulders. Harch then turned to Ibn Mahan, saying, "I see that you're engaged with the Chief Courier and with our master Ibn al-Fadl. Have we come at an inconvenient time?"

Unable to hide his interest, Ibn Mahan laughed and said, "Under the circumstances, there's no doing without astrologers, especially if their predictions are reliable." Then he addressed himself to Salman. "Have you discovered anything that might interest us, Malfan?"

"I may have," he replied, as if placing no great trust in himself.

Harch then intervened. "The news you're whispering about," he said, "was known to us hours ago!"

"What news is that?" asked Ibn Mahan in mock ignorance.

Harch signaled to Salman, who, seeing what was wanted, said, "Al-Rashid's death is no news to me. But that's just the beginning. If I were to perform a divination tonight, perhaps..."

Chapter 22

Taken by Surprise

Taken by surprise, Ibn Mahan looked at the Chief Courier as if expecting him to be equally astonished. But it was Ibn al-Fadl who took the initiative, asking whether there was any news besides the death of al-Rashid.

"Al-Rashid, may God rest his soul, was ill before he left," came the reply. "All of us expected him to die. But the mirror has revealed certain other matters that I will divulge to you if you promise to keep them from our master al-Amin until he hears of them from others." By saying this, he hoped to achieve the opposite: that is, to encourage those present to spread the news, as a crafty strategist will do when seeking to spread word of some accomplishment. The insistence on secrecy, and the apparent fear of exposure, only make a person more likely to disseminate the news (in confidence, of course) and thereby make the one revealing the secret seem all the more formidable.

Provoked by his reticence, Ibn al-Fadl said eagerly, "If you know something of interest, then telling our master al-Amin about it can only work in your favor. But what is it that you know?"

"A secret that concerns Ibn al-Fadl more than anyone else."

Surreptitiously moving closer to him, Ibn al-Fadl asked, "What is it? And why should it matter to Ibn al-Fadl in particular?" He was confident that Malfan Sa'dun did not know who he was.

"Because it concerns his father, the vizier Ibn al-Rabi—that is, your father."

Ibn al-Fadl was surprised to be recognized, but was more interested in knowing what the secret was. He turned to Ibn Mahan.

79

"That's quite a claim you're making," said the latter to Malfan Sa'dun. "Say what you have to say and let's see if we believe you. If your prediction comes true, we promise to make you our master's confidant."

"If by that you mean the Commander of the Faithful, to be his confidant is a great blessing. We are his servants, nothing more."

Startled by Malfan Sa'dun's use of the title, Ibn Mahan asked, "Why are you calling him Commander of the Faithful? As far as we know, he's the heir apparent. Al-Rashid is dead, true; but is al-Amin already caliph?"

"He is caliph, and he alone! Thus the matter has come to pass."

"What do you mean, he alone?" asked Ibn Mahan, realizing that Malfan Sa'dun indeed had something new to tell him.

"It came to pass thanks to the efforts of the vizier, Ibn al-Rabi," said Salman, pointing to Ibn al-Fadl, the vizier's son.

Suddenly the room was all ears. Keenest of all was Harch, who broke in saying, "This is news to me too. You've clearly discovered something since I last saw you. Tell us what you know!"

Sitting up straight in his seat, head bowed, Salman told them what he had heard from Behzad, as if reading from a document spread before him. The others sat silent, hearts pounding in wonder, especially Ibn al-Fadl, who swelled with pride at what his father had achieved on behalf of al-Amin. He had heard intimations of his father's plans; and now, hearing from Salman that those plans had come to fruition, he forgot his doubts. Unable to contain himself, he went up to him and clapped him on the shoulder in admiration. "God bless you!" he cried. "You're a marvelous astrologer!"

For his part, Ibn Mahan refrained from expressing his admiration. "Are you certain of this, man?" he asked.

"That's what the mirror revealed," replied Salman with a shrug. "I've never known it to deceive me before."

Knowing himself outdone, the Chief Courier felt nothing but disdain for the news he himself had brought, and said nothing at all.

Ibn Mahan turned to Harch. "If what Malfan Sa'dun is saying is true, something serious is afoot, and I congratulate him in advance on his appointment as chief astrologer in the Caliph's palace. For now, though, keep this secret until we see what happens." From under his seat-cushion he pulled a bundle of coins and offered it to the astrologer. "This will cover the cost of your journey and the price of your incense."

Salman clasped his hands behind his back and moved away in horror, leaving Ibn Mahan with his hand in the air clasping the bag. Salman turned to Harch as if surprised. Laughing, Harch took the bag and put it back, saying, "Our astrologer doesn't ply his trade for profit. He gives us his knowledge in return for our friendship."

All present expressed their admiration for this high ideal. "If that's what he prefers," said the police chief. "He'll earn many times more if he gets as close to the Caliph as I think he will."

At that point Salman rose to go, saying, "Please excuse us! We've disturbed you and now we're keeping you up late."

All condescension gone, Ibn Mahan was unable to stop himself from rising in respect, realizing how useful the man's knowledge might be to him. So it is when people encounter a real expert: though at first they may show him respect only as a matter of form, let him prove his expertise and they will feel genuine esteem. You may sit with a man whose shabby appearance inspires contempt, making you feel superior to him, but let him speak: if he turns out to be a learned man, your contempt will give way to respect, and you will concede that he is superior to you. You may have ignored him when he came in, but by the time he leaves, you are happy to rise and escort him out, lavishing him with compliments. So it was with Ibn Mahan, who had received Malfan Sa'dun half-heartedly, convinced that he was merely seeking favors. But when he witnessed his display of learning and his indifference to material gain, Ibn Mahan rose in admiration to escort him to the door, asking him to return the next day.

As he bid goodbye to Harch, Ibn Mahan lavished praise on him for having introduced him to the astrologer. "I've done nothing to deserve your praise," said Harch to Ibn Mahan, "and your kindness to us seems endless." Then he remembered his protégé Hamid, who was still waiting outside. Calling him in, he presented him to the police chief. "This is a young man I don't let go lightly," he said. "I'd like to see him among the Shakiriyya at the Caliph's palace. I'm asking you to have him admitted."

The young man came forward, bent over Ibn Mahan's hand and kissed it, and then straightened into a decorous posture.

"Go to the pages' quarters," said Ibn Mahan, "and tomorrow you'll be one of the Shakiriyya." He turned to Harch. "Rest easy; it's all taken care of." Harch bowed and went out.

Of them all, Ibn al-Fadl was the most gratified, thinking, as he did, that the astrologer might prove useful to him. He accompanied Salman to the door and, when everyone but Harch was out of earshot, whispered that he had a job for him that had nothing to do with the caliphate. He insisted that the astrologer come to see him. Gesturing his assent, Salman left with Harch. Then he bid the latter goodbye, mounted his mule, and rode off. It was nearly dawn.

For his part, the Chief Courier did not sleep at all, preparing himself instead to report to al-Amin. He should have conveyed the news as soon as he received it, but he could not resist divulging it to the police chief first. As day broke, he made his way to the Palace of Eternity to tell al-Amin what he had learned.

Chapter 23

The Oath of Allegiance

The people of Baghdad, who so far had no inkling of what was afoot, awoke to hear town criers in the streets announcing the death of al-Rashid and the accession of al-Amin. For the members of the Hashimite family and the high officials, the most pressing matter was the tendering of the customary oath of allegiance.

Early that morning—19 Jumada II, 193 AH (April 9, 809 AD)—Sa'dun made his way to Ibn Mahan's residence. The police chief welcomed him[71] and surreptitiously included him into his retinue so he could witness the accession ceremony. When they reached the Palace of Eternity, the party dismounted amid the crush of soldiers and dignitaries on their way inside. They were admitted at the Commoners' Gate, and Sa'dun went in alongside Ibn Mahan.

Attending the ceremony were the senior members of the Hashimite family then present in Baghdad, along with the commanders and state officials. Together they formed a crowd that filled the hall. On the throne sat al-Amin. He was twenty-three, with a muscular build and a long beard and sideburns that gave him a manly appearance. He was tall, brave, and daring enough to face a lion without flinching. He was also handsome, with fair skin, small eyes, a slightly hooked nose, and lank hair. His face bore the scars of smallpox.[72] He had been dressed in the caliphal regalia, with the jewelled turban on his head and the mantle of the Prophet on his shoulders. The mantle, along with the staff and signet ring, had been collected by his brother Salih and brought from Tus by Raja' the Retainer. With the ring on his finger and the staff in his hand, al-Amin looked particularly handsome

---

71 Abu al-Fida, II; al-Mas'udi, II; *Siyar al-muluk.*

72 Idem.

and regal. Before him were the Hashimite family, sitting on chairs. Other dignitaries were seated on cushions or carpets. The rest of the attendees were standing. Whether in mourning for al-Rashid or out of deference to al-Amin, all had their heads bowed.

The first official to come forward was Sallam, the Chief Courier, who pronounced his condolences on the death of al-Rashid and acclaimed al-Amin as caliph. Then came the Hashimites, who offered their condolences and clasped al-Amin's arm to declare their allegiance. The commanders and senior officials, including Ibn Mahan and Ibn al-Fadl, made their oaths to Sulayman ibn al-Mansur, the senior member of the Hashimite family, who was empowered to receive them on the Caliph's behalf. Standing in the press of people, Malfan Sa'dun attracted no notice at all.

When the tendering of oaths was completed, al-Amin rose to address the crowd. All those present craned their necks to hear him. After praising God, he said, "People! Dignitaries of the 'Abbasid house! In wait for all those who live and breathe, by a divine decree that cannot be averted or denied, lies Death. So turn your hearts away from sorrows past to pleasures present, that you may be rewarded for your fortitude and recompensed for your gratitude to God."

No one had expected him to speak so boldly, and the sermon caused some surprise. Then, following the custom that dictated that a caliph upon his accession should ensure the loyalty of his troops by paying their stipends, he ordered that the army receive twenty-four months' worth of pay.

After all the oaths were given, al-Amin's poet, Abu Nuwas, spoke, combining condolence and congratulation:

Bereaved, we feel a shared delight
As Time's one stroke brings weal and woe;
With weeping eyes but smiling lips,
We mourn, then to a wedding go.

Tears for al-Rashid still on our cheeks,
We greet al-Amin, the king to be;
We hail two moons: one in Tus interred,
The other rising in Eternity.

Throughout the ceremony, Ibn al-Fadl remained preoccupied by the matter he intended to discuss with Malfan Saʿdun. When the ceremony was over, Ibn al-Fadl, seeing that Saʿdun was preparing to leave, caught up with him and asked him to come along. But Salman—who was determined to find his master Behzad—pleaded urgent business and offered instead to see him later that day. "Come this evening, then," said Ibn al-Fadl, "to our residence in Rusafa."

Bidding him farewell, Salman hurried away towards al-Maʾmun's palace.

Chapter 24

At Home in
Al-Ma'mun's Palace

Al-Rashid's death had struck a grievous blow to the residents of al-Ma'mun's palace. Most affected was Zaynab, who had adored al-Rashid. She wept bitterly when she heard the news. Dananir, though she did not yet know what Behzad knew—namely, that al-Ma'mun had been ousted from the succession—was well enough acquainted with court intrigue to suspect that a *coup d'état* was in the offing. Even so, she continued to wait for word from her master. If al-Ma'mun indeed became governor of Khurasan now that his father had died, as stipulated on the day the expedition left the capital, then he might send for his daughter and the other members of the household. Amid the tumult, she wished she could consult with Behzad the physician about what to do. If nothing else, she needed his help in caring for Zaynab, who despite her youth had been deeply affected by her grandfather's death. Normally full of laughter, the girl had withdrawn into herself and stopped showing interest in anything. She refused to leave her room or to eat, and her health began to suffer. She lost color and began to feel dizzy. Dananir, who remained at her bedside, could do nothing to comfort her. Worried, Dananir asked if she might call in some of the palace doctors. Zaynab refused but Dananir insisted. Finally the girl asked, "Where's the doctor from Khurasan?" Knowing that Behzad was the one Zaynab was most comfortable with, and the only one capable of healing her spirit as well as her body, Dananir awaited his return with mounting impatience.

'Abbada too, was saddened by al-Rashid's death. Not only had he been like a son to her, as we have seen, but his death meant that Zaynab could no longer intercede with him on her behalf, as the girl had promised. Admittedly, 'Abbada could take some consolation in the prospect of a *coup d'état* that would redound to her benefit. Yet such an event was unlikely

given the machinations of al-Ma'mun's enemies, who were equally the enemies of the Persians, herself included. She decided that her most urgent
task was to join Dananir in trying to console Zaynab. If she could manage
to be alone with the governess, she could broach the subject of what might
happen next.

As for Maymuna, she paid little attention to what was going on around
her, distracted as she was by her heart's desire to see her beloved and ascer-
tain his feelings for her. Love has a way of insulating a person from her sur-
roundings. When her beloved is absent, she becomes scatterbrained, inca-
pable of thinking about anything but his return. Nothing will make her
forget her longing or renounce her passion, and thoughts of anything else
will prove fleeting. Then, when she joins her beloved, an impenetrable wall
rises to block off all awareness of outside events. She becomes deaf to everything but his voice, blind to everything but the sight of him, and mute
except when she answers him. She hears and sees, certainly, but like one listening through a wall or staring into the darkness. Should events intrude,
they concern her only to the extent that they bear upon her lover's ability
to be near her, or the possibility that he might move away. It was only in
this last respect that al-Rashid's death mattered to Maymuna. She was still
unsure of how Behzad felt about her, especially in view of how he had bid
her goodbye the day before and then rushed away in so odd a manner. The
day passed with no sign of him or of his servant, whom she regarded with
affection and hoped to see so that she could ask him how long his master
was likely to be gone.

Maymuna thus spent the day troubled, but for reasons that had nothing to do with the grief that reigned in the palace or the clamor that filled
Baghdad during the ceremony of accession, even among those far from the
center of activity. She occupied herself by sitting with Zaynab and consol-
ing her as best she could. All the while, she was listening for footsteps, her
eyes on the door, hoping someone would bring news of Behzad. When she
overheard Dananir telling 'Abbada that she hoped the doctor would arrive
soon, her heart pounded but she remained quiet and anxious. By sunset she
had eaten nothing, the bereaved denizens of the palace having forgotten to
tend to her needs.

It was then that Maymuna saw one of the page boys approaching as if
bearing news. She roused herself to meet him, but then stopped, remembering that he might well be coming to see Dananir on palace business.
Pretending to have risen for reasons of her own, she walked slowly to the

door. She saw the page stop, greet Dananir, and announce that Salman, the doctor's man, had asked to see her.

Maymuna's heart pounded and the consternation she felt at the mere mention of Behzad nearly showed in her face. Dananir, meanwhile, was saying, "Bring him in! I hope he's here to say his master's on the way. We certainly need his help!"

A moment later, Salman, dressed in his ordinary clothes, made his appearance, walking heavily as if in mourning. At the edge of the room, he bowed and waited for permission to come in. Dananir spoke first: "What brings you here, Salman? Have you seen what misery has befallen us?" She stopped, choking on a sob.

Eyes averted, Salman came forward until he reached Zaynab's couch. He bowed as if to kiss her hand, looking all the while as if on the verge of tears. Then he turned to Dananir and said in the most mournful and self-effacing manner possible: "It is a great loss, my lady. The passing of the Commander of the Faithful is a bitter blow indeed. May God grant long life to our master al-Ma'mun and his children, and make him a worthy successor to a worthy sire." Swallowing, he backed away and stood against the wall.

Motioning for him to sit, Dananir asked whether he had seen the doctor.

"No, my lady, not since we parted yesterday. I was thinking he might be here."

"He hasn't come, Salman," she said reproachfully. "Under the circumstances, we were expecting him. Our mistress has fallen ill and refuses to see any other doctor."

"When he arrives, I'm sure he'll have a good explanation. He'll be here soon: I can't imagine him waiting until tomorrow or..."

"Don't you know where he is?" interrupted 'Abbada.

"No," he replied. "No one knows a thing about his comings and goings."

"We're accustomed to not seeing him for days at a time and then having him arrive unexpectedly," said Dananir. "But..."

"I think he's gone back to his house in Ctesiphon," said 'Abbada.

Salman shrugged as if to disavow any knowledge of his master's whereabouts.

Maymuna had been listening to the conversation but had been too shy to take part in it. But then curiosity got the better of her and she said, feigning innocent indifference, "I think he is in Ctesiphon, with his door locked, working on alchemy, or treasure hunting, or whatever it is they say he does." For all her circumspection, she was unable to finish speaking without blushing and glancing at Dananir, who was studying her face and smiling. Feeling even more embarrassed, Maymuna looked away and then went over to a pillow along the wall, where she sat and busied herself with adjusting her veil.

Salman, pretending not to notice any of this, said to 'Abbada, "People accuse my master of all kinds of unlikely things. When he hides away in his house, it's to read books on medicine or philosophy. In any case, if I knew he was there I would go now and fetch him. I don't think he'll be gone much longer, but if he doesn't come tonight or tomorrow morning, we'll search for him in Ctesiphon, or wherever he may be."

In exaggerating her fear for the doctor, Dananir hoped to placate Zaynab. She was also thinking of Maymuna, who, as she knew, was too shy to express her concern and needed someone else to do so on her behalf. Hearing Salman's promise, she said, "We must look for him tonight, if at all possible."

He stepped back, and, eyes averted, said, "I will do as you command. I hope to have something to report to you tonight or tomorrow morning."

Dananir thanked him, then glanced wordlessly at Maymuna, who gave her a look full of gratitude. Smiling, she turned to 'Abbada, asking, "Don't you agree?"

"Of course," came the immediate reply. "If Salman is too busy to search, I can go look for him in Ctesiphon, since I know his house well. It would be an easy trip for us." Scratching behind one ear, she continued, "Or, if you want Salman to search elsewhere, we'll go look in Ctesiphon."

When Maymuna heard 'Abbada's suggestion, her face lit up, since the idea was the one she would have proposed if she could. It was as if her grandmother had spoken for her.

As for Salman, he had promised to search for Behzad only out of deference to Dananir. He was planning to honor his appointment with Ibn al-Fadl, hoping thereby to make progress in the quest that had brought him to the palace. Moreover, he saw no good reason to worry about his master, knowing as he did the number of things the man had to take care of. But he nevertheless promised, as he took his leave, to go and look for him.

Chapter 25

Ibn al-Fadl

Leaving them thus, Salman went out, changed his clothing, mounted his mule, and made his way to the mansion of Ibn al-Rabi. The mansion was located in Rusafa, on the east side of Baghdad, overlooking Maydan Street. The lot had originally been granted by al-Rashid as a fief to 'Abbad Ibn Khasib but was now the property of Ibn al-Rabi,[73] who lived there with his family. Though it too was on the east side, it was far from al-Ma'mun's palace. Salman cut through Mukharrim to reach Maydan Street, which started at the Tuesday market and ended in Shammasiyya, where it was called Khudayr Street. It was there that Chinese manufactures and other precious goods were brought for sale.

It was nearly sunset when Salman reached the mansion gate to find Ibn al-Fadl, Ibn al-Rabi's son, waiting for him. The young man had described Malfan Sa'dun for the guards and told them to escort him in. Thus it was that Salman reached the gate and dismounted without being stopped by the guard, who before he could identify himself, asked if he was Malfan Sa'dun. When Salman replied in the affirmative, he was told that the master was waiting for him inside.

Head bowed, Salman made his way slowly through the garden, tapping with his stick and muttering under his breath as if reciting scripture or chanting a spell. A second guard raced ahead to inform Ibn al-Fadl. When they reached the inner door, they found that the host had come out to meet the visitor. He welcomed Malfan Sa'dun, shook his hand, and escorted him through the reception room, across a great hall, and into a private room accessible only to the young man and his intimate friends. It was furnished with a couch, two chairs, a costly rug, and a corner stand where several

---

73 Yaqut, *Dictionary*, 4: 108.

candles had been lit. Seating himself on the couch, Ibn al-Fadl invited Malfan Sa'dun to take one of the nearby chairs.

Still muttering to himself, Malfan Sa'dun sat down, holding one elbow close against his body as if to protect some precious object under his arm. After settling into his seat, he pulled out a packet bundled in a piece of silk and slowly untied the knot. The wrapping contained an ancient codex of parchment pages with holes in the cover. He laid it carefully in his lap. Visible through the holes was writing in a script illegible to man and jinn alike. Then, making a show of completing his muttered recitation, he passed a hand over his face from brow to chin, turned to Ibn al-Fadl, and thanked him for his kind reception.

"You are most welcome," said Ibn al-Fadl, beaming. Then, hoping to break the ice before divulging the secret he intended to confide, he began speaking with him in a jesting manner, trying thereby to put him at ease and gain his confidence.

"You are far too kind, Vizier," said Malfan Sa'dun, smiling.

Though he assumed that Malfan Sa'dun had called him vizier because he had foreseen his accession to that position, Ibn al-Fadl feigned ignorance, hoping thus to confirm what he suspected. "You called me 'Vizier,' but it's my father who's the vizier."

"The son of a vizier is a vizier too, my son," said Malfan Sa'dun. "Command me, and I shall obey."

"Since you've called me a vizier, I'll call you Chief Astrologer in the Caliph's palace."

Salman realized that Ibn al-Fadl was promising to secure that position for him—a promise he could keep, given his father's influence and al-Amin's willingness to listen to both of them. Hoping to confirm the promise, he said, "Bless you, Ibn al-Fadl! I know that you're a man who keeps his word. In any event, I'm at your service."

Ibn al-Fadl sat deep in thought for a moment. "I've called you here," he said, "because I need your help with something. It's something I'm determined to have, but it must remain a secret."

"The matter my master is referring to," said Salman, "is a secret to everyone but myself, Malfan Sa'dun, from whom nothing is concealed."

Startled, Ibn al-Fadl tested him: "So you know my secret?"

Salman had heard one of al-Ma'mun's palace servants talking about Ibn al-Fadl's love for Maymuna. He had also overheard 'Abbada telling the story to Dananir the day before. In those days, servants were well acquainted with their masters' secrets, since their masters thought nothing of speaking freely before them. "I think I do know," he replied, "unless it's something besides your love for that young woman who imagines that no one knows her ancestry."

Taken aback by this frank declaration, Ibn al-Fadl threw discretion aside. "Well, since you already know, I won't try to hide the fact that I'm utterly, completely, and painfully enamored of her." As he spoke, his eyes shone and he blushed, looking lovelorn.

Salman shook his head, laughing. "There's no force like love," he said. "So you love her?"

"I do. But does she love me?"

"I don't know. Perhaps if she were here now I could see into her heart, though I would need to use divination."

"Let's assume she doesn't care for me," said Ibn al-Fadl. "In fact, that seems to be the case so far. What can I do? That's why I called you here for help. What do you think?"

Salman lifted the codex from his lap, opened it, and began turning it in his hands as if reading from it. Then he would re-read a passage, bow his head, raise his eyes to the ceiling, and then look down at the pages again. Next he scrutinized Ibn al-Fadl's face as if trying to fathom his thoughts. Finally he looked down with his hand on his beard as if giving deep thought to some regrettable circumstance. Then he said: "Your beloved has moved."

"Where did she go? And where was she before?"

"Wasn't she in Ctesiphon?"

"Of course."

"She's not there any more."

"Where is she? Where did she go?"

"I know that she's left Ctesiphon, but I don't know where she's staying now. To know that, I need to do more searching."

"Perhaps she's on the road somewhere," said Ibn al-Fadl, certain that, if she were somewhere in particular, Malfan Sa'dun would be able to tell.

"Perhaps so," said Malfan Sa'dun. "But it makes no difference. There's nowhere in Heaven or on Earth that can hide her from me."

Relieved, Ibn al-Fadl smiled. "May God reward you! Do whatever you think is best, and spare no expense. I'm willing to spend all I have to obtain her. And by that I mean marry her according to God's law: I'm sincerely in love with her, and I don't know why she resists me."

Salman smiled dismissively. "I think you know why. Aren't feuds passed on from parents to their children?"

Ibn al-Fadl was again surprised by how much his visitor knew. "You're right," he said. "That is the reason. But if she knew how much I loved her, and how I would make her forget what my father did to hers, I'm sure she would change her mind."

"She does know, but she didn't change her mind. But no matter, she will." Pointing to a pen-case stuffed into his waist-band, he said: "This pen can turn stone to water and back again. It can certainly soften the heart of a girl!"

"Do as you see fit," said Ibn al-Fadl, "and spend whatever you need."

"Weren't you there yesterday when I visited the police chief?" asked Salman, looking at him with narrowed eyes. "Why do you insist on insulting your friends? Well, it's not your fault, I suppose: you're more accustomed to the company of sycophants and flatterers."

Ibn al-Fadl hastened to apologize. "Forgive me! I'll accept this as a favor from you, but please accept my help in asking the chief of police to appoint you Chief Astrologer to the Commander of the Faithful. In fact, we'd be doing a great service to the Caliph: having you at his court would be a great boon to him." Then he asked: "What is that you're doing now?"

"Let me try to find out where she is," said Salman. "Then I'll write a letter for you. If you can deliver it to her—and I'll tell you how to do so—she'll come prepared to do anything for you."

Thunderstruck, Ibn al-Fadl rose involuntarily to his feet. "Do you really mean that? I don't know how to thank you. When will you write the letter?"

"When I finish my search. Don't lose hope, and don't do anything rash."

"Then proceed as you see fit," said Ibn al-Fadl. "But I do ask that you grant me one request."

"What's that?"

"Stay here tonight and come with me tomorrow morning to the Caliph's court so I can present you to him and he can make you the Chief Astrologer."

"I'll come to the palace," said Salman. "But I won't spend the night here. I'll come tomorrow morning if you wish."

"No, stay here," said Ibn al-Fadl. "The mansion is big. You can choose the room you want, and no one will bother you. I've already sent word to the police chief to escort us to the audience inside the Round City. Now that al-Amin's been acclaimed caliph, the court has moved from the Palace of Eternity outside Khurasan Gate to the interior of the City."[74] He clapped his hands and his page came in. "Prepare a table for dinner, and tell the houseman to prepare a room for Malfan Sa'dun to spend the night."

Seeing that Ibn al-Fadl would not take no for an answer, Salman was reluctant to refuse and possibly undo all the work he had done to win him over. A moment later, he rose for dinner, and later spent the night at the mansion.

---

74 Ibn al-Athir, VI; and *Tales of the Kings*.

Chapter 26

The Citadel of AL-Mansur

The next morning, Ibn al-Fadl, dressed in the black robe required when appearing before the 'Abbasid caliphs, rode out with his entourage. Salman, dressed as Malfan Sa'dun, mounted his mule and rode with them westwards out of Rusafa. Crossing the bridge, they reached the road that led to the Palace of Eternity, but did not take it, al-Amin having moved after his accession from there to al-Mansur's palace, the Golden Gate, as mentioned above.

The Citadel of Al-Mansur was circular in plan. Its fortifications consisted of three walls, of which the middle one was the largest. This middle wall was 20,000 cubits in length, ninety cubits wide at the base, and sixty cubits high, narrowing to a width of twenty-five cubits at the top.[75] It was surrounded by a ring of open space, equally wide, encircled by an outer wall flanked with bastions and turrets. Around this outer wall was an embankment of baked and well-cemented brick and a moat filled with running water. Beyond the moat were passages for pedestrians and vendors, and beyond that were the allotments. Inside the great middle wall was another, smaller wall. Between the two was an open ring containing buildings for the market traders. Between the walls was a thoroughfare paved with flagstones.

Piercing the walls were four gates—the Gates of Khurasan, Syria, Kufa, and Basra—each named for the direction it faced. Each consisted of multiple entryways topped by gatehouses with balconies and peepholes. Entering any gate from outside the city, one passed through a paved court and then

---

75 A cubit, at least during the reign of al-Ma'mun (813-833 AD), measured 48.25 cm or about 19 inches. By that standard, the walls of Baghdad would have been 9650 meters or 6 miles long, 43.4 meters or 142 feet wide at the base, 28 meters or 91.8 feet high, and 12 meters or 39.3 feet wide at the top. Other sources, however, give quite different figures. *Translator's Note*

into the first of the four entrance halls, which were vaulted with bricks set in mortar. This gateway hall of the great wall was set with double doors of iron so heavy that it took a company of men to close them, and so high that a horseman could ride through with a banner, or a spearman with a lance, without lowering the banner or lowering the lance. From there one passed into a vaulted arcade of bricks and mortar set with Byzantine windows made in such a way as to let the sunlight through while keeping the rain out. In the arcades were the lodgings of the Caliph's pages. Atop each of the gateways was a vaulted and gilded cupola surrounded by sitting rooms and belvederes commanding a view of the gate. The cupolas were reached by a gangway built upon arches, some of unburnt bricks and some of baked bricks set in mortar, marvelously arranged in order of increasing height.

When Ibn al-Fadl and his entourage, accompanied by Malfan Sa'dun on his mule, reached the Khurasan Gate, the guards made way for the son of the vizier. Ibn al-Fadl and Malfan Sa'dun rode through the gateway of the outermost wall, attendants at their side. They crossed the paved court, where their horses' hooves clattered on the flagstones, to the hall of the great middle wall. Apprised of Ibn al-Fadl's approach, the gatekeepers pulled back one of the heavy iron doors, which swung open with a piercing creak. The party rode through on horseback with plenty of room to spare between their heads and the top of the door frame. Sa'dun gazed across the great open space to the vaulted arcades and the Byzantine windows, where the pages had gathered to look down on the cavalcade. When they had passed through the gate into the space before the arcades, he turned his eyes to the great vaulted cupola overhead, noticing the gilding, the belvederes, and the elevated gangways, all of which, in their grandiose dimensions, were a spectacle to behold.

Chapter 27

The Palace of
the Golden Gate

After passing the arcades, Ibn al-Fadl and Salman reached another gate, this one inside the walls, and went through it into the great open space in the center of the city. In the middle was the Palace of Al-Mansur, called the Golden Gate after its gilded portal. Beside it was the Friday prayer hall called the Mosque of Al-Mansur. They proceeded for a great distance through an expanse where no building stood, finally reaching the palace and the mosque in the middle of the great space. There they passed one building, which stood by the side of the road that led to the Syria Gate, where the Caliph's personal guard resided. There were also two porticoes supported by pillars of bricks and mortar, one for the chief of police and the other for the chief of the guards. The only other structures were on the perimeter of the great space. These included residences built for al-Mansur's younger children and intimate slaves and servants, the treasury, the armory, the chancery, the land-tax bureau, the office of the privy seal, the bureau of the army, and the other government offices. Between the sections of the arcade were lanes and passages named after al-Mansur's freedmen, dependents, and commanders.

Every time Ibn al-Fadl approached a gate, the guards there would rise in respect. Entering the great space, the party was greeted by the neighing, whinnying, and braying of the horses, mules, and asses that swarmed across the courtyard, as well as the riding animals being led away to the stables after carrying commanders and officers wishing to pay their respects to the new caliph, or riders on other errands. Sa'dun—that is, Salman—observed all of this activity and kept his mule close to Ibn al-Fadl. As they drew closer to the palace, the latter turned toward the portico of the chief of police to meet Ibn Mahan, who was to present them to the Caliph. One of the servants was sent ahead and returned to say that Ibn Mahan was in the presence of the Commander of the Faithful and had sent for them only moments ago.

Ibn al-Fadl was not surprised to hear this, though he had wished to see Ibn Mahan before entering al-Amin's presence in order to confer with him about presenting Malfan Sa'dun. Now, however, he had no choice but to dismount. Sa'dun followed suit, and they walked to the palace gate. The guards rose to salute them, surprised to see someone of Sa'dun's appearance, a pen-case stuck into his waistband, hobbling along with his staff, a pace behind Ibn al-Fadl. Crossing the court that led to the inner gate of the palace, Ibn al-Fadl and Salman joined the knots of princes, poets, and commanders seeking an audience with the new caliph. Al-Amin was generous and free-spending, especially with the troops, whose loyalty he needed in view of his precarious position. It was for this reason that he had given them two years' pay on the day of his accession. The troops were overjoyed, as were the people of Baghdad, since those funds would be spent in the city as the soldiers paid back their debts and bought whatever vessels, foodstuffs, and clothing they needed. It was no wonder that the Baghdadis had welcomed the appearance of a new caliph ever since the custom had been established of paying a bonus upon accession.

Many of those standing in the court recognized Ibn al-Fadl as the vizier's son and greeted him hoping to win his regard, since in those days it was the vizier who held the reins of power. Ibn al-Fadl asked why they were waiting outside. "The Caliph has been busy with the police chief," they said, "ever since that messenger appeared." They pointed to a man standing on the edge of the court: a man whom Ibn al-Fadl recognized as a freedman of his father's. Though he had not dared accost him when he saw him come in, the man hastened over and kissed Ibn al-Fadl's hand when he saw his master's son looking at him with a smile. "What's happened?" asked Ibn al-Fadl. "What brings you here?"

"My master the Vizier sent me with a letter for the Commander of the Faithful."

"Where's my father now?"

"He's close to Baghdad. He sent me to announce his arrival."

"Did you bring any letters from him?"

"I gave a letter to the Commander of the Faithful. It may be the reason that they haven't let anyone in to see him yet, as you can see. They did admit the police chief, though."

Ibn al-Fadl felt a strong urge to see al-Amin when no one else was allowed to do so, if only to show off his closeness to the Caliph. So he set off, Sa'dun at his side, toward the palace gate, where the troops of the Shakiriyya detachment stood with their weapons. Seeing him, they stood at attention. The chamberlain came forward to greet him, looking and sounding apologetic about not being able to admit visitors. But Ibn al-Fadl preempted him, saying, "Ask the Commander of the Faithful permission for me and my companion to enter," pointing to Sa'dun.

The chamberlain hesitated, not daring to say flatly that the Caliph had given orders to admit no one. Deciding, finally, to do as he was asked, he went back inside to ask permission. All eyes fell on Ibn al-Fadl as he waited, the others expecting him to be turned away instead of being admitted ahead of them all. He himself expected to be admitted, on account of his father's ascendancy. A moment later, the chamberlain returned. "Please come in," he said smiling.

In the anteroom, Ibn al-Fadl and Sa'dun removed their shoes, which were whisked away by servants. They crossed a carpeted reception room and passed from one hall into another, the chamberlain leading the way, until they reached al-Amin's audience room. Across the entry hung a silken drape embroidered in gold. Drawing the drape aside, the chamberlain cried, "My master Ibn al-Fadl and his companion!"

"Bring them in!" said al-Amin.

Chapter 28

An Audience with al-Amin

Al-Amin was sitting at the far end of the room, on a couch of ebony inlaid with ivory but without gemstones or gilding, as it was the throne used by al-Mansur in the days before the 'Abbasids began to indulge themselves in luxurious refinements and use gold and gemstones in their furnishings and appointments. On the floor were costly but unadorned velvet rugs strewn with cushions and chairs. The Caliph, who was still receiving visits from well-wishers and persons offering their oaths of allegiance, was dressed as he had been on the day of his accession. As they came in, Ibn al-Fadl and his companion saw Ibn Mahan, the chief of police, sitting on a cushion apparently unconstrained by any need for formality. Al-Amin was less awe-inspiring than his father had been, especially for those of his intimates accustomed to sitting with him at drinking parties and concerts. He rarely stood on ceremony with counselors like Ibn Mahan, whose help and advice he needed. He had great faith in both Ibn Mahan and Ibn al-Rabi, and consulted them in all his important undertakings. That morning, he had received Ibn al-Rabi's message, in which the Vizier had reported that he would soon be arriving in Baghdad with al-Rashid's men and supplies and would provide a full account of what he had done. Excited by this message, al-Amin had sent for Ibn Mahan in order to share it with him, asking that no other visitors be admitted. When Ibn Mahan arrived, al-Amin handed him Ibn al-Rabi's message, which he had barely finished reading when the chamberlain announced Ibn al-Fadl and his companion. Al-Amin asked who the companion was. "A learned man of Harran," said the chamberlain, "a *malfan* or a rabbi, apparently."

"What does he want?"

Knowing who the visitor was, Ibn Mahan smiled. "I believe it's Malfan Sa'dun of Harran. He's a great man, with an extraordinary ability to discern the unseen."

Al-Amin turned to Ibn Mahan. "Do you know him?"

"If it's Malfan Sa'dun, then yes. I've seen him do marvelous things."

Al-Amin shook his head. "I don't have much faith in fortune-tellers."

"He's no fortune-teller, Sire. He's an astrologer."

"We have plenty of astrologers. Their predictions rarely come true."

"You'll see: it's different with him. If you admit him, he'll tell you something you don't expect. 'To see a man do his best, there's nothing better than a test.'"

Al-Amin motioned to the chamberlain, who went out and returned with the visitors.

Ibn al-Fadl greeted al-Amin in the manner due a caliph, and remained standing until invited to sit. Al-Amin turned to Malfan Sa'dun, who greeted him as well. "Sit down, Malfan," said the Caliph.

Salman sank to his knees on the carpet and rested there politely with his eyes averted, silent.

"Our police chief tells us that you're an astrologer," said al-Amin.

"I'm a servant of the Commander of the Faithful," said Salman.

"Is your astrology accurate?"

"I practice my art according to its rules, and I will faithfully report to the Commander of the Faithful whatever I find. To believe or not to believe is for him to decide."

Al-Amin turned to the police chief as if asking how to test the astrologer's claim.

"Here we have the letter from the vizier," said Ibn Mahan, "saying that he'll report to the Commander of the Faithful on what he did in Tus. Let's test Malfan Sa'dun on that."

This suggestion appealed to al-Amin, who turned to Sa'dun and said, "We have just received a letter from our vizier saying that he is on his way to us. Can you inform us of what he'll tell us when he arrives?"

With a respectful bow, Malfan Sa'dun put his hand inside his garment and extracted his codex. Untying the cloth, he began turning the pages as if reading and trying to understand exactly what it was he was seeing. Then he lifted his eyes to al-Amin and said, "The Vizier—may God guard him!—is bringing you some important news concerning the caliphate."

Al-Amin snickered. "Well, of course he is! He knows I've received the oath. There's nothing unseen about that."

"Yes, Sire," said Malfan Sa'dun. "The Commander of the Faithful is quite right. But the Vizier is bringing news about your brother al-Ma'mun. Would it distress you to know that Ibn al-Rabi has removed him from the line of succession?" With a shrug, he continued. "From what I see on these pages, it seems to me that that's what he's done, and without meeting any resistance. If this action of his should distress the Commander of the Faithful, that is no fault of mine."

Pretending to find the idea of his brother's removal distasteful, al-Amin asked, "Would Ibn al-Rabi do that? I can't imagine it. Be very careful in what you say! What you've told me is enough to warrant a beheading."

Undeterred, Malfan Sa'dun replied, "As I have told my master, my words are not my own: I am simply reading what I find before me. When I close the book, I forget all I've said."

"It's slander!" said al-Amin, feigning anger. "You should be punished!"

"Forgive me, Sire," continued Malfan Sa'dun, his composure unruffled. "I am not to blame for what I read. I read aloud what I see, and my art has never deceived me."

"Enough!" cried al-Amin, making an excessive display of truculence. He turned to Ibn al-Fadl. "Has your father told you any of this?"

"Not at all, Sire. He hasn't written anything," said Ibn al-Fadl, not daring to report what Malfan Sa'dun had told them the night before.

Al-Amin then rounded on Ibn Mahan. "I told you these astrologers will say anything to gain our favor!"

Smiling in a placating manner, Ibn Mahan said softly, as if speaking in confidence to al-Amin, "I know from experience that Malfan Sa'dun is reliable. Let my master test him, if he wishes. The Vizier will be in Baghdad tonight or tomorrow morning. When he arrives, let my master hear his report, and then judge as he sees fit."

Malfan Sa'dun, who was busy leafing through his codex and muttering as if oblivious to what the others were saying, heard al-Amin call for a servant. When the chamberlain appeared, the Caliph said, "Tell the majordomo to take Malfan Sa'dun to the guest house, and let him stay there, well cared for, until I ask for him." Then he turned to Malfan Sa'dun. "Go, then, if you like; you have nothing to fear until we summon you."

Rising, Salman silently cursed the necessity of staying, knowing that the women of al-Ma'mun's household were anxiously waiting for him to bring news of Behzad. But he could see no alternative but to obey. He was courteously escorted to an accommodation near the commoners' kitchen, and orders were given to supply him with food and drink.

Chapter 29

The Test

Salman tossed and turned in his room, almost regretting the visit that had taken up the entire day. The next morning, the Caliph's messenger came to summon him. After seeing to his appearance and touching up his costume, he was taken to attend al-Amin. He arrived exuding every appearance of simplicity and good will. As on the day before, Ibn Mahan and Ibn al-Fadl were in attendance as well. Al-Amin asked him to sit down, saying, "Our vizier Ibn al-Rabi will arrive shortly. We'll ask him about this matter in your presence, and see what we shall see."

Salman bowed in assent and remained standing. Al-Amin again commanded him to sit, and he sat. Then the chamberlain came in. "The vizier Ibn al-Rabi, Sire!"

"Bid him enter!" said al-Amin, brightening.

The chamberlain backed away and raised the drape. Ibn al-Rabi, looking travel-strained, entered and greeted al-Amin as caliph. "May the Commander of the Faithful forgive me," he said, "for attending him before seeing to my appearance."

Ibn al-Rabi was then a man of middle age, with a graying beard and a furrowed brow—though his brow was only partly visible under his tall cap. He was dressed in the black robe required of those presenting themselves before the 'Abbasid caliphs.

Beaming, al-Amin bade him sit on a chair beside him. Ibn al-Rabi conveyed his condolences on al-Rashid's death and offered his congratulations on al-Amin's accession. His gaze, meanwhile, flitted from one visitor to another, as if hoping to be left alone with the Caliph to make his report.

Al-Amin came directly to the point. "Since you've come to report something to us, go right ahead."

"Now?"

"Yes," said al-Amin. "Say what you came to tell us. This astrologer claims to know what it is, and I want to see if he's telling the truth. If he is, we'll reward him; if not, we'll punish him severely."

"May I say something?" asked Ibn Mahan.

"Speak!"

"If Malfan Sa'dun is lying, kill him. If he's telling the truth, will my master consent to appoint him Chief Astrologer to the palace, so that we might avail ourselves of his knowledge?"

"Agreed," said al-Amin. Then he turned to Ibn al-Rabi and asked: "Tell us what you've done concerning al-Ma'mun and the caliphate."

Surprised to hear the question put this way, Ibn al-Rabi said, "I did what I thought would most benefit the dynasty. As the Commander of the Faithful well knows, our master al-Rashid solicited an oath of loyalty to your brother al-Ma'mun and gave him command of the expeditionary force after his death. But he did this only because he was led to do so by certain persons with ulterior motives. There was already an oath of allegiance sworn to you, al-Amin, who sits on the throne before us. When al-Rashid died, we felt that honoring the oath to al-Ma'mun would divide the caliphate and foment sedition. I consulted my colleagues, and we agreed to put matters back the way they should have been. So we repudiated the oath to al-Ma'mun and affirmed that the caliphate belongs to you, our master, the Commander of the Faithful, and to you alone."

"But...what did you do to al-Ma'mun?"

"We've done nothing to him. He remains governor of Khurasan, as he was intended to be, in addition to being heir apparent."

Before he had finished speaking, al-Amin, his astonishment plain to see, had turned to Malfan Sa'dun, who was sitting quietly, eyes downcast, but quite unruffled.

"Damn you!" cried al-Amin, unable to contain himself. "How can you see the unseen?"

"I deserve no credit," said Malfan Sa'dun, lifting his head. "Mine is a science familiar to astrologers. But those who employ it truthfully are few."

"What I like," said the Caliph, "is that you're honest and don't boast. I hereby declare you Chief Astrologer!"

Malfan Sa'dun rose to his feet, bowed, uttered a prayer for the Caliph, and said, "It's an honor I don't deserve."

"But you do," said al-Amin. "It's the reward for your honesty." He clapped his hands and the chamberlain appeared. "Tell the majordomo to arrange a residence and a stipend for Malfan Sa'dun. He's now the Chief Astrologer." He motioned for Malfan Sa'dun to sit.

Salman bowed, repeated his prayer, and sat down, saying, "The Caliph's realm is vast: no matter where I stay, I will enjoy his benevolence and bounty. If he would allow me to choose my own residence, I would be able to serve him better, since my work requires me to spend time alone in my house practicing divination or reading astrology. I could still be available to the Commander of the Faithful whenever he needed me. And if it were possible to decline his gift, I would beg him to accept me into his service without stipend or reward, for the true practitioner of my art must mortify his soul and renounce luxury and worldly pleasures. But the gifts of the Commander of the Faithful may not be declined."

Such self-denial surprised al-Amin, who had never heard the like of it before. As far as he knew, men like Malfan Sa'dun sought enrichment by association with the Caliph. Bewildered, he turned to Ibn Mahan for help.

"That's Malfan Sa'dun's nature," said Ibn Mahan. "The Commander of the Faithful may do as he wishes."

"But what if we need him and can't find him?"

"I will stay in the palace if I have permission to go to my house whenever I deem it useful, without anyone stopping me. I'm quite sure there will be no trouble finding me when I'm needed."

"Let it be as you wish," said al-Amin.

During this exchange, Ibn al-Rabi was scrutinizing Malfan Sa'dun with frank astonishment, as if suspicious of him.

Eager to hear more from Ibn al-Rabi, the Caliph tossed his staff onto the throne and moved from his seat, signaling to the Vizier to stay. Seeing that he wanted them to go, the others rose and went out. Salman found his mule and set out for al-Ma'mun's palace.

Chapter 30

To Ctesiphon

When we last encountered them, the residents of al-Ma'mun's palace were waiting for Salman, who had left two days earlier with a promise to return with news of Behzad. After one day passed with no word, they spent the night anxious and miserable. The next morning they expected that Behzad would certainly appear or that Salman would arrive with news of him. But when most of that day passed without news their distress became extreme, all the more so since al-Ma'mun's daughter Zaynab had awoken that morning with a high fever. In her grief, she had eaten and drunk only at odd times, so her stomach became upset and her temperature rose. Frantic, Dananir asked Zaynab for permission to summon one of the palace physicians, among whom were skilled specialists of all kinds. But the girl refused to see anyone but Behzad. Pages were accordingly sent to keep a lookout for him on the road and along the shore. Terrible misgivings beset everyone in the palace, especially Maymuna, who had furthermore to endure the fear of what might happen if the others learned why she was so much more anxious than everyone else.

Yet as soon as Maymuna saw that Zaynab had contracted a fever, she was able to disguise her anxiety as fear for the girl's well-being. She took to standing for a time on one of the balconies overlooking the road, then moving to one of the gates that led to the shore, hoping to see Behzad arriving on horseback or aboard a boat. When she tired of keeping watch, she would sit in her bedroom, her mind dulled by worry and her face pale, drawn, and somber. She lay on her bed, thinking of a thousand reasons why Behzad had not come, and reliving what had passed between them at the moment of their parting—the thought of which only made her more eager to see him and reassure herself of his feelings. As the sun sank in the sky and darkness fell, she could no longer bear to remain where she was. She went out, expecting to run into someone who knew where he was, or to hear his voice in the anteroom. Anyone who desires something intensely imagines that the wish must somehow come true—all the more so in this case, since Behzad had promised to return.

Maymuna walked through the anteroom to the doorway that overlooked the Tigris. Staring at the boats that passed before her on their way up and down the river, she hoped to see Behzad aboard one of them, even imagining more than once that she did see him. After several disappointments, she began to think that he would never come. She sat at a window seat with a view of the river, trying to guess when he would appear, spinning stories that would bring him in a moment, then imagining events that would prevent him from arriving, as one does when tormented by anxiety but has nothing to do and no way to distract oneself. Seeing a bird fly through the air, she would tell herself that if it landed on a certain tree, Behzad would come that night. If the bird turned right or left, she would take it as a good or bad omen respectively. If the bird did the opposite of what she wished for, she would convince herself that she had wished for something different. Then she would do the same with a fly that was buzzing around her: if it landed on her face, she would say to herself, he would come; and if it landed on her hand, she would find a way to tell herself that this meant that her wish would come true.

So time passed until, as darkness fell, she was roused from her reverie by the slap of shoes on the wharf. Heart pounding, she peered out, but saw no one. She leapt up and hurried to Zaynab's room, where she found her grandmother at the girl's bedside and Dananir sitting on a couch nearby. Zaynab's cheeks were pink with fever, and the room was silent. Seeing Maymuna look in, Dananir cried out, "Do you see how the doctor has treated us?"

"He hasn't come," said Maymuna. "But there must be a good reason."

"What's even more surprising," said 'Abbada, "is that Salman hasn't come either, even though he promised to search for him. I'm quite sure that Behzad is in Ctesiphon. I wish I'd gone to look for him there this morning."

"If he doesn't come tomorrow, we'll send someone after him."

"My grandmother and I will go there tomorrow," said Maymuna, "and try to find him at his house."

"It'll be a strenuous trip for you," said Dananir.

"Not at all," exclaimed 'Abbada. "I doubt anyone knows how to find him better than we do. We know the town and we know his house. If he doesn't come tonight or tomorrow morning, and if Salman doesn't arrive with some news, Maymuna and I will go search for him there."

"God bless you both," said Dananir. "We'll wait until tomorrow, then. If it turns out that you have to go, then you'll take one of the palace boats, with sailors and servants. If only our mistress would agree to let some other doctor treat her, we could ask one of the palace doctors to come, and spare you the journey."

Chapter 31

On the Tigris

Maymuna rejoiced at this resolution but continued to fret until it came time to go to sleep. They arose the next day to find Zaynab feeling better, her fever having abated. Even so, Maymuna pressed her grandmother to insist on going to Ctesiphon to repay their hosts for the hospitality they had received. 'Abbada accordingly pleaded with Dananir to prepare a boat to take them to Ctesiphon. Dananir gave the order, and the boat, along with sailors and an escort of palace pages, was ready by noontime. Maymuna and 'Abbada boarded, and the latter told the captain to head south. He turned the rudder and unfurled the sail, and they were off. Maymuna sat on the port side, hoping to see Behzad riding along the shore, while 'Abbada turned her gaze to the river, hoping to see him aboard another vessel.

Though the boat raced along, carried by the current more than by the sail, Maymuna still thought it moved too slowly. To her it seemed to be standing still, so eager was she to arrive at their destination. 'Abbada sat silently beside her. The others were silent too, and there was no sound but the splashing of the prow as it cut through the water.

Suddenly they heard a clamor astern. Turning around, Maymuna saw another vessel speeding along behind them. Looking closely, she saw that it was a well-crafted boat decorated with designs painted in gold. Its prow was shaped like the head of an elephant, complete with trunk and tusks. Startled, she pointed the boat out to her grandmother. "That's the Caliph's boat," cried the old woman. "Al-Amin has five boats shaped like different animals: there's a lion, an elephant, an eagle, a snake, and a horse. He spent a fortune on them."[76]

---

76 Ibn al-Athir, VI: 120.

Maymuna's heart beat faster and she flushed, then suddenly turned pale. "Oh no! They're following us. What do they want?"

Her grandmother motioned for her to hide behind the mast, then hastened over to the captain, telling him to drop sail, slow down, and head for shore, making way for the boat behind them. The captain turned the rudder. Throwing her veil over herself, 'Abbada crept over to where Maymuna was hiding.

Al-Amin's boat was gaining on them. From the sounds coming from her, they could tell that she was carrying soldiers and Ruffians. One of the men on board laughed drunkenly and said, "Not much to hope for out of this mission!"

"How can you be so greedy?" said another. "Aren't you happy with what you've gotten out of the Treasury? Twenty-four months' worth of pay: that's four hundred eighty dirhams a man, all at once, not to mention your share of the spoils![77] You lot are never satisfied. The only living we Ruffians make comes from plunder—no one pays us anything."

The first man laughed. "You Ruffians make more than we do: you're always going on private missions like this one and making more at one go than we make in months. If you manage to catch this man from Khurasan, you'll make a bundle."

"I don't think the Commander of the Faithful will pay that much for him," scoffed the Ruffian. "We've caught plenty like him before, and made only a few dirhams."

The soldier guffawed. "The reward depends on who the captive is. Do you expect to make as much from catching a common thief as you will from catching someone like him?"

"So what makes him so special? Don't get my hopes up."

"This Khurasani," said the soldier, whispering in the Ruffians' ear but in a voice loud enough for Maymuna to hear him, "means a lot to the Commander of the Faithful. That's what we found out when the Vizier came this morning."

Hidden behind the mast, Maymuna overheard the entire conversation. When she heard the soldier speak of the man from Khurasan, her heart leapt in fear at the thought that it might be Behzad he was talking about. Her knees trembling, she pricked up her ears. She heard another man

---

77 *History of Islamic Civilization.*

116

saying, "What's all this yammering? If our chief Harch hears you, he'll give you an earful. We didn't come here to argue; we came to catch this man in disguise, and if we do it, we'll all make money."

By that time, the other boat had come alongside al-Ma'mun's. Hearing them mention her beloved, Maymuna could not prevent herself from rising and turning to look at the men who were speaking. She saw a clamorous crowd of well-armed soldiers and Ruffians, laughing riotously as if drunk. At one end of the boat was a short, fat man who seemed to be in charge. She nudged her grandmother and asked, "Do you recognize any of them?"

'Abbada looked up and, recognizing the man, whispered in her ear, "That's Harch, chief of the Ruffians."

At that moment, one of the Ruffians happened to see Maymuna, whose fear made her seem all the more alluring and vulnerable. "I see a pretty girl!" he shouted. "Maybe she's a singer. Tie up, Captain, and let's hear her sing!"

Maymuna shuddered and the blood froze in her veins. Her grand-mother, seeing what was happening, rose to urge the helmsman to flee or prepare to defend the vessel. But then she heard one of the men on the other boat say in a low voice, "Mind your own business! Don't you see the flag she's flying?"

As their boat shot past, several crewmen crowded to the rail to look at the pennant flying from the prow. "It's al-Ma'mun's," they cried. "The boat belongs to the Caliph's brother. Leave her alone!"

Though relieved at their near escape, Maymuna was now more worried than ever about Behzad. Fearing that it was he they were searching for, she turned to her grandmother, tears in her eyes: "Oh no!" she cried, forgetting that her love was supposed to be a secret. "They're looking for Behzad!"

"Don't worry, dear," said 'Abbada, unaware of the real reason for Maymuna's fear. "I don't think they're looking for him. Even if they are, we'll arrive before they do and warn him in plenty of time for him to escape, God willing." Rising, she ordered the helmsman to hoist the sail and fol-low the other boat at full speed.

Chapter 32

At Wit's End

The boat shot forward. Maymuna, beside herself with anxiety, stood staring first at the boat and then at the shore, too agitated to make a pretense of hiding her feelings. Anticipating her thoughts, her grandmother said, "Don't be afraid, child. We'll reach Behzad before they do, even if their boat is faster." Scrambling to the bow, 'Abbada began scrutinizing the shoreline on the port side, trying to see as far ahead as she could, while Maymuna, shuddering, her knees trembling, clasped her shoulder to steady herself. The boat sliced through the water, the sail snapping in the wind. Even so, al-Amin's boat was faster. For two hours, the two vessels sped along at close quarters, with al-Amin's some distance ahead. All the while, 'Abbada stood silently, her eyes fixed on the horizon. Then, glimpsing a great building looming in the distance, she cried, "There's the Arch! We're almost at Ctesiphon."

Turning to the captain, she shouted, "Do you see that waterwheel ahead?"

"Yes, mistress," he said. "I see it."

"Stop the boat there." She turned to Maymuna. "If we get out here and go to Behzad's," she whispered, "we'll reach his house long before they do."

The crew dropped the sail and the captain turned the rudder. Within moments, the boat drew up near the waterwheel. 'Abbada took Maymuna's hand and they disembarked. "Wait here," said 'Abbada to the captain, "until we come back."

"Don't you want servants to accompany you?" he asked.

"No."

"As you wish."

'Abbada dashed off, Maymuna running along behind her. It was nearly sunset. 'Abbada knew every turn and every shortcut on the path, but after half an hour she was ready to collapse from exhaustion. Maymuna, however, was too worried to find running strenuous, and went on, oblivious to her grandmother's plight. Soon, 'Abbada was panting, sweat running down her face, and unable to run any more. She stopped, sat down on a rock, and began mopping her brow. Fretting at the the delay, Maymuna wished she had wings to carry her to Behzad's house. She wondered whether to leave her grandmother there and go on alone. She didn't know the road, and she was reluctant to leave 'Abbada by herself. But if she waited for the old woman to recover, it might be too late. So she helped 'Abbada wipe the sweat from her brow and encouraged her to get up. At first too tired to speak, 'Abbada finally said, "We're near the house. Don't you see the tall palm tree?"

The sun had dropped behind the palm trees on the west bank of the river where they had landed. Looking eastwards to the horizon, Maymuna saw the tree and exclaimed, "Isn't that the tree that casts a shadow when we leave the house?"

"That's the one."

"Then we're near Behzad's house," said Maymuna. "Let's finish the journey, even if it's difficult. I'm afraid that rabble will get to him before we do."

"Don't worry," said 'Abbada, gritting her teeth and rising to her feet. "They're still splashing around in the Tigris." She set out again and Maymuna followed, willing herself not to press her to walk more quickly. By the time they had crossed the marketplace and approached the house, it was nearly sunset. They could see that the door was closed and there was no one about. Cautiously they made their way forward, suddenly aware that they were now far from the river. Seeing no one coming, Maymuna was reassured that Behzad's enemies had not yet found the house. But they found the door locked. They pounded on it but no one answered.

After a good deal of fruitless knocking, 'Abbada noticed that the door was locked from the outside. Realizing that Behzad must have left, she felt a load lift from her shoulders. She told Maymuna, who breathed a sigh of relief. "Thank God he's not here, and those men can't find him!" she said. "But where do you think he is?"

"In Baghdad, perhaps, or in some other town," said 'Abbada, sitting down to rest on a stone by the door.

"But what if he's on his way back here now and they catch him?" said Maymuna. "O dear God! What do we do? I say we stay here so if he comes we can warn him."

"But who will protect *us*?" asked her grandmother.

"What else can we do? I'm afraid that he might be on his way here now, and—since he doesn't know about the soldiers—he'll fall into their hands. If we're going to save him, we have to finish the job." Then, realizing that she had revealed too much, and still afraid to confess her love for him, she caught herself, saying, "After all he's done for us, we have to do all we can for him, even if it's dangerous."

Pleased by her generosity of spirit, 'Abbada said, "True! We have to do whatever we can to help him. But what can we do? I can already hear that rabble coming from the river. Listen: they're racing toward us! Come on! Let's move away before they get here." Taking hold of Maymuna's gown, she rose and struck out to the east with the young woman in tow.

As they moved away from the house, they found themselves stumbling over little hillocks and blocks of stones that had formed part of some ruined monument. "This looks like an ancient Persian ruin," said Maymuna. "Was it a palace?"

Hurrying as best she could given her age, 'Abbada said, "It was, dear. These mounds and stones are all that's left of a palace that used to stand here—not the palace of Chosroes, but the palace of Shapur.[78] It's where al-Mansur stayed before they built Baghdad, and it fell into ruin after he left, as you can see."

"Behzad seems to have chosen a house near here because he wanted to be near the remains of our ancestors," said Maymuna, racing ahead of her grandmother, and trying to recall what the mention of the palace reminded her of. Safely away from the house, she remembered: "Once I heard him say that he goes often to Chosroes' palace to look for medicinal plants that grow in the ruins. What if he's there now?"

"Maybe he is," said 'Abbada. "Follow me, then, and let's look for him before the sun goes down."

---

78 The building today called 'the arch of Chosroes' was evidently a Sasanian royal palace, though it is unclear who built it and when. Among the candidates are Shapur I (r. 241-272 AD), Khosrow I Anoshiravan (r. 531-79 AD), and Khosrow II Parviz (r. 590-628). *Translator's Note*

Chapter 33

The Arch of Chosroes

They raced toward the palace, which stood outside the town, to the east. As they left town, they worried that someone would guess where they were going, so they wrapped themselves up in their veils and head-coverings and made their way as inconspicuously as possible. The palace stood as high as a mountain, its ruined condition making it seem all the more desolate. The sun had sunk below the horizon, the shadows had lengthened, and darkness had gathered. Sunset is the bleakest hour: it marks a transition from light to darkness that man finds hard to face without a tremor. And if it seems a lonely hour even for those surrounded by family and friends, how much more desolate must it be for one who finds himself before a lonely ruin where all he hears is the hooting of owls? Inhabited, the palace was an imposing sight; now ruined, it was terrifying. Ruins, moreover, are desolate even by day; by night, they overwhelm.

Full of anxious thoughts of Behzad, Maymuna was able to keep her fear at bay. Otherwise, she might have seen the ruined palace for what it was: a great lesson in the swift end of worldly glory. She might have thought of those who lived there once upon a time: the emperors and margraves, the nobles and the knights, all of them with ambition enough to span the earth; or of their horses, filling the courtyard; or of all those crowned heads who once passed through that place, draped in silk and brocade, polo sticks in hand; or of all the kings and princes who came to plead for truces and offer gifts. She might have thought of all the generals brought here in defeat, and all the captives dragged here in chains, in the days when the palace swarmed with women and children and thousands of slaves, male and female, brought here as prisoners or given as gifts, among them the sons and daughters of princes, all of them dragging silken trains and sleeping on mounded pillows of eiderdown, embroidered in colors to dazzle the eyes, amid melodies to thrill the ear. She might have imagined the belvederes of the palace hung with painted curtains, with ravishing slaves peering down at the horse races and polo matches in the courtyard. Everyone would have been joyous, imagining that life would always be so blessed. If only one could see them, and then return with Maymuna on that evening to see the palace crawling with vermin, the pillows crumbled to dust, the vines and mosses hanging heavy on its sides, its carpets run to thorns and stones, its walls collapsed, its columns fallen, its pillars cracked asunder, he would surely draw a fearful lesson, even if he were a hardy soul. What then of Maymuna, who had known nothing but ease and comfort? Looking around, all she could see was a wasteland filled with ruins; and in her fear and trembling regretted having come. But then her longing for her beloved gave her new strength, and her faith in her grandmother made all things seem possible.

'Abbada, for her part, was overcome with fatigue, and felt less fear than Maymuna. Leaning against a column that lay fallen among the ruins of the palace, she asked Maymuna whether she had seen or heard anyone. Straining to pick up any kind of sound, the young woman answered that she had not. "But that doesn't mean that Behzad isn't inside the building, looking for herbs or plants. Since we've come this far already, let's go inside. If we don't see anyone, we'll hurry back before it gets too dark. Shall we try it?"

Unwilling to argue, and thinking the plan a sound one, 'Abbada agreed; and the two went forward, probing the ground with their feet as they went, hoping not to stumble over a stone or a thorn bush. The world had fallen quiet and the birds had returned to their nests. When they reached the gate, they stood in awe of its great size: thirty-four cubits across and thirty-two high. Standing before the great arch, they heard the sound of wind and felt a cool draft. Maymuna recoiled as if a cold hand had touched her face. She whirled around but saw no one.

"What's wrong, child?" asked her grandmother.

"Do you hear that? The sound of a breeze? And a cold draft? Or is it the breathing of the jinn? Just now when we were outside, there was no wind. So why is there a whistling noise now? And a chill?"

"You've never been inside the palace before, have you?"

"No. Are there jinn here?"

"Don't be afraid, child," said 'Abbada. "There's no one here at all, human or jinn. What you hear are the air shafts outside the walls."

"But there wasn't any wind before. Where did it come from so suddenly?"

"The palace was built using techniques that no one today has been able to discover. It was designed so that the air moves around inside it, even if the air outside is hot, and goes out through vents in the walls that no architect today knows how to build. The builders came up with an ingenious way to keep the breeze blowing in the emperor's throne room even on the hottest days. So there's nothing to be afraid of. Do you want to go back?"

By that time they had already crossed the threshhold and entered the Hall of the Arch, which had given its name to the whole palace. When it was first built, the span measured sixty cubits by sixty, or a hundred by fifty according to another report. It had been adorned with a single carpet, embroidered and studded with gems, big enough to cover the entire floor.

Chapter 34

A Grim Sight

In the days of the Sasanian emperors,[79] the Hall of the Arch contained a golden throne studded with precious stones. Above it was a spangled dome containing a fan made of ostrich feathers, and on either side of it were seats for the emperor's attendants and nobles. The Muslims plundered all of these treasures during their conquests. At that time, they were a desert people, and so they broke apart the furnishings, sliced up the carpets, and tore apart the drapes. Theirs was a victory of nomadism over settled civilization, and left nothing in its wake but stones and a few warped and splintered pillars.

Looking at the walls that towered around her, Maymuna noticed colored pictures, but it was too dark to see them clearly. When her grandmother suggested going back, she was relieved. She found the place terrifying, not least because it was swarming with vermin of the kind that gathers in ruins. She was about to reply in the affirmative and turn back when suddenly she heard footsteps from outside the Arch. Her heart leapt in terror. She wanted to scream, but her tongue froze in her throat. Sensing her panic, her grandmother, who was equally frightened, took her hand and pulled her inside. "Those Ruffians may have thought as we did and come here looking for Behzad too," she whispered in Maymuna's ear. "Thank God he's not here! But if they find us they may kill us. Let's hide behind those pillars." Her voice shaking, she pulled Maymuna along behind her. They scrambled over the ruins as quietly as they could, but they were unable to do anything about the rustling and crackling they made as they stepped on the weeds and thorns that grew between the stones. Too alarmed even to notice the rats, hedgehogs, and other creatures wriggling underfoot, they raced forward, finally reaching a broad alcove, possibly even the one where

---

79 The rulers of the Persian empire that had been overthrown by the Arab Muslim conquests of the 630s and 640s. *Translator's Note*

the throne had stood in the glory days of the Persians. In front of the alcove were some scattered columns that blocked the view of anyone entering the hall. Too frightened to breathe, they crept into a corner of the alcove and trained their terrified eyes and ears on the door. Now they regretted the risk they had run. Hidden in her corner, a trembling Maymuna clutched at her grandmother, who was doing her best to comfort her, all the while imploring God silently to come to their aid.

A moment later the footsteps stopped. From the direction of the door, Maymuna heard whispering, as if someone were fearful of being overheard. Then the voice stopped and a flint was struck. As she watched, the Hall of the Arch was pierced by rays of light. A tall figure swathed in a black muffler and cloak was approaching, silent and invisible but for the hand that held the lamp. Behind him came a knot of men dressed the same way he was. Terrified that he would come forward far enough to see her, Maymuna, her heart pounding, huddled closer to her grandmother.

Stopping in the middle of the hall, the figure carrying the lamp looked left and right, asking the others if they had seen anyone there. Finally he seemed satisfied that the place was empty. "Who would come here now anyway?" he said. "We must have scared some animals away." Glancing around as if searching for a place to put the lamp, he noticed a column that had fallen away from its base. He put the lamp down on the base and then removed his other hand from under his gown. He was carrying a polished black box, which he put down next to the lamp. He turned to his companions, who were six in number.

"Are we safe here?" he asked softly.

"Yes," said one. "Speak freely."

As soon as the first man had spoken, Maymuna thought he sounded familiar: his voice resembled her beloved's. Her heart thudded and her eyes gleamed; she thought she must be dreaming. Then she watched the tall figure remove his cloak and spread it on the ground. The others did the same. He invited them to sit down and they did, though he remained standing. With their cloaks removed, it was clear that they were dressed in a manner unusual in Baghdad. Each man wore a green gown and a tall cap with a green turban, along with a sword belt and a bow slung over the shoulder, as if going to war.

Maymuna concentrated on the first speaker, who had turned his back to her. It was now obvious that it was Behzad. She stared hard at him and fought her impulse to call out. She pointed him out to her grand-mother, who despite her poor eyesight recognized him too. She motioned for Maymuna to sit still and keep quiet. Steeling herself to be patient, Maymuna looked over the other men. She could see from their faces and beards that they were Persians, though she did not recognize any of them. Behzad, meanwhile, had turned toward the base of the column, picked up the box, and placed it before the group. Sitting down cross-legged, he said: "Swear by what is in this box that you will keep our meeting a secret."

One of the group, a thin, slightly built man whose features suggested irascibility, keenness of mind, and outspokenness, spoke up first. "You haven't told us what's in there," he said, "even though you promised to show us before we go any further."

Behzad took a key from his sleeve and unlocked the box, saying, "Look, but don't say a word."

They looked, then took a step back, astonished. "'We belong to God, and to Him we return!' What's this?"

"This is our sign, beginning today. This is the head of our martyred leader. Swear by it that you will keep our meeting a secret, and that you will avenge his death, and the death of the ones who were killed before him."

Still on his knees, he shut the box. Together, they recited the Opening Chapter, then each of them swore to spend his blood and treasure for the sake of revenge.[80]

---

80 The Opening Chapter (al-fatiha) is the first verse of the Qur'an. It is often recited by Muslims when committing to some new undertaking. *Translator's Note*

Chapter 35

The Emperor Chosroes

Rising to his feet, Behzad returned the box to its place, then picked up the lamp and approached the walls of the Arch. "Do you see the images on this wall?" he asked, lifting the lamp.

"It's the Emperor Chosroes," they said, "laying siege to Antioch."[81]

"He captured it, did he not?"

"Of course."

"Like him, we shall triumph in the end," said Behzad. "Was he not a just king?"

"Just and wise."

"Are you not his sons and successors?"

"We are!"

"Did you not come to the aid of the Arabs and help them conquer the world?"

"We did."

"Was it not your ancestors who gave their lives for that cause? Did they not shed their blood and prove their valor? Did they not commit great misdeeds in the service of their imam, killing on suspicion, and practicing treachery and deceit, all for the sake of this dynasty? And how were they rewarded?"

"They were betrayed!" cried the men in unison. "May God have mercy on Abu Muslim."[82]

---

81 Khosrow I Anoshiravan (r. 531-79 AD) captured the northern Syrian city of Antioch in 540 AD. *Translator's Note*

82 Abu Muslim of Khurasan led the uprising that overthrew the Umayyad dynasty and brought the 'Abbasids to power in 750 AD. He was later executed by the second 'Abbasid caliph, al-Mansur, who seems to have feared his power and popularity. *Translator's Note*

"Abu Muslim wasn't the first of our martyrs. But he's the greatest victim of Arab treachery, murdered by them after bringing them to power. Do you want his blood to lie unavenged, like the blood of your fathers?"

One of the group, an elderly man of imposing mien, said, "You're asking us to commit to a dangerous enterprise, but you haven't told us who you are. You're a fellow Persian, true enough, and a fellow conspirator. But we want to know your real reason for bringing us out to these ruins when we have enough to worry about at home."

"People may call this place a ruin," said Behzad, "but it isn't. It's a living monument to the greatness of our civilization. After betraying Abu Muslim, al-Mansur tried to demolish it, but could not. If the Arch can survive, so can our empire. I think it's fitting for us to talk of vengeance in this of all places, where Chosroes the Just seems to see us and hear what we say. If we pledge loyalty to one another here, the pledge will have greater meaning."

Then, lifting the lamp as high as Chosroes' head, he said, "Look! He's reproaching you, as if to say: 'You've shirked your duty to your nation, submitting to a people who have exploited you, humiliated you, and stabbed the best of you in the back. How can you bear this affront when you, the Persians, were great lords, wise men, and leaders of armies? Have you forgotten Rustum, Cyrus, Darius, Shapur, Parviz, Anushirvan, and Bozorgmehr? Or that you once fought Greece, Rome, India, and Sogdiana, conquering countries and capturing cities? How could you let yourselves be defeated by Arabs who once came to you to beg for food to eat and clothes to wear? The best of them fought for you as vassals, but then turned their swords against you. You rushed to their aid, but they betrayed and slew your lords, and placed their feet on your necks. And yet: are the keys to power not in your hands? Are the viziers, the generals, the scholars, and the statesmen not all Persians like yourselves? How can you bow your heads to weaklings who overcame you only by trickery and stealth? Fortitude is worthy, but forbearance too long extended is a sign of weakness.' Such is the speech of Chosroes; it is the reason I summoned you here today. As for who I am: if you would join me in avenging Abu Muslim, then know me to be the emissary of your brothers in Khurasan. What say you?"

By the time he finished his speech, Behzad had forgotten the need for secrecy. He had raised his voice, and his face glowed with passionate intensity. Listening to him call for revenge, Maymuna was elated. At the same time, she found herself wondering about what was in the box. From what the men had said, she understood that it contained the head of some victim of tyranny. She was intensely curious to know who it was. In the meantime, though, she allowed herself to be distracted by the happiness she felt at the sound of her beloved's call for vengeance against the ruling dynasty.

His speech finished, Behzad stood, lamp in hand, looking at the group. The elderly man rose and asked, "Are you the envoy sent by our brothers of the Khurrami sect in Khurasan?"[83]

"I was sent several years ago."

"So why did you wait until now to summon us?"

"I was waiting for the right moment," said Behzad. "Success depends on good timing. Al-Rashid, the man who outflanked us and outwitted us by killing our leader, is finally dead, and his successor is an untried youth who thinks of nothing but eating, drinking, and..."

"But we've already founded a Persian dynasty in Khurasan," interrupted the man. "Al-Ma'mun is heir to the throne and will become caliph soon enough. As you know, he's putty in the hands of Ibn Sahl, who embraced Islam and became his favorite to await the moment when he could act on our behalf. So when al-Ma'mun becomes caliph, we'll have what we want with no trouble."

"Didn't I tell you that you don't know how to protect your own interests? The stripling and his allies are already plotting against us, and if they succeed, all of Ibn Sahl's efforts will come to naught. Just as al-Mansur founded the dynasty by betraying and killing Abu Muslim, and al-Rashid saved it by betraying and killing Ja'far, so now the stripling is trying to thwart Ibn Sahl by betraying al-Ma'mun and removing him from the line of succession."

"Has he done it?" cried the man.

"He has," said Behzad, "and, if you keep your heads in the sand, it won't be long before he starts killing al-Ma'mun's partisans. Ibn Sahl's efforts can only be sustained by clever politicking, and if you don't lend him a hand

---

83 'Khurrami' is a term used in Arabic sources to refer to an Iranian sect, or group of sects, that rallied against Muslim rule in the expectation that Abu Muslim, or some other messianic figure, would return from hiding to lead them to victory over the Muslims. The idea of messianic return is a Shi'ite one, but the Khurramis were distinct from mainstream Shi'ites, who looked to the family of the Prophet Muhammad for leadership. *Translator's Note*

quickly all will be lost. Neither his being a Muslim nor his closeness to al-Ma'mun will do us any good then."

"Are you sure al-Ma'mun's been removed?" asked the man.

"Unlike you, I've been vigilant. For the past few years, I've been look-ing out for your interests. I have spies, even in the Caliph's palace, and I know everything that happens in al-Amin's household. I know what the lower orders are feeling and what the elite is thinking. I've learned, without a shadow of a doubt, that al-Amin has deposed al-Ma'mun, and now might well go further than that. The lower orders are a pack of rabble who care about nothing except making money. As for the elite, the elite is you, and now is the time to act: the flood is head high and rising!"

The men sat silently for a moment, heads bowed. Then the distin-guished-looking man rose and said quietly, "If al-Ma'mun has been deposed then the matter is serious. But we'll never succeed in our mission unless we proceed with caution. Nothing can move the common people except reli-gion. This cause of ours began in Khurasan and will never triumph unless it arises from there."

"Our next move is easy," said Behzad, "because Khurasan is indeed where our strength lies. And yes, religion is the way to unite the common people; and that, too, can be arranged in Khurasan. These green gowns will see to that, God willing."

Understanding that Behzad meant that Shi'ism would serve as a weapon, the man said, "When the caliphate adopts green instead of the 'Abbasid black, then victory is ours. But how can we accomplish that?"

"We can accomplish it, God willing, in Khurasan," said Behzad. "Blood will be shed. You must look after our Shi'ites in Baghdad.[84] When the moment comes, each of us will be judged by his deeds." Pointing to the box, he said, "Our real standard is what you saw in this box. To it I'll add another head; when you see it, you'll know that you've spent your blood and treasure in a worthy cause. If you are Khurramis, then you are fighting for an ancient imam and a great leader: Abu Muslim of the black banners, founder of the 'Abbasid dynasty. He calls on you from his grave to overthrow the 'Abbasids and bring back Persian rule with the help of

---

84 Shi'ites were Muslims who believed that 'Ali Ibn Abi Talib (d. 661 AD) and certain of his descendants were the only fully legitimate leaders of the Muslim community. Here Zaidan assumes that Shi'ites, being enemies of the caliphate, would have been sympathetic to the oppressed Persians. *Translator's Note*

the Party of 'Ali,[85] whose call to revolution was so shrewdly perverted by al-Mansur. 'And those who have oppressed you shall know what fate awaits them.'"

---

85 The 'Party of 'Ali' is another name for the Shi'ites, who are partisans (in Arabic, shi'ah, from which comes 'Shi'ite') of 'Ali Ibn Abi Talib (d. 661 AD), the cousin and son-in-law of the Prophet Muhammad. They believe that 'Ali, not Abu Bakr, 'Umar, or 'Uthman, should have succeeded the Prophet Muhammad as leader of the Muslim community, and that 'Ali and his descendants have priveleged insight in matters of faith and practice. *Translator's Note*

Chapter 36

To the House

Transported by zeal, his brow bathed in sweat, Behzad roused his little band of followers, inspiring them with his enthusiasm and courage, so that the ruined arch seemed crowded with armed men and the speaker to be Chosroes himself. Before that night, they had known Behzad as a Persian doctor resentful of the 'Abbasids, but it had never occurred to them that he might be the envoy of one of the secret societies that had arisen in Khurasan with the aim of toppling Arab rule. Among the most famous of these societies was the Khurrami faction. Though ostensibly a religious sect, it was a political party used by ambitious men to help them attain power. Among its members were the relatives and partisans of Abu Muslim, including his daughter Fatima, whom the Khurramis venerated and addressed in their prayers. The Khurramis played an important role in Islamic history. Whenever they gained in strength, they emerged into the open; when they weakened, they retreated into the shadows. In every city of Islam, their spies and agents worked together in secret. Among them were Muslims, Zoroastrians, and Magians, all of them Persians.[86]

Not surprisingly, there were many Khurramis in Baghdad, including the ones who had come with Behzad. They were wealthy and influential men who resented the caliphs for having killed Abu Muslim, Ja'far the Barmaki, and others. They had shared these grievances among themselves in secret while waiting for circumstances to change. They had pinned their hopes on al-Ma'mun, never expecting that al-Amin would go so far as to remove him from the succession. When Behzad told them what had happened, they were provoked to anger. One of them rose and said, "We stand

---

86 On Zoroastrians, see note 35. 'Magians' (*majus*) are Zoroastrian priests, or Zoroastrians in general. Zaidan seems to think of them as a distinct group. *Translator's note*

by our oath to spare neither blood nor treasure in our cause. But we must act with deliberation."

"That is our resolution," said Behzad. "Continue as you were until the day comes. I know where to find you, so be ready." Turning aside, he put down the lamp he had been holding. "It's time to leave," he said. "This is the last time we'll have a meeting like this here. Soon enough, we'll be able to gather without trouble or fear, God willing."

Throwing on their cloaks, his companions rose to leave. Behzad picked up his cloak, put it on, extinguished the lamp, and went out, leaving the lamp where it was. The Arch went dark. Unable to bear the thought of remaining in her hiding place, Maymuna was on the verge of calling out, but her grandmother seized her hand, telling her to be quiet until the men had dispersed. Then 'Abbada rose, beckoning Maymuna to follow her as quietly as she could. Maymuna obeyed, her knees shaking so violently that she could barely walk and her teeth chattering as if she were suffering convulsions. When they reached the center of the Arch, they could see the men shake hands with Behzad, bid him farewell, and mount their horses.

Left alone, Behzad turned to where his horse was tethered. Then he heard footsteps behind him. Turning around, he saw two specters in the garb of women. "Who's that I see?" he asked, unfazed.

Maymuna ran to him and clutched his arm, "It's Maymuna, with my grandmother 'Abbada!"

Behzad felt her tremble but steeled himself to speak firmly. "And what brings the two of you here?"

"We came to look for you," said 'Abbada. "You were gone for so long, and we were worried. Our mistress, al-Ma'mun's daughter, has a fever, and she refuses to let anyone but you treat her. When you didn't come back, we thought we were the best able to come find you, since we know your house and the roads you use."

With one hand on his horse's reins and the other holding the box, he bowed his head in thought. "But why did you come to this place? How did you know I was here?"

"It was divine providence that brought us here," said Maymuna. "But the story will take time to tell. Now you need rest, and so do we."

"We'll go to my house," he said. Then he turned to 'Abbada. "I imagine you're more fatigued than we are. Climb onto the horse: you ride and we'll walk."

"Forgive me, my lord," she said, "but I wouldn't dream of it: no one but you may ride your horse. But where are we going?"

"To the house."

"The house in Ctesiphon?"

"Yes."

Seizing his hands in hers, 'Abbada cried, "No, by God! Don't go there!"

"Why not?"

"It's dangerous!"

"Why?" he asked, without slowing his pace.

"We saw the soldiers and the Ruffians coming to look for you there," she said, and went on to tell him quickly what they had seen. "I'm afraid something will happen to you."

"You may be afraid," he said with sudden resolution, "but I'm not."

"Please do as we ask," she pleaded. "Come with us to the river. There's a boat waiting for us there."

"I need to go to the house, my lady."

Unable to keep silent any longer, Maymuna was about to beg him to change his mind when suddenly she heard the sound of hurried footsteps. All three turned and saw a figure approaching from the direction of Ctesiphon.

"Oh no!" cried Maymuna, flinching. "He must be a Ruffian!"

"Not at all," she heard the man say, and all of them recognized the voice.

"Salman?" said Behzad.

"Yes, master," said Salman, reaching them and pausing to catch his breath.

"What's wrong?" asked Behzad.

"The house is surrounded," he said, his voice breaking with fatigue. "There's a lot of them, all sent by al-Amin to capture you."

"How did you happen to be here and see them? I thought you were still in Baghdad."

"I heard about the plan to come to Ctesiphon and did everything I could to get here as quickly as possible. When I reached the house I found them already there and discussing how to break into it, and I understood that you weren't there. Then I remembered that sometimes you go to the Arch, so I came hoping to find you and warn you."

"So I should flee?"

"What else can you do?" asked Salman. "Why risk your life? Please listen to me."

"I can't," said Behzad. "But I want you to take Maymuna and her grandmother to their boat. I need to go to the house, and if I find soldiers there, God will decide what is to become of me."

Unable to keep her thoughts to herself any longer, Maymuna said, "Do you think we fear for ourselves? Yours is the life that matters. Do you think we didn't hear your speech? We know what your mission is, and I want to know what you have inside that box."

"Perhaps I'll show it to you later," he said. "Now, though, I have to go home. I'm not used to running away."

Now Maymuna was even more impressed with him. Seeing no way to dissuade him, they said, "We'll all go together, come what may."

Behzad handed the reins to Salman and began walking. Salman moved to take the box, but Behzad refused to let it go. 'Abbada came along slowly and painfully, making every effort to look as exhausted as possible. Maymuna and Salman did the same, as if they were being led to the slaughterhouse; and Behzad slowed his pace to match theirs.

Chapter 37

A Lover's Colloquy

Torn between hope, fear, joy, and sorrow, Maymuna was suffering agonies that defy description. Walking along with the others, she felt as if she were swimming through a sea of wild surmise. Thinking back to what she witnessed under the Arch, she felt her heart leap with joy at the thought of his coming to the aid of the Persians; but then she recalled his speaking of a journey to Khurasan, and she could feel her spirit shrivel. To make matters worse, she still did not know whether he cared for her. She felt an urge to be alone with her thoughts. When she imagined being alone with him, she was overcome with nervous embarrassment.

It was now completely dark. Silent, they felt their way slowly forward along the rough, rubble-strewn path, each wrapped in his own thoughts. As they approached the town, they grew ever more anxious about the soldiers. When they reached the markets, Salman asked permission to walk ahead. He disappeared, then returned, saying, "The soldiers broke down the doors and plundered the house, but they're gone now."

"There's only one thing in the house that I care about," said Behzad. "If they've left it, that's enough."

Thinking he meant his books and papers, Salman said, "They took the books and ripped up the papers."

"That's not what I mean," said Behzad, walking on. When they reached the house, they went in through the broken doorway. Salman went ahead to where the lamp-stand was and returned with a lamp to light their way. The house had obviously been pillaged. Still carrying the box, Behzad was examining the floor. The group passed into a broad courtyard full of relics indicating that the house had been built atop the palace of Shapur, where al-Mansur had taken up residence before Baghdad was built. From the courtyard they passed through the inner door of the house, which was also open. Behzad was still examining the ground, and the others wondered at his silence and his indifference to what had happened to the house. As they proceeded through the anteroom, he suddenly turned toward an alcove set in the right-hand wall and, joy brightening his face, took down a pickax that was resting there. "Keep this with you," he said, handing the pickax to Salman. Then he marched on, turning neither right nor left, until he reached a large room in the middle of the house. There on the floor was a rug soiled with footprints and strewn with papers thrown about by the intruders. After inviting 'Abbada and Maymuna to sit on the cushions that lay against the walls, he ordered Salman to follow him through a door into a chamber at the opposite end of the room. The two men went inside and shut the door, leaving the lamp in the room outside.

Alone with 'Abbada, Maymuna saw that she was gasping for breath and her head-scarf was soaked with sweat: her grandmother needed rest. Hoping that she would fall asleep and give her a chance to speak with Behzad, Maymuna left her undisturbed. Seeing her droop and yawn, she said, "Take a pillow, Grandmother, and rest." She rose and brought her two pillows. "Wake me when Behzad comes out," said 'Abbada, lying down.

"I will."

Within minutes 'Abbada was asleep, leaving Maymuna as if stranded in some stormy sea, racking her brains for a pretext she might use to speak with Behzad.

Suddenly the door opened and she recoiled, startled. She turned to see Behzad, now wearing a light cloak and a small turban, coming out of the room, followed by Salman with the pickax. Behzad motioned for Salman to take the pickax outside. Salman went out and Behzad remained behind. Maymuna rose out of respect, but averted her eyes, feeling shamefaced and lovesick. Placing a hand on her shoulder, he said, "Sit down, Maymuna— last of the Barmakids!"

When she heard him address her by her family's name, which he had never before shown any sign of knowing, she sat down, shaken. He quickly found a cushion, folded it in half, and motioned for her to sit on it, saying, "Take this cushion, daughter of Ja'far."

Though this sudden openness on his part left her even more astonished than she had been, Maymuna forced herself to make the most of this opportunity. Head down, cheeks crimson, she asked, "Why are you calling me by a different name now?"

Taking another cushion for himself, he said, "I'm calling you by your real name, even though you thought I didn't know it. May God have mercy on Ja'far, and restore him to us!"

Eyes shining with tears of love, voice breaking with emotion, she raised her face to him and, trying to hide her feelings behind a smile, asked, "Do you expect the dead to rise again in this world?"

"Even if his body cannot arise," he said, "his memory will. Ja'far is not dead, Maymuna. Though al-Rashid could kill his body, he has no power over the good name he left behind."

Shrinking at the mention of her father's murder, she toyed with the end of her sleeve, saying, "I'm grateful for your kindness, my lord. You've been generous to us, and concealed our poverty, for such a long time." So saying, she burst into tears.

Seeing her weep, he felt his heart break, and was on the verge of baring his soul to her, but thought better of it. "Ja'far encompassed all of us with his generosity," he said, hoping to sidetrack her. "Every Muslim and non-Muslim owes him a debt of gratitude. What thanks do we deserve for paying back some small part of it?"

Maymuna was disappointed. She had expected him to say something else: that he loved her. Afraid that she had been deluding herself, she wiped the tears off her face with her hand. Taking her wrist, he pulled her hand away, asking in a choked voice, "Why are you crying?"

Eyes still averted, but feeling an electric current running from his hand through her every vein, she replied, "I'm sad, my lord. Let me cry out my sorrow!"

"Why are you sad?"

"How can you ask me that when you know the reason? Who could be more miserable than a girl who's lost both her parents and lives in fear of being discovered? I'm the daughter of Ja'far and I have to live among those people. That's one of the reasons I'm miserable." Swallowing hard, she pulled her hand from his.

Taking her hand back, he pressed it between both of his. "God forbid that you should be as miserable as you say you are."

"But I am," she said, trying to pull her hand back. "Why shouldn't I be? Tonight I've learned that…" She stopped speaking, swallowed, and looked at him instead. Not knowing what she meant to say, he studied her face, his love for her suffusing his features. As the poem says, the eye conveys more than the tongue:

Should love or hatred lie concealed
The eye will either state reveal;
Despise a thing, and all will know
When you gaze upon it so;
Forbid your tongue to speak a word:
The truth will from the eye be heard.

From the look in his eye, Maymuna understood that Behzad loved her. All the same, she wanted to hear him say so. She glanced at her grandmother, who was asleep and snoring. Then she dropped her gaze again, saying nothing.

"Go on," he said. "What is it that you've learned tonight, Maymuna?"

"It's painful to talk about," she said. "Let me be. I don't want you to be worried about me. You have more important things to take care of. I don't want to distract you with my silly dreams."

"I may be dreaming the same dreams," he said. "Tell me."

Feeling that he was close to coming out and saying he loved her, she looked up at him with a sort of lovelorn reproachfulness, and smiled, tears sparkling in her eyes. "Forgive me, my lord, for my childishness. I'm sure that I'll be disappointed: how likely is it that Behzad, the great leader, should be suffering what I'm suffering? It's his business to gather partisans and overthrow dynasties and stir up nations; why should he notice a girl like me? His mission is to slay hundreds of enemies and trample on their skulls! Why should he concern himself with the heart of a poor orphan girl?" Her hand had been lying between his hands; she pulled it free, covered her face, and wept.

Hearing her speak and seeing her weep, he was overcome by passion, but then restrained himself. "Do you want me not to go away?"

"If only you would stay," she sighed. "But then what good would that do me? No...I want you to stay, but..." She fell silent.

"But what?" he cried. "Tell me!"

Chapter 38

Unconditional Love

Suddenly angry at herself for trying to trick him into admitting he loved her, Maymuna looked away, embarrassed. Heartbroken and bewildered, she knew that she had tried to manipulate him only because she loved him so much. Now, though, she feared that he would say something to destroy her hopes. She responded with defiance. Angry with herself for sinking so low, she recoiled from him; and, determined to cut the conversation short, rose to go. Surprised at her sudden change of attitude, he seized the end of her gown and pulled her back. "Where are you going, Maymuna?" he said reproachfully.

Without looking at him, she said, "Let me go, Behzad." She swallowed hard and tried to slip away.

"Sit down, Maymuna. There's nowhere to go. You're a stranger here, and you have no home of your own."

His words struck home. Reminded of her misfortunes, she stood up, put her face in her hands, and collapsed in tears.

His heart breaking for her, he found himself unable to speak. After striving to conceal his feelings, he was now at a loss for what to do. Finally he said, "There was something you wanted to say. Tell me!"

Still standing, she tried to fight down her emotions but found she could not. She felt helpless and unequal to the task of putting a brave face on her predicament. Her knees were knocking together and she was too weak to remain standing any longer. So she sat down and dried her tears on her sleeve. Then she looked into his eyes and saw something that seemed to show what was in his heart. She was on the verge of telling him frankly what she wanted to hear, but modesty held her back. He was smiling at her, his eyes sparkling with love, but she was nevertheless afraid to speak and so remained silent.

"Tell me, Maymuna," he repeated, his voice constricted.

She looked at him with tear-reddened, half-closed eyes that seemed more alluring than ever. "I see that you're trying to be kind. But there's no need to mock me. Say that I make no difference to you, and your responsibility will end there."

"But you make a great deal of difference to me," he said. "Can't you feel that? You're pretending even more than I am. Or do you have no heart at all?" he asked hoarsely.

Brightening, she looked him in the eye as if to take the measure of his words. Tears still streaming down her cheeks, she smiled, as a child does when you finally give her a long-forbidden toy. But then, checked again by modesty, she said, "I make a great deal of difference to you. Does that mean that you…"

He knew what she meant but pretended not to. "What do you want me to say, Maymuna? You say it first!"

"Do I need to? Don't these tears speak for me? You say it! By God, say you love me…or else leave me alone!" So saying, she turned her face from him, so buffeted by love, mortification, and fear that she could hardly breathe.

Though remembering the mission he had undertaken, and fearing that a declaration of love might interfere with his plans, Behzad was unable to restrain himself any longer. "It's so obvious that I shouldn't have to say anything. Yes, I love you!"

Hearing his words she was overcome with joy. She nearly laughed, but she choked on her laughter as she had choked on her tears. Tears streaming uncontrollably, she exclaimed, "You love me, Behzad? You love me? Is this real or is it a dream? Am I awake or asleep? My beloved Behzad! Do you love me?"

Seeing her excitement, he thought again of the distressing predicament he was in. "Yes," he said, his expression troubled. "I…" He swallowed, scratched his chin, and fell silent.

Afraid that he was now regretting his admission, she looked at him with a mixture of hope and fear. "What's wrong? Why are you hesitating? What happened? Don't you love me?"

"I do," he said. "But…"

"But what?"

"I have something else to tell you."

"Now that you've said you love me," she said bashfully, "you can say anything you want." Then she interrupted herself. "No…Wait! Don't say anything. I'm afraid you'll threaten to go away."

"It's not a threat," he said. "But it is a condition of loving me."

Her heart pounding, she gave him a reproachful sideways look. "So you're setting conditions," she said in a low, soft voice. "But I love you without any conditions."

He bowed his head, abashed at her gentle remonstrance. "You're right," he said, lifting his eyes to hers. "Conditional love is no love at all. But what I'm asking is for your own good. Let me explain it to you, and then do as I ask."

"I love you unconditionally," she said. "Absolute love means that I accept no impediments. So place whatever conditions you wish."

"You know that I have to leave," he said. "But I'm leaving to serve you. You may think you know everything there is to know about me and can easily reach a judgment about my future. You've heard that I'm an emissary of the Khurrami sect. That's true enough, but I'm more than that. I cannot enjoy love until after I've had my revenge. If I succeed and come back alive, I will count myself fortunate to have avenged your father and his predecessor as well. If I fail, then I was fated to fail, and there is nothing I can do about that. I know that this is a difficult condition for you to accept, and it's unfair of me to impose it. But I have no choice." Then, getting to his feet, he said, "Go to bed now."

She rose, her heart flailing wildly. Though she dreaded not knowing when they would be together again, she was gratified to learn that he sought to avenge her father. She was also curious about his claim to be more than she knew him to be. "Who could he be, then?" she wondered. But she did not dare ask him directly. Instead, she did as he asked and rose to go to bed. Pointing to a door that led to the bedroom, he picked up the lamp and led the way. Her thoughts in a whirl, she followed him into the bedroom, where she saw a rug made of pelts, a pillow, and a blanket. "That's your bed for the night," he said, leaving and taking the lamp with him. A moment later the room went dark. She removed her head-scarf and lay down.

Chapter 39

Sleeplessness and Worry

Maymuna lay down and covered herself with the blanket. The house was quiet except for the sound of her grandmother's snoring, which continued to disturb the silence now that darkness had fallen. Left alone, Maymuna again fell prey to worry. She thought again of all that had befallen her that day, from the frightful experience of hiding in the Arch to the moment when she learned to her great joy that Behzad did love her after all. She also remembered what she had meant to do before being distracted by her conversation with Behzad: to find out what was in the box. Still intensely curious, she resolved to find the answer on some other occasion.

For an hour or two, she tossed and turned. Though mentally and physically exhausted, she was still too excited by the conversation to sleep. She lay awake until she could no longer stand to be in bed. On a sudden impulse she rose, but found that it was too dark to go anywhere. So she forced herself to lie down again and wait until the break of day.

As she lay pensive and sleepless, the stillness making her feel even more desolate, she heard something moving on the other side of the wall. Straining her ears, she recognized the sound of a spade striking the earth. Her heart pounded, and for a moment she thought that she was imagining things. Then she heard the sound of whispering voices. Alarmed, she leapt up and turned to face the wall. Above her bed was a window through which she could see a few faint rays of light. Putting her head through the window, she saw that there was an empty space between the house and the courtyard wall. On the ground was a lamp that she recognized as Behzad's. She saw a hole in the ground, and a tall man, his sleeves and trousers rolled up and his head uncovered, turning the earth over with a spade. Looking carefully, she saw that it was Salman. With him was a second man whom she recognized as Behzad. Her heart beat faster, her knees trembled, and her body began shaking so hard she nearly fell. She pulled herself together and leaned against the window, trying to avoid being seen. Then she heard Behzad say, "It must be here. Keep digging!"

"I'm afraid you may be mistaken, my lord," said Salman. "We've moved a lot of earth and there's no sign of the body."

"No, I'm not mistaken. Isn't this the site of Shapur's palace?"

"It is."

"The old man told me that al-Mansur used to sit under the portico where this house now stands. He said they buried the body in the palace garden. The garden must have been in this open space, and we've dug up every part of it except this one. So dig!"

"If only that old man were here tonight to show us the spot!"

"Didn't I tell you he was dead?" said Behzad. "Thank God he lived long enough to tell us about this place. He was certain about it because he was a young man in al-Mansur's time and never recovered from the shock of what he witnessed. Keep digging! We're on the right track."

"No sign of the corpse, master," said Salman, resuming his digging.

Meanwhile, Behzad was studying the earth that flew out of the pit. Suddenly he stooped and pulled out a piece of fabric. Knocking the earth off it, he said, "Isn't this a piece of that rug?"

Salman stopped digging and took the piece of fabric. "Yes," he gasped, breathless with exhaustion. "That's what it is, all right." He went back to digging with new energy. Watching him, Maymuna could make no sense of his movements.

A short time later, Salman, gasping and sweating, was too tired to continue. Breathless, he stopped and leaned on the spade.

"We have no choice but to finish tonight," said Behzad, "but you're exhausted. Give me the spade." He took it and applied himself to the pit with speed and vigor. Not long afterwards, Maymuna heard the spade strike something solid, like a stone. She saw Behzad stop digging, reach down, and pull out a long piece of bone. "Here's a thigh or a shinbone," he called out. "We're on the right track."

Salman came forward, lowered himself into the pit, and began scooping away at the earth until he found something that he took up between his thumb and forefinger and handed to Behzad. "Here's a ring."

Behzad took it and went over to the lamp. "It's his signet ring," he said.

"How do you know, my lord?"

"God rest his soul! Do you remember when he came from Khurasan at al-Mansur's request? He told his scribe to ignore any messages sealed with his full signet but to accept instead only the ones sealed with half the signet."

"I remember."

"Look at this ring. It has his name on it, but half of it has been rubbed out. The ring is his and the bone is too. Look for the skull!"

Salman began pawing through the soil and pulling out tattered bits of fabric and worm-eaten bones. Finally he found the skull and handed it to Behzad, who brushed the dirt off it, the elation on his face turning slowly to sorrow. Looking pale, he said, "That's his head: the head of one unjustly done to death. Finding his head is worth half the caliphate. If we avenge his death, we gain the entire caliphate!" Unable to restrain himself, he kissed the skull. Salman, too, bent over it and kissed it, then began gently and reverently wiping the dirt off with the end of his sleeve as Behzad looked on, his expression altogether altered and his eyes flashing with anger.

"I congratulate you, my lord, on your find," said Salman. "Now that you've found what you were searching for, our work is done. Let's go back to the house and rest. It's been a tiring night for you." He picked up the lamp in one hand and the skull in the other. Wrapped in silent anger, Behzad followed him stiffly.

Seeing them turn back toward the house, Maymuna returned to her bed, exhausted and full of misgivings. Too intimidated to go out at such a late hour and ask Behzad about what she had witnessed, she resolved to be patient until morning. She spent the rest of the night as if tempest-tossed, unable to close her eyes until shortly before dawn. Then she fell into a deep sleep, awakening only when her grandmother roused her. Opening her eyes, she saw 'Abbada standing by her bedside, saying, "Maymuna, get up! We're ready to leave."

Chapter 40

Parting

Alarmed, Maymuna leapt up, wishing she had not slept so heavily. She threw on her veil, put on her shoes, and followed her grandmother out through the reception room. A horse whinnied, and she turned around. There was Behzad, shrouded in a cloak, with the box before him on the saddlebow. He turned to the women and waved goodbye. "Go with Salman," he said, and spurred his mount.

Maymuna felt as if her heart had been torn out. As he rushed away, she thought of trying to stop him. Stricken, her blood seemingly frozen in her veins, she forgot herself and burst into tears. She regained her senses to find that her grandmother had taken her hand. "Let's get back to the boat," she was saying. "Salman's waiting for us by the shore. The doctor will find us at al-Ma'mun's palace."

Maymuna set off in a daze, her eyes following Behzad until he vanished. Her grandmother, meanwhile, knew nothing of what she was thinking—or perhaps she had an inkling of it but pretended to overlook it out of consideration for Maymuna's feelings. If so, 'Abbada was acting contrary to the custom of old women, who are inquisitive even about matters that do not concern them. They enjoy gossip, especially when they have nothing else to keep them busy. Should an old woman notice a change in her neighbor, she will leave no stone unturned trying to discover the reason for it. Yet 'Abbada, raised in the house of a prominent man, had witnessed reversals and marvels of all kinds. She had devoted herself to Maymuna, assuming full responsibility for her upbringing and sticking as close to her as a shadow. As a result, she had no fear that her charge might commit any impropriety. Had the young woman evinced interest in a man who would make a poor match, she would have intervened. As it happened, she favored

Behzad even more than Maymuna did. She therefore thought it best to keep her own counsel and see what fate would bring.

The party walked slowly toward the river, Salman enveloped in his usual cloak. When they reached the Tigris, they saw the boat waiting for them. They boarded and ordered the captain to return to Baghdad. He turned the tiller and raised the sail. 'Abbada sat down in the middle of the boat beside her granddaughter. Each was wrapped in her own somber thoughts. Salman sat near the captain, keeping an eye on the shoreline on either side as if expecting something to happen.

They had been sailing for less than an hour when they saw another boat approaching from Baghdad, slicing through the waves as it came. It was flying a flag that Salman recognized as that of al-Fadl Ibn al-Rabi. Realizing with dismay that the boat belonged to the Vizier, Salman hurried to Maymuna and 'Abbada and motioned for them to leave their seat and conceal themselves. Seeing his frenzied gestures, Maymuna grew frightened. Keeping her eyes on the other boat as it drew closer, she saw that it was fitted out with rugs and cushions. Standing on board were several attendants, and sitting amidships was a good-looking man whom Maymuna recognized as Ibn al-Fadl. He turned toward her and saw her looking at him. Certain now that it was he, she felt misery seize her heart and drain the blood from her face. Looking away, she busied herself with her veil.

'Abbada looked at Salman as if seeking his counsel. With a reassuring smile, he said in a low voice, "Don't be afraid, Mistress. That boy doesn't dare do anything as long as we're in al-Ma'mun's boat."

"And what if we weren't?"

"He might stop us and ask who we're carrying, since he's going to Ctesiphon to look for..." He glanced at Maymuna.

"Damn him," she said. "Won't he give up?"

"He's consulted with astrologers and had them write up charts," he said smiling, "all in the hope of winning her over. They told him that she'd left Ctesiphon, but it seems he didn't believe them and had to go see for himself."

Maymuna could hear what Salman was saying but pretended out of modesty that she couldn't. Though she was surprised that he knew about Ibn al-Fadl, she let her grandmother do the talking.

"Shame on him, the wretch!" said 'Abbada. "He'll not touch a hair on her head so long as I'm alive."

Meanwhile Ibn al-Fadl's vessel had come alongside theirs. Some of the attendants had gathered at the gunwale to examine the passengers, but they saw no one but Salman. Even if they had noticed the women, the fear of al-Ma'mun would have dissuaded them from harrassing them.

As Ibn al-Fadl's boat passed alongside, Maymuna trembled with fear and loathing. After the other vessel had passed them, Salman, hoping to cheer the girl up, said, "My mistress seems quite averse to the Vizier's son even though he's dying of lovesickness."

Looking up at him, she saw that he was smiling, but felt too bashful to reply. "We can't stand the sight of that fellow," said her grandmother.

"Or his father either, I suppose."

'Abbada had always thought that Salman had no idea who they were, and was startled to hear him say what he had said. She gave him a disapproving glance but he spoke first: "You have every right to hate him and his father too, Mistress. Don't be surprised that I know about them. I'm here to take over whenever my master the doctor isn't able to protect you. I'm at your service, and you can trust me and rely on me for anything you need."

Sensing that he meant what he said, 'Abbada was reassured. As for Maymuna, when she heard Salman mention Behzad, she regained her senses and asked, with a great show of innocence, whether the doctor was preparing for a journey.

"Yes," said Salman. "He's going to look for some medicinal substances." Then he laughed.

Maymuna knew that he was jesting with her, and that he doubtless knew all of his master's secrets. Warming to his good spirits, she smiled to show him that she understood. Then she asked, "Do you think he'll be leaving soon?"

"Of course you're only asking," he said with a laugh, "because you're worried about our mistress Zaynab, al-Ma'mun's daughter, who refuses to see any other doctor. How kind of you! Yes, I think he's leaving soon. But the truth is that predicting what he'll do is all guesswork. We could easily be wrong: whenever he decides to act, he moves suddenly and without any warning."

"It seems to me you're playing dumb, Salman," said 'Abbada. "As far as I can tell, the doctor never hides anything from you; but now you're telling us you don't know when he's leaving."

Seeing that 'Abbada was speaking seriously, Salman tried to give her the impression that he was not as well informed as she thought, even though he knew she was too discreet to reveal anything he told her. "My master the doctor is tireless in pursuing his aims, but he's very secretive as well. He may well intend to travel, but he would never tell me so directly." He turned to Maymuna. "Perhaps he has told you, Mistress."

Even if Maymuna had not had the same reasons to keep silent as Salman did, propriety alone would have stopped her from revealing any knowledge of Behzad's doings. Blushing, she looked away. Satisfied, Salman took the opportunity to change the subject. Turning to the captain, he asked if they were still far from Baghdad.

"Aren't those the mansions of Kalwadha?" asked the captain, pointing forward.

Salman looked to the horizon. "So they are," he said. "And if that's Kalwadha then we're near the City of Peace." A moment later he added, "Yes, we're coming close. Soon we'll see the minaret of al-Mansur's mosque and then our master's palace."

Hearing Salman mention the palace, Maymuna remembered they would have to explain their failure to bring the doctor back with them to treat Zaynab. She wondered what she would say to Dananir. Should she tell her the truth or keep it a secret? As she mulled this over, she saw Salman come over, looking perturbed. Addressing 'Abbada, he said, "My mistress doubtless understands that everything concerning Behzad has to remain a secret."

"What do I tell Dananir when she asks where he is?"

"We'll say we couldn't find him."

"Agreed," said 'Abbada.

Chapter 41

The Journey

The day before, we had left Dananir worried about Zaynab's health and eager to see 'Abbada and Maymuna return with the doctor. As the day wore on, she became increasingly anxious; but by evening the girl felt better. Soon she had left her bed and resumed her usual games as if she had never been ill.

Those at the palace spent the night expecting to see 'Abbada and Maymuna the next morning, but when noontime came and went with no sign of them, Dananir began to worry, as she could imagine a thousand reasons why they might have been delayed. Finally, in the late afternoon, a servant brought word that the boat had returned. Dananir went out to the wharf and saw that the doctor was not aboard. She welcomed 'Abbada and Maymuna and then, seeing that Salman had come with them, asked him about Behzad.

"We saw no sign of him," said Salman. "Did he come here?"

"No," she replied. "How odd! I wonder where he is."

"I don't know," he said. "But that's how he is: he disappears whenever he has secret business to take care of. I'll look for him in Baghdad."

During this exchange, they had entered the palace, where Zaynab, looking bright and healthy, came to meet them. 'Abbada and Maymuna kissed her, distracting her from asking about the doctor. After they had settled in, Salman declared that he would go into the city to look for his master. He left and the women waited for him to return.

The next day he arrived looking preoccupied and asked to meet Dananir. Told that he was waiting for her, Dananir, who was with 'Abbada and Maymuna in the garden, rushed away, leaving her guests at a loss. Most distressed was Maymuna, who was desperately eager to learn what the matter was.

Meanwhile Dananir had joined Salman, who came up close to her and said confidentially, "I found my master, the physician, on the bridge. He intended to come here, but when he saw me he gave me a message to convey to you."

"What is it?"

"He told me that he received an urgent summons from our master al-Ma'mun."

"A summons from the heir apparent? Is anything wrong?"

"Not at all," he said. "But he's ordered him to Marv without explaining why. My master told me to pass this message on to you and ordered me to remain here at your service."

"Will he be gone for a long time?"

"He didn't say."

Dananir bowed her head thoughtfully for a moment. This sudden trip was unwelcome news to her, as she had come to find the doctor's presence comforting and to rely on him, especially with regard to Zaynab, as we have seen. "May God forgive him!" she said. "But we have to accept his excuse, I suppose. What led our master al-Ma'mun to summon him so urgently?" Turning back toward the garden, she asked Salman, "Are you staying with us now?"

"I can't stay," he said, "but I'll be here whenever you need me. You can rely on that."

Returning to the garden, Dananir saw that Maymuna had left her grandmother sitting in her place and was coming toward her with an anxious expression on her face. Seeing her, she remembered the young woman's attraction to Behzad and realized that the news of his departure would be hard for her to bear. Dananir decided to adopt a nonchalant attitude and to keep the journey a secret. Maymuna was looking at her, too embarrassed to ask a direct question. Guessing what she wanted to know, Dananir spoke first, asking, "What's wrong, dear? Why have you left your grandmother all by herself?" She gently put her arm around the young woman's shoulders and felt her tremble. "You're shaking," she said.

Maymuna looked up affectionately, grateful for Dananir's kindness. "What did Salman have to say?"

"He brought a message from the doctor."

"What is it? Has he left?"

Dananir was surprised at the accuracy of her guess. "Was it your heart that told you that?" she asked teasingly. "A lover knows her lover's mind, or so I'm told."

The young woman, who had never before realized how much Dananir knew of her secret thoughts, blushed at this phrase, and, ignoring the hint, busied herself with rebraiding her hair and said, "Why do you say that, Aunt? I'm only concerned because I know our mistress, daughter of the heir apparent, is so attached to him."

"How very generous of you!" said Dananir, smiling. "If you learned he was leaving, would that trouble you for Mistress Zaynab's sake as well?"

Still feigning innocence, Maymuna said nonchalantly, "So, has he really left?"

"Yes, he has," she replied, examining the young woman's face and seeing her sudden dismay reflected there: the embarrassed blush had given way to a stricken pallor. "But he'll be back soon enough," Dananir added quickly. "His heart won't let him stay away."

Afraid that if she spent any more time with Dananir her secret would soon be out, Maymuna made up a reason to excuse herself and set off toward her room to be alone. Waiting for her in the corridor was Salman. Seeing him, she felt her heart pound in dismay, and asked without preamble, "Has Behzad really left?"

"Yes, Mistress," he said.

"Where has he gone?"

"To Marv, in Khurasan, where our master al-Ma'mun lives now."

"How could he leave us?" she asked, swallowing hard.

"He's left all of us except for you. For you, he wrote a letter," he said, handing her an object wrapped in a handkerchief.

She took it, and through the cloth could feel the letter. Her face brightened. Slipping the letter into her sleeve, she turned toward her room, stopping only when Salman asked her if she needed anything else. Apologetic about rushing away without addressing him, she said, "Thank you, Salman! I won't forget your kindness. What would I do without you? You said that he asked you to watch over me, so do as you think best."

"I'm at your service," he said. "I'll be back to take care of anything you need." So saying, he departed.

Chapter 42

Behzad's Letter

Maymuna raced to her room. Alone, she sat on the rug, untied the handkerchief, and took out a roll of paper. Paper had only recently come into use for writing letters. The credit belonged to her father Ja'far, who introduced it as a replacement for parchment in government offices. Frantically unsealing the roll, she read:

From the lover called Behzad to Maymuna, daughter of the martyred Ja'far son of Yahya:

I would have written to you in the language of our glorious ancestors, if only you could understand it; but the circumstances of our age force us to communicate in the tongue of the nation that oppresses us: a nation destined to defeat us by treachery, slay our leaders, reduce our generals and scholars to servitude, and tyrannize us. One day, we will turn about to face them and exact our revenge, 'and those who have oppressed you shall know what fate awaits them.'[87] I hoped to see you before my departure and bid you farewell in person, and would have done so if not for fear that my heart would overcome me, as it did during that meeting when it forced from me a secret I kept hidden for many years, intending to conceal it until I had undertaken such deeds as would make me worthy of your regard. Yet you would accept from me nothing less than a declaration of my love. So I said then, and I say again now, that I love you, Maymuna. I love you boundlessly: I say so now without fear that my words will prevent my fulfilling that intention that I formed at our first meeting, and even earlier. Were I in your presence now, I would not have confessed this, lest passion compel me to accede to your wishes, and indeed to my own, by remaining with you and thereby let slip away the fruits of a lifetime of labor. But here, where no such course is open to me, there is no impediment to revealing the secrets of my heart. Know, my love, that I

---

87 Qur'an 26:227. *Translator's Note*

161

have dedicated my life to you and to avenging your father. I am not Behzad, nor am I a physician, nor an alchemist, nor an emissary of any group nor sect; rather, I am one whom you will come to know and be proud to love.

I will not tell you who I am until the time comes. Before then, there will be battles and bloodshed. I travel to Khurasan not by a summons from al-Ma'mun, or by order of anyone, but to finish an undertaking which I began and which I must complete. I travel in obedience to a cry rising from grave upon deep-buried grave, calling upon brave men to take up arms against oppression. As for the box, I wanted to show you what it contains; but I feared that the sight would pain you. One day, I will open it for you, as I have opened my heart; 'for every deed comes a day.'[88] *Remain in Baghdad, in God's care. I have told my faithful servant Salman to attend to your needs; you may trust him. Keep secret what I have told you until a true report reaches you from Khurasan of a day when fortunes turn and truth triumphs over falsehood. Should I fail, I shall die comforted by the thought of having done as men must do. The most that can be expected of any man is to give up his life and soul in defense of what is right. Let us trust in God's purpose, 'for He is all-powerful.'*[89]

By the time she had finished reading the letter, she had turned pale and her expression had changed. She could hear her own heart pounding in her ears. Feeling faint, she thought for a moment that she must be dreaming, and rubbed her eyes. Deciding that she was awake, she rolled up the letter and hid it in her sleeve. Then she lay down on the rug and let her thoughts drift. In her mind's eye, she revisited her first meeting with Behzad in Ctesiphon and his attentions to her and her grandmother—attentions she mistakenly thought were offered out of charity, but which she now understood, thanks to his letter, were expressions of his love. Now she regretted all the chances she had missed to make her own feelings plain.

Then, recalling some of the hints and promises in the letter, she felt an urge to read it again, so she took it out and read it through twice more, fearful all the while of being surprised by a visitor or observed by some hidden watcher. Hearing footsteps nearby, she hid the letter and pretended to be sleeping. When the footsteps receded, she fell back into a trance, recalling the expressions her beloved had used. She saw now that he was risking his life, and she was transfixed with fear for him. She wished he had

---

88 Qur'an 13:38. *Translator's Note*

89 A refrain that appears 163 times in the Qur'an, beginning with 2:20. *Translator's Note.*

renounced his vow and stayed with her, that she might revel in the sight of him; but then, when she recalled his determination to avenge her father, she could face with greater equanimity the thought of how far away he was. She imagined his triumphal return, and how proud she would be; and how she would be rewarded for all the distress she had suffered.

Chapter 43

The Shakiri

But if Maymuna's beloved was not Behzad the physician or an envoy of the Khurrami sect, then who was he? Her speculations proving fruitless, she resolved to accept whatever fate had in store for her. As she lay deep in thought, she began to feel drowsy, and had nearly fallen asleep when she was roused by a knock on the door. She rose and opened it to find that Dananir had come alone to visit her. Pretending to have been asleep, Maymuna welcomed her. The governess asked with a smile what she was doing all by herself.

"I lay down on this rug to rest. I had a headache and I fell asleep."

Pretending to believe her, Dananir turned to go, saying, "Then sleep, dear: you'll see him in your dreams."

"What do you mean?" said Maymuna, taken aback.

"Don't worry, Maymuna," said Dananir, looking back at her. "Your grandmother isn't here, and you can be honest with me. I'm a governess with a good deal of experience and I can tell you that secrecy does no good. In this case, the writing is on the wall!"

Though she knew that Dananir had not seen her letter, Maymuna imagined that she was somehow referring to it now. "What writing do you mean?" she asked, bewildered.

"Not a letter," said Dananir, turning around. "I mean that the signs of love are plain to see. The first time I saw you together, I could tell that you loved Behzad; and I'm sorry that he left before you could..." She winked.

Maymuna was embarrassed. At the same time, she was relieved to learn that her letter was still a secret. She was also relieved to hear that Dananir had divined her secret. A lover loves to confess, provided she trusts the one she confesses to. She smiled and averted her eyes.

Dananir, who was drawing her out in the hope of helping her fulfill her wish, could sense that Maymuna was on the verge of confessing. Placing a hand on her shoulder, she invited her to sit, then sat beside her, smiling and encouraging her gently to unburden herself. "May God forgive our doctor!" she said. "How could he go away without proposing? Don't be embarrassed, Maymuna: your love for him is pure, as is his, no doubt. He's a fine young man, and I pray that God will not keep him from you."

Summoning her courage, Maymuna asked, "Is it shameful to be in love, Aunt?"

"God forbid! I said no such thing. Don't let the separation trouble you: he'll be back soon. Don't worry."

Maymuna sighed and sat quietly, her happiness plain to see. Then she said, "I'm a poor orphan. Perhaps God has taken pity on my misery and decided to console me. But whatever the case may be, I need your help: I'm here under your protection and in your care."

"You're my mistress and the daughter of my mistress," said Dananir. "I'll never forget your father's generosity. May God have mercy on his soul! You can be sure that I'll do what I can to help you. And our mistress Zaynab thinks the world of you as well!"

She had hardly finished speaking when she heard the sound of footsteps hurrying toward the room. A trembling voice called out, "Where is the governess?"

Realizing that one of the pages was looking for her, Dananir clapped her hands. The page came to the door and asked permission to enter.

"Come in," said Dananir. The page came in and greeted them, looking stunned.

"What's wrong?" she cried.

"There's a trooper from the Shakiri regiment at the gate saying he has a letter for you."

"A Shakiri? What's a Shakiri doing here? They deliver messages for the caliph, and there aren't any men here. Perhaps he's in the wrong place."

"I asked him, and he said that he was carrying a message for the person in charge of the palace. He named you by name."

"Go," she said, "and bring the letter."

The page went out. Dananir stayed where she was, mulling over this strange turn of events. Maymuna was at her wit's end, fearing that the message had to do with her, or would convey some news that would upset her. Anyone who has suffered successive tribulations always expects news to be bad. Often that expectation proves to be correct.

Chapter 44

The Letter

A short time later the page returned with a letter. He handed it to Dananir and left. She recognized the seal as that of al-Fadl Ibn al-Rabi, vizier to al-Amin. This she took as a bad omen, and her hands trembled as she unsealed the letter. Seeing her look of dismay, Maymuna expected the worst. With the young woman following her every move, Dananir opened the letter and read it, a look of astonishment spreading across her face. It was all Maymuna could do not to tear the letter from her hands. Dananir finished reading it, and, with evident consternation, read it again. Then she gathered herself to leave. Unable to contain herself, Maymuna seized her hand and cried, "Where are you going? Tell me: is it about me? I can see Ibn al-Rabi's seal on it. It must be about me!"

"It may be about you," said Dananir, "but it's addressed to me."

"So it *is* about me! Tell me: what does he want from me? Please tell me!"

Dananir pulled away and rose, saying, "It's nothing to do with you."

Maymuna followed her, took her hand, and flung herself upon her. "I beg you to tell me the truth! Please tell me. Don't hide anything! And forgive my excitement."

Gently extracting her hand, Dananir said angrily, "That man's effrontery knows no bounds. Who does he think he is? Just because my lord is absent he thinks he can frighten us into obeying his orders. Damn him!"

Now even more persuaded that the letter was about her, Maymuna cried, "Whatever that letter says, I want to read it; what happens after that is up to you. I want to see it even if it kills me. Let me read it!"

Seeing that the young woman would not be dissuaded, Dananir handed her the letter. Maymuna took it into her trembling hands and read:

From al-Fadl Ibn al-Rabi, Vizier of the Commander of the Faithful, to the governess Dananir:

The Commander of the Faithful has learned that a girl named Maymuna has recently taken refuge in the palace of our master al-Ma'mun. He wishes to see her and ask her certain questions. He herewith calls on you to send her to him with the Shakiri, the bearer of this letter.

She had hardly finished reading the letter before tears rushed to her eyes and her hands began shaking so violently that she nearly dropped the letter. "Oh no!" she cried. "Bad luck follows me wherever I go. What do I do now? Let me leave the palace: there's no reason you should suffer the Caliph's anger on my account."

"There's nothing to worry about," said Dananir comfortingly. "You're staying here and we're not handing you over to anyone. You're our guest and you're under our protection. Have no fear." She went out, leaving Maymuna alone. In the passageway, she clapped her hands to summon the page. "Tell the Shakiri to go," she said. "We decline to reply to his letter."

Shaking with anger, she returned to Maymuna's room. Overcome, the young woman began bemoaning her fate, and Dananir did her best to comfort her. As they were thus occupied, 'Abbada, who had no notion of what had happened, came and found them in this sorry state. "What's wrong?" she asked. "What happened?"

Maymuna spoke up first. "We must leave the palace! Otherwise we'll bring the Caliph's anger down on everyone here." So saying, she gathered herself to rise.

Surprised, 'Abbada asked what had happened.

"That evil vizier sent a letter summoning me. He's claiming that the Commander of the Faithful wants to ask me about something."

'Abbada thought for a moment. "I know what's going on," she said. "That letter cannot have come from the Caliph. Ibn al-Rabi must have written it himself for reasons of his own—reasons that we all understand. The best thing would be for us to leave now before we bring some misfortune upon you."

"You're our guests," cried Dananir, "and you're not leaving. Does that wretch think he can have his way with the heir apparent's guests? Not if I can help it!"

Maymuna thought of Salman and wished he were there to offer advice. "Where's Salman?" she asked. "He said that Behzad asked him to keep an eye on us."

At the mention of Salman, Dananir felt calmer. "When he comes, we'll ask him what he thinks. His judgment is sound. Then we'll see what happens."

Chapter 45

Ibn al-Rabi's Audience

That morning, Salman had left al-Ma'mun's palace to return to his own room. Changing his clothes, he transformed himself into Malfan Sa'dun. Then he made his way into the Citadel of Al-Mansur. Leaning on his staff and running his hands through his beard, he headed for the Golden Gate Palace. With his book tucked under his arm, he went looking for the room that had been prepared for his use during his stay by order of al-Amin. Once there, he pretended to be absorbed in reading and in divining secrets of interest to him. He maintained this pretense until evening, expecting someone to come and consult him, knowing, as he did, that in every doorway were spies who reported secretly to the police chief on everyone who came and went.

At some point he heard the sound of hoofbeats approaching his dwelling. Straining his ears, he heard the rider turn and gallop toward his door. From the perfume that suffused the air, he recognized the caller as Ibn al-Fadl; and from the sound of his racing footsteps, he could tell that he was excited about something. He nevertheless remained seated until he heard the knock on the door. He rose, opened the door, and welcomed his visitor with an unwonted lack of enthusiasm. Ibn al-Fadl, remembering that Malfan Sa'dun could see the unknown, maintained a deferential attitude. Greeting him with a smile, he said, "How is Malfan Sa'dun today?" The latter replied by motioning wordlessly for him to come in and sit down. "What's wrong?" asked Ibn al-Fadl, taking the initiative. "You seem angry."

"Come in, son of the Vizier, and sit down. Who am I and what does my anger matter? Though I must say that this new generation seems to live on trickery and lies." So saying, he again invited him to sit.

"There's no need for me to sit," said Ibn al-Fadl. "I haven't come for any particular reason except to invite you to meet my father."

"If your father is like you, and doubts me and refuses to believe what I tell him, then what's the point of meeting him?"

Ibn al-Fadl was surprised to hear this allusion to what he himself had done: going to Ctesiphon to look for Maymuna after Sa'dun had told him that she was no longer there. Trying to bluff his way through, he asked, "What's all this hinting? When did I ever doubt you?"

"Did you take the trouble to go to Ctesiphon because I told you she wasn't there? And did you find her?"

Caught, Ibn al-Fadl felt abashed, and changed the subject. "We'll talk about that later," he said. "For now, come along to see my father. He has something important to ask you regarding the dynasty and the caliphate."

Naïve though the request was, Salman realized that it offered him the chance to achieve his end more quickly than he expected. "I'm at the service of the Vizier," he said. "Where is he now?"

"He's in the police chief's room in the palace."

Sa'dun strapped on his sandals, put his book under his arm, picked up his stick, and followed Ibn al-Fadl outside, trying to guess what questions he might be asked. He knew that the problem uppermost in their minds was that of Behzad. He had deduced this from the evidence around him, and from Ibn al-Fadl's remark that his father would ask him about a matter of state. Nevertheless, he was apprehensive about meeting Ibn al-Rabi. The Vizier was a shrewd and perceptive man, as was evident from his discovery that Behzad was coming to Baghdad and from his attempt—unsuccessful though it was—to arrest him. On the other hand, as Sa'dun walked along behind Ibn al-Fadl with his head bowed, muttering his spells, he thought that he was not afraid of Ibn Mahan, having learned that the police chief was a feeble and conceited man.

A few moments later they had reached the police chief's audience hall. Ibn al-Fadl went in without asking permission, but Malfan Sa'dun remained standing outside until Ibn al-Fadl invited him in. Entering the room, he saw Ibn al-Rabi reclining on a large cushion, his brow furrowed and his expression grave. In his hand was a fly swatter, which he waved back and forth over his face and shoulders, not because there were flies about, but as a sort of nervous tic developed in response to his many cares and responsibilities. Beside him on another cushion sat Ibn Mahan, his beard dyed with henna to a bright shade of red, spread across his chest. Refusing to acknowledge, even to himself, how old he was, he fought a constant battle against time. Though he could have reclined without constraint in the presence of Ibn al-Rabi, he nevertheless sat cross-legged, afraid that sitting more comfortably might be taken as a sign of frailty and decrepitude.

Ibn al-Rabi sat motionless as his son entered the room, and, looking at Sa'dun, asked, "Is that Malfan Sa'dun? The one I saw here yesterday?"

"Yes, Father," said Ibn al-Fadl. "He's the Chief Astrologer to our master al-Amin."

Ibn al-Rabi motioned for Sa'dun to sit. He did so, maintaining an air of ingenuousness despite his wariness of Ibn al-Rabi, who had received him so coldly. In his anxiety he nearly gave himself away, but then composed himself with an effort and set about straightening the silken cloth that held his ever-present book. No sooner had he sat down than Ibn al-Rabi asked him, "So you're the Chief Astrologer?"

"So they tell me, Master, but I hardly deserve such a title."

"You may deserve a good deal more than that, if my brother here, the police chief, is right about your marvelous abilities to glimpse the unseen."

"If I can," said Sa'dun, "there's nothing marvelous about it. The credit goes to this book and to the rules I've learned for how to practice divination. I report what I see, or what the voices tell me. Sometimes I don't even know the meaning of what I'm saying."

Ibn al-Rabi turned to Ibn Mahan as if to ask his opinion, and the latter confirmed with a nod that he believed everything that he had heard. But Ibn al-Rabi smiled skeptically. "Let me test him, then. 'To see a man do his best, there's nothing better than a test.' Will you answer any question I put to you?"

Malfan Sa'dun raised his head and addressed the fly swatter, as if thinking himself unworthy to address the Vizier directly. "Ask whatever you like," he said. "Only God knows the truth. If something is revealed to me, I repeat it; if not, I admit failure, without shame or embarrassment. That's how I've always worked."

"That's right," said Ibn Mahan and Ibn al-Fadl in unison, as they had already seen him at work.

Sitting up, Ibn al-Rabi asked, "I'm going to ask you about an important matter of state and I want you to tell me what you see. Keep in mind that I already know the answer. That's the test."

Ibn Sa'dun gave an ingratiating smile. "If you don't trust me you'd bet-ter dismiss me because I…"

"Not before I find out whether you're telling the truth," interrupted Ibn al-Rabi. "So if you have the knowledge you claim to have, tell me what I'm thinking about."

Sensing the hostility in his tone, Sa'dun spoke soothingly. "My master can do as he likes: he can let me go, imprison me, or kill me, if he wants to—test or no test."

Ibn Mahan, thinking that Sa'dun resented Ibn al-Rabi's way of express-ing himself, intervened. "The Vizier has nothing against you," he said. "But he's seen too many quack astrologers at the Caliph's court. When we told him about your abilities, he decided to let you prove yourself. So tell us what you see regarding the caliphate."

Chapter 46

The Astrologer at Work

Sa'dun opened his book and began turning the pages, muttering with his head bowed. The others waited silently for him to speak. Finally he addressed himself to Ibn Mahan. "Didn't I tell you what was to happen to the caliphate before anyone else knew?" he asked.

"Indeed you did. But now we need to know what our enemies are doing."

He went back to searching through the book, reading until the effort showed on his face and sweat broke out on his brow. Taking a chunk of incense from his sleeve, he put it in his mouth and chewed on it. Then he asked for a goblet of water and a censer. A small brass fire-box was placed before him and he cast the incense into the fire. Then he took up the goblet and looked into the water as if afraid of what he might see. Suddenly he exclaimed: "To Ctesiphon, to the palace of Shapur!"

He went back to scrutinizing the water, saying, "Isn't that Shapur's palace? But who was staying there?" Then he fell silent, stealing a glance at the others to see if they were thinking of Behzad. Seeing Ibn Mahan gesture in the affirmative, he saw that he had guessed right. But then, feigning fatigue, he put away the goblet, took up his handkerchief, and wiped the sweat from his brow. Realizing that he was not saying anything more, Ibn al-Rabi asked, "What happened at the palace?"

Tossing another chunk of incense into the fire, Sa'dun looked into the goblet and said, "I see soldiers and Ruffians disembarking from boats and rushing inside."

"Then what?"

"Their efforts were in vain, Master. They did not find him in the house."

Ibn al-Rabi brightened. "Good for you!" he said. "You've read my mind." Then, looking perturbed, he said, "I was looking for the man who lives in that palace. Do you know his name?"

Malfan Sa'dun bowed his head as if listening to what a voice was telling him, then said, "They call him Behzad, the doctor from Khurasan."

Ibn al-Rabi could not hide his surprise. "He's the one I want! Where is he now? Tell us!"

Malfan went back to the codex and paged through it, tossed in some incense, and looked for a moment into the goblet before putting it away. Then he clapped his hands and pointed. "He's outside the city," he said, "on horseback in a distant desert, dressed like a traveler."

"He's fled!" cried Ibn al-Rabi. "That damned Khurasani has fled. Do you see his servant?"

Turning back to the goblet, he said, "I see no one with him."

"Do the stars tell you anything about his servant or companion?"

Knowing that he himself was meant, Salman understood that whoever had told Ibn al-Rabi about Behzad had mentioned his companion, saying that the two had come from Khurasan to Bagdad on a quick mission. Learning of this while in Khurasan, Ibn al-Rabi had ordered the two arrested as soon as he reached Baghdad, but they had eluded him. When Salman learned that the Vizier was tracking them and had sent soldiers after them, he used that knowledge to save Behzad, as recounted earlier. Now, when Ibn al-Rabi asked him about Behzad's companion, he feigned ignorance, saying, "I see that he has a companion they call Salman."

"Yes, Salman! Where is he now?"

At that, Salman trembled, but had no choice but to tough it out. He looked into the goblet, cast glances right and left, and said, "He's in Baghdad. I think he's inside the Citadel of Al-Mansur. But he's concealed: there's a thick veil hiding him from any astrologer who tries to find him. I might be able to see through to him on some other occasion."

"If we catch Salman in Baghdad, we'll make up for losing Behzad. But I've heard that Salman puts on a different disguise and takes on a new appearance every day."

"That's why he appears to me here in disguise," said Salman, "but he can't remain hidden from Malfan Sa'dun forever. Even if he wears the stars as a belt, the sun as a turban, and the moon for shoes, his day will come."

Then, deciding to take advantage of this opportunity to further the anti-'Abbasid cause, he said, "Does my master think it better for Behzad to have fled than to have stayed here?"

"He left Ctesiphon to escape us. Or do you see something else?"

Opening the book, he turned two pages and said, "He's on his way to help a great notable in Khurasan."

Realizing that he meant al-Ma'mun, Ibn al-Rabi said, "What good does his help do when he's so far away?"

"That great notable has power conferred on him by the Commander of the Faithful, and there's reason to fear that he might use it against him if the Caliph doesn't clip his wings now, while there's still time."

By saying this, Salman hoped to incite Ibn al-Rabi to depose al-Ma'mun and widen the rift between the brothers. Understanding what he meant, Ibn al-Rabi exchanged glances with Ibn Mahan. At that moment, the two men resolved tacitly to encourage al-Amin to depose his brother. Of the two, Ibn al-Rabi was the keener, knowing as he did that al-Ma'mun bore a grudge against him. Nevertheless, he feigned indifference and changed the subject, saying, "Well done, Malfan!" Turning to his son, he said, "We were unfair to doubt the Chief Astrologer. I'm afraid we've been remiss."

"I never doubted Malfan Sa'dun," said Ibn al-Fadl. "But you made me doubt him, and that's why we did what we did."

Salman was unaware that Ibn al-Fadl had written to Dananir about Maymuna. Looking at Ibn al-Rabi, he said, "I hope you haven't done something you shouldn't have."

"I only doubted you when I saw you didn't know where that girl was staying," said Ibn al-Fadl. "Then we learned from our spies that she was staying at al-Ma'mun's palace. So I wrote to the governess asking her to send her here. But the governess sent our envoy back empty-handed, and wasn't very nice about it either. So we sent some soldiers to fetch her by force."

Though worried about what harm might befall the young woman, Salman feigned ignorance and said, "It's not my place to argue with my master"—motioning towards Ibn al-Fadl—"but I did tell him, before she went to al-Ma'mun's palace, that the girl was no longer in Ctesiphon. If he had asked me later, I could have told him where she was. I was hoping to use this book of mine to bring her along willingly. I wish he hadn't been so hasty," he said, pained by the thought of the brutal expedients that might have been used.

"It was ill-mannered of the governess to send back the Shakiri," said Ibn al-Rabi. "But she may not have known the whole story. The family has fallen from favor, but we want to do our best for the girl because this son of mine is enamored of her."

Chapter 47

"She Didn't Come Alone"

At that moment the chamberlain appeared. "The Vizier's messenger is at the door!"

"Let him in," said Ibn al-Rabi. Turning to the others, he explained, "This is the man who took the troops to al-Ma'mun's palace. Let's see what he has to say."

The Shakiri page entered the room and greeted the assembly.

"Report," said Ibn al-Rabi.

"Now?"

"Yes. Did you bring the girl?"

"We did. But she didn't come alone."

"Who came with her?"

"Our mistress Umm Habiba, daughter of the heir apparent."

"God help us!" said Ibn al-Rabi, recoiling. "Why did you bring her? Who told you to do that?"

"No one, and we didn't want to bring her. But she came with us anyway. She took hold of the girl and hung on to her clothes, and said, 'If you take her then you have to take me, too.'"

"What a disaster!" said Ibn al-Rabi. "Couldn't you have stopped her somehow?"

"No, sir. She was clinging to the girl and wouldn't listen to anything we said, even when we threatened her. We were even going to leave them there. In the end we brought both of them... and the governess Dananir as well."

"Dananir too?"

"Yes, sir. She was ready to die, saying that she'd rather be killed than give up her guest. So we brought all three of them."

"Where are they now?"

"In the women's quarters. And Umm Habiba is asking to see her uncle the Caliph."

Seeing that matters had gotten out of hand and might well cause him embarrassment, Ibn al-Rabi's face fell. Yet he was certain of his ability to manipulate al-Amin, especially since he could say that the girl was the daughter of Ja'far the former vizier and that he had ordered her siezed so that the Commander of the Faithful could decide what to do with her. He rose to go, then turned to Ibn Mahan. "Whoever said that haste begets regret was right. If we had asked Malfan Sa'dun's advice, we wouldn't have run into this problem. But no matter." He turned and saluted Malfan Sa'dun as he left.

Salman had risen out of respect, and now bowed his head in gratitude. He felt sure that no harm would come to Maymuna so long as Zaynab was with her. Al-Amin would learn of her situation and look after her out of courtesy to his niece, keeping her safe from Ibn al-Fadl.

Salman left the audience room to find that the sun had set and the great lights known as "al-Amin's candles" had been lit.

At that moment, al-Amin himself was sequestered with his singers and boon companions at a gathering that had been set up under a portico between two great halls of the palace. In the center was a pool fed by pipes shaped like the heads of serpents. Around the pool were garlands of sweet basil and seats for the guests and the singers. The company was served by eunuch attendants and cup-bearers dressed in splendid women's attire, their hair falling in single and double braids. Some of them carried tamborines, flutes, or lutes, and played and sang. There were also beautiful slave women dressed as page boys, given to him by his mother Zubayda. Al-Amin went to great lengths to acquire eunuchs from distant lands, spending great sums in the process.

That night he was dressed in his gala evening clothes: an iridescent yellow mantilla and a light turban. He was seated on a couch of ebony inlaid with ivory. Before him was a table laden with food, drink, and basil. The smell of musk and other perfumes filled the air.

At some point during the evening the chamberlain announced: "The daughter of the heir apparent is at the door."

Startled, the Caliph thought the chamberlain had made a mistake. "My niece?" he asked.

"Yes, Sire."

Al-Amin found himself at a loss for what to do. He was loath to let his niece see him presiding over a drinking party. He may have been powerful and mighty, but he could still be put to shame by a girl whom others might buy off with an apple or a toy. The dictates of good breeding and the fear of scandal will always hold greater sway than political authority and brute strength. For this reason, breeding has a certain power, and refinement commands respect from the wise and foolish alike. A vicious man, no matter how great his power, will still retain—however depraved he may have become—a residue of respect for virtue and its exemplars. Have you not seen how great transgressors who make light of their own crimes will nevertheless recoil from having those crimes attributed to them? In this way, they are humbled, no matter how high their standing; be they heroes on the battlefield, or sovereigns on the throne, they can still be made to cringe before their fellow beings. A transgressor is judged and condemned by his own soul, which despises him for violating the norms of good conduct as well as those of religion. This holds true even for absolute rulers who need fear no opposition. Even if his heart is made of stone, even if punishment and reward hold no meaning for him, the tyrant still trembles before the intangible tribunal of what he imagines people to be saying of him, even if their words can neither help nor harm him; since he too was raised to think always of reputation, without which men would be no more than beasts that live to eat and sleep—except for those few whose faith suffices to make them immune to temptation.

Thus it was that al-Amin, despite his depravity and drunkenness, and his knowledge that his conduct violated both divine and human law, and who had never been dissuaded by any kind of remonstrance, was ashamed to face his niece, a little girl, for fear that he would be diminished in her eyes, knowing, as he did, of her purity of heart and clarity of conscience. The fair sex, in particular, command special respect in this regard.

Told that Zaynab had requested permission to enter, he hesitated before giving his assent. At the same time, he was unwilling to rise and meet her in another room, as if he, the Caliph, holder of supreme power over his subjects, was ashamed to be seen at such a gathering. Nor could he send her away, as he had no good excuse for doing so. Forced to give his assent, he said, "Admit our niece!"

Chapter 48

Zaynab and Dananir

The goblet was still in his hand, and he put it down on the table. He tried to assume an appearance of decorum, as far as such a thing was possible for someone who had been chairing a drinking party. Seeing this, his companions fell silent, assumed deferential postures, and put aside their cups and glasses. Al-Amin gestured for the slave girls and pages to withdraw. The company sat stiff and silent, as if each of the guests had a bird perched on his head; and an air of propriety settled over the assembly.

Zaynab came in wearing a silken shawl around her shoulders and a brocaded veil that covered all but a small part of her face, which shone with a modest purity and wholesomeness. The innocence of childhood is a splendid thing to see: it commands the respect of anyone who encounters it, and provides an object lesson to the wise. For moral philosophers, it offers evidence that man is born with an inclination to the good, and is drawn to evil only because of the temptations of ambition and exposure to noxious influences. Should he do evil, he does so in defense of life and property; such that, even if he seems belligerent, you would find, if you could examine his conscience and be privy to his innermost thoughts, that his aggressiveness arises from motives of self-defense.

As exemplars of pure, untainted humanity, children know nothing of lies, flattery, or deceit; they speak their minds without fear or circumspection, especially if raised as Zaynab was by Dananir: that is, with as much attention to the cultivation of the intellect as age permits. When Zaynab saw that the soldiers did not mean to let her have her way where Maymuna was concerned, their refusal had quite an effect on her. Thwarted, she had wept, and then come with them, as we have seen. And now she was coming to confront her uncle, her eyes shining with tears.

When al-Amin saw her, he could not help smiling and rising to greet her. Everyone present did the same, and then, understanding that they were best advised to leave the Caliph alone with his niece, the guests departed, leaving behind them the tables strewn with jugs, goblets, flowers, and garlands, the scattered pieces of fruit, the cups of wine, the blossoms, and the candles that glowed from the corners of the portico, with al-Amin wishing that they might be doused to hide the sight of his dissipation!

Zaynab crossed the room to her uncle and then flung herself into his arms, weeping. "There, there," he said, embracing and kissing her. "What's wrong, niece?"

Smelling the wine on his breath, she looked around in surprise.

"What's wrong?" he asked, hoping to cut off any questions she might have about his banquet. "What do you want? Why haven't you gone into the women's quarters?"

"I was there," she said, "and I wanted to see you. I didn't know you were at table."

Happy to see that she thought he had been dining, he asked, "Is there anything I can take care of for you?"

"Yes, there is," she said, looking back at the door. "Where's Dananir? She'll explain what happened."

Al-Amin froze. Knowing, as he did, of the harm he had done to the young woman's father, he could imagine a thousand reasons for this visit. But then he realized that it was unlikely that she would have heard the news. So, feigning innocence, he asked, "Is your governess with you?"

"Yes," she said. "She was with me in the women's quarters, and she didn't want me to disturb you." Looking at the vessels scattered on the ground, she said, "Your table looks different from ours, Uncle! Perhaps this is what a caliph's table looks like."

She spoke entirely in innocence, but her words struck al-Amin forcibly as a kind of unintended reproach.

"It's a table laid for some guests who were here tonight," he said. Then, unwilling to remain there any longer for fear of being reproached again, he said, "Let's go into the women's quarters."

Taking Zaynab's hand, he rose and guided her to the women's quarters, to an empty room furnished with rugs and cushions. He sat her down beside him, eager to hear her complaint and find out what was going on. He clapped to summon a page and ordered him to summon Dananir.

A short time later, Dananir, fully veiled and eyes averted, came into the room. She gestured as if to kiss his hand, then stood, waiting politely.

"What brings you here, Dananir?" he asked.

"We're sorry to have disturbed the Commander of the Faithful and interrupted his assembly," she said. "But my lady Umm Habiba insisted on coming tonight, and I couldn't stop her."

"So what's wrong?"

"Did you not send us a message asking for our guest?"

"Which guest is that?"

"Maymuna."

"I don't understand what you mean," he said. "Explain."

Seeing that Ibn al-Rabi had indeed acted on his own, Dananir said, "Two days ago, a strange young woman named Maymuna came to stay with us. My lady Zaynab has come to know and love her. Then a letter came from your vizier, Ibn al-Rabi, asking for her in your name. I couldn't hand her over, since she's a guest and has a right to asylum. So he sent soldiers to take her by force. When my lady saw that they intended to take her away, she clung to her and insisted on coming along. Since I'm responsible for her, I came as well."

Though taken aback by Ibn al-Rabi's use of his name without permission, al-Amin maintained his composure. "Who then is this Maymuna? Is she a dependent of ours?"

"She's an orphan," said Dananir, "with nowhere to live and no one to support her. There may be dozens or hundreds like her in the palace of the Commander of the Faithful."

"Where is she now?"

"In these quarters, Sire."

"Bring her here and let me see her."

Dananir went out. Al-Amin, who had his arm around Zaynab, hugged her affectionately and said, "You went to all this trouble for that girl?"

"I love her, Uncle. She's kind and sweet. You'll see her. I told the soldiers to leave her alone but they wouldn't. Can't you give her to me?"

Finding her simple manners charming, he said, "I'll do as you wish. Don't worry."

A moment later, Dananir returned with Maymuna, who came in with bowed head, her cheeks red and her eyes bleary from weeping. Crossing the room, she threw herself at al-Amin's feet, crying, "I am the slave of the Commander of the Faithful!"

Impressed by her beauty and moved by her tears, al-Amin ordered her to rise. "No harm will come to you," he said, "so long as you have come as a guest of our niece, who thinks so much of you. Rise!" Then, turning to Dananir, he said, "Take her to the women's quarters and spend the night there. Tomorrow we'll see what's to be done with her. You're our guest, too, Zaynab. Don't worry: I can't refuse you anything."

Innocent as she was of politics, and knowing nothing of what had happened between al-Amin and al-Ma'mun since her grandfather died, Zaynab felt a surge of affection for her uncle. As he hugged her and smiled at her, she thought of her father. "Uncle, when is my father coming back?"

Her question struck him to the heart. "Soon, God willing," he said, and fell silent.

Sensing that he was disinclined to say any more, though unable to explain her feeling, she looked away and let the matter drop. In so doing, she reached a judgment as women do: that is, by instinct rather than logic. If you ask a woman whether some plan of yours will succeed or not, she will tell you what she thinks; but if you ask her to explain why she thinks so, she will not be able to furnish any kind of proof, and will instead say: "It's how I feel." Using her emotions, a woman is as likely to be right as a man is when he uses his intellect. Even so, not all persons of the same sex are created alike. Just as men differ in their ability to use logical inference and reach valid conclusions, so too do women differ in the strength of their feelings, as determined by how sensitive they are and how sound are their instincts. Such feelings cannot be separated from intellect; but in women they are the dominant force, just as the intellect is for men. Yet if a man has no feeling, he becomes a scourge on mankind for, though he works on the basis of intellect, he lives with his fellow creatures on the basis of feeling. People possess feeling to different degrees: those with little of it are unpleasant to be with and are commonly avoided, even if they are respected for their sagacity or their strength of character. I have seen many an intelligent and hard-working man shunned by others for just this reason. A lack of sociability is an impediment to success: a person without sensitivity or feeling cannot win the confidence of others or gain their affection by making himself agreeable. Despite her youth, Zaynab possessed both a sharp mind and a refined sensibility; and so when her uncle gave her an unrevealing answer, she could tell—without being able to explain why—that he preferred to say no more.

Hoping to end the conversation quickly, al-Amin clapped to summon a page boy. "Call the palace forewoman," he said.

When that lady arrived, he said, "Take our niece into the palace and make her as comfortable as possible. And take good care of Maymuna, as you would any of our slaves." Turning to Zaynab, he said, "I'm sure you need rest, and something to eat. Don't worry: everything will be as you wish." He patted her on the shoulder and stood up. Zaynab rose as well, and followed her governess to the women's quarters.

Left alone, al-Amin remembered what he had heard: that Ibn al-Rabi had written a letter asking al-Ma'mun's household to hand over the girl. He thought about calling the Vizier in to explain himself. But then he lapsed back into the mood of revelry he had been enjoying before Zaynab arrived, and returned to the portico. No sooner had he seated himself than his guests came swarming from all directions and resumed their singing, drinking, and table talk; and the page boys and slave girls picked up where they had left off.

As for Ibn al-Rabi, we last saw him leaving his audience room and praying that no harm would come to him as a result of his hasty pursuit of Maymuna. He began preparing his excuses, which was not a difficult task given his closeness to al-Amin and his influence over him. Thus occupied, he waited for al-Amin to summon him and demand an explanation.

As for Sa'dun, or Salman, though he was sorry to see Maymuna fall into the hands of the Caliph, he was gratified at having succeeded in widening the rift between al-Amin and al-Ma'mun, which he had been able to do because men with political ambitions pay no attention to the demands of the heart. All they care about is reaching whatever goal they have set for themselves, and they will scoff at any objections made on the basis of emotional considerations or good judgment. At the same time, Salman was aware of how much the young woman meant to Behzad, and remembered his promise to look after her. He thus began to think of ways to make her plight easier to bear and of guaranteeing her safety until he could discern what fate had in store for them.

Chapter 49

Al-Amin and Ibn al-Rabi

The next morning, al-Amin sent for Ibn al-Rabi, who came to attend him in the Privy Palace. Seating the Vizier beside him, he began questioning him gently about the incident involving Maymuna.

"The Commander of the Faithful doubtless thinks it odd that I dared to use his name to demand her from his brother's house," said Ibn al-Rabi. "I did so because I had no choice: for the sake of the dynasty, I had to act. Does the Commander of the Faithful know who that young woman is?"

"No," said al-Amin.

"If you look closely, you'll see the resemblance to her father. She's the daughter of Ja'far, the former vizier, who was executed for treason by the Caliph al-Rashid."

Stunned, al-Amin looked hard at Ibn al-Rabi. "She's the daughter of Ja'far Ibn Yahya? Are you serious?"

"Certainly, Sire. If you had asked her she wouldn't have denied it. I learned yesterday morning of her arrival at the palace of our master al-Ma'mun, and so I sent a message to the governess there, telling her that the Commander of the Faithful wished to see the girl. But the governess rebuffed the Shakiri, so, to preserve the sanctity of the Caliph's name, I had the girl brought here by force. I could not have known that the Caliph's brother's household held persons fallen out of favor in such high regard. The residents of his palace should have helped us catch such persons, not shelter them. It's true that she's a girl and poses no threat, but she may be able to answer some questions for us, because I suspect that..." He fell silent, swallowing as if afraid to say any more.

"Out with it," said al-Amin.

"The Commander of the Faithful is aware of our position at the moment. Far be it from me to interfere between him and his brother, but I cannot remain silent when the interests of the dynasty and the rights of Muslims are at stake. Why should we feel compassion for the daughter of Ja'far, who was executed by al-Rashid for interfering in the succession? Isn't Ja'far the one who pushed al-Ma'mun to seek the heir apparency, which was to have been the sole right of the Commander of the Faithful, and more besides? How do we know that he doesn't want the caliphate for himself?"

At this allusion to the caliphate, al-Amin recoiled, then glared at Ibn al-Rabi with narrowed eyes. Had he been any less familiar with the Caliph, Ibn al-Rabi would have found this expression terrifying, especially since al-Amin was a strong, intimidating man, who had faced down lions without fear.

"I don't mean," said Ibn al-Rabi hastily, "that our master al-Ma'mun is seeking the caliphate for himself. But I am afraid that, as time goes by, some of his Persian entourage might incite him, hoping to gain something for themselves."

By raising the subject of al-Ma'mun and the caliphate, Ibn al-Rabi had managed to distract al-Amin and avoid being blamed for using his name to demand Maymuna. He had also made the idea of removing al-Ma'mun more enticing. His motive was fear for himself. He was certain that, should al-Ma'mun accede to the caliphate, he would seek revenge on him, if he was still alive, or on his family, in all likelihood inflicting some kind of public chastisement. His only hope of escaping such a fate was to remove al-Ma'mun as governor of Khurasan, thus dispersing his supporters and weakening his cause.

"Those Persians," said al-Amin, "are at the root of all our troubles. Ever since the days of Abu Muslim, they've defied us, or treated us with condescension, because they think that we couldn't have seized the caliphate without them, even though they couldn't have won it except in our name, as you well know. So now they're urging my brother to seek power for himself while I'm still alive?"

"If the Commander of the Faithful has his doubts," said Ibn al-Rabi, "let him ask the Chief Astrologer about the man from Khurasan. On the day I arrived, I suggested—without giving my reasons—that you arrest him. The man from Khurasan is an envoy of al-Ma'mun's partisans in Khurasan, sent here to plot against us. I was informed of this by a spy in Tus who told me where these people have their headquarters. When I reached Baghdad I sent people after the Khurasani, but they didn't find him at home. Yesterday I met the Chief Astrologer, Malfan Sa'dun, and asked him what he knew. The police chief was there as well. Malfan Sa'dun identified the man and said that he had left Baghdad to join his partisans, who are working to restore Persian power. No doubt, they're using the name of our master al-Ma'mun to further their aims, since without Qurashi blood they cannot rule. If they do come to power, I can't imagine that they'll spare anyone, not even al-Ma'mun himself. Don't be angry: I'm saying all of this for the good of the dynasty. Go to Malfan Sa'dun, who's alive and well, or my master Ibn Mahan, the chief of police, whom you trust. Ask him and then decide for yourself, O, Commander of the Faithful."

Ibn al-Rabi made this speech with a great display of concern for the future of the dynasty. Looking troubled, al-Amin took it all in, but decided not to express an opinion until he spoke with Ibn Mahan. "We'll look into this matter," he said, then returned to the subject they had been discussing earlier. "As for Maymuna, the one you say is the daughter of Ja'far the Barmaki, she's in our palace with our slaves. Let us not harm her, or harm anyone on her account, unless we discover some reason to do so. My niece asked me to treat her kindly, and that's what I intend to do."

"The decision belongs to the Commander of the Faithful," said Ibn al-Rabi, who was less interested in the young woman than in the deposing of al-Ma'mun. His son, who had been raised in affluence and lacked political experience, and who had spent his life dependent on his father, would have preferred seizing Maymuna, even if it meant the end of the dynasty. The young man was infatuated with her, and his intentions toward her were indeed perfectly honorable. Were she not already in love with Behzad, and had she not hated Ibn al-Rabi, she would have had no reason to refuse him.

Seeing that al-Amin wanted to end the audience, Ibn al-Rabi rose and left. The Caliph sat alone, weighing the promise he had made to his niece to release Maymuna against the danger that Ibn al-Rabi had explained to him. He was at a loss for what to do. Finally he rose and went into the women's quarters, where he asked after his niece and was directed to where she was staying.

Since entering the Caliph's palace, Maymuna had felt greatly oppressed. It now seemed to her that she had lost everything she had hoped for, knowing as she did that her beloved intended to try his hand against al-Amin. Despite Dananir's attempts to comfort her, she had not stopped weeping since she had entered the palace. Zaynab, who had grown even more concerned about her and even more determined to save her, reassured her that her uncle had promised to release her. But Maymuna spent the night in despair, knowing that Ibn al-Rabi would reveal her identity to al-Amin in order to escape a reprimand for what he had done.

The next morning, Dananir and Zaynab again came to Maymuna and set about trying to cheer her up; but she remained despondent, finding comfort only in weeping, especially since she felt all alone without her grandmother and without any knowledge of where Salman might be. Sitting silently with tears coursing down her cheeks, she looked defeated and humiliated. The more despondent she became, the more Zaynab pitied her. But Zaynab still had faith in her uncle's promise. At that juncture, they heard a commotion among the servants, and a slave appeared, saying that the Commander of the Faithful was coming to see his niece.

Zaynab rose to greet him at the door, and Dananir and Maymuna rose respectfully as well. Al-Amin came in and sat down on a cushion, inviting Zaynab to sit beside him. "Do you miss your own palace, Zaynab?"

"I am happy wherever the Commander of the Faithful tells me to go," she replied.

Admiring this politic reply, especially from one so young, he said, "Go with your governess, then, under our protection. I've ordered the forewoman to prepare a camel litter to carry you to the Tigris, and a boat to take you home."

"And Maymuna?" asked Zaynab, looking at him expectantly.

"She'll stay here as our guest for another day or two," he said, smiling. "Then we'll send her to you with full honors."

"But... you said you'd send her back with us!"

"I did. But now I think she should stay here as our guest, just as she was yours. Do you think she'd refuse the hospitality of the Caliph's palace?"

The girl could sense that, despite his affable manner, her uncle had no intention of changing his mind. She looked pleadingly at Dananir. Al-Amin turned to the governess and said, "Tell your mistress that Maymuna will stay as our guest and then we'll send her back to you."

Seeing his determination to keep Maymuna there, Dananir could guess why. She had heard rumors that al-Amin had met privately with Ibn al-Rabi that morning. At a loss, she finally said, "The Caliph's command must be obeyed. It is an honor to his servant, and a kindness on his part, that she remain in his palace."

Understanding that she had no choice but to stay, Maymuna stood silently, tears running down her cheeks. Al-Amin glanced at her and felt so sorry for her that he nearly ordered her released. But then he remembered what Ibn al-Rabi had said and restrained himself. He rose, saying to Zaynab, "God keep you safe, niece! Take good care of her, Dananir." Turning to Maymuna, he said, "Everything will be all right." Going out, he ordered the forewoman to arrange for the return of Zaynab and her governess to al-Ma'mun's palace. Zaynab wanted to cling to Maymuna and refuse to go, but Dananir held her back and gently gave her to understand that the Caliph's orders had to be obeyed lest he become angry; in this way no harm would come to Maymuna.

Alone with Zaynab and Dananir after al-Amin's departure, Maymuna wept so hard she nearly fainted. Dananir tried to comfort her, promising to inform Salman, who would do his best to get her out; and resolving to seek help elsewhere if necessary. None of this did any good. Face to face with the inevitable, Maymuna whispered to Dananir to do her best to console her poor grandmother, who had given up so much for her sake. Dananir promised to do so, and then took her leave, heartbroken. When she bid goodbye to al-Amin's palace forewoman, she asked her to look after the girl, and the woman promised to do so.

Chapter 50

'Abbada and Zubayda

When she reached al-Ma'mun's palace, Dananir saw 'Abbada waiting for them on the wharf. The old woman had seen her granddaughter dragged off roughly to the Caliph's palace. She had wanted to go with her, but feared that her presence might make matters worse for the young woman. Dananir had told her to wait at the palace until she returned, and had promised to bring Maymuna back. For the rest of the day and the following night, 'Abbada had been sleepless and frantic. The next morning found her waiting at the wharf and watching the boats as they passed. Finally she saw one she recognized as belonging to al-Amin. When the boat docked and she saw no sign of her granddaughter, she cried, "Where's Maymuna?"

Taking her by the hand, Dananir told her quickly what had happened and promised her that the young woman would be back soon.

"No, she won't," retorted 'Abbada. "When al-Amin finds out who she is, he'll hurt her. Oh, why didn't I go with her, and suffer the same fate? All I've done for her has come to nought!" Bemoaning her fate, she wept like a woman bereaved, and Dananir tried vainly to comfort her.

Some time later, 'Abbada regained her composure and began thinking about what she could do to rescue her granddaughter. Her hand fell upon the little emerald box in her pocket, and it occurred to her to put it to use. For some days, people had been saying that Zubayda, al-Amin's mother, had come from Raqqa with al-Rashid's treasures. "I'll go to her," thought 'Abbada, "and appeal to her in her husband's name. If I gain her sympathy with these tokens of his, perhaps she'll agree to ask her son to release Maymuna." This plan gave her a certain peace of mind. She consulted Dananir, who agreed that it was a good idea. "We have no other door to knock on," she said. "Perhaps when she sees her husband's relics

197

and hears about your misfortune, she'll forget her grudge. We can only try, with God's help!"

At noon, 'Abbada left for Zubayda's palace, called the Abode of Permanence. It was no easy journey, but she undertook it gladly for Maymuna's sake. Leaving al-Ma'mun's palace by boat, she disembarked on the shore near the Abode of Permanence, and went from there on foot, dressed in her black robe and leaning on her cane. She looked not only aged but heartbroken, sorrow being all the easier to see in the faces of the aged. It was late afternoon before she reached the palace gate, which was manned by a group of armed Shakiri guardsmen. She greeted them but, taking her for a beggar, they ignored her; so she approached one of them and asked, "Is my mistress Zubayda at home?"

"She is," said the man. "What do you want with her?"

"I want to see her and kiss the hem of her robe for a blessing."

"She's not receiving anyone now. If you're looking for charity, today's not the day."

"No, my boy," she said, "I'm not looking for charity. I have something to tell her."

"What is that, lady?"

"It's for her ears only. Please, let me see her."

Scoffing, the man turned to his comrades, who were listening to the exchange. Then another Shakiri came forward and asked, "Are you asking to see our mistress the Caliph's mother herself?"

"Yes," she replied. "I beg you: ask them to let me in, and do it quickly. I've had a tiring journey and I can't stay on my feet much longer."

"I see you've fallen on hard times," said the Shakiri. "I'll ask the fore-woman to give you something and spare you the trouble of trying to see our mistress Zubayda. She rarely admits anyone."

These words were a bitter blow. Once, she had lived in splendor; now, those who looked at her saw nothing but a beggar. Fighting tears, she said, "Dear boy, I'm not looking for charity. I have something to say to our mistress Zubayda, and I have to tell her myself. So ask them to let me in. God bless you!"

Moved by her tears, the Shakiri went in to ask, leaving her at the gate. Exhausted, she sat down. A moment later the Shakiri reappeared. "She asked me for your name," he said.

Unsure what to do, she thought a moment, then said, "Tell her my name is Mother of al-Rashid."

Taken aback, the guardsmen scanned her face, not knowing what she meant. "You're the mother of al-Rashid?" one of them asked. "Which al-Rashid do you mean?"

"Didn't she ask for my name? Tell her that Mother of al-Rashid is at the gate asking to see her."

The Shakiri went back in and she waited, pleased to have presented herself as al-Rashid's mother, hoping that the name would prove a good omen for her meeting with Zubayda. A moment later the Shakiri returned, saying, "Go on in, lady."

Leaning on her cane, she followed him inside. They crossed a garden and reached the door of the residence. She removed her shoes and entered the reception room. From there one room led to another, and slim-waisted slave women passed by, looking at her in surprise. Head down, she kept on, finally reaching a large room redolent with perfume. Looking in, she saw a pavilion of sandalwood covered in sable, brocade, and brightly colored silks. It was hung with curtains suspended on hooks of gold and embroidered with lines of poetry. The floor of the room was covered with a single rug on which stood a splendid array of cushions and chairs.[90] Yet 'Abbada was not impressed: during her ascendancy, her son's palace had been full of such luxuries, and she had grown accustomed to them. On this day, her only concern was to gain Zubayda's help and rescue her granddaughter.

---

90 See the novel by Jurji Zaidan: *The Caliph's Sister – Harun al-Rashid and the Fall of the Persians (Al-'Abbasa Ukht al-Rashid)* .

Chapter 51

Face to Face

When she reached the door, she saw Zubayda on the other side of the room, reclining on a cushion of silk brocade atop a couch of ebony inlaid with jewels. Leaving her cane outside, she called out a respectful greeting and stood looking at Zubayda, awaiting an invitation to come in or sit down. Zubayda was dressed in a striking sky-blue gown and a jeweled headband decorated with a peacock design—it was the sort of thing she rarely wore and she seemed to have put it on deliberately only a moment before. 'Abbada remained standing while Zubayda busied herself with picking up some crumbs of musk that had fallen from an ivory chalice onto the cushion. Thinking she had not heard, 'Abbada cleared her throat. Zubayda looked up and asked scornfully, "Who are you?"

Taking heart, she came forward, saying, "Your servant, 'Abbada." When she reached the middle of the room, Zubayda gave her a sidelong glance, then pouted and raised her eyebrows in distaste. "'Abbada? They told me that the Mother of al-Rashid was asking to see me."

"I'm your servant, Mistress. Look at me: am I so pale that you can't recognize me?"

"I recognize you, 'Abbada," she laughed. "Are you still alive?"

'Abbada found this question tasteless and rude, but held herself in check and said, "Yes, unfortunately."

"That's your reward for ingratitude, 'Abbada," said Zubayda with a chuckle. "Sit down."

Shaking with repressed anger, she sat down. She was sorry she had come, but then she remembered Maymuna's predicament and found her ordeal easier to bear. "I have never been ungrateful, Mistress. But God does as He wills."

"True enough. He does as He wills, and rewards every soul according to its deeds. You and your husband and your children tried to take the caliphate from us, and this is the result—the wages of treason! This is your punishment for defying your master: God dropped you into the pit you dug for us. I thought you had perished of grief over your son, but here you are, still clinging to life."

'Abbada listened to this speech with her head bowed, and when it was over, said, "Mistress, I did not come here to discuss the reckoning that befell us. I've come to appeal to your kindness. You are a mother, and you know the love a mother has for her child. You're now a grandmother, too, and you know the love a grandmother has for her grandchildren..."

"So now you've discovered what it means to be a mother and a grandmother? Where was all this tenderness when your son, the one we executed, tried to take the right of succession away from my son and give it to the son of Marajil?" By "the son of Marajil" she meant al-Ma'mun.

Her chest tight with misery, 'Abbada said in a choked voice, "As I told you, Mistress, I've come to appeal to your kindness. I don't claim any merit of my own. I beseech you in the name of the one who gave me these relics." From her pocket she took out the little emerald box with the golden key, then stood and held it out. With a great show of disdain, Zubayda made no move to take it, leaving 'Abbada with her hand outstretched like a beggar's. Finally she asked, "What relics are those?"

Her hands trembling with old age and emotion, 'Abbada worked the key into the lock and opened the box. Then, coming forward, she placed it on the cushion in front of Zubayda and returned to her place. Zubayda looked down and saw a lock of her husband's hair and a few teeth, all scented with musk. "What are these?" she asked.

"That's a lock of hair belonging to our master al-Rashid, and those are his baby teeth. Don't you remember that I was his nurse? Didn't he call me 'Mother of al-Rashid'? By these relics I implore you to hear my grievance and take pity on my weakness: not for my sake, but for the sake of a girl who has never sinned against anyone. She was a baby when all those things happened. She spent her infancy in prosperity and comfort, but now she's an orphan and an outcast with nowhere to go and no one to help her. Whether she lives or dies depends on you. For God's sake, can you not speak the single word that will save her life?" She finished her speech choking on her tears. What sight could be more pitiable than that of an old woman weeping and pleading for mercy?

Hearing her appeal, and seeing her husband's teeth and hair, Zubayda nearly succumbed to pity. She sat silently for a moment, 'Abbada watching her with no doubt in her mind that her cry had struck home.

Then she saw Zubayda close the box. "Didn't you once appeal to al-Rashid using these same tired relics when he was alive?"

"Yes… I did."

"Why?"

"So he might pardon my husband Yahya."

"And what did he say?"

At a loss for how to respond, 'Abbada swallowed hard. In the end she had no choice but to tell the truth. "He turned me away, Mistress."

"Do you expect me to know better how to treat you than he did, 'Abbada?"

"I appealed to al-Rashid," she replied, "because I thought he owed me something. Today, I'm beseeching you to be merciful, without thinking you owe me anything. I'm asking you to be kind to a young woman who bears no responsibility for anything we may have done. If you think I've trespassed against you, then here I am: punish me! My life means nothing to me. But the poor girl has done nothing."

"What girl do you mean?"

Taking the question as a good sign, she said, "The last remnant of my son's ill-fated line. She was miserable enough to escape the disaster that struck her father, her uncles, and her grandfather. She survived, and I did too, to support her and raise her. We spent years in hiding, living like beggars, but accepting our lot in life. Then, as bad luck would have it, we were denounced to the Commander of the Faithful and the poor girl was carried off to his palace. I'm afraid they'll trick him into killing her, and I have nowhere to turn but to you. I came with those relics hoping that they might inspire you to pity the poor girl and give the command that will spare her life. If you ask the Commander of the Faithful to release her, I'll take her away and we'll spend the rest of our lives in some wretched hut, or we'll leave and go anywhere you tell us to go. Please take pity on her! By the head of your son and your tenderness toward him, I beg you to hear my plea. You know I've never appealed to anyone in this way, not even al-Rashid, may God have mercy on him!" She could not restrain her tears.

Expecting to hear a kind word from Zubayda, 'Abbada instead heard her ask, "What's the girl's name?"

"Maymuna, Mistress."

Zubayda broke into a smile so laced with vengeful antipathy as to make it clear that mercy was out of the question. "Maymuna!" she exclaimed. "You want me to save Maymuna? Why don't you ask her Khurasani lover instead—the one who's declared war on the whole House of 'Abbas? He'd drink our blood if he could!"

'Abbada was shaken. She wondered how Zubayda had learned what was supposed to be a well-kept secret. What she had forgotten was the espionage that was an ever-present feature of life in that age. Everyone spied on everyone else; even fathers and sons spied on each other. Zubayda had agents in al-Ma'mun's palace who kept her informed of everything that went on there. She had learned of the Khurasani the day before and decided to tell her son, not knowing that the man had left Baghdad and escaped her toils.

Stunned, 'Abbada was unable to reply. Then, fearing that her silence would be taken as an admission of guilt, she said, hoping to divert the accusation as best she could, "I don't understand what you mean, Mistress, or who this Khurasani might be. We can barely fill our bellies: what have we to do with plots and vengeance? I beg you to accept my appeal. I no longer care for myself at all; all I'm asking is that you release the girl from the Caliph's palace. Do that, and I will do whatever you ask of me."

Turning away, Zubayda held out the box and said, "Enough, 'Abbada! Take this box. Perhaps it will do you some good somewhere else. If you need food or money, you can have it."

Chapter 52

Fury

'Abbada saw that her appeal had fallen on deaf ears and that Zubayda was now dismissing her. Taking the box back, she said, "I would accept your gift, Mistress, if I had any will to live. Forgive me for my presumption. I pray God to preserve your good fortune and sustain your son's caliphate." So saying, she turned to leave, expecting Zubayda to relent; but she reached the door without hearing a sound or seeing her move from her place. Suddenly, she rebelled against the thought of leaving in humiliation and defeat. Thinking of the high rank she had enjoyed while her son was still in power, remembering all she had suffered at Zubayda's hands, and seeing how cruel and vindictive she was, 'Abbada turned around. Zubayda was sitting on the couch with her eyes on the cushion, still engaged in picking up the crumbs of musk, but now smiling, her expression conveying a volume's worth of arrogant and vindictive contempt.

Zubayda, who had not yet vented all her spite, was hoping she would return, and for that reason had not replied to her farewell. She was enjoying her conversation with this woman whom fate had crushed and delivered into her hands. She had killed her son, brought her husband low, scattered her family, seized their lands and property, and made their name strike fear in all those affiliated with them—for it was at her urging that al-Rashid had toppled the Barmakids. She was enjoying her victory, which is the sweetest of all delights.

If you analyze happiness carefully, you will discover that it arises from victory, or some similar feeling. One who triumphs in battle enjoys victory in the simplest sense, as when a general sees his army triumphant and his enemy's forces vanquished. Those who seek wealth do not do so because they fear going hungry, since even the poorest of men can find enough to eat to satisfy his hunger, but in order to achieve their aims or attain a higher political or social position, all of which imparts a sense of power and prestige. Those who seek fame, in all its varied forms, seek it for the same reason. One who seeks it through politics, when he is praised for his accomplishments, enjoys the feeling of having triumphed over others by virtue of his intelligence and regards their praise as an acknowledgement of his superiority in that respect. One who seeks fame through scholarship, poetry, or any other literary endeavor revels in people's admiration of his writings and ideas, just as the general revels in his victory over his enemies. So it was that Zubayda delighted in her ringing victory over the Barmakid family. 'Abbada's visit, and her abasement, served to heighten her pleasure, which she enjoyed to the point of forgetting—or pretending to forget— the emotion of pity; or perhaps she suppressed it deliberately, just as the Barmakid family had deliberately tried to bring down her son and take power from her husband.

When 'Abbada turned back, Zubayda continued to concentrate on plucking the bits of musk off the cushion, her heart pounding as she waited to see what this defeated woman and mother would do now. "So am I to go," said 'Abbada, "having gotten nothing from you but vindictiveness and scorn, even after appealing to you by the sacred right of your husband who lies buried in Tus? Are you satisfied with saying that God has done this to us as a punishment for our crimes? I'm glad you understand that, because God is capable of doing the same thing again anywhere and anytime He chooses."

Hearing this, Zubayda could not stop herself from looking up. No longer humble and conciliatory, 'Abbada's expression was now one of fury and disgust. Her eyes were red, her tears had dried on her cheeks, her lips trembled, and her limbs shook so violently that she seemed on the verge of collapsing; but, having taken up her stick and put her weight on it, she stood her ground. Saying no more, she began looking for her shoes so she could put them on and leave.

"'Abbada!" cried Zubayda. But 'Abbada, pretending not to hear, continued through the reception room.

"'Abbada!" she called again. "Mother of al-Rashid!"

Addressed by this title, 'Abbada felt a glimmer of hope and turned back, repressing her anger in the hope of helping Maymuna. One hand on her cane and the other at her waist, as if holding herself erect by sheer force of will, she turned to look at Zubayda, hoping to see some evidence of pity or sympathy or willingness to help Maymuna; but she found that nothing had changed. If anything, she looked even more threatening now that she was angry. For several moments, 'Abbada remained where she was, searching Zubayda's eyes for any sign of sympathy and seeing nothing there but anger. Even so, she kept hoping against hope. Then Zubayda spoke. "Are you praying for the death of my son?" she asked in a strangled voice.

"God forbid, my lady," said 'Abbada. "I pray God to spare you any sorrow on his account. Indeed, I pray that He guard all children everywhere, including my poor granddaughter," she said, choking back tears.

"Didn't you pray for that once before?" interrupted Zubayda, referring, as 'Abbada understood, to her days of glory before her son was killed.

"Woe is me!" she cried. "I used to wish for long life for my son, but I never wished it as fervently as I do now. In those days, I had not yet suffered. I thought that my good fortune would last forever. Instead, it fed me a poison like none other in this world. And when fate turned against me, the whole world did too: since then, I have known only catastrophe and lived only with heartbreak."

Realizing that 'Abbada was alluding to what might happen to herself, and unwilling to prolong the conversation lest she hear something even more distressing, Zubayda stood and began adjusting her necklace and headband as if preparing to depart. 'Abbada, having said enough, bent to put her shoes on, and went out, feeling that, even if she had failed in her mission, she had said what she wanted to say to Zubayda.

So rousing was her encounter with Zubayda that 'Abbada, forgetting her weakness and old age, made short work of the trip back to al-Ma'mun's palace. There waiting for her was Dananir, who when she heard the story expressed her sorrow for the old woman's disappointment and did her best to comfort and console her.

Chapter 53

Behzad's Arrival

Let us leave the people of Baghdad and look to what became of Behzad after his departure from the city. As we read in his letter to Maymuna, he intended to depart for Khurasan, which he did only after explaining to Salman what needed to be done in his absence. Then strapping the box to his saddle, he left the city on horseback and set off on the shortest route. Whenever he stopped at an inn, he presented himself as a physician carrying a box of medicinal substances. He spent days crossing mountains, plains, valleys, and rivers, until he reached the outskirts of Marv-e Shahegan, the capital of Khurasan in that era. The city was located on a plain and surrounded by a quadragonal wall. In the center was an enormous citadel called, in local parlance, *qahanduz*, visible to travelers from a long way off, and seeming to be a city in itself, with gardens planted on the roof as if atop a mountain. Having grown up in Marv, Behzad paid this sight no attention, but rode directly to the residence of al-Fadl Ibn Sahl.

Originally from Sarakhs, Ibn Sahl was raised a Magian, and was an expert astrologer. He had entered state service at the hands of Yahya the Barmaki during the reign of al-Rashid, but embraced Islam—of the Shi'ite variety—only in 190 AH (805 or 806 AD), and only to further the cause of the Persians in Khurasan.[91] He was ambitious, and Yahya promoted him from one post to another until he became a member of his inner circle and eventually his majordomo. In al-Ma'mun, Ibn Sahl perceived clarity of mind and nobility of character, and predicted that he would one day become caliph. Accordingly, he entered his service, gained his confidence, and became one of his inner circle. Al-Ma'mun in turn thought very highly

---

91   Here, as throughout, Zaidan assumes that the aggrieved Persians would have gravitated to oppositional movements such as Shi'ism. The real situation was rather more complicated; see the Afterword. *Translator's Note*

of him, and became instrumental in his advancement. Ibn Sahl had set his hopes on nothing less than the vizierate. It is said that, in the days before al-Ma'mun became caliph, one of his tutors, seeing how highly al-Ma'mun regarded Ibn Sahl, reported this to Ibn Sahl, saying, "I imagine you'll make no less than a million dirhams from him." Furious, Ibn Sahl replied: "By God, I did not join him to turn a profit, no matter how great; I joined him so that my writ would run from east to west."

When al-Rashid staged the oath of allegiance to his sons as heirs apparent, he gave Iraq, Syria, and the west to al-Amin, who was to succeed him as caliph; and gave Khurasan and the rest of the east to al-Ma'mun, who was to succeed his brother al-Amin. This arrangement came about as a result of the efforts of Ja'far and other partisans of the Shi'ites, including Ibn Sahl. When in 192 AH (808 AD), al-Rashid set out for Khurasan, he ordered his son al-Ma'mun to remain in Baghdad until he returned. Al-Rashid being ill, Ibn Sahl feared that he might die on the road and all his efforts would come to naught. So he went to al-Ma'mun and said, "We can't say what might happen to al-Rashid, but Khurasan is your province, and al-Amin is ahead of you in the line of succession, and the least he'll do is depose you. Al-Amin is the son of Zubayda, his uncles are from the tribe of Hashim, and Zubayda is rich, as you know. So ask the Commander of the Faithful to let you go with him." Al-Ma'mun accordingly asked his father, who at first refused but then relented. The initial refusal was for a reason: al-Rashid knew he had little time left to live, and believed that his sons had set spies to observe him and count his every breath, hoping to see him expire at any moment.

Al-Ma'mun thus departed with his father. Ibn Sahl came along as well, and during the journey did his best to promote al-Ma'mun's cause. He solicited oaths of allegiance to him from all the commanders and officers in al-Rashid's camp, and had al-Rashid declare his son heir to all the property he had brought along with him.

By the time al-Rashid fell gravely ill in Tus, al-Ma'mun had settled in Marv, the capital of Khurasan. Meanwhile, al-Amin, who was still in Baghdad, had partisans who were keeping their eye on al-Rashid. The most protective of them was Ibn al-Rabi, who had succeeded the Barmakid family as vizier to al-Rashid. Learning that his father was failing, al-Amin wrote to Ibn al-Rabi and others, urging them to solicit oaths of allegiance to himself.

When al-Rashid died in Tus in 193 AH (809 AD), Ibn al-Rabi took advantage of al-Ma'mun's presence in Marv and exercised his ingenuity on the officers, urging them to swear allegiance to al-Amin. Eager to return to their families in Baghdad, they did as he asked, ignoring the oaths they had sworn to al-Ma'mun, and carrying all the supplies they had with them back to al-Amin. Al-Amin was then acclaimed as caliph, as we have seen.

When al-Ma'mun learned that his father had died and that his men, in violation of their oaths, had carried all his wealth and supplies back to his brother, he feared for himself. Assembling his inner circle in Marv, he revealed the weakness of his position, saying that he could not defeat his brother, and asked their advice. They encouraged him as best they could and promised him that the matter would be resolved to his satisfaction. Meanwhile, Ibn Sahl continued to keep his eyes open for any opportunity to further the cause for which he had converted to Islam. He knew Behzad as a leader of the Khurrami sect and he admired him for his enterprise and his dedication to Shi'ism and to the Persians. Before al-Rashid's death he had arranged for Behzad to be dispatched as a physician to al-Ma'mun's household, along with his servant Salman, who was also a member of the sect. A secret correspondence sprang up between Ibn Sahl and Behzad. When al-Rashid died and al-Amin took over the caliphate, it came time to act in Khurasan. Thus it was that Behzad rode there to join Ibn Sahl in managing the campaign.

On the day Behzad arrived in Khurasan, Ibn Sahl was sitting in his residence with his brother al-Hasan. When the chamberlain announced Behzad, Ibn Sahl called him inside. Still dressed in his traveling clothes, Behzad entered the room, set his box down by the door, and greeted the brothers, who welcomed him and invited him to sit at the front of the room. Then in middle age, Ibn Sahl was of lymphatic temperament, slightly built, and pale, though healthy and vigorous. In his eyes, one could glimpse his ambition, his craftiness, and his willingness to weave elaborate schemes and wait patiently for them to bear fruit. His brother al-Hasan was of a less devious temperament. He was more likely to speak his mind or let his intentions show on his face; when angered or pleased he would look it. Ibn Sahl, by contrast, never let his emotions show and never displayed anger or joy. He would not allow his temper to influence his goals or let emotion undermine his efforts. In this respect he differed from persons of sanguine or nervous temperament, who cannot bear any kind of affront and lack the ability to repress their anger. If provoked, such people lose their temper and, unlike those of a lymphatic cast, may utter a single ill-considered word that undercuts all the efforts they have made to achieve their aims.

When Behzad had taken a seat, Ibn Sahl and his brother asked him to report on what he had accomplished. He told them, impressing both of them with his courage and his devotion to the Persian cause, even if he himself did not think very highly of his efforts.

When Ibn Sahl asked him about the members of the Khurrami sect in Baghdad, he replied, "They are devoted to our cause, and are prepared to sacrifice their lives and their fortunes."

"What of the boy?" he asked, meaning al-Amin.

"Still occupied with wine and slaves."

"His days are numbered," said al-Hasan, "but…"

"But that does us no good," said Behzad, "unless we're the ones doing the numbering."

Ibn Sahl gave a triumphant laugh. "We will be, God willing. What we need to do is widen the rift between him and his brother until one of them asks for our help against the other. At that point we'll be able to dictate our own terms."

"You should be hearing more news along those lines from our friend Salman soon enough," said Behzad. "Otherwise, you'll have become Muslim for nothing!"

Ibn Sahl found his frankness distasteful. Although his conversion was widely considered insincere and—like Behzad's—opportunistic, he did not like to hear it said that he had converted for the sake of worldly gain. Or perhaps, having embraced Islam, he had come to believe in it. In any event, he made no reply. He did, nevertheless, want to reinforce Behzad's commitment to their cause, seeing in him, as he did, a great capacity for moving their work forward after his return from his mission, and expecting to have need of his abilities again. So, looking at al-Hasan, he laughed as if uncertain whether to speak his mind; and al-Hasan, understanding what he meant, smiled at Behzad. The latter remained silent. Al-Hasan then addressed him, saying, "We're grateful for all you've done on behalf of all Persians, and one day you'll enjoy your share of the fruits of victory."

"Why not reward him today?" interrupted Ibn Sahl. "Can you think of anyone better suited to Buran?" Buran was al-Hasan's daughter, and famous throughout Khurasan for her spectacular beauty and her good sense.

At the mention of Buran, Behzad flinched, having given his heart, as we have seen, to another. Even so, he could hardly spurn such a princely offer. Wiping the stunned expression off his face, he bowed gratefully and said, "That would be a favor I hardly deserve. I haven't yet done anything to merit such a reward, and our mission has barely begun."

Ibn Sahl admired his deft response. It never occurred to him that Behzad might not want to marry Buran, who was desired by all the grandees of Khurasan. "That would be in addition to your appointment to a state position as soon as possible."

"Forgive me, my lord," said Behzad, "if I ask to be exempted from holding a post. I will serve my nation in another way—one I hope is equally satisfactory." Then, gathering himself to depart, he said, "Will you excuse me? I need to go home, change my clothes, and rest." So saying, he found his shoes, put them on, picked up the box, and made for the door.

"What's in the box?" asked Ibn Sahl.

"Medicinal substances, Master," he said, and went out.

Chapter 54

Fatima

After he left the residence, Behzad mounted his horse, plunged into the narrow alleyways of the city, and rode all the way to the edge of town, lost in thought. He was unhappy about Buran, as he believed that Ibn Sahl really meant to marry him off to her. He was unaware that Ibn Sahl had made the suggestion only as a way of encouraging him to continue fighting the 'Abbasids. Had Ibn Sahl known him better, he would have known that no such incentive was necessary. This train of thought led Behzad to Maymuna. He berated himself for leaving her in Baghdad even as relations between al-Amin and al-Ma'mun soured, making war increasingly likely. Then he remembered that she was staying in al-Ma'mun's palace, which seemed a safe enough place for her to be.

When he finally roused himself from these disquieting thoughts, he saw that he had ridden past his destination. Turning around, he found the lane he wanted, and then followed it as far as a certain doorway. There he dismounted and, box in hand, rapped out a signal. A moment later, the door was opened by a tall, elderly slave. As soon as he saw Behzad, he bent down, seized his hands, and began kissing them, saying, "Is it really you, my lord? You were gone for so long!" He reached for the box, but Behzad would not let him take it. After leading the horse to the stable, the slave locked the door and then hurried joyfully ahead of Behzad through a reception room that led to a broad courtyard. From there they turned off into a room where an old woman was sitting. Her hair was white and her brow furrowed, and her eyebrows had grown so long that they covered her eyes. She was sitting with a scarf wrapped around her shoulders.

"Mistress!" cried the slave, looking into the room. "My lord is here."

"He's here?" she said, bewildered. "Where is he?"

Behzad crossed the room, flung himself at her feet, and kissed her hand. She looked up, embraced him, and held him close. Kissing him and weeping, she said in a choked voice, "Welcome back, dear child! Welcome, Kayfar! You're here! I've waited for so long... I was afraid that I wouldn't see you again, and die without fulfilling my vow." She stopped, weeping so hard that she was unable to speak.

"Why are you crying, my lady?" he asked, trying to maintain his composure. "We should be thanking God for this meeting."

With an effort, she stopped weeping and said, "I do thank God that you've come back safe. Where are you coming from?"

"Baghdad."

"Did you do what you needed to do?"

"I did," he said. "And I've brought you what you asked for."

"You've brought his head?" she asked, astonished.

"Yes, my lady."

"Where is it?"

He pointed at the box. "There."

Suddenly feeling as vigorous as a young girl, she reached for it, saying, "In that box? Open it... and show me my master's head. Show me! Let me revel in the sight of him before I die."

Sitting up, he looked back at the slave and gestured for him to leave the room. Alone with the old woman, he applied himself to the box, finally opening it and taking out a skull. He placed it before her. The reek of moldy soil filled the room. Looking intently at the skull, she shouted, "That's the head of Abu Muslim, my father, the hero! You've brought him back to life, my child!" Choking on her tears, she began kissing the head.

Though on the verge of weeping himself, Behzad pulled himself together and said, "You'll rejoice even more when I've avenged him!"

Recovering some of her composure—though her hands still trembled—she said, "Yes, you must avenge him. That's why I called you Kayfar: your name, my child, means 'vengeance.' You will punish those who betrayed and murdered him. But how did you find his head? We heard that they had thrown it into the Tigris."

"That's what I thought as well," he said. "But I was fortunate enough to find an old man who had witnessed the murder. He took me to the site in

Ctesiphon and helped me identify where the body was. Look at it carefully: that's Abu Muslim's head, no doubt about it."

"Yes," she said, looking at it again with tear-dimmed eyes. "The beating of my heart tells me so. It's the head of my father, Abu Muslim. What a great deed you've done, Kayfar! You'll be the one to avenge him. Is it time?"

"It is, my lady. And it's time for you to tell me who I really am, and to give me the legacy you promised I would need to fulfill my mission."

"It's ready, my child. Wait a moment, though: before you take it, let me tell you the story. Sit down. Don't you want something to eat?"

"No, my lady."

Chapter 55

A Noble Lineage

Invigorated, the old woman rose from her seat, her back as straight as it had been in her youth. Laying a hand on Behzad's shoulder to stop him from rising with her, she walked over to a cabinet that stood against the wall. She took a key from her pocket and opened the cabinet. As Behzad watched, fascinated, she took out a long bundle wrapped in silk and placed it before him.

"I am Fatima," she said, "the daughter of Abu Muslim of Khurasan, as you know."

"I know," he said.

"Everyone, including you, believes that you never knew your parents and that I raised you."

"And…"

"And that I'm the only one who knows who your parents are."

"Right."

"The Khurramis honor me," she said, "because the blood of Abu Muslim runs in my veins. What they don't know is that it runs in yours, too."

"In mine? How?"

She smiled. "Because you're my son."

"Your son?" he said, startled. "I'm your son?"

"Yes, child," she said, embracing him. "You're my very own."

He kissed her hand. "But how…"

"I was married, but no one knew that your father and I had a child. Everyone believed that you were a poor little boy and I took you in and raised you."

Flabbergasted, Behzad could not keep silent. "But how am I your son?"

"There's nothing to be surprised at. My husband, Muhriz Ibn Ibrahim, died when I was already middle-aged. No one expected that I would ever get pregnant, but when he died, I already was. I kept my condition hidden until it was time to have the baby. After you were born, I kept you hidden for a time. Then I told everyone that I had taken you in and meant to raise you. When you grew older, I taught you to admire your grandfather Abu Muslim, and I named you Kayfar, 'Revenge,' because those tyrants broke my heart when they betrayed and murdered him in such a horrid way. From the time I was married, I promised myself that I would have a child and raise him to avenge his grandfather, who had no male children to take up the cause. I had to wait a long time, but when you came I vowed that you would be that child." She began to unwrap the bundle. "One of the things your grandfather left behind was a dagger that never failed him. Whenever he took it with him, he was victorious." She freed the dagger and pulled it from its sheath. The blade flashed like lightning. She handed it to him, saying, "Strike with this, and avenge Abu Muslim!"

Behzad took the dagger and turned it over. Then he returned it to its sheath and slid it into his pocket. "So I'm the grandson of Abu Muslim of Khurasan," he said, as if in a dream. "I was fighting for revenge for your sake, because you raised me," he said. "But now I'm fighting to avenge my own flesh and blood." His eyes flashed, his passion flared, and he thought of Maymuna. A lover thinks of his beloved whether he is happy or unhappy. If he is happy, he wants to share the feeling; if unhappy, he wants to draw strength from her in his suffering. Thinking of Maymuna, Behzad remembered that there was something else in his box. Reaching for it, he said, "Here's the head of another victim who demands revenge." Holding the head by a few locks of hair stiff with dried blood, he lifted it up. The skin had dried out, darkened, and shrunk so tightly over the bones that the whole skull seemed made of the blackest bone.

Fatima looked at the head but did not recognize it. "Whose is it?" she asked.

"Look carefully," he said. "Don't you recognize it?"

She examined it closely but had to admit defeat.

"It's the head of Ja'far, the second of our martyrs."

"Ja'far the vizier? The son of Yahya?"

"Yes, Mother," he said. "Ja'far, who was also betrayed and killed." He felt an impulse to tell his mother about Maymuna, but then decided to put the subject off to a later occasion. Then he fell silent as he thought back over all the strange things he had just learned about himself.

"How did you find it, child?"

"Al-Rashid betrayed him and killed him, as you know, but that wasn't enough: he cut his body in half and displayed the two parts on two different bridges in Baghdad. Then he set up the head on a third bridge. The corpse was exposed to heat and cold and sun and rain until al-Rashid left for Rey two years later. When he returned, he resolved to live in Raqqa. On the way, he passed through Baghdad, and ordered Ja'far's corpse to be taken down and burned. Meanwhile, I had given Salman the task of trying to get the head. When they took the corpse down, he bribed the official who was supposed to burn the body, and took the head. I've kept it in this box, and now I've got my grandfather's head to lay alongside it."

Impressed with what her son had accomplished, she kissed him and said, "Leave them both in the box, and put the dagger in with them. When the time comes to unsheathe it, gird it on and be victorious, God willing. Meanwhile, don't breathe a word of what I've said to anyone. The day will come when you'll need that dagger to dispatch your enemy and kill the descendants of your grandfather's murderer. But don't reveal your plan to anyone; and if you're summoned to battle, don't agree to serve as a general or commander."

"That's what I've resolved," he said. "All I care about is revenge."

She sighed. "I wonder if I'll live long enough to see that day."

"I pray that you see it and rejoice in it."

"You'll be meeting the Khurramiyya," she said. "Let them continue thinking of you as they have been: that you are their leader because you're my stepson. So long as you repeat that story our plan will be safe."

Chapter 56

A Letter from Salman

The sun was setting. Food was prepared for them and they ate. Behzad, or Kayfar, passed the night feeling infused with a new energy, as if invigorated by the spirit of Abu Muslim. Thinking back to what he had learned of the parlous state of the caliphate in Baghdad, he expected that the opportunity to gain his revenge would come when al-Amin deposed his brother, an event he knew to be inevitable given the groundwork that Salman had laid. Now he was even more eager to accomplish his mission.

The next morning, he went to meet the members of the Khurrami sect in their secret gathering place. Limiting the meeting to a few prominent leaders, he reaffirmed the importance of what they were doing and described the readiness of their comrades in Baghdad to spend all they had to help them. Then they discussed what they needed to do to prepare for the day when they would strike. Meanwhile, he was still waiting for word from Salman.

Over the next days, indeed weeks, he continued his work without calling on Ibn Sahl or receiving any news. Then he awoke one day to find that a man on camelback had brought him a message, which he had hidden inside his shoe for fear of discovery. Taking the letter, he could see from the seal that it was from Salman. He opened it and read:

From Salman, servant of the Khurrami sect, to their leader and chief, Behzad:

Yesterday we reached the goal we have been striving for—one which you know well. When Ibn al-Rabi came to Iraq after breaking his oath to al-Ma'mun, he was afraid of what might happen to him if al-Ma'mun ever became caliph, and began taking steps to save himself. The Chief Astrologer urged him to press al-Amin to remove his brother as heir apparent and solicit the oath to his own son Musa instead.

Ibn Mahan seconded this view, and al-Amin has great trust in that conceited old man. So al-Amin, ignoring all advice to the contrary, has decided to proceed. He has appointed Ibn Mahan 'Leader of the Call to Allegiance and Representative of the Dynasty,' and may well appoint him commander-in-chief of the army. If war breaks out, his appointment is a bad omen for the Caliph, as the man has far too high an opinion of his own abilities. I also learned this morning that al-Amin has written to all his governors asking them to include Musa in their prayers as heir apparent. I expect he will also write to al-Ma'mun asking him to remove himself from the succession. Do as you think best. All is well here. Goodbye.

Reaching the end of the letter, Behzad, realizing that he was now a giant step closer to fulfilling his goal, felt a great sense of relief. He was spending the day at his mother's house, and he showed her the letter. "The time is near, child," she said happily. "I'm sure Ibn Sahl knows well enough what he needs to do now. But do you?"

"Tell me," he said.

"When conflict breaks out between al-Amin and al-Ma'mun, the Persians will side with al-Ma'mun on condition that he support them and respect their rights. If they try to get rid of him and claim power for themselves without a caliph, their cause is lost, since the lower orders can only be ruled using religion. If two contenders ask for their loyalty, they'll follow the one who's a caliph."

"But we have a caliph," he said. "We'll rule through al-Ma'mun."

"And will al-Ma'mun live forever? When he dies, he is to be succeeded by one of his relatives. Who can say whether that relative will favor us or not? He might resent us, as al-Rashid did, and make us suffer for it."

Her words struck home. Marveling at her shrewdness, he remembered the conversation he had had with the Khurrami leaders in Ctesiphon on the night of the Arch. "So what do we do?" he asked.

"The smart thing to do is to prepare a stable future for your descendants, starting now. If the head of state must be an Arab caliph, let him come from the partisans of 'Ali, who, of all the Arabs, are the most affectionate towards us. So tell al-Ma'mun that you'll take his side only if he chooses a Shi'ite as his successor. If you do that, you'll get what you want. But do it through Ibn Sahl: present the idea to him as your own, but do it secretly. And be cautious!"

Hearing this advice, he bent and kissed her hand, then excused himself to go and show the letter to Ibn Sahl and discuss their next move.

He reached the residence by mid-morning and went straight in, the chamberlain knowing that he enjoyed his master's favor. As he walked through the grounds toward the room where Ibn Sahl and his brother—who lived there together—held their audience, he saw a kiosk in the middle with a page boy standing at the door. Thinking that Ibn Sahl must be sitting inside, he made for the kiosk. Suddenly a young woman appeared at the door, her relaxed manner making it clear that she was unaware of his presence. When her eyes fell on Behzad, she blushed and backed away, looking startled. For a moment she stood still as a statue, debating whether to beat a timorous retreat into the kiosk or to greet the visitor, since the two were known to each other. She was wearing house clothes, including a light head-cloth that covered only part of her face. Behzad was taken aback by her natural beauty, her radiant face, and her sparkling eyes, which exuded both intelligence and modesty. Embarrassed at having inadvertently disturbed her, he spoke first: "Forgive me, Mistress! I seem to have disturbed you. I'm looking for my master Ibn Sahl, and I thought he was in the kiosk, since I've known him to sit there in the mornings."

"You're looking for my uncle Ibn Sahl?" she asked with an air of unpretentious good will. "He went out with my father early this morning to meet al-Ma'mun. You haven't disturbed me at all. Unless I'm mistaken, you must be Behzad." She stopped and waited for him to reply.

"Yes, my lady; I'm called Behzad."

"My father and my uncle think very highly of you, and if they were here they'd be happy to see you. Please have a seat, if you like."

Impressed that so young a woman could be so intelligent and tactful, Behzad recognized her as al-Hasan's daughter Buran. Recalling Ibn Sahl's allusion to her, he saw that she was indeed worthy of the best of men. Were his heart not otherwise engaged, he would think himself fortunate to win her. "Thank you for your kindness, my lady," he said. "I would enjoy remaining here, but I must go to al-Ma'mun's audience to attend your father and uncle. With your permission," he said, turning and going out. He then made his way to al-Ma'mun's palace, or the governor's palace, as al-Ma'mun was then governor of Khurasan.

Chapter 57

Al-Ma'mun

As we have seen, al-Ma'mun had come to Khurasan with his father al-Rashid. When the latter died, Ibn al-Rabi, in violation of his oath, had returned to Baghdad with the expedition's troops and supplies. Learning of this, al-Ma'mun asked the advice of his Persian advisers in Marv. All of them, except for their leader, Ibn Sahl, advised him to take a detachment and go in pursuit of Ibn al-Rabi. As for Ibn Sahl, he warned him not to leave Khurasan for any reason. "If you leave the province," he said, "you'll be delivering yourself as a gift to your brother. Instead, send a messenger with a letter reminding them of their oath of allegiance and asking them to affirm their loyalty to you."

Al-Ma'mun followed this advice, but his letter had no effect. He began to fear for his position, but Ibn Sahl reassured him. "Here you've settled among your mother's family," he said, "and they've sworn loyalty to you. Be patient, and I can guarantee you the caliphate." He advised him to make a show of piety, as the common people are most easily led by displays of religion. Encouraged, al-Ma'mun waited to see what would happen next. He was a thoughtful, deliberate, kind, unassuming, soft-hearted man who loved learning. In Khurasan, where there were many learned men, he had given himself over to study and spent his day in discussions with scholars, having studied the ancient sciences, especially philosophy. He was a man of medium height, of a light complexion, good-looking, with a long beard and thin hair, with a narrow forehead, a mole on one cheek, and eyes that shone with benevolent sagacity. His forgiving nature became proverbial.[92] Trained by the Barmakids and later by Ibn Sahl, he had been raised as a Shi'ite and favored their sect.

---

92 *History of Islamic Civilization*, II.

Al-Ma'mun remained in Khurasan, spending his time reading and studying the sciences, and waiting to see what his brother al-Amin was going to do. Then, on that day, a delegation came to ask him to swear allegiance to al-Amin's son Musa, to place the latter's name first in the Friday sermon, and to visit Baghdad, because al-Amin missed him. Alarmed by these demands, al-Ma'mun sent for Ibn Sahl. The meeting took place in the governor's palace and was attended only by the inner circle of commanders, led by Ibn Sahl and his brother al-Hasan.

"My brother has sent envoys;" said al-Ma'mun, "who are asking me to place his son Musa ahead of myself in the line of succession, and to visit Baghdad."

"The first request is a violation of the oath of allegiance," said Ibn Sahl, "and defies the will of God. As for the invitation, if you accept it that's your choice; but then you'll be throwing away every hope of defending yourself. That's not only my opinion: everyone else in Khurasan thinks so too. For example, ask Hisham," referring to the leading figure in the province.

Hisham was duly sent for and asked his opinion. "When we gave you our oaths of allegiance," he said, "you promised that you wouldn't leave Khurasan. If you do, then we can do nothing for you except to wish you well. If I see you preparing to leave, I will restrain you with my right hand. Cut it off, and I will restrain you with my left. Cut it off, and I will restrain you with my tongue. Behead me, and I will have fulfilled my duty toward you."

Hearing this, al-Ma'mun was heartened. "That is how the whole province feels," said Ibn Sahl, "and they're your maternal uncles." To further poison the relationship between the brothers, he advised al-Ma'mun to drop al-Amin's name from the Friday sermon and from the robes of honor, and to stop the couriers from carrying news to Baghdad. In gratitude, al-Ma'mun gave Ibn Sahl full control over military and civilian matters, with the title 'Dual Vizier.'

In the course of this meeting, a page boy announced the arrival of Behzad the physician. Al-Ma'mun asked who he was. "He's the physician who serves your palace in Baghdad," said Ibn Sahl. Remembering him, al-Ma'mun bid him enter.

Behzad came in and greeted the assembly, then sat when invited to do so by al-Ma'mun. Asked about Baghdad, he replied, "When I left, the city was bemoaning what has befallen people of good character. As for the

Commander of the Faithful's family, I left them in health and strength, but…"

"But what?"

"I don't know what may have happened to them now that men of base ambition have grown strong enough to violate their oaths of allegiance, nor do I know how safe it is for them in Baghdad. If the Commander of the Faithful were to summon them here, it might be the best thing."

"You're quite right, Doctor," said al-Ma'mun. "I'll do that, God willing."

Behzad had suggested this only in the hope that Maymuna would come along as well and thus escape her enemies. Salman had not told him anything about what had happened to her in al-Amin's household.

"How was Umm Habiba when you saw her?" asked al-Ma'mun.

"In perfect health," he said, "but she misses her father."

Thinking of his daughter, al-Ma'mun smiled. He adored her, and marveled at how wise she was for someone so young. He well knew that it was dangerous for his family to remain in Baghdad after the coup d'état and resolved to summon them to Khurasan. He turned to Ibn Sahl, who was sitting beside him. "How does the ascendant look today?" he asked. "Is it propitious to send people to fetch my family?"

From his pocket Ibn Sahl took a small golden astrolabe that he kept with him at all times. He went over to a window, looked out, and studied the instrument. Then he came back and said, "Today is good enough, my lord, but tomorrow would be better."

Al-Ma'mun ordered his servant Nawfal to depart the next morning. Then he turned back to Ibn Sahl. "What do I tell the delegation?"

"The Commander of the Faithful knows best," he replied. "If he asks my opinion, I would suggest that he turn them away emptyhanded. Here among your uncles you're safer than in Baghdad among al-Amin's men, who will tell him anything to advance their own interests. The best thing is to treat him gently. Write him a friendly letter that reveals nothing of your intention to defy him, and try to win him over. That, I think, would be the politically astute thing to do."

Al-Ma'mun approved of this suggestion and wrote the following letter to his brother:

I have received the letter sent me by the Commander of the Faithful. I am no more than an executor of his wishes, commanded by al-Rashid to man the frontier. For me to remain here is assuredly more useful to the Commander of the Faithful and more beneficial to the Muslims than for me to leave, delighted though I would be to enjoy his company and witness the blessings that God has conferred upon him. Should the Commander of the Faithful wish to confirm me in my governorship and exempt me from attending him, let him do so, God willing.

Al-Ma'mun gave this letter to the head of the delegation, then gave a signal that the meeting was over. Of all those present, the keenest to leave was Behzad, who wanted to tell Ibn Sahl about his mother's idea of appointing a member of the house of 'Ali as heir apparent—an appointment that would be a condition of siding with al-Ma'mun.

Behzad waited until Ibn Sahl had returned home, then followed him and asked for a private meeting. When they were alone, Behzad began by praising the judicious advice that Ibn Sahl had given al-Ma'mun. Then he gave him Salman's letter and asked him to read it.

Before he had finished reading, Ibn Sahl was laughing. "If Salman is right and al-Amin has given Ibn Mahan command of the army, then we're as fortunate as could be. That's exactly what I'd been hoping and working for. Not only is Ibn Mahan feeble and conceited, he was also governor of Khurasan under al-Rashid, and alienated the people with his oppressive rule. Al-Rashid dismissed him, and the people were happy to see him go.[93] When they fight him, they'll be fighting in anger. Better yet, he expects them to side with him, as some of them wrote to him promising falsely to support him. This is what I've been hoping for ever since this conflict began. That's why I said we're fortunate."

"But what do you mean by 'fortunate,' Master?"

"I mean that we'll defeat al-Amin and depose him and make al-Ma'mun ruler in his place."

"But how does that benefit us?" asked Behzad. "Aren't they both Arabs and 'Abbasids? Aren't they both the sons of Ja'far's killer al-Rashid? And the grandsons of Abu Muslim's killer al-Mansur?"

93 Ibn al-Athir, III: 96.

"But al-Ma'mun is our cousin, and a Shi'ite like us. We've created him, and he does as we tell him. In the end, we're the ones in charge."

"Are you sure he'll always be with us? And even if he is, what about his successor? How can you trust the 'Abbasids after they've betrayed us—and others too—so many times?"

Ibn Sahl had been listening with his head bowed as if suddenly aroused from sleep. Now he raised his eyes and said, "Behzad, you're right. I understand what you're getting at. You've hit the nail on the head, and we have to reconsider what we're doing, starting now." He looked down again and rubbed his chin. "To rule, we need a caliphate, and the caliph must be a Hashimite of the Prophet's line. The ones most sympathetic to us are the family of 'Ali. One of them, 'Ali Ibn Musa, called al-Rida, is among us at the moment. He's a descendant of Husayn, son of 'Ali Ibn Abi Talib.[94] He's an intelligent and thoughtful man, and al-Ma'mun is fond of him. If I tell al-Ma'mun to make him his heir apparent now, the caliphate will be transferred from the 'Abbasids to the 'Alids when he dies. Then our victory will be complete." He beamed.

"An excellent plan, my lord!" said Behzad. As he rose to go, Ibn Sahl said, "If you get another letter like that one from Salman, let me know."

Behzad returned to his mother's house. Worried about Maymuna, he was waiting impatiently for al-Ma'mun's family to arrive, thinking that she would be with them.

---

94   'Ali Ibn Abi Talib (d. 661 AH) was the cousin and son-in-law of the Prophet Muhammad. Shi'ite Muslims believe that he and certain of his descendants (including his son al-Husayn) are the only legitimate guides (imams) to correct faith and practice, and that only the wickedness of their enemies has prevented them from assuming their rightful places as leaders of the Muslim community. The Twelver Shi'ites, so called because they believe that there have been twelve such imams, consider 'Ali al-Rida (d. 818 AH), the figure mentioned here, to be the eighth. He was indeed made heir apparent by al-Ma'mun, though he died before he could succeed as caliph. Today, Twelver Shi'ites believe that the Caliph forced him to accept the position of heir apparent as a device to placate the Shi'ites and later poisoned him to clear the way for a reconciliation with the 'Abbasids of Baghdad. *Translator's Note*

Chapter 58

Ibn Mahan's Campaign

In 195 AH (810 AD), al-Amin publicly removed his brother from the succession. The coins that al-Ma'mun had struck in Khurasan bearing his own name only, al-Amin declared void. He gave his son Musa the title 'Speaker of Truth' and decreed that he be mentioned in the Friday sermon. He had al-Ma'mun's name dropped altogether, and solicited the oath of allegiance to a second son, Abdullah, giving him the title of 'Rising in Truth.'

Al-Ma'mun, meanwhile, was seeking Ibn Sahl's help to raise an army. Ibn Sahl seized the occasion to stipulate that al-Ma'mun appoint 'Ali al-Rida, the leader of the Shi'ites in Khurasan, his heir apparent. Though reluctant to take so momentous a step, al-Ma'mun realized he had no choice but to comply. He promised Ibn Sahl that if he won the war, defeated his brother, and became caliph, he would name 'Ali al-Rida his successor. Applying himself to the matter of recruitment, the Dual Vizier assembled an army under the command of Tahir Ibn Husayn, 'the man with two right hands,' and dispatched him to Rey to stop al-Amin's army if it tried to capture Khurasan. Tahir was a brave commander, though he was a good deal younger than his rival Ibn Mahan.

During this time, Behzad was waiting impatiently for the arrival of al-Ma'mun's family and for any news from Salman. When Ibn Sahl offered him the command of the army, he refused it. Then, when he felt he could wait no longer, he received the following letter from Salman:

My efforts have paid off and my expectations have been fulfilled. Ibn Mahan has been named commander of the army that is coming to fight you. Even as I write, the troops are leaving Baghdad; al-Amin has come in person to see Ibn Mahan off. Ibn Mahan thinks that the people of Khurasan will welcome him, as some of them have sent him letters promising to join him when he arrives. When he learned that Tahir Ibn Husayn was leading al-Ma'mun's forces, he dismissed him, saying, 'Tahir is a thorn but I am the branch. The likes of him cannot command armies.' Then he told his companions: 'The moment he learns we have reached the pass at Hamadhan, he will crack like a branch in a storm. A lamb cannot battle a butting ram, nor can a mule hold his ground against a lion. If he stays where he is, he will fall to the blades of our swords and the tips of our lances. As soon as they hear that we've reached Rey and will soon be upon them, their arms will tremble in despair!'

Al-Amin believed Ibn Mahan and put him in command. He has added all the towns of Jabal to his estates and made him military governor and tax collector for the province. He has given him a free hand with the treasury and equipped 50,000 riders for him. He has also ordered Abu Dulaf 'Ijli and Hilal Hadrami to join him, and supplied him with more and more men and money. The people of Baghdad imagine that, given his great age, he will certainly be the victor. When he went to bid farewell to Zubayda, as is the custom, her concern was to make sure that when he captured al-Ma'mun, he treated him gently. 'Ibn Mahan,' she said, 'although the Commander of the Faithful is my son and my most beloved, I would not wish to see any harm befall al-Ma'mun either. My son is a king, challenged in his royal right by his brother, and forced to defend it. But his rival has dignity of birth and family, which you must respect. Do not speak roughly to him, as you are not his equal. Do not treat him like a slave, or insult him with manacles and fetters, or forbid him his servants and slave women, or impose a strenuous pace on him, or ride alongside him, or gallop ahead. Take his stirrup, and if he curses you, bear it patiently.' She handed him a shackle made of silver. 'If he falls into your hands, restrain him with this.'

He promised her to do as she asked, and promised the same to al-Amin.

I have learned that our master al-Ma'mun has sent for the members of his household. They will reach you soon. I know that you expect to see Maymuna among them, but do not be grieved when you do not, as she has remained here. I did not tell you of this before, so as not to worry you. Now, however, I cannot keep the news secret any longer, as you will soon be hearing it from Dananir or someone else. Maymuna is living in the Caliph's palace but is safe. Dananir will explain to you how she came to be there. Don't worry: as long as I am at my post, I will see to her safety. Goodbye.

Behzad read the letter and felt the world darken around him. Though the letter was full of promising news, the part about Maymuna made him furious with jealousy at the thought that she was living at the mercy of his enemy. He was also angry at Salman for keeping the news from him. He was at a loss for what to do. Should he leave Marv and join the battle against Ibn Mahan in Rey, or stay where he was until Dananir came so he could find out what had happened to Maymuna? In the end, it was passion that won out: he decided to stay and wait for news of Maymuna and then join the army. In such matters, lovers have no will of their own.

Surprised to find him still at home after the army left for Rey, his mother said, "The dagger's there in the box. When are you leaving?"

Embarrassed, he picked up the box and said, "I'm leaving now. I came to say goodbye. Pray for me!"

Baring her breast, she looked up to heaven, spread her arms, and cried, "May God succour you against the oppressors who murdered your grandfather, took what is ours, and robbed us of the fruits of our toil!" Then she rose, clasped him to her breast, and, kissing his neck, held him close for a long time. Feeling hot tears and warm breath on his neck, he realized she was crying, and was deeply moved. He nearly wept himself, but then controlled himself, asking, "Why are you weeping, mother?"

Lifting her head, she stepped back, her eyes wet with tears and a mournful expression on her face. "I'm crying, child, because I don't know whether I'll see you again."

"I pray I'll return alive, well, and victorious, God willing, and find you in health and strength, ready to rejoice in our vengeance."

So saying, he kissed her hands and breast. Then he picked up the box, took out the dagger, and hung it around his neck. He put on his traveling clothes: a cloak slung over his tunic and trousers, and a headcloth wound around a tall cap and thrown across his face. His horse was brought out to him and he mounted it. When he reached for the box, his mother took it, saying "Leave this here. It contains two precious heads. Either you'll put the heads of your grandfather's killer or killers alongside them, or they'll stay here where I can mourn for them until I die."

Moved, he said, "I pray that you not have to mourn any more, Mother."

Leaving the box with her, he turned the horse's muzzle and rode off. After a short distance, he realized what he had done: he had let his mother shame him into going on this journey. Yet he could not bring himself to leave Marv before he had a chance to see Dananir and ask about Maymuna. He was angry at Salman for not explaining more about what had happened.

Letting his horse lead the way, he rode through the markets of Marv. When he found himself outside the city, he told himself that he could ride out and meet al-Ma'mun's caravan before it reached Marv. Having bid farewell to his mother and told her he was leaving, he could not bring himself to turn back.

Chapter 59

Dananir's Story

Behzad traveled for days, his eyes constantly scanning the empty horizon. Every time he saw a caravan, a rider, or a group of travelers, he thought he had found al-Ma'mun's party. On he went until he was only a few stages from Rey, where Tahir's army was camped. One morning he spotted a caravan that even from a distance seemed to be carrying women of noble families, as it included camel litters, bundles of clothing, and tents, and had an escort of slaves and pages. He accosted the caravan leader, who told him that the travelers were members of al-Ma'mun's family. Behzad asked to see Dananir. Intimidated, the members of the escort led him toward her. Then some of the pages recognized him and helped him find the right litter. Seeing him approach, Dananir ordered her attendants to kneel the camels and set their loads down for a moment. Dismounting, Behzad said, "Salman wrote to me that Maymuna's in the Caliph's household. What took her there?"

Dananir related the whole story to him, from the day the Shakiri appeared at the gate to the day that she and Zaynab returned from al-Amin's empty-handed.

"What happened to her after that?"

"She's safe enough where she is," said Dananir. "Al-Amin promised his niece that he wouldn't let anyone harm her. And Salman seems to be doing his best to look after her."

Thinking she knew where his servant was, Behzad asked, "Do you know where Salman is?"

"I have no idea," she answered. "He'll go missing for months and suddenly turn up again. I saw him before we left and he told me to set your mind at rest about Maymuna. His letter may have reached you before we did because letters travel by fast camel while we plod along with all these provisions."

Behzad could see no alternative but to hurry on to Baghdad and look for Maymuna. But he also remembered that it was his duty to fight. "Have you seen al-Amin's army?" he asked.

"We rode alongside them for most of the way."

"Where are they now?"

"Ten parsangs from Rey," said Dananir.[95] "They say the commander, Ibn Mahan, is an arrogant man who thinks his army is too big to be defeated. If what I've heard is true, then Tahir's in real trouble."

"How so?"

"Ibn Mahan is supposed to have fifty thousand troops but Tahir has only four thousand."

Behzad bowed his head thoughtfully. "Victory is not always granted to the many, but to the brave and steadfast."

"True enough, but how can four thousand stand up to fifty?" She went on: "I've heard that Tahir's taken the few troops he has out of Rey with Ibn Mahan camped only five parsangs away. If he had stayed in the city he could have held out in the citadel."

"He did the right thing," said Behzad. "If he's routed, the people of Rey would be just as dangerous to him as Ibn Mahan's soldiers. Another good move would be to take the initiative and attack before they see how small his forces are."

"That's what he seems to be doing," she said. "I thought he had made an error and I didn't want to believe what I had heard. One of his men said to him, 'Your men are few, and they're intimidated by the size of al-Amin's army. Why not put off the fight until your men feel more confident about it and have a better idea of the enemy's weak spots?' To that, Tahir replied, 'If anything does us in, it won't be inexperience or indecisiveness on my part. We're few and they're a big, numerous force. If I put off the battle they'll see how few we are, and they'll start waving carrots and sticks at my men until I can't rely on them to stand their ground. Instead I'm going to put my infantry and my cavalry up against theirs, and trust my men to follow

---

95 An originally Persian measurement corresponding to the distance that could be covered on foot in one hour. In Islamic times it was fixed at 5.985 kilometers or 3.718 miles. *Translator's Note*

orders and do their part. I'm going to see it through as if expecting victory, but eager to die a martyr. I pray God takes our side; if not, I won't be the first to fight and fall, and the hereafter is better anyway.'"

Behzad marveled at Tahir's valor and resolve. Then, to put an end to the conversation, he asked, "So you're on your way to Marv?"

"Yes. What about you?"

"To Rey and then Baghdad. Where's Umm Habiba?"

"In her litter. Do you want to see her?"

"I wish I had time. Give her my regards." Then, excusing himself, he mounted his horse and bid her farewell. He rode off, torn between two impulses. Duty demanded that he go help Tahir against Ibn Mahan, while his heart urged him to rescue his beloved from the enemy. The latter impulse had grown stronger since his talk with Dananir, who had explained that the reason for Maymuna's capture was Ibn al-Fadl's desire to marry her. Despite Dananir's assurances that the young man had no access to Maymuna so long as she stayed in the Caliph's household, Behzad found the thought unbearable. Lovers, as a rule, are fearful and suspicious creatures.

Chapter 60

The Battlefield

Bundled up in his cloak, his muffler wound around his face, his sword and his dagger strapped on under his clothes, Behzad rode on. By mid-morning, he was passing Rey. There he learned that Tahir indeed meant to strike before his enemies learned how few men he had. He had not gone much further when he heard the beating of war drums. As the clamor grew louder and the dust clouds rose, he climbed a hill that overlooked a plain. Below he saw the two armies drawn up for battle. The difference in size was obvious, and he felt a pang of fear for Tahir. But he resolved then and there not to leave until he saw al-Ma'mun's side victorious, even if it cost him his life.

Ibn Mahan had arrayed his armies in a three-part formation—right wing, left wing, and center—and set up ten banners, each for a hundred men. He brought the banners forward one by one, placing them a bowshot apart. He ordered the commanders to take their banners up one by one, letting the men of the first banner fight for a time and then withdraw, allowing the men of the next banner to take their place. Ibn Mahan himself took position with the bravest of his comrades. For his part, Tahir had arranged his men into squadrons, each composed of troops arrayed in rows, with his own in the middle. He marched them forward, urging them to fight bravely and stand their ground. Behzad noticed with chagrin that some of Tahir's men had gone over to Ibn Mahan. Ibn Mahan, however, did the wrong thing: instead of rewarding the deserters, he ordered them flogged, humiliated, and tortured, which only discouraged the others from following their lead. Behzad remained where he was, his eyes trained on the field, his heart beating with eagerness to join the fight, but waiting for the right moment.

As Behzad stood watching, Tahir Ibn Husayn suddenly rode out ahead of his troops toward Ibn Mahan's army. He held a leveled spear. On its tip was a great sheet of parchment that Behzad recognized as a copy of the oath of allegiance given to al-Ma'mun. Poised between the two armies, Tahir asked for safe conduct and Ibn Mahan gave it. Tahir then lifted the spear and held the oath aloft. "Have you no fear of God?" he cried. "Isn't this the oath that you, of all people, swore to uphold? Fear God, for you are standing on the lip of your grave!"

Provoked by this insult, Ibn Mahan ordered his men to capture Tahir, but they could not. Though too far away to hear what Tahir had said, Behzad nevertheless understood the message. Soon enough, he saw the two armies move forward and clash. Ibn Mahan's right wing attacked Tahir's left wing and sent it reeling back in retreat. Ibn Mahan's left wing did the same with Tahir's right and crushed it. Dismayed, Behzad nearly let his rush of fellow feeling carry him into the thick of battle. Again, though, he held back, waiting for the right moment. Meanwhile, he set himself the task of rounding up the men in flight and urging them to turn and fight. Darting here and there on his charger, his face half-covered by his scarf, he harangued the men in Persian, mocking the idea of retreat and heaping ridicule on Ibn Mahan and his men. His words struck home. One by one, Tahir's men turned around. Meanwhile, Tahir, too, was urging them to stand their ground. So they stood firm, feeling a new sense of resolve. They charged the foe at the center, pushing their enemies back and killing many of them. Ibn Mahan's banners were forced back one after another, and his right wing gave way. With Behzad shouting at them, Tahir's right and left wings had regrouped and rejoined the battle. The center renewed its efforts and the whole army surged forward as if Behzad had infused them with a brave new spirit. All up and down the line, Ibn Mahan's army faltered and fell back.

Seeing his army scuttling back, a panic-stricken Ibn Mahan leapt up and began urging his men to stand their ground, promising them money and lashing out at Tahir and his men. Behzad saw his chance. Unless he killed the commander, this setback would only be temporary. His hand on the dagger, he charged like a thunderbolt, indifferent to the storm of arrows that fell all about him, and to the spears that shivered and broke. Reaching Ibn Mahan, he cried: "Halt, sir! Never say I attacked you from behind."

Ibn Mahan turned around. He did not recognize the figure wrapped in the muffler, but he drew his sword and struck. Behzad dodged the blow, whipped out his dagger, and stabbed him in the chest, killing him. Deciding that he had done enough, Behzad rode away from the battle and disappeared from sight. Through Tahir's camp the rumor spread that one of Tahir's men had killed Ibn Mahan with an arrow. Ibn Mahan's hands and feet were lashed together, as was done with animals; and his body was carried to Tahir, who ordered it tossed into a well. Full of gratitude to God for his victory, Tahir embraced the page boys who were standing nearby. Utterly routed, al-Amin's army fled at swordpoint, turning to fight twelve times in two parsangs, and being routed each time. Tahir's men were busy killing and capturing until night fell, by which time they had collected a vast amount of plunder. When Tahir announced that mercy would be granted to anyone who laid down his arms, al-Amin's men tossed away their weapons and dismounted. He then returned to Rey and wrote the following letter to al-Ma'mun and Ibn Sahl:

In the name of God, the merciful and compassionate. As I write to the Commander of the Faithful, Ibn Mahan's head is before me, his signet is on my finger, and his army is under my orders. Farewell.

The letter arrived by courier three days later, having traversed some two hundred and fifty parsangs. Ibn Sahl, the Dual Vizier, presented himself before al-Ma'mun and congratulated him. Then the residence was thrown open to visitors, who came in and acclaimed al-Ma'mun caliph. Two days later, the head arrived, and was paraded through Khurasan.

Chapter 61

Zubayda's Procession

Let us return to Maymuna, whom we left in al-Amin's household in Baghdad, alone, friendless, and terribly anxious about what might happen next. She had not seen Salman and had no idea where he was. Accordingly, she imagined that he had died or gone off to rejoin Behzad. She missed her grandmother and felt wretched at being cut off from her, all the more so since she did not know where she was. She spent her days hiding from others, pretending to be feeling dizzy or indisposed. Whenever she was alone, she would take out her beloved's letter, kiss it, and reread it, hoping to feel closer to its author. Every time she read his expressions of resentment toward the 'Abbasids and his threats of revenge, she would tremble with fear of what would happen if the letter fell into the hands of her enemies. She kept it carefully hidden, trusting none of the slave women and attendants that surrounded her. The only one she had any faith in at all was Farida, the forewoman of the palace, whom Dananir had asked to take care of her. Farida, as it turned out, was a friend of Dananir's, and an admirer of her intelligence and sagacity. Though Maymuna felt she could trust her, she was still afraid of revealing her secret, knowing as she did that there were spies everywhere. So she said nothing about the letter or about Behzad. In any event, she had no further news of him, nor was there any way to contact him except through Salman, who had vanished; even though—unbeknownst to her—he was in the same palace, only a stone's throw away, and was avoiding her for reasons of his own.

She spent several days wondering what would become of her, indifferent to the games and laughter and music and singing that kept the slave women of the palace occupied. Whenever she saw them gathering, she would hide away in her room, take out Behzad's letter, and begin reading it. If she heard footsteps or voices, she would hide the letter in her pocket.

One day, it so happened that she was lonely and wanted to seek solace in her letter. When she reached into her pocket for it, it wasn't there. Feeling as if her heart had stopped, she searched for it, more carefully this time, but found no trace of it. She grew frightened and now felt even more lost and alone. More than ever, she wished she had someone there to talk to. She could think of no better expedient than to invite her grandmother to come and see her. So she wrote a note to Dananir complaining of her loneliness and asking after 'Abbada, and begged the forewoman to smuggle the note to al-Ma'mun's palace. Farida, who had been hoping to render some service as a tribute to Dananir, did as she was asked, quickly and in secret.

When the note reached Dananir, she resolved to help Maymuna because she loved her and wanted her to feel as comfortable as possible. After showing 'Abbada the letter, Dananir did her best to arrange a visit. "Send me to her," said 'Abbada, "and let me die there. I thought they would let her go in a few days, but now it seems that she'll be there indefinitely."

"Will you go in disguise?"

"I'm afraid that if they recognize me they'll take it out on her."

"Let me send you to my friend Farida. I'll tell her that you're Maymuna's nurse, and ask her to let you stay with her. I'm sure she'll agree."

Thanking her for all her efforts, 'Abbada dressed, bid her goodbye, and took a donkey to the Citadel of Al-Mansur in the company of a messenger who, once they reached the palace, presented Dananir's letter to the forewoman. Farida knew full well who 'Abbada was, just as she knew all about Maymuna; but she feigned ignorance in both cases, hoping to keep the court ignorant of their identities. She had been among the beneficiaries of Barmakid largesse, and like the others was forced to express her gratitude in secret.

There is no need to describe Maymuna's happiness at the sight of her grandmother: she was so delighted that she no longer cared how long she stayed in the palace. She also decided it was time to tell her of her relationship with Behzad, including all the professions of love they had exchanged, up to the receipt of the letter, which, as she told her, had disappeared. Though she had not noticed all the signs she might have, 'Abbada was not entirely surprised by these confessions. She was much perturbed, however, by the loss of the letter, which under the circumstances was worrisome indeed.

Salman, meanwhile, was doing his best to use Ibn al-Rabi and Ibn Mahan to help him persuade al-Amin to remove his brother from the succession altogether. Ibn al-Rabi, who feared for himself if al-Ma'mun ever became caliph, was especially insistent. Al-Amin was still reluctant, if not for fear of the consequences then out of respect for the arrangement dictated by al-Rashid, or out of some fraternal feeling toward al-Ma'mun. With Ibn al-Rabi urging him on, he began to regard the idea more favorably. Even so, he would not move ahead without consulting his mother Zubayda, whose judgment he held in the highest regard. At that time, she was in residence at her palace, called the Abode of Permanence, near the Palace of Eternity. Al-Amin was not sure whether he should ride out and see her or invite her to visit him at the Palace of Al-Mansur. He thought about the problem for a while, but then went back to amusing himself, in this case with fishing. On the palace grounds was a big pond stocked with fish. He would fish there with a rod and hook, surrounded by eunuchs dressed as women who would bait his hooks or drive the fish from the edges of the pond to the part closest to the Caliph. Some held nets and others busied themselves with rods, hooks, and the like. Al-Amin himself was enraptured with the game. He delighted in performing feats of strength at the expense of his attendants: he would pick one of them up and toss him into the pond, and the others would laugh and praise him, then make a point of showing that they were too weak to do the same. The truth is that al-Amin was physically very strong: on one occasion he reportedly wrestled a lion to the ground.

As he was enjoying this diversion, a page appeared and announced that the Caliph's mother and her entourage were approaching.

Al-Amin was glad: he remembered that he wanted to consult with her. He ordered that the palace be made ready to receive her. The foremen and forewomen began arranging the male and female attendants in rows. Among them were a troop of beautiful, slim-waisted slave women given to him by his mother Zubayda. Noting his preoccupation with male servants and page boys and his indifference to women, she dressed this troop of women as page boys, complete with turbans, forelocks and side-curls, tunics, earrings, and belts, a uniform that showed off their waists and buttocks. She sent them to him and had them parade before him. Much taken with them, he showed them off[96] both to his inner circle and to the common people, some of whom imitated the fashion for themselves.

96 Mas'udi, II.

That day, learning that his mother was coming, al-Amin knew that she would enjoy seeing those slave women among those lined up to receive her. He ordered the foreman to arrange the slaves in rows, with Kawthar, with whom he was famously infatuated,[97] in front. Besides the eunuchs and women, the 'Cricket' pages and the Ethiopians, called the 'Crows,' took their places, each troop in their distinctive clothes and colors. There were long garments and short, in many colors: red, blue, sky blue, pink, and yellow. There were boys dressed as girls, and girls dressed as boys, as well as lutenists, pandore players, and pipers.

Thus arrayed, the rows of attendants stretched from the door of the great hall out to the main gate of the palace. In front were more page boys, some burning incense, some holding flowers, and others reciting poetry. Al-Amin walked between the ranks as far as the gate to receive his mother. She was sitting in a sort of sedan chair made of sandalwood inlaid with silver and ebony and hung with brocaded curtains on hooks of silver and gold. The sedan was mounted on a litter carried by two mules saddled in silver and led by pages wearing embroidered silken tunics painted with the slogan of the dynasty, as the pages were soldiers. From a distance came the scent of musk.

When the litter reached the palace gate, all those standing in attendance stepped back except for the head eunuch, who helped Zubayda descend from her perch. Then al-Amin came forward. He kissed her between her breasts and she kissed him on the head. She was wearing shoes studded with gemstones[98] and a veil woven with golden thread and bordered with designs made of precious stones. Through the veil glinted her jeweled headdress, necklaces, and earrings. Draped around her shoulders was a gold-colored scarf that hung down her sides. Underneath it was a gown of pink silk that hung low in the back but opened in the front to show off her gem-studded shoes, Zubayda being the first to wear studded shoes in Islam. Yet her clothes, sumptuous though they were, did not distract from the fetching beauty of her countenance, or from her splendid bearing and dignity of carriage.

She had hardly passed through the gate when word of her arrival spread through the palace. When the news reached 'Abbada, she trembled and her heart began to pound, and she wished she could hide somewhere so no one

---

97 Ibn al-Athir, VI.

98 *The Book of Songs.*

would notice. Maymuna, on the other hand, was eager to see the procession, having heard a great deal about the Caliph's mother and her splendid entourage. So she joined the courtiers who were crowded around the peepholes. She was duly impressed by Zubayda's beauty even as she found her grandiosity intimidating.

Chapter 62

Al-Ma'mun Deposed

At Zubayda's request, she and al-Amin passed through to a private chamber, she having indicated that she had something of special importance to discuss with him. He was glad about this, as he wished to consult her as well. Before she took her seat, a troop of ladies' maids disencumbered her of some of her garments. Other attendants, male and female, plied fans and flyswatters, while others again set about preparing food and drink. But she said to al-Amin, "I want to see you alone, and I don't want anything to eat."

At al-Amin's signal, the attendants went out and left him alone with his mother. She sat on the divan and beckoned him to sit beside her.

"What a happy coincidence," he said. "It's as if you knew exactly when to come. Just this morning I was saying I should come to see you, or else invite you here, because there's something I want to discuss with you. And here you are! I'm taking that as a good omen."

She smiled indulgently at her son, but her eyes flashed with anger. "That's all very nice. But I came to see you about something that concerns both of us."

"What's that, Mother?" said al-Amin, interested.

"Is that misguided bit of unfinished business still here with you?"

"What do you mean?" he asked, baffled.

"I mean our enemy's daughter—the enemy who tried to remove you from the succession, and tricked your father into demanding an oath of loyalty to the son of Marajil!"

He realized that she was talking about Maymuna, the daughter of Ja'far. "Yes, my lady," he said. "She's still in the women's quarters."

"Why have you let her stay instead of getting rid of her?"

"She's a poor orphan who can't do any harm to anyone. I couldn't let her go, and my niece told me to take care of her, so I kept her here to prevent her from causing any trouble."

"A poor orphan! Call her a backstabbing traitor instead. And what's even odder is that you would let your niece vouch for her: her father is even more dangerous to you than your enemies are. Hasn't he rallied the people of Khurasan against you? And don't you think that if he could push you off this throne he would do it? And who do you think gave him such an inflated idea of himself? Wasn't it Ja'far, the father of this girl? Your father, may God rest his soul, was a better judge of character than you: he killed Ja'far in the most painful way possible, and if he hadn't you wouldn't be sitting where you are right now. After all that, you tell me she's a poor orphan and your niece told you to look out for her? Your brother has more Persian blood in his veins than Hashimite: he takes after Marajil more than his father al-Rashid. That's why he's going to his maternal uncles for help."

As Zubayda spoke, her anger flared. Her face paled, her lips went white, her cheeks drained, and her eyes flashed. As it happened, what she was saying matched up with al-Amin's desire to remove his brother from the succession. But he wanted it to be her idea. So he asked, "Didn't my father have an oath of allegiance sworn to me and my brother and hang the text of the agreement inside the Ka'ba?"

"That agreement is worthless," she said, in a voice full of suppressed fury. "It was written at the behest of that treacherous vizier, who wanted to use your brother to take the caliphate away from the House of Hashim. Do you think the sons of slave women are worthy of being caliphs when the sons of free women are there for the taking? Could any son of the slave Marajil measure up to the son of Zubayda? Do you know who Marajil was, and how she got close enough to your father to bear al-Ma'mun?"

"No," he answered.

"I'll tell you, then. Marajil was a slave, along with Mariya, Farida, and God knows who else. Your father, may God have mercy on his soul, was spending most of his time visiting a singer named Dananir who belonged to his vizier Yahya. I complained about it to his uncles, and they advised me to distract him by giving him new slaves as a gift. So I gave him ten slaves, of whom one was Marajil.[99] She was a Persian, and she bore him al-Ma'mun. Ja'far raised him from infancy to love the Persians, and turned

---

99 The Book of Songs, XVI.

him into what he is today. How can someone like that be your equal? That agreement you mentioned: send someone to bring it from the Ka'ba and then rip it up! It was written under false pretenses."

Relieved, al-Amin asked, "So you think I should remove my brother from the line of succession?"

"You mean you haven't already?" she asked. "Remove him before he removes you!"

He sat up. "I was meaning to consult you about this. My vizier Ibn al-Rabi says the same thing."

"Remove al-Ma'mun and ask for oaths of allegiance to your son Musa, even though he's a child. That way the caliphate will remain firmly in the family of Hashim. You're the only caliph born to Hashimite parents on both sides, and your children have a better pedigree than the rest of the 'Abbasids."

Pleased, al-Amin bowed his head and fell silent. Zubayda pressed on. "Now let's go back to that treacherous girl," she said. "It would be a good idea to kill her and be done with her."

"Kill her?" he asked. "What has she done? And what can she possibly do to harm us?"

"You pay no attention to what goes on around you," said Zubayda. "You're too busy enjoying yourself to notice that you're being fooled. But I've been keeping my eyes open and I know what's going on in your palace, even in your very bedrooms. I'm telling you that keeping that girl here is more dangerous than keeping your brother in the line of succession. Kill her!"

Al-Amin was surprised at her vehemence, not knowing what justification there was for it. "It wouldn't matter if I killed her," he said. "There are hundreds, maybe thousands, like her in the palace. But I promised Umm Habiba to keep her safe and..."

Losing her temper, Zubayda rose to her feet. "You're naïve, and you'll fall for anything! The fact that it's al-Ma'mun's daughter who's interceding for her should make you suspicious. Well then: you should know that this Maymuna is engaged to the greatest enemy of the 'Abbasids. From their correspondence it's clear that he intends to take revenge for Abu Muslim the Khurasani and Ja'far the Barmaki, and he calls the 'Abbasids liars and traitors. If you don't believe me, read this letter yourself." So saying, she pulled Behzad's letter out of her pocket and handed it to al-Amin.

Al-Amin took the letter and began reading it. Even before he finished reading it, his hands were shaking, as the letter was full of rage against the 'Abbasids and threats against them. Furious, he looked over at his mother, who was reclining on a cushion.

"So you see: your poor orphan's fiancé says that we came to power through treachery and lies. How can you keep her here among your slaves where she can see your every move? How can you keep anything secret, or make plans, with her here?"

Impressed by his mother's efforts on his behalf, he asked, "How did you get this letter? Who brought it to you?"

"I had it brought to me from your palace because I pay attention and you don't, and talking to you about it wasn't doing any good."

Roused to action, he said, "I'll have her thrown to the bottom of the Tigris this minute!"

"What? Without asking her any questions first?"

"I'll be rid of her!"

"You have a lot to learn," said Zubayda. "With someone like her, you have to learn what you can from her before you kill her. No doubt, she knows our enemies' secrets. Once you've learned what you need to know, behead her, or drown her, or do whatever you want."

"What if I call her right now and we can question her together?"

"Go ahead."

Al-Amin clapped and a page appeared. "Bring me Maymuna the slave!"

Maymuna and her grandmother had hidden themselves away in the most distant room of the palace for fear that Zubayda might see them. 'Abbada was praying that Zubayda would leave without laying eyes on her. Then they heard the page summoning Maymuna to appear before the Caliph. 'Abbada was petrified. Suspecting that Zubayda had come to urge her son to do away with her, she wished she had never gone to see her. Maymuna, who had no choice but to obey, followed the page to the meeting room. When they reached the door he went in and announced, "The slave is here, Master!"

"Bring her in!"

Abashed, Maymuna went in, her head bowed and her knees trembling in fear. She saw Zubayda reclining on a cushion, her anger making her look all the more terrifying; and al-Amin sitting next to her, looking like one of her page boys. She stopped at the door and saluted them.

"Come forward, Maymuna," said al-Amin.

Her eyes averted, she came forward, shivering with terror. And suddenly he was holding out the letter and asking, "Do you know whose this is?"

When she saw the letter she recognized it immediately, and knew that her secret was out. Her hand was shaking too violently for her to hold on to the paper, which fell from her trembling fingers. She bent to pick it up off the carpet and collapsed on the ground. Unable to stand, tears pouring down her cheeks, she tried to feign reading the letter as if unaware of its contents, but could not. Overcome by weeping, she walked on all fours to al-Amin and kissed his feet, unable to speak.

"What's wrong?" screamed Zubayda. "Why are you crying? Do you think tears will save you? Who is this Behzad? Isn't your lover the one who wants to avenge himself on the 'Abbasids?" Then, realizing that she would have to be more artful in eliciting a confession, she spoke more gently. "But don't worry: the truth will save you. Tell us: where is he now? And what do you know about the plans afoot in Khurasan? If you tell us the truth, we'll release you and let you live. If not, you're a dead woman."

"Believe me, my lady," said Maymuna, her voice choked by weeping. "Everything I know is in this letter. If you've read it you know that everything in it about him was new to me, and I swear by the head of the Commander of the Faithful that I have learned nothing more about him since."

Zubayda laughed scornfully. "You swear by the head of the Commander of the Faithful?"

"Yes, because I'm telling the truth."

"Be honest, girl, and you have nothing to fear," said al-Amin. "Otherwise we'll bring the Chief Astrologer here right now and he'll find out whatever it is you're hiding. If you deny anything he tells us, you'll suffer the consequences."

"The Commander of the Faithful may do as he wishes," she said. "I have nothing more to say."

Chapter 63

Divination

Al-Amin clapped his hands and ordered the page to summon the Chief Astrologer. After Maymuna rose to her feet and composed herself, al-Amin ordered her to sit down. She had no idea that the Chief Astrologer was none other than Salman, whom she had not seen in such a long time that she thought he must have fled or died.

After a short time, Malfan Sa'dun appeared. He was wearing a large black turban, a long cloak over a honey-colored gown, and a sash that held his pen-case, and had put on thick sideburns ending in a dense beard streaked with white. That is, he was dressed like a *dhimmi* from Harran, and not in the manner that Maymuna was used to. Had she suspected who he was, she might have recognized him from his eyes and nose.

Sa'dun entered the room, saluted, and stood waiting politely, his book under his arm. Glancing furtively at the people in the room, he recognized Maymuna and Zubayda. He also noticed Behzad's letter in front of al-Amin. He recognized it immediately, he being the one who had delivered it to Maymuna. In an instant, he had guessed why he had been summoned. Even so, he feigned ignorance. Al-Amin ordered him to sit without a curtain or partition between them, and he knelt down, eyes fixed on the ground.

Al-Amin spoke first. "We've called you here, Malfan Sa'dun, to ask you to tell us what this girl's secret is. We've asked her, but she denies everything; so we threatened her with having you divine her secret for us. So go ahead."

Zubayda, meanwhile, was looking at the astrologer without saying a word, waiting to see how much he knew. She put little faith in astrologers, but she went along with the plan hoping that the sight of this one would frighten Maymuna into confessing.

Sa'dun took out his book and asked for a censer stocked with olive wood, claiming that olive—which was easy enough to find in the Caliph's palace—was the only sort of wood that worked for divination. A sort of censer made of silver, with the fire already lit, was placed before him on a platter. All the while he busied himself reading and muttering. The others were silent. Removing a chunk of incense from his sleeve, he threw it into the fire. Then he asked for a goblet of water. Taking it between his thumb and forefinger, he stared into it for a time. Next he asked the Caliph's permission to have Maymuna come forward and put her hand on his book. Trembling, she did so. Then he took her other hand and examined the lines on her palm. Removing her hand from the book, he told her to sit down. For a moment he read from the book in a whisper. Then, nodding and smiling triumphantly, he said, "There's a good deal more to this young woman than meets the eye!"

Zubayda snickered at this declaration, which conveyed nothing in particular. Knowing what she was thinking, Sa'dun looked discreetly in her direction, though he avoided looking her in the face for fear of giving offense.

"I don't say so in order to be vague," he said. "What I mean is: she's not an ordinary young woman. She may be a slave today, but she's from a very old and distinguished line…"

"If you're sure about that," interrupted Zubayda, "then tell us who she is."

"In her presence?"

"Go ahead."

He looked into the goblet again, then back at her face. "She's the daughter of a vizier who died a violent death."

When she heard this, Maymuna shuddered and turned pale. Al-Amin turned to his mother with a smug expression, and saw that she was no less impressed than he. But, giving nothing away, she said, "You may be right about that." Then she stretched out her hand and took Behzad's letter. "What's this?" she asked.

"A letter!" he said.

"Brilliant!" scoffed Zubayda. "A child could see that. But if you're really the Chief Astrologer, tell me what it says."

"My lady, I'm sorry to see that you hold my science in such low esteem. Given what I've heard, it may be best for me not to reveal what I know. But

I'll tell you: it's a letter that can kindle a flame. Indeed, fire would be easier for your delicate hand to bear. That letter was sent to this young woman from a certain Persian. It contains expressions that praise the Persians and insult the 'Abbasids, in such a way as to distress you as well as my master the Caliph. If this general description doesn't convince you, I can give you the details. I can't be sure that my art has led me to the truth, but I've never known it to mislead me before."

Stunned, Zubayda could only confess her admiration. "You're right, Malfan. And now that you know what's in the letter, tell us where the writer is."

"He's far away, my lady. He's in Khurasan."

"What relation is this girl to him?"

"They've only known one another for a short time. If she claims otherwise, she's lying. There's no point in asking her about the threats in the letter since she knew nothing about them until she received it, nor has she heard anything further from its author."

Hearing this, Maymuna was the most astonished of all, since the man seemed to have read her mind. Had she been able to explain what she knew, she could hardly have done it better than he had. A look of relief spread over her face, and she gave al-Amin a look of silent appeal.

Though she still hated her, Zubayda was no longer determined to hurt the girl. "Do you believe this girl is innocent?" she asked Sa'dun.

"From the divination, it seems that she is," he answered. "My art has always been reliable. I think you'll find that the Commander of the Faithful has some experience of that."

She motioned for Maymuna to leave the room, and the young woman went out, hardly able to believe that she had been spared. Then Zubayda turned to Malfan Sa'dun. "I'm sure your art is reliable, Malfan, but I still feel uneasy about her."

"Because you hate her," he said, "and with good reason: her father did harm to you and to the Commander of the Faithful. If you wish, I can perform the divination again at another time. And if the Commander of the Faithful permits me to meet with her alone, I will be able to find out more about them."

"Permission is granted, Malfan," said al-Amin, giving his mother a meaningful look. As Sa'dun set about collecting the pages of his book and preparing to leave, Zubayda broke in. "Now that we've seen your art at work, tell me what the Commander of the Faithful and I are most concerned about."

Guessing that the issue of most concern to them was the activity of al-Ma'mun and his partisans in Khurasan, he said, "There are many subjects that concern you, but the most important is a man from Khurasan who has reason to fear you as you have reason to fear him. You fear him, but he fears you more."

"You're right," she said, since that was her own feeling as well. "What do you see happening next?"

He looked again at the book until his expression grew grim and sweat beaded on his brow. Finally he said, "I see no choice but to fight."

"Who will draw his sword first?" she asked.

"The first to draw will be victorious," he said. "But the future is known only to God."

She turned to al-Amin as if to say, "Didn't I tell you to depose him before he deposes you?"

"Our vizier al-Fadl Ibn al-Rabi has advised us to depose al-Ma'mun," said al-Amin, "and, if he doesn't accede to our wishes, to send an army against him. If we do that, will we win?"

Sa'dun picked up the book again, turned several pages, read a bit, and looked through the window at the sky. Taking a pen out of his sash, he dipped it into some ink and scribbled some calculations. Then he said, "As I told my master, only God knows the future, not I. But from this calculation it seems to me that the side led by al-Fadl will be the victor."

Chapter 64

The Secret Revealed

Al-Amin was now firmly convinced that it was necessary to remove his brother from the succession. He complimented Malfan Saʿdun and gave him a gift. Seeing that he was being dismissed, Salman collected his papers and pen case and went out.

Then Zubayda rose to go. Her ladies' maids entered and dressed her in the clothes that they had removed upon her arrival. As she bid goodbye to her son, she suggested that he take up residence in the Palace of Eternity, closer to her, and he promised that he would. Then she and her entourage returned to the Abode of Permanence.

After she left, al-Amin formally removed his brother and named his own son Musa heir apparent. He sent notice to Khurasan, as we have seen, then amassed an army. He intended to place it under the command of Ibn al-Rabi, but the Vizier urged him to appoint Ibn Mahan instead and the Caliph complied. The troops then marched to Rey to engage Tahir Ibn Husayn. After seeing them off, al-Amin moved to the Palace of Eternity with his inner circle, leaving Maymuna and Saʿdun in the Citadel of Al-Mansur with orders that they be well cared for.

Maymuna had left al-Amin's presence dazed but ready to dance for joy. She found her grandmother, who was waiting in an agony of suspense, and told her what had happened, lavishing praises on the skillful Chief Astrologer. Astonished, ʿAbbada said, "May God reward him! God must have used him to save us from our predicament. Without him, that evil queen would have settled for nothing less than our deaths."

"Now that Salman's given up on us," said Maymuna, "God sent someone else to rescue us. Praise be to God, who comes to the aid of the oppressed!"

Though al-Amin had moved to the Palace of Eternity, 'Abbada and Maymuna remained where they were. They had no inkling of events outside, and Maymuna could no longer divert herself by rereading Behzad's letter. Salman had been gone so long she nearly forgot about him, and might have except for his association with Behzad. How could she forget the one appointed by Behzad to watch over her, the one who had delivered his letter? She was desperately eager to find her beloved so she could tell him where she was; perhaps he would try to rescue her. But how could she manage that while locked inside four walls, with no source of news and no visitors? It was all 'Abbada could do to keep the young woman's spirits from flagging.

As they were sitting together one day, the palace forewoman came to tell them that the Chief Astrologer was asking to see Maymuna. Startled, she asked, "What does he want with us?"

"The Commander of the Faithful commanded me to admit no one to see you except the Chief Astrologer, whenever he wishes. Don't worry: he won't hurt you."

Her surprise turned to pleasure as she thought to herself that if they got along, she could ask him to tell her where Salman or Behzad was.

"Is he coming to us," she asked the forewoman, "or do we go to him?"

"He asked to see you alone in his room."

"See him alone in his room?" She recoiled. "But he's a strange man!"

"Will you let me join her?" 'Abbada asked the forewoman.

The forewoman gave her consent, and the two women rose and put on their veils. A page escorted them to Malfan Sa'dun's dwelling, which was in a distant part of the palace. The page knocked on the door, announced their arrival, and withdrew. Malfan Sa'dun, dressed in his usual attire, opened the door and welcomed them. He ushered them in and locked the door behind them. Maymuna found the room unpleasant. Wherever she looked, she saw nothing but tools and vessels that made no sense to her: tubes, beakers of different sizes and shapes, and tablets covered with drawings and script, some of which made sense and some of which looked like gibberish. Malfan Sa'dun had taken off his cloak and was now dressed in his honey-colored gown and sash, with a small turban on his head. He invited Maymuna and her grandmother to sit on the velveteen rug next to his mattress. They sat down, saying nothing. He sat down across from them and said, "Maymuna, do you know that I saved you from being executed?"

Astonished that he knew her name, she responded, "Yes, sir. I won't forget the great debt I owe you. God bless you!"

"I ask for no reward. But I will ask you to give me an honest answer to one question. Will you do that?"

"I will," she said. "I have to: you can tell what I'm thinking!"

"Do you love Behzad very much?"

She blushed and modestly averted her eyes.

"You don't need to be ashamed," he said. "Tell me!"

She sighed, but continued to look away in silence. 'Abbada spoke up: "I imagine that the Chief Astrologer knows her answer without hearing her say it."

Turning to the old woman, he said, "After all the horrors you've seen, do you still recognize the signs of love?"

Having heard of his ability to peer into people's thoughts, 'Abbada was not surprised at his reference to her identity. She said nothing.

Running his fingers through his beard, he said, "I see you love Behzad. But does he love you?"

Head bowed, she shrugged as if to say she did not know.

"If he did," he said, without waiting for an answer, "he wouldn't have left you here and disappeared. You might end up here for the rest of your life. But since I care for your well-being, I've come up with a way to guarantee your safety and happiness. If you do as I say, you'll be making the right choice."

"What is that, sir?"

"I know a young man—one of the finest in Baghdad, and the noblest. He loves you to the point of misery, but you don't care for him." He stopped and cleared his throat. Realizing that he was talking about Ibn al-Fadl, the son of Ibn al-Rabi, she couldn't help but shudder. She turned to her grandmother as if asking her to answer on her behalf. 'Abbada started to speak, but Sa'dun spoke first, saying, "I know what you're going to say, but refusing him won't help. He's a powerful man, and if he asks the Commander of the Faithful for you, he'll hand you over to him. So you're better off accepting of your own accord. That's my advice. Behzad is far away. And who knows? You may never see him again."

Hearing this, Maymuna felt her chest tighten. Her emotions surged, and she wept. 'Abbada rose, bowed to Malfan Sa'dun, and said in a pleading tone, "Since you can read minds and you know who we are, I beg you to be a friend to us, not an enemy." She swallowed hard.

Gesturing for her to sit down, he asked, "And what is it you want?"

"The young man you've mentioned can hope for nothing from us, and you know why. We'd rather die than accept his proposal. Instead I'm asking you to use your art to address a matter that concerns us."

"Which is..?"

"We've lost track of someone who might be of great help to us," she said. "Behzad left him to take care of us. He delivered the letter to Maymuna and then disappeared. Could you use your divination to find him for us?"

"It's Salman you're looking for, is it not?"

"Yes."

"The Vizier is looking for him too!"

"Is he in Baghad?"

"He's in this palace."

"In this palace?" asked Maymuna, startled.

"And in this room!" he said.

At that moment, 'Abbada felt as if scales had fallen from her eyes. Maymuna, remembering Salman's voice, cried, "Salman…Salman!"

"Don't raise your voice," he said. "Yes, it's Salman, and the Chief Astrologer too!"

Her face lit up, and she could not stop herself from laughing. Her heart beat joyfully, the prospect of receiving news of Behzad making her almost as happy as she would have been to see him. But she no longer knew what to ask Salman, or how to pose a question. She tried to speak but stammered incoherently. Salman took the initiative, saying, "You'll blame me for staying in hiding for so long, but I did it for your own good. When it seemed like the right time, I reappeared. It seems I chose the right time!"

"You saved our lives," said 'Abbada. "God bless you and…"

"Where is Behzad now?" asked Maymuna, interrupting her grandmother.

"In Baghdad, or just outside it."

"In Baghdad? Won't he come here?"

"Do you think it's so easy? He won't appear until he's ready. And Baghdad has changed a good deal since the last time he was here. He has the partisans working in secret again, and they're making life difficult for that boy who holds the caliph's staff."

"How wonderful, Salman! How noble you are! Behzad is back from Khurasan. Have you seen him?"

"I've seen him and spoken to him."

"Where did you see him? How?"

"We have a secret place where we meet."

"Then he's here and we'll see him?" she asked, beaming. "When?"

"When the time is right," he said. "Don't be so demanding!"

"As you wish, then," said Maymuna. "What about now? What do you plan to do with us?"

"Stay here, as you were, and don't tell a soul what you've seen until the right time. I think you trust me, right?"

"It's been a long time," said 'Abbada, "since we've heard anything about al-Ma'mun and al-Amin and what's going on between them."

"Let me assure you, my lady," he said, "that God will see you, and all of us, avenged. Al-Amin removed his brother from the line of succession, and al-Ma'mun did the same to him. The Persians rallied around al-Ma'mun because his mother was Persian. They put together an army under the command of Tahir Ibn Husayn, and al-Amin sent an army under the command of Ibn Mahan, who was the police chief. The two armies met in Rey, and al-Ma'mun's side won. Ibn Mahan was killed and his troops were scattered. When al-Amin heard the news he didn't know what to do, so he sent for me. I went to see him at the Palace of Eternity. He asked my advice and I told him to send Ibn al-Rabi to lead the second expedition, making this a condition of winning the war. I said that knowing full well that Ibn al-Rabi wouldn't go; and in fact he went into hiding. The second expedition was defeated too. Al-Amin's condition grew worse and his own men thought so little of him they tried to depose him. But they failed because I wouldn't support them. If I had wanted it to happen, they would have done it; but all I wanted was to weaken him."

Maymuna was impressed with Salman's shrewdness, especially with the way he had manipulated Ibn al-Rabi and his son.

"Stay here in al-Mansur's palace and the forewoman will take care of you. I may go see the Caliph and spend a few days in the Palace of Eternity."

He clapped for his page. "Take these two ladies to the palace and deliver them to Farida, the forewoman, and tell her that I'm coming to see her."

After they had left, Salman dressed and ordered the page to prepare his mule for the journey to the Palace of Eternity. On the way, he stopped to see the forewoman and told her to take care of Maymuna and 'Abbada. She signaled her assent. Then he turned toward the Palace of Eternity, the page at his side. As he rode past, people stared at him and stepped aside, having heard stories about his miraculous skill as an astrologer.

Chapter 65

Al-Amin and his Ring-Fish

Salman rode on to the Palace of Eternity, where he found a crowd of Ruffians instead of soldiers guarding the gate. One of them recognized him and rose to salute him, then made way. As he rode into the court on his mule, he met Harch riding out on horseback. Spotting Sa'dun, the Ruffian chief stopped his horse and greeted him. Sa'dun asked him why his men, not the soldiers, were at the gate.

"The army's angry with the Commander of the Faithful."

"Why?"

"It's a long story," said Harch, "and I can't tell you all of it while we're on horseback. It's probably not news to you, either. Here's the short version. After Tahir and his men won the battle at Rey and killed Ibn Mahan, the Caliph's men lost their fighting spirit and fled. Then Tahir advanced and took the provinces of Jibal. Al-Amin sent another army, but they got beaten too. His grip on power weakened to the point that his own generals tried to oust him, but they didn't follow through, as you know. Tahir and his army kept on advancing: they got to Ahwaz, then took over Wasit, and Ctesiphon, and then Sarsar close by. Meanwhile the Caliph was collecting money and paying it out to his men. When Tahir's men heard about it, they got greedy, and a group of them went to al-Amin. He gave them money, drenched their beards with perfume and treated them very well. His troops became angry because he never did that for them, and they scattered. At which point he sent for me and told me to bring my men to help him."

Sa'dun interrupted him with a laugh. "One man's misfortune is another man's blessing! I don't doubt al-Amin paid you well. But what's good for you is good for me. And you certainly deserve what you're getting more than those treacherous commanders of his, not to mention the viziers. I heard that when Ibn al-Rabi saw things going against him, he disappeared, even though he's the cause of this catastrophe." Bidding Harch goodbye, he turned his mount away; but the Ruffian chief stopped him, saying, "When you see the Caliph, you'll understand why matters have gotten out of hand."

Sa'dun did not know what he meant. But no sooner had he passed through the third of the palace gates and entered the grounds than he saw that something was wrong.

Handing the reins to his page, he set off through the grounds, leaning on his stick. Everywhere he looked he saw page boys, some of them barefoot and bareheaded, running to and fro. Something about the scene frightened him. He continued along one of the paths until he reached a pool set amid the gardens in front of the palace. All around the pool the pages had gathered. Some had taken off their clothes and dived in, while others were staring into the water. Then he saw al-Amin himself coming toward him, looking distraught. The Caliph was dressed in his banquet clothes, but in the excitement had lost his tall cap. Sa'dun thought it likely that some plot to assassinate him had been uncovered and that the pages were busy searching for the plotter, thinking that he had gone into the pool in the hope of escaping into the Tigris. The pool was fed by a channel that ran under the palace wall, and an escapee who was a good swimmer could follow the canal down to the river, the only barrier being an easily removed grate that lay across the outlet of the channel.

But then Salman heard al-Amin shouting, "Where's my ring-fish? Where did it go? Who took it? Sa'id! Jawhar! Kawthar! Come here! I think it's in the pool! Find it! Cast the nets!"

Now Salman, remembering what Harch had said, understood what was happening. The reason for all the fuss and commotion was that al-Amin had lost his ring-fish. Caught for him when it was small, the fish had two pearl-studded gold earrings attached to it,[100] and the Caliph would frequently amuse himself by playing with it. Just as Sa'dun was coming in, the fish disappeared, and al-Amin had the whole palace busy looking for it. Seeing this, Sa'dun stepped back to wait until the Caliph regained his wits or found his fish. "How can a dynasty headed by a caliph like this possibly endure?" he thought. "Will anyone be surprised to see his brother, who spares no effort in his own cause, and has loyal troops to fight for him,

---

100 Mas'udi, II.

triumph in the end? This Caliph has no one on his side but flatterers who want his money. Such are the wages of hubris. It won't be long before this dynasty falls, and justice triumphs over falsehood."

As these thoughts were passing through his mind, he saw that al-Amin was looking at him, his dissipation and frolic giving way to concern. The Caliph beckoned him, and Saʿdun followed him through the inner gate of the palace. At the end of the reception hall was a domed structure called a "folly." It was made of sandalwood and measured ten cubits on a side.[101] It was padded with silk, brocade woven with golden thread, and other precious fabrics. At the door stood a knot of important-looking men who made way for the Caliph as he passed. Salman recognized only two of them: Ibrahim Ibn Mahdi, the Caliph's uncle; and Sulayman Ibn al-Mansur, one of the senior members of the clan of Hashim. Al-Amin invited Salman into the folly and dismissed the others. Leaving his stick and shoes at the door, Salman followed him inside. Al-Amin took a seat on the other side and invited Salman to sit as well. As he did so, he marveled at the change in the Caliph. Looking around, he saw that a singing and drinking party had been going on before he arrived. There were cups scattered about, and pitchers here and there, some full and others empty, and plates of different sorts of fruit lined up in rows. In front of al-Amin was a crystal drinking bowl that looked big enough to hold five pints of wine. It had been knocked over and broken. There were two more bowls like it perched on cushions where members of his inner circle had been sitting—perhaps Sulayman Ibn al-Mansur and Ibrahim Ibn al-Mahdi, who were the highest-ranked of his companions.

Saʿdun saw immediately that al-Amin had been sitting with his companions when he learned of the loss of his ring-fish and rushed off to look for it. Still finding it odd to see the Caliph shift so abruptly from jest to earnest, he waited for him to speak first. Sweeping the broken bowl aside, al-Amin looked at Saʿdun, sighed, and said, "I have no one left to trust except you. All my men have scattered. None of them stayed loyal; all they wanted was my money. You know so much and you can uncover secrets, and so I sent for you to ask you what to do. I'm sorry that you found me caught up in that silliness with the page boys, and then came in here and found that we've been enjoying ourselves even though there's plenty we should be worried about." He sighed even more deeply. "But I do it to forget that I'm

---

101 A cubit, at least during the reign of al-Maʾmun (813-833), measured 48.25 cm or about 19 inches. *Translator's Note*

desperate. I sent for some of my uncles, and they brought singers and wine. We drank and listened, but it didn't make me feel any better. Actually, it made me feel worse: the women kept singing verses that were bad omens—whether on purpose or not, I don't know. One of them sang:

'They slew the king and took his throne
'As the nobles did in Ctesiphon

"By God, I'm afraid of everyone around me. It's like the court of Chosroes: no one cares about me.[102] Even Ibn al-Rabi, my vizier, has abandoned me and disappeared. And then just to make me feel worse, one of the singers got up for some reason and tripped over this bowl and broke it. It's my special bowl that I've been drinking from for years and nothing's ever happened to it before." In a strangled voice, he asked, "Am I right to think it's a bad omen?"

"May no harm befall you, Sire!"

"Even you," interrupted the Caliph, "didn't tell me the truth that time...or maybe it was your astrology that lied."

"How so?"

"Remember when we were in al-Mansur's palace and I asked you what would happen if I fought my brother and you told me I would win?"

Sa'dun bowed his head as if mulling over the problem. Then he said, "If my master thinks back to what I said that day, he will realize that I was right. I said that my art told me that 'the side led by al-Fadl will be the victor.' Did al-Fadl Ibn al-Rabi lead the last campaign?"

"No. I wanted to send him, but he dodged it. When he saw that I meant to insist, he decided he didn't want the responsibility. That's when he disappeared. I haven't seen him since, and I have no idea where he is."

Salman shook his head as if in disbelief. Then he sat pensive for a few moments, rubbing his brow. "It seems that my divination was accurate in another way, too. I just remembered that your brother's vizier in Khurasan is also named al-Fadl: al-Fadl Ibn Sahl. He's doing for your brother what

---

102 The Sasanian emperor Khosrow Aparwiz II (called Chosroes in Greek and Kisra in Arabic, but not to be confused with his predecessor Chosroes or Khosrow I Anoshiravan, r. 531-79 AD) was assassinated in 628. *Translator's Note*

the other al-Fadl has been unable to do for you. I have faith in my art. If there's a mistake, it's in the interpretation of the results."

His faith in the astrologer restored, al-Amin said, "As you know, I have no more troops and no more money. I melted down all the gold and silver vessels in the palace to mint coins, and sold off everything I could. I even collected whatever I could from the merchants[103] to pay off the army. But none of it has done me any good: here I am, as you can see." He swallowed hard, and Sa'dun could see tears in his eyes. But he felt no pity for the Caliph. If he seemed to show compassion, it was only to further his aims. In this case, his aim was to poison the relationship between the two brothers and prevent any sort of reconciliation. If the two did manage a truce, all the Persians' efforts would be in vain. Feigning grief over the Caliph's predicament, he asked, "Did you look for valuables in your brother's palace? I recall al-Ma'mun's man Nawfal had been keeping some property there since the days of our master al-Rashid."

"Nawfal had a million dirhams, and we took them. We also confiscated his properties and estates."

Bowing his head to hide his delight that al-Amin's coffers stood empty, Sa'dun said, "You need the money to keep the army happy. But there's another army here that will fight without pay—they'll collect it by pillage."

"You mean the Ruffians and Bandits?"

"That's right. They fight naked, and their only weapons are slingshots and sacks of palm fiber, but they can do more damage with their chunks of gravel than soldiers can with swords and spears.[104] There are about fifty thousand of them in Baghdad right now. Why not order their chief to mobilize them for you?"

"Did you imagine I hadn't thought of that?" said al-Amin. "Harch was just here. I told him to prepare his men and he promised he would. I think he's also going to round up peddlers and prisoners and pickpockets and all the rabble and riffraff he can find in the markets. If they fight, they'll destroy the city. But..." He fell silent.

---

103 Ibn al-Athir VI; *Tales of the Kings.*

104 According to the Arabic chronicles, the Ruffians who defended Baghdad used the fibrous leaves of palm trees to weave armor, shields, and helmets for themselves. Lacking horses, they would ride on one another's backs. Despite these disadvantages, they were reportedly so ferocious that they could hold their own against al-Ma'mun's armored cavalry. *Translator's Note*

Sa'dun saw that he was holding something back so he waited and said nothing. Al-Amin then spoke. "Some of the few loyal advisors I have left have told me to take my remaining men and leave Baghdad. I've got seven thousand horsemen of the Sons. They say I should take them and get out through one of the city gates at night and then go to Northern Iraq or Syria. There they can collect taxes for me and I can have a big kingdom to rule. I'll leave Baghdad to those who want it, and wait for God to do as He wills. What do you think?"

From al-Amin's point of view, at least, it was a very good suggestion. If he followed it, Sa'dun realized, he might survive, and his survival meant the undoing of all that the Persians had worked so hard to achieve.

"Does the Commander of the Faithful really think it's a good idea to flee?" he asked. "And how can he take seven thousand men through a gate with the city surrounded on all sides by the enemy? If, God forbid, he should fall into their hands as a refugee, they may take liberties with him that they wouldn't under other circumstances."

"Is there no way to get out of Baghdad?" he said.

"If the Commander of the Faithful agrees," said Sa'dun, "we can climb up to the top of one of the minarets and look out over the whole city and see just where his enemies are. Then he can decide what to do."

Chapter 66

A Mother's Intuition

Al-Amin agreed to this proposal and got to his feet, saying, "There's a tall minaret in this palace that we can climb without anyone knowing." Sa'dun followed him out. They climbed the minaret and from the top gazed out over Baghdad and its palaces. Turning first to the west, Sa'dun said, "Sire, do you see where Harthama Ibn A'yan is camped there by Nahrabin beyond the Tigris? And those are the tents of 'Ubayd Allah Ibn Waddah in Shammasiyya, with a vast army; they're holding the biggest of the bridges. Tahir's army controls the Khurasan road; I don't see any way to flee in that direction. Over to the west, there's Tahir and his army on the grounds by the Granary Gate. I can see them advancing with their standards. They've entered Karkh and surrounded the Kufa Gate. They're in all the districts to the west and the south, and they've nearly got us encircled. The Ruffians are fighting them off with their slingshots: do you see the chunks of rock flying above the rooftops?"

Pallid and miserable, al-Amin was watching the scene with growing certainty of his imminent defeat. He said nothing. Then he looked north and saw that Harbiyya was burning. "My God!" he said. "What's that?"

"It's the rabble and the prisoners," said Sa'dun. "With everyone busy fighting, they've set fire to the buildings to make them easier to pillage. Let's go down, Sire, to your palace. It's well fortified and you'll be safe there."

Al-Amin climbed down with Sa'dun behind him. When they reached the residence they found everything topsy-turvy. Attendants were running to and fro as if searching for someone. The moment they laid eyes on al-Amin, they jumped back, crying, "Here's our master, the Commander of the Faithful! He's here!"

A moment later, the Caliph's mother Zubayda appeared, then ran towards him and clasped him to her chest, tears running down her face. "My child!" she cried. "Where have you been? I was so worried when I couldn't find you! They told me that you had been sitting right here, but then they couldn't find you, and they said you hadn't gone out, either. To lose you at a time like this! I was frantic."

Seeing his mother so excited, al-Amin couldn't help weeping as well. But then he pulled himself together and, with a great display of composure, said, "What are you frightened of, Mother? Everything is fine. I was busy with the Chief Astrologer. What brings you here at this hour?"

Zubayda took hold of al-Amin and led him into a nearby room, with Sa'dun on their heels. After the door closed behind them, she said, "I'm here for a good reason. As you know, I've been thinking hard about how to help you. All along I had a feeling that the man from Khurasan, Behzad, poses some kind of threat to us. I've been sending spies to look for him. I've learned that he's in Baghdad, but I don't know where he lives. Then, as I was waiting to hear more, I had a bad dream. I don't want to tell anyone about it: I only want to forget it. But now I can't wait any longer for this Behzad to come out in the open. Arresting him will be as good as defeating half an army. From the minute he arrived here, we've been retreating, while Tahir's forces get stronger. Behzad is a powerful leader with influence over some of the most important men in Baghdad. I've told you many times that he's the head of secret societies that include some of the biggest merchants in the city." So saying, she sat down.

Al-Amin took a seat as well and gestured for Sa'dun to do the same. Then he asked his mother, "So where is he?"

"I don't know," she said. "But I'm going to send for that girl and see whether she can tell us, and save us a great deal of trouble."

Al-Amin turned to Sa'dun as if soliciting his opinion. The latter nodded as if to say that Zubayda might be right.

"But what do we need the girl for if we have the Chief Astrologer right here?" said al-Amin.

"Tell us, Malfan," she said, sitting up on her cushion next to her son, "what your art tells us about that Khurasani."

Sa'dun took out his book and read a bit. He put a piece of incense in his mouth and chewed on it. Then he said, "He's in Baghdad, my lady."

"But where exactly?" she asked.

"It looks as if he's between two bodies of water, but not in the river. I need more time and better weather to tell you exactly where. The girl, by the way, doesn't know where he is. And how could she? She's been locked up in the Caliph's palace without making contact with anyone."

Zubaydah thought for a moment. "I know that Ibn al-Fadl's in love with her and she doesn't want him. If it weren't for his father's disappearance I would marry her off to him against her wishes." Then she said, "That Ibn al-Rabi ran away just when we needed him. He's the cause of all these disasters. He's the one who pushed al-Amin to depose his brother and send armies after him. God damn that traitor!" Zubayda swallowed hard, as if sensing the danger that surrounded her son. Looking grave, she went on. "But I have faith that he'll come back. We'll see!"

Sensing her anxiety, al-Amin tried to reassure her. With an effortful show of composure and a forced smile, he said, "Don't curse anyone, Mother. All traitors will get what they deserve. Go back to your palace and don't worry. Pray for victory, and don't be fooled by all the enemy soldiers you see. God willing, we'll beat them in the end. The Ruffians will do their job."

Seeing that al-Amin wanted her to go, Zubayda rose; but even as she prepared to depart, she felt an impulse to stay. Her heart would not let her leave her son, as if warning her that he was in danger. She was on the verge of sitting down again, but then felt that doing so would make him uncomfortable. For a few moments she hesitated, busying herself with her veil and her headdress. Then she put her arms around al-Amin, showering his neck with kisses. Feeling the warmth of her tears, he pushed her gently back and kissed her between the breasts, fighting his own impulse to weep. Then she hurried out, feeling as if her heart had been torn from her breast. Assembling her entourage, she returned to her palace.

The sun was setting, and Sa'dun made motions to leave. "Does my master have any orders for me?"

"Stay here," said al-Amin. "Don't leave me. I'll need you tonight."

Unsure what that might mean, Sa'dun studied the Caliph's face. He noticed an anxiety there he had not seen before. He rose to go to one of the guest rooms, but al-Amin motioned for him to stay. Then he clapped to summon a page. "Bring me wine, and light the candles." After the page had gone, al-Amin unwound his turban and groaned. "They reproach me for being addicted to drink," he said, "but what else is a desperate man to do? Wine will dull the pain until God decides my fate."

Sa'dun sat down, politely ignoring this remark. The pages came in carrying a table laden with wine and fruit, and lit the big candles named after al-Amin. "Is my uncle Ibrahim here?" al-Amin shouted at the page. He meant Ibrahim Ibn al-Mahdi, the singer.

"No, Sire."

Al-Amin gestured for the page to fill the goblet. He picked it up and gestured for another, saying to Sa'dun, "Won't you drink, Malfan?"

"If the Commander of the Faithful commands it, I will," he said. "But I never have before. Drink and divination don't mix."

"Don't pour him any, then," said al-Amin to the cupbearer. "We need his art tonight. And tell the man at the door that if a messenger comes, to let him in, no matter how late it is."

Now more curious than ever about what al-Amin was thinking, Salman waited to see what he would do next. After a few goblets, the Caliph regained his good cheer. Turning to Sa'dun, he said, "Do you know why I've kept you here after sending all the others away?"

"No, Sire."

"If there is anyone who should know this secret, it would be my inner circle; but I don't trust any of them now that I've seen how many of my enemies are disguised as friends. All of them want to betray me and take my money. Take my vizier: he caused this rift between me and my brother. He's the one who pushed me to fight al-Ma'mun, and now that everything's gone wrong, he fears for his life and disappears, without caring about the danger I might be in. He's not the only one, either. All my officials stayed with me until I had spent my coins, sold off my jewels, and melted down my gold; and then, when they saw I had nothing left, they abandoned me. Now my enemies have me under siege, and they've even cut off the food supply." As if afraid of bursting into tears, he toyed with his wine and fruit. Handing a piece to Sa'dun, he said, "How can anyone cursed with advisers like mine ever hope to prosper?"

Delighted by this complaint, Sa'dun felt certain that the dynasty would soon fall. But he feigned dismay, saying, "The Commander of the Faithful must not despair. God will take his side. Let us rely on Him!"

"For a long time now," said al-Amin, "I let myself be deceived by false hopes. I believed whatever those rotten flatterers told me, and made a fool of myself. Now that I'm at war with my brother, I see how much more loyal his men are, and how much firmer his commanders stand; and I can see things as they really are. But even if I wanted to have a reconciliation, I couldn't, because no one will act as a go-between. I'm telling you things I've told no one else, not even my mother."

Sa'dun gestured as if to say that the secret would go no further.

"I'll tell you something more. When I realized I had no more men and no more money, I sent a message to Harthama[105] on the east bank, asking for safe passage. I'm waiting for his answer now. Do you think I did the right thing?"

---

105 Harthama Ibn Ay'an (d. 816 AD) was a long-serving 'Abbasid general who played a major role, along with Tahir, in the siege of Baghdad. Unlike Tahir, he was well-known to al-Amin. *Translator's Note*

Chapter 67

Flight

Putting on a mournful expression, Saʿdun raised his eyebrows and said, "Yes, it was the right thing to do. There's nothing shameful about asking for safe passage, especially since you'll be under your brother's protection, and blood always stays loyal to blood. But…" He fell silent.

Al-Amin was peeling an apple as he listened. When Saʿdun stopped he said, "But what?"

"I'm not sure it's a good idea to tell Harthama but not Tahir, since it's Tahir who has this part of the city under siege."

With a sigh, al-Amin tossed the apple away. "No," he said. "I won't go to Tahir. He gives me a bad feeling, and I don't like him. Once I dreamed that I was standing on a wall made of mud brick that reached all the way up to the sky. It was very broad at the bottom, too: it was the highest and widest wall in the world. I was wearing my black raiment, my sash, and my sword. At the bottom of the wall was Tahir. He was hitting the wall. He kept hitting it until it collapsed, and my cap fell off my head. So I don't like him. But Harthama is one of our dependents. He's like a father to me, and I trust him."

Saʿdun was overjoyed at this piece of news, but feigned approval of al-Amin's choice, saying, "Our master has the last word."

Meanwhile a page had appeared. "The Caliph's messenger is at the door."

Looking surprised, al-Amin said, "Let him in immediately."

The messenger came in dressed in the attire of a merchant. Al-Amin rose and asked, "What is it?"

"Shall I tell it all?"

"Go ahead."

"I met Harthama," said the messenger, "and conveyed your offer. He said that he was at your disposal, and would consider it an honor to welcome the Commander of the Faithful. But he would prefer you to come out to him tomorrow night, not tonight, and..."

Al-Amin was leaning forward to hear every word, forgetting in his excitement to ask the man to sit down. After hearing the beginning of the message, he motioned for him to sit and then asked, "And then? Go ahead, don't be scared. Why did he postpone the meeting?"

Sitting down politely, the messenger said, "Because he's certain that having the Commander of the Faithful come to him will upset Tahir. Tahir is nearby, and he's tightened the siege the way he has in the hope that the Commander of the Faithful will choose to surrender to him. It's a matter of pride. Tahir's got spies planted all over this area. Harthama told me that he's seen suspicious activity on the riverbank, and he doesn't want any misfortune to befall the Commander of the Faithful."

Al-Amin seemed to understand that Tahir was a threat to him, but said, "I'm going to Harthama, and it has to be tonight, since I'm all alone here. My guards and freedmen have all scattered, and I'm afraid that if Tahir finds out he'll come in after me."

Looking distressed, he rose and called for white clothes and a black cape. He put them on and wrapped a light turban around his head. Then he called for the page to bring his two sons. Meanwhile, Sa'dun had risen to his feet out of respect. "Does my master have any orders for me?" he asked. "I would give my life for his!"

"Stay with me until I leave," said al-Amin. "I feel so alone."

His two sons were brought in. Weeping, he embraced them and bid them farewell, saying, "I give you into the care of God." Wiping his eyes on his sleeve, he walked over to a mule that had been readied for him and mounted it. He gestured his farewell to Sa'dun, who was standing beside him. Sa'dun kissed the mule's stirrup, saying, "May God watch over your path!"

Al-Amin asked him to look after his family. Then rode away toward the river, where Harthama's boat awaited him. He boarded and the captain turned the rudder toward the far shore. Harthama himself was on board, along with a number of his men. When the Caliph came on board, they rose, except for Harthama, who pleaded an affliction of gout and fell to his knees, then embraced him, held him close, and seated him on his lap to comfort him. It was a cold night: the Caliph's departure took place on Sunday, 25 Muharram, 198 AH, or September 28, 813 AD.[106] Seeing movement on the shore, Harthama ordered the boatmen to row hard. A number of skiffs that belonged to Tahir had been moored along the bank. Suddenly they sped out to Harthama's vessel, and the men on board pierced her hull and showered her with bricks and arrows. The boat foundered and capsized. Harthama and al-Amin fell into the water. Al-Amin tore off his clothes and swam to shore, followed by Harthama. Happy to have made it safely off the boat, the men put al-Amin on a donkey and rode off looking for a place to hide.

For his part, Salman, after bidding farewell to al-Amin, had begun thinking about how to kill him. As long as the Caliph was alive, there was still a chance of reconciliation, which would do the Persian cause no good. Stripping off his astrologer's costume, he had raced to the riverbank ahead of al-Amin and told Tahir's men that the Caliph was on his way to Harthama's boat. Tahir's forces were thus lying in wait for the Caliph. When they saw him board the boat they scuttled it, as we have seen. Learning that al-Amin had survived the sinking, Salman joined the search, and managed to join the men who were taking the Caliph to a new hiding place. After noting the place, he returned to Behzad.

Since arriving in Baghdad, Behzad had been urging the Shi'ite to take al-Ma'mun's side. Among those who joined him were the members of the Khurrami sect who had promised to do so. Although he did not make himself known to Tahir, he took every opportunity to assist his troops, as he had done at Rey. His leadership of the Khurramis in Baghdad proved of great help to al-Ma'mun's forces as they worked to weaken al-Amin's partisans, undermine his cause, and force him to surrender. Behzad did not advocate taking the Caliph prisoner. Instead, he hoped to meet him in battle, confront him, and kill him with his dagger, thereby fulfilling his vow to his mother, and return to her in triumph with the head. During his stay in and around the city, he would meet up with Salman and ask him for news, particularly news of Maymuna. Salman would reassure him, all the more so in order to prevent Behzad's romantic preoccupations from interfering with the completion of their task. As far as the mission was concerned, Salman had as much at stake as Behzad, though his aspirations were for Khurasan

---

106 Ibn al-Athir VI; General Calendar. [The date actually corresponds to September 25. *Translator's note*]

rather than Baghdad. It may be, too, that he envied Behzad his meeting with his beloved, and thus did his best to keep them apart. In any case, he continued to tell each of the parties that the other was well, and Behzad did not insist on going to see Maymuna, for fear that his love might prevent him from carrying out his appointed task.

Chapter 68

Execution

Much time passed in this manner, until the siege closed in, as we have seen. By then, Behzad was staying at the house of a Khurrami in Karkh. Based on what he heard people saying about al-Amin, he expected the Caliph to surrender. One night, as midnight approached, he had undressed, hung his weapons on the wall above his head, and fallen asleep when a boy woke him to tell him that Salman had arrived. Knowing that Salman would not have come at such an hour except for a good reason, Behzad rose and asked the boy to admit him. Salman came in dressed neither as the Chief Astrologer nor as Behzad's manservant. He looked exhausted.

"Salman, what's wrong?" cried Behzad.

"Victory is nearly ours," he said.

"Of that I have no doubt. But what's happened?"

Salman reported everything, ending with: "Al-Amin is in hiding, in a private house on the east side. When I left him, he was wearing nothing but his trousers and a turban, with a ragged piece of cloth around his shoulders. There with him is Ahmad Ibn Sallam, head of the Grievance Court; they met by chance during his escape. I heard al-Amin asking him who he was. Then he recognized him and relaxed a bit. I heard him say, 'Hold me; I'm alone and afraid.' So Ahmad embraced him and gave him a padded jacket he had with him. Then I heard him say, 'Ahmad, what happened to my brother?' He said, 'He's still alive.' Al-Amin said, 'Damn their couriers! They told me he was dead,' as if he were trying to justify going to war against him, though I'm sure he knew better. 'Damn your viziers!' said Ibn Sallam. The last thing I heard al-Amin ask was, 'What do you think they'll do with me? Will they kill me or keep their promise to spare me?'

283

Ibn Sallam answered that of course they would keep their promise. But he's wrong," said Salman, clearing his throat.

Realizing that Salman intended to break the promise of safe conduct, Behzad asked, "What do mean? Do you intend to violate our oath?"

"Do you intend to let that man live?" replied Salman. "If they take al-Amin to his brother, they'll be reconciled, and all our work will be wasted. Why did you bring that dagger with you from Khurasan? You said you'd vowed to avenge Abu Muslim and Ja'far, and now you have the chance: the man is in our hands, and killing him will complete our victory. How will you fulfill your vow by letting him escape?"

"You know that I'm the greatest enemy of that dynasty," said Behzad. "I've dedicated my life to defeating them, and now I've succeeded, thank God. It's one of my most fervent wishes to kill that Caliph by my own hand using that dagger, and add his head to the two I left in Marv. But I want to kill him on the battlefield. I want him to be armed and ready. I don't want to stab him in the back while he's unarmed and afraid and under our promise of protection. How can we break our oaths when the reason we hate this dynasty most for is breaking oaths and betraying our heroes? Every traitor is himself betrayed in the end."

Seeing the conviction in his eyes, Salman was disappointed, as he could see no reason for such generosity. He himself was a man of shrewdness and artifice, concerned only with achieving his aims, undaunted by obstacles, and untroubled by the lies, tricks, and betrayals that were necessary to attain his goals. Conscience had no hold on him, nor was he bound by his word. For this reason, the supreme commander in Khurasan had chosen him for this mission, which required precisely those characteristics. In this respect he differed from Behzad, who led with honor, and acted in accordance with the generosity, honesty, and bravery that were part of his nature.

Listening to Behzad, Salman, though not surprised, regretted having tried to assign the task to him. Pretending to have been convinced, he said, "You're right, Behzad. What a noble fellow you are!" Then, feigning sleepiness, he lay down. Behzad, too, lay down, thinking of how far their mission had progressed, and wondering how it would end. Toward the end of the night, he was suddenly awakened by a scraping sound. He opened his eyes to see a shadowy figure standing beside his bed, hands raised to the wall. He jumped up and said calmly, "Who's there?"

He saw something drop from the man's hand onto the bed. Looking hard, he saw that it was his dagger, and that the man was Salman. "What are you doing?" he asked.

"Nothing," came the reply. "It's already done. Here's your dagger: take it."

Picking up the dagger, he saw traces of blood. "What have you done?" he asked. "Did you kill him?"

"We've killed him, and may God never resurrect him. You wanted to let him live as a stumbling block in our path, but now he's dead and we're well rid of him."

"You killed him?" cried Behzad. "With my dagger?"

"Your dagger, as you yourself said, was sworn to that purpose. I decided to take responsibility for the killing and let you keep your noble ideals and purity of heart intact." Salman shook his head. "I've never seen anyone found a dynasty without cunning or guile, the way you wanted to do. Even Abu Muslim wouldn't have won if he hadn't resorted to treachery. Al-Mansur would never have established his rule without it; and if al-Rashid hadn't double-crossed Ja'far, he might have lost the caliphate. Go back to the first days of Islam. 'Ali and his sons failed as statesmen for one reason: they were honest and loyal, and never resorted to plots and schemes. If Mu'awiya hadn't been shrewd and crafty, he would never have founded a state. The descendants of 'Ali inherited his love of justice and his scrupulous loyalty, and they were all defeated, just as he was. Now it's our turn, and we need to do our own double-crossing. But remember: I didn't ask you to commit the crime. I took responsibility for it myself."

Impressed as he was with this explanation, Behzad still protested. "But every traitor is himself betrayed in the end, as history shows." Then he fell silent, relieved that al-Amin had been disposed of by someone else, leaving him blameless. "How did you do it? How did you kill him, for God's sake?"

"I stole your dagger and I put on the uniform of a Persian soldier. I raced back to where I had left al-Amin. It was already past midnight, and pitch-dark. At the gate I found some Persians with drawn swords. I joined them and went in with them to find al-Amin. He was sitting down when we came in, and when he saw us he got up. He looked terrified. He said, 'We are of God and to Him we return.[107] I'm going to die a martyr! Is there no one to save me? Are none of the Sons here?' More of us came in. He had

---

107 Qur'an 2:156. *Translator's Note*

a cushion in his hand and he tried to protect himself with it, saying, 'Damn you! I'm the cousin of the Prophet of God! I'm the son of al-Rashid! I'm the brother of al-Ma'mun! Fear God and don't hurt me!'"

Salman continued the story. "I was afraid that the soldiers would take pity on him and ruin everything, so I urged on the man in front of me, who had drawn his sword. I shouted, 'Get him!' The man struck al-Amin on the head and al-Amin threw the cushion at him. So I stepped up and stabbed al-Amin in the gut. That was the blow that got him. He kept saying, 'He's killed me!' Then the others came forward, beheaded him from behind, and took his head to Tahir.[108] Here's your dagger back. If you think I deserve to be punished, then go ahead and judge me."

"It seems they were going to kill him no matter what," said Behzad. "But you made sure it was my dagger that did the killing so that my vow would be fulfilled. May God have mercy on al-Amin, and my congratulations to you: our mission is over."

"So then we're going back to Khurasan tomorrow?"

"What's the hurry?"

With a malicious squint, Salman said, "You've completed your task and made provision for your future: Maymuna's ready and waiting. Whether you stay here or go somewhere else doesn't matter. But I've got business to take care of in Khurasan, and I want to get back there quickly."

"But aren't you going to get Maymuna out of the place where you've locked her up?"

"Right you are," said Salman, laughing. "She's in the Palace of Al-Mansur, and tomorrow I'll hand her over to you, with her grandmother too. Will that satisfy you?"

"Of course," said Behzad. "I'm very grateful to you. It's about time for us to treat one another as equals: from now on, you are my brother and friend. With the end of our mission, you are no longer a servant."

Salman thanked him. The next morning they rose early. "I'm going to the Palace of Al-Mansur," said Salman, "dressed as the Chief Astrologer, to make it easier to get in and get Maymuna out. What about you?"

"I'll follow you," said Behzad, "or you can follow me, so we don't waste time."

"Very good," said Salman.

---

108 Ibn al-Athir, II.

Chapter 69

Al-Amin's Head

Dressed as the Chief Astrologer, Salman mounted his mule. Behzad, wearing the cloak, tall cap, and trousers of a Persian dignitary, mounted his charger. They passed through the markets of Karkh as dawn was breaking. Turning toward the Kufa Gate, they were taken aback at the size of the crowd gathered there. They were also surprised at how many Ruffians were still shooting chunks of gravel from the walls, though they pressed on undeterred through the rain of projectiles. As they approached the gate, they saw crowds of people, not only troops from Khurasan but also market traders, rushing toward the park where Tahir's army was camped. Then they saw a head mounted on a spear. At a glance, Salman could see that the head was al-Amin's, brought by Tahir and brandished from one of the turrets that topped the wall around the park.

Seeing the head, the people were stunned and horrified, though some were doubtless rejoicing that the war was over. When his glance fell on the head, Behzad cried, "May God be our refuge! Praise be to Him, who is living and immortal! Today a dynasty falls and another takes its place—if Ibn Sahl knows how to take advantage of our victory."

"What do you think Tahir's going to do with the head?" said Salman.

"I think he'll send it to al-Ma'mun in Khurasan, along with the Caliph's mantle, signet ring, and staff, as quickly as possible, to reassure everyone that victory is ours. Tahir will be richly rewarded and al-Ma'mun alone will reign as caliph."

As for the denizens of the Palace of Al-Mansur, Salman had left them the day before with no idea of what was happening at the Palace of Eternity. Farida, the forewoman, was going about her business when the chamberlain came in to announce Ibn al-Fadl, the son of Ibn al-Rabi. She knew that Ibn al-Fadl was close to the Caliph, and, thinking that he had arrived on urgent business, ordered him to be admitted. As we have seen, Ibn al-Fadl and his father had spent some time in hiding, though they remained in Baghdad, and kept abreast of what was happening there. That evening, Ibn al-Fadl had learned that the situation had grown dire indeed, and that the city would shortly fall into the hands of the Khurasanis. He had been keeping track of Maymuna's whereabouts and had tried his best to claim her. The previous morning, he had gone to Zubayda and persuaded her that he could force Maymuna to tell him where Behzad was. He had also given her to understand that he loved her. Zubayda had said, "If you can find out where that man is, she's yours." He had then asked her to give him permission to see her. That evening, seeing the chaos that reigned everywhere, he hired some Ruffians to help him abduct Maymuna if the forewoman refused to hand her over. Then he went to the Palace of Al-Mansur.

At the palace, the forewoman received him graciously and asked him what he wanted. He handed over the letter he had received from Zubayda. The forewoman remembered that Sa'dun had told her not to let anyone take Maymuna away, but she could see no harm in letting Ibn al-Fadl in to see her. So she went to Maymuna's room and told her that the Vizier's son had come to visit her. 'Abbada, who was with her granddaughter, cried, "We don't want to see him!"

"He's brought an order from our mistress Zubayda."

Hearing that name, 'Abbada trembled and expected the worst. She begged the forewoman to send the young man away, but to no avail.

Ibn al-Fadl made his way to the room. The candles had been lit, and Maymuna, her complexion altered by the stream of misfortunes she had suffered, sat in her black gown, her pallor making her look more fragile than usual. Looking lovelorn, and smiling in an ingratiating manner, the young man came into the room. When she saw him, she shuddered and remained seated, her eyes averted. He came forward, greeted her, and said, "Don't you recognize me, Maymuna?"

Turning her face away, she said, as coldly as she could, "No."

"Don't you recognize the young man who loves you? Who worships you? Don't you recognize Ibn al-Fadl?"

"I've heard the name," she said, "and it pains me to hear it. It's his father who put me into these clothes."

"If that's true," he said as kindly as he could, "then I'll be responsible for finding you something new to wear, and turning your days of mourning into days as bright as snow."

"I'm used to black," she said with a vindictive look. "I'm not interested in wearing anything else."

"Wear what you want, and do what you want," he said, "but have pity on a man who loves you to the point of misery. I love you, Maymuna, but luck is against me: you don't love me."

So saying, he knelt before her and tried to take her hand, but she snatched it away as if he were a scorpion poised to sting her.

Wounded by her rejection, he stood, saying, "Maymuna, I came here to beg you in the name of love. But if my begging inspires no pity, then I'll have my way by other means."

"You'll never have your way with me," she said. "Leave me alone and look for someone else. There are many other women in the world."

"You're the one I've chosen," he said, "as you can see from my faithfulness to you despite your aversion to me. Isn't it time you reconsidered?"

Turning away from him completely, she said, "Leave me alone!"

"I warned you: if you don't reconsider, I'll have to resort to harsher measures, though it pains me to do so."

"What can you do to me here in the Caliph's palace?" she said, still looking away.

"I can carry you off by force. I have a troop of soldiers and an order from the Caliph's mother."

'Abbada, who had been listening to the conversation, cried, "I thought you were an honorable man who listens to reason. Haven't you heard enough? Leave the girl alone! If I were you and knew she didn't love me, I would leave her be."

"I would leave her without a second thought," said Ibn al-Fadl, "but I won't let myself leave empty-handed after waiting so long. Even though I love her, I have to show her who I am, and teach her that someone like me can't be treated this way. Baghdad is full of girls, the daughters of princes and commanders, who would be grateful to have me." Turning to Maymuna, he said, "Think it over! I want what's best for you. Don't make me use force. There's a troop of Ruffians outside waiting for my orders."

"Oh no!" cried Maymuna, rocking back and forth in misery. "Where's the army? Where are the guards?"

"Spare us your brutality, young man," said 'Abbada, rising to her feet. "Since you know who we are, have pity on us! Haven't we suffered enough?"

At that moment they heard a commotion from outside. Thinking the Ruffians had come to take her away, Maymuna cried, "Oh God! If I have to suffer any more, let me die now!" She began weeping and calling out heedlessly: "Where's Salman? Where's Behzad? How miserable I am!" Weeping, her grandmother stood beside her, trying to comfort her.

Ibn al-Fadl, meanwhile, had realized that the noise had nothing to do with the Ruffians. Going out to see what was the matter, he heard the servants saying that Zubayda had arrived. Everyone was surprised that she should come at such an hour: it was already well past midnight.

After Zubayda had left the Palace of Eternity that evening, afraid, as we have seen, for the safety of her son, she had returned to her own palace, where she continued to worry, as if her heart were warning her of imminent danger. She lay down but could not sleep. At some point after midnight, her palace forewoman roused her. Panicked, Zubayda rose and asked what was wrong.

"A Shakiri trooper from the Palace of Eternity is here," came the reply. "He's asking for the Commander of the Faithful."

"My son?" she cried. "But why here? Where is he, then? When I left his palace two hours ago, he was there. Bring me the Shakiri!"

When he was admitted, she asked him where the Caliph was.

"We don't know, my lady. We looked for him everywhere in the palace and we can't find him."

Zubayda rose, wrapped herself in a shawl, and rode to the Palace of Eternity, where she searched for him everywhere but to no avail. Thinking he might have gone out for some reason and would soon return, she waited as if on burning coals until the first glimmer of dawn. Then it occurred to her that he might have gone to the Citadel of Al-Mansur, which was equipped to withstand a siege. So she rode there and asked the forewoman if she had seen the Caliph. She answered that she hadn't.

"I saw some Ruffians at the door," she said. "Who brought them here?"

"Ibn al-Fadl," answered the forewoman. "He had a letter with him, from you, saying he could talk with Maymuna."

Hearing that name, Zubayda grew furious, imagining as she did that the young woman was the cause of all her troubles. "Where is she?" she shrieked.

"In her room."

Unwilling to wait for the young woman to be summoned, Zubayda headed for the room in a state of high dudgeon. At the door she saw Ibn al-Fadl, who stepped aside. Going in, she found Maymuna standing there with her grandmother beside her. "You too?" she screamed. "You miserable old woman! You're the reason for all my troubles! What on earth are you doing here?"

'Abbada looked away silently, unable to offer an explanation for her presence. Turning to Maymuna, Zubayda said, "Isn't it time you told us where that damned traitor called Behzad is hiding? I know he's in Baghdad, and all of this is his fault! Where is he?"

"I don't know, my lady," said Maymuna in a terror-stricken voice. "I'm a prisoner here. I don't receive news and I have no idea what's going on outside."

"How can you lie to me? I know there's a servant named Salman who delivers messages between the two of you."

"Ask the forewoman," said Maymuna. "I've seen no one, prince or pauper. For God's sake, have pity on me. I've suffered enough!"

"Have pity on you?" said Zubayda. "Why? If I could strangle you myself, I would." Looking outside, she saw Ibn al-Fadl standing there. "Take this girl!" she screamed. "I give her to you to do as you will. And I'll give that ill-omened crone the punishment she deserves."

Hearing this, 'Abbada knelt before her, saying, "Do as you please with me but deal kindly with the girl. She's done nothing! I pleaded with you once before and you sent me away. But you're a mother who knows what it means to care for a child, and now I'm begging you once again to have some pity on her. As for me, I don't care if I live or die."

At the mention of caring for children, Zubayda, conscious as she was of the danger her son was in, felt her resolve weakening, especially since she still had no idea whether al-Amin was alive or dead. People never truly understand the misfortunes of others until they themselves suffer the same misfortunes, or fear they might. An unmarried man can hear about parental bereavement without any feeling; if he hears a child's cry, he fumes at the parents and gestures for them to beat the little one. But if the same man becomes a father himself, the sound of a child crying out in pain or hunger will break his heart and send him running to help. Even parents cannot fully understand the grief of losing a child unless they themselves have lost one, or fear they might, as was the case with Zubayda on that day. 'Abbada had invoked her son before to no effect, but today the same plea inspired a surge of pity. Zubayda fell silent as if struck mute and, with a tear rolling down each of her cheeks, fought to control herself so as not to appear weak. Feigning anger, she rose to her feet and said, "I told you, there's no way to save her unless she tells us where Behzad is. Otherwise she belongs to Ibn al-Fadl." She motioned for him to take her.

Without anyone noticing, the day had dawned. Ibn al-Fadl came forward to take Maymuna, thinking she had given in. But she began wailing and shrieking, "No, no, I'm not going! Kill me right here! Behzad, where are you? Is this my reward for waiting so long?"

Chapter 70

A Matter Resolved

Ignoring her protests, Ibn al-Fadl went to fetch the Ruffians to help him seize her and carry her away. Outside he heard the servants saying that the Chief Astrologer had arrived. Ibn al-Fadl decided to ask him to try persuading Maymuna to come along quietly. When he inquired after Sa'dun, he was told that he had gone in to see Zubayda. Afraid for her son, she had gone into the main hall to think over her predicament. When the Chief Astrologer was announced, she had sent for him immediately.

Salman and Behzad had arrived a few moments earlier. The denizens of the palace still had no idea that the city had surrendered. When they reached the courtyard, Salman and Behzad saw a number of Ruffians gathered there. Paying them no attention, Salman went to the gate and found it shut tight. Hearing the commotion inside, he knocked. When no one answered, he pounded on the door. From a spyhole above the gate, a servant looked out and asked, "Who's there?"

Salman looked up and, recognizing the servant, shouted, "Open up! Now!" Recognizing him in turn, the boy raced down and opened the gate. Salman rode his mule straight into the courtyard with Behzad behind him. They dismounted, gave their mounts to the page, and looked around. The palace was in turmoil, with attendants rushing in and out of the interior gate. The astrologer asked the page where the forewoman was.

"With our mistress Zubayda," came the reply.

Salman was unhappy to hear that Zubayda was on the premises. "Call the forewoman right now," he said. "Tell her that the Chief Astrologer needs to see her on urgent business." He turned to Behzad. "No doubt she'll ask me about her son, and possibly about you, too. Shall I go alone?"

"No, I'll come with you."

Salman turned back to the page. "Tell the forewoman that the Chief Astrologer has a companion who must be admitted as well."

The page went away and came back. "Follow me," he said, leading them into the main hall. Sa'dun went in first and greeted Zubayda. Behzad followed him, but the Caliph's mother was too worried to notice him. She was sitting cross-legged with a pillow on her lap, her elbows on the pillow, and her head between her hands. "Where were you?" she cried when Sa'dun came in. "And what made you come here just when I needed you?" She motioned for him to sit and he did. Behzad did too, though she didn't notice him.

"I tried hard to find Behzad," said Salman, "and I finally did."

With a fierce grin, she cried, "Where is he?"

"Right here," he said, pointing.

She stared, recoiled, and turned red. She looked hard at Behzad, seeing a handsome, dignified, serious-looking man. Unable to stop herself, she cried, "You're Behzad?"

"I am."

"How dare you come here? Aren't you afraid of what the Commander of the Faithful will do to you?"

"I never feared him when he was alive," he said, calmly and with dignity. "Why should I fear him now that he's dead?"

Stunned, she shuddered violently and struck her cheeks with both hands in disbelief. "The Caliph? My son? What are you saying? Are you making fun of me, you wretch?"

"No, my lady," he replied. "I'm telling you the truth. I'm sorry to say something so painful, but you asked me and I told you the truth."

Dazed, she turned to Salman. "Sa'dun! Don't lie to me. Where is the Caliph? This man must be mad. Where is my son? My beloved boy, where is he? Tell me!"

Coldly, Sa'dun replied, "I saw his head hanging from the wall near the Kufa Gate. The matter is concluded." So saying, he rose.

Zubayda struck her cheeks again with both hands and wailed.

At that moment, Behzad heard Maymuna crying for help.

Leaping from the room, hand on his dagger, he called back, "I'm coming, my love!"

Outside he saw a group of Ruffians dragging Maymuna away by her hair, and Ibn al-Fadl standing by, saying, "Take that ungrateful girl away!"

Behzad drew his dagger and pounced on Ibn al-Fadl, striking him a blow that killed him instantly. Turning to the Ruffians, he cried, "Run, you bastards, or you'll have Behzad to deal with!"

Hearing him shout, and seeing Ibn al-Fadl lying lifeless on the ground, the Ruffians broke and ran. Maymuna had never suspected that Behzad was nearby, but when Ibn al-Fadl ordered the Ruffians to carry her off and she had given up all hope of rescue, she began shouting his name in despair. When she saw him strike down Ibn al-Fadl, she fainted. 'Abbada, meanwhile, rushed up to Behzad. "Where did you come from, you angel?" she asked. "I'm afraid those awful men might hurt you."

"Don't be afraid, my lady," he said. "Baghdad is ours, and al-Amin's head is hanging from a wall where everyone can see it."

When the attendants heard this bit of news, they ran in a panic back to Zubayda. They found her with her hair unbound, wailing, "My son! Killed by tyrants and oppressors!"

Moved by her cries, 'Abbada made her way to her, and seeing her in that state, felt a surge of pity for her. Bending over her hands, she kissed them, saying, "Don't torment yourself, my lady. It's the will of our Master." Then, remembering the death of her own son, she began weeping as well.

Hearing these compassionate words, and seeing her tears, Zubayda, who had expected 'Abbada to rejoice at her misfortune, gazed at her, heartbroken and mortified, humbled as only the bereaved can be. "You were right, dear 'Abbada: no one knows the bitterness of bereavement but those who have tasted it. Oh, my little boy! May God have mercy on your Ja'far and my Rashid, and on my Amin! Is he dead? Is he really dead? Have they killed him? Have they exposed his head, as they did to your son? Please tell them to be gentle with his body. He's not used to feeling pain. He can't bear the hot sun, or the cold at night. How could you hang him up and leave him in the open air? Shame on you: he's just beginning the best part of his life. Couldn't you have killed me and let him live? Take him down and hang me instead! You were right, dear 'Abbada: I didn't listen to your plea because I had never known this pain!" Her hair hanging loose, she began pacing frantically back and forth across the room, weeping and wailing, until everyone in the room was shedding tears as well. Then the others began to think about how to save themselves.

Taking Maymuna away from the clamor, Behzad did his best to comfort her. She herself felt as if she were dreaming. She would look at him without quite believing that she was seeing him, or that he had arrived in the nick of time to save her life. As she walked through the palace leaning on his arm, she noticed Ibn al-Fadl's corpse on the ground. "I'm sorry that young man had to die," she said to Behzad. "He thought highly of me, and he wanted to take care of me. But he tried to force me to love him, and I only love my dear Behzad."

"When I saw him shouting at you and threatening you," said Behzad, "I couldn't stand it, so I killed him. But what do we care about other people? It's over. Come on. Salman! Let's go."

Salman lent a hand to 'Abbada, and Behzad took Maymuna, and they left the palace, mounted their riding beasts, and departed, leaving the denizens of al-Mansur's palace to their mourning.

Chapter 71

To Die Content

With the death of al-Amin, the struggle between the brothers came to an end. Baghdad fell to al-Ma'mun, and the caliphate was his. Even so, he remained in Khurasan, and wrote to Tahir Ibn Husayn ordering him to hand over Baghdad and the other territories he had captured to Ibn Sahl's brother al-Hasan.

Having completed the task he came to accomplish in Baghdad, Behzad wanted to return to his mother in Marv to give her the good news and tell her of his love for Maymuna so they could be married with her blessing. Late in the afternoon of the day they left the palace, he, Maymuna, 'Abbada, and Salman departed for Khurasan. Maymuna could still not quite believe that she was finally with her beloved, and as much as she looked at him it was never enough. She was again curious about who he really was, where his family came from, what his objective had been, and what secrets he was carrying around in that box of his. She thought about asking him during the journey, but her modesty, and her grandmother's presence, stopped her. She told herself that she would find out what she wanted to know as soon as they reached Khurasan.

Fatima, Behzad's mother, and the rest of Khurasan were waiting impatiently to learn whether their efforts had borne fruit. From al-Rashid's death in Tus to that of al-Amin in Baghdad, some five years had passed. During that time, al-Fadl Ibn Sahl, al-Ma'mun's vizier in Khurasan—the one given the title of Dual Vizier—had been administering the state on his behalf.

When news arrived of al-Amin's death and the surrender of Baghdad, there was great rejoicing. Tahir sent al-Amin's head, along with the Caliph's mantle, staff, and signet ring, to Ibn Sahl. The head was placed on a shield and brought before al-Ma'mun. Upon seeing it, he prostrated himself to God in gratitude. Ibn Sahl, meanwhile, laid the groundwork for using the

Shi'ites to restore power to the Persians. At his behest, al-Ma'mun named 'Ali al-Rida, leader of the Shi'ite faction, his heir apparent, and ordered that the black uniforms of the 'Abbasid dynasty be replaced with green. This announcement was strongly opposed by the 'Abbasids in Baghdad, who wrote to al-Ma'mun reproaching him and threatening retaliation. Ibn Sahl, however, intercepted the letters, and used his considerable influence to ensure that al-Ma'mun never saw them.

Having reaped the fruits of his labors, and won his beloved as well, Behzad returned to Khurasan. Salman, on the other hand, though he too had done his duty, had yet to win his prize. When they reached Marv, Behzad asked if he might take his betrothed home. Salman replied, "Don't forget that you've completed your task, but I'm still waiting for my reward."

"You'll be a leader of the Khurramiyya," said Behzad. "It's already been arranged. Isn't that enough?"

"No," said Salman. "I'm hoping for something that means more to me than power. I helped you get what you wanted, so now help me."

"What do you mean?"

"Didn't I help you win Maymuna? What I want is to marry Buran, daughter of al-Hasan Ibn Sahl. So long as her uncle agrees, the matter should be a simple one. I think, after the miracles I've accomplished for the cause, that I deserve no less."

Behzad thought about this demand and concluded that it was not so very farfetched. Remembering the conversation he and al-Fadl had had about Buran before his return to Baghdad, he saw that marrying her off to Salman would solve his problem nicely. "We'll see about that tomorrow," he said. "First, though, I have one last favor to ask."

"What?"

"I need al-Amin's head. Can you spirit it out of its burial place, as we did with the heads of Ja'far and Abu Muslim?"

"That's easy enough," said Salman, understanding his reasons. "Give me until tomorrow, and I'll deliver the head to your house."

As soon as Salman had taken his leave, Behzad, with Maymuna and 'Abbada in tow, headed straight for his mother's house, hoping that she had survived his absence. He knocked on the door but heard nothing. Heart pounding, he knocked again. This time he heard footsteps. The door opened and the slave who had welcomed him the last time stood there again, but this time with a mournful expression on his face. "How is my mother?" said Behzad.

The slave welcomed him and said that Fatima was well, though feeling indisposed because she missed him so much. Telling him to make their two guests comfortable, Behzad rushed in to see his mother. Entering her room, he found her lying in bed, her sunken eyes and prominent cheekbones making her look infinitely old. Unsure whether she was dead or alive, he stood before her and greeted her in a faltering voice.

When she heard him speak, Fatima awoke, opened her eyes, and, with a great effort, turned her head and smiled weakly at him. He knelt by the bed, bent over her hand, and kissed it. She motioned for him to come closer. She kissed his forehead and gave him an inquiring look.

"I've brought what you asked for, my lady," said Behzad. "We've defeated our oppressors and killed their stripling caliph. Our cousin al-Ma'mun now rules the Muslims. After him will come 'Ali al-Rida, head of the Shi'ites, and then sovereignty will be ours again. I've avenged my grandfather with his dagger, as you asked me to do." Taking the dagger out, he showed her the traces of blood on the blade. "And I've avenged Ja'far as well."

Fatima's face shone with pleasure. She breathed a sigh of relief and then, marshaling her strength, said in a faltering voice, "Bless you, child! You've washed away the shame of your people and made your mother proud." Then, twisting and gasping for breath, and summoning what strength she had left, she asked, "Where is the last head?"

"It will be here tomorrow morning," he answered. "We'll bury all three together, as we promised."

Fatima raised her hand to the sky as if praying for him, then touched his face to bless him. Her hand felt cold and dry, as if her fingers were made of iron. She beckoned him closer. He leaned over her and she kissed him again, then whispered in his ear, in a voice so low he could barely hear it, "Bury them with me tomorrow."

Looking at her pale, shriveled face, he saw that tears had gathered in the corners of her eyes but could not fall because of how deeply her eyes had sunk into their sockets as she lay on her back. Realizing that she had little time left, he spoke in a rush: "You've given me your blessing, mother; and now I beg you to bless a young woman who will share my life, as she's shared all our afflictions." Turning to the door, he ordered the servant to summon the two guests. Too weak to talk, Fatima looked at Behzad inquiringly. With a gesture, he implored her to wait.

When Maymuna heard Behzad ask the servant about his mother as soon as they arrived, she realized that this was his home. She was still intensely curious about his ancestry. Now, coming in to see his mother, she was taken aback by how old and frail she looked. Understanding her reaction, Behzad spoke first, saying, "For a long time you've wanted to know who I am. The lady lying here is my mother. She's also the daughter of Abu Muslim, who led the 'Abbasid revolution and founded the 'Abbasid dynasty before being betrayed and murdered, just as your father was. No one in Khurasan knows that I'm the grandson of their hero except for my mother and our servant. People think I'm her stepson because I was born after my father died and she claimed that she had adopted me. She dedicated my life to avenging her father, and gave me the name Kayfar. And now it's time to tell you what's in the box. It contains two precious heads: my grandfather's and your father's."

Maymuna shrunk back and blanched, but Behzad continued to explain. "I kept them here until I could bring al-Amin's head, which makes three. It'll be here tomorrow, and we'll bury the three together. Then I'll have fulfilled my mother's vow, and brought the daughter of Ja'far into the bargain."

"So you're Abu Muslim's grandson?" she asked.

"Yes," he answered, "and you're Ja'far's daughter. It was our destiny to avenge ourselves on our enemies."

Fatima, meanwhile, had fallen into an exhausted sleep. Having told Maymuna what he wanted her to know, Behzad took her hand and brought her to his mother's bedside. "This is Maymuna, daughter of Ja'far son of Yahya, who was murdered by al-Rashid. Good fortune guided me to her. She'll be my wife, so give her your blessing."

Raising her hand, Fatima motioned for Maymuna to come closer. When she did, the old woman kissed her and rubbed her face with her sleeve. Mumbling, she pointed toward Maymuna's black gown, then made a gesture as if to say, "No more." Understanding that this meant that she should put away her mourning clothes, Maymuna signaled her assent. Then Behzad asked 'Abbada, who had been standing beside him, to come forward. "This is Ja'far's mother," he said. "Do you recognize her?"

Fatima peered at her near-sightedly, then smiled painfully as if to say, "I do."

"I've known you since I was young," said 'Abbada. She bent over the woman in the bed and kissed her hands. Exhausted, Fatima brushed her with her lips, as if trying to kiss her. She was suffering a tightening of her chest and a shortness of breath, and it was clear to the group that she was dying. Even so, a smile of triumph played on her lips until she finally gave up her soul, with all of them looking on as she opened and closed her eyes. When she had taken her last breath, they wept. The next day, Salman brought the head. They added it to the others, then buried all three with Fatima, as she had asked.

Chapter 72

A Friendless Traitor

A few days later, Behzad and Maymuna were married. Behzad sent for Salman and named him chief of the Khurrami sect. Salman then reminded him of his promise to intercede with Ibn Sahl. The next day, they rode to the Vizier's residence. With the ascendancy of al-Ma'mun and the nomination of 'Ali al-Rida, Ibn Sahl had reached the pinnacle of his career: his word was law and his orders overrode even the Caliph's. When Behzad and Salman were announced, he told the chamberlain to escort them in. The audience room was crowded with petitioners, among them dignitaries and generals. Al-Hasan, however, was absent, having gone to Baghdad, as we have seen. Ibn Sahl welcomed Behzad and invited him to sit next to him on the divan. He motioned Salman to a chair in the place where the notables were seated, and he took it without complaint. In response to Ibn Sahl's questions, Behzad said that he had come from Baghdad and had witnessed the fall of the city.

"Were you there the day al-Amin was killed?"

"Yes," he said. "I was there with my friend Salman, and we saw al-Amin's head on the wall of the park by the Kufa Gate."

Ibn Sahl laughed triumphantly. "A tyrant paid back in his own coin!"

Their host then took up the business brought to him by the petitioners, and Behzad waited quietly for him to finish. It wasn't until after the noon call to prayer that everyone else departed, leaving Behzad and Salman alone with Ibn Sahl.

Behzad then addressed Ibn Sahl. "It's a pleasure to tell you about the miracles accomplished by my friend Salman during this campaign. Without his intelligence and his strong hand on the sword, we might never have fulfilled the commands of the Dual Vizier."

Ibn Sahl smiled. "We'll reward him with the governorship of an important province. Or is he like you in his aversion to official positions?"

Behzad laughed. "It would be most generous of you to give him a governorship. But I'd like to see him enjoy an even greater blessing: one that would make him stand out among his peers."

"What would that be?"

"The hand of your niece."

"Which niece do you mean?"

"Buran."

Ibn Sahl sat back, his expression altered, and shook his head. "Is he asking for her?"

"I'm asking for her on his behalf, if it pleases the Vizier," he said. "Salman is among the worthiest of men."

"It pains me to say no to you, Behzad," said Ibn Sahl, "but Buran is engaged."

For a moment Behzad thought that he meant to him, and was about to ask; but Salman spoke first. "To whom?"

Annoyed by this interruption, Ibn Sahl looked at him and said, "To the greatest man in Islam today."

Realizing that he meant al-Ma'mun, Salman realized that he had lost her. Bitter and angry, he said, "The Dual Vizier seems to have forgotten his promise!"

"What promise?"

"Didn't we have an agreement?"

"When did we ever have an agreement?" asked Ibn Sahl in a forbidding tone.

"Shall I speak frankly?"

"Speak as you wish."

"When you renounced Zoroastrianism and became a Muslim, hoping for advancement, we promised each other to work together. At the time, you had nothing, and Buran was a child. Now things have changed: you're the Dual Vizier and the master of all you survey. But remember that we had an agreement, and I've done my part. Will you do yours?"

Clearly irked by what Salman was implying, Ibn Sahl said, "I have no recollection of what you're talking about. But do you really think we can turn away her current suitor and marry her off to you? In any case, the matter is up to her father, and he's not here."

These words struck Salman like an arrow to the heart. He turned pale and his mustache twitched. Then he rose to go. Seeing what was happening, Behzad wanted to continue the conversation, but then he saw Ibn Sahl pick up his flyswatter and move as if preparing to leave. At a loss, Behzad stood as well, and he and Salman departed after receiving a tepid farewell from Ibn Sahl. Outside, Behzad tried to calm his friend down, but Salman would have none of it. As Salman turned to go, Behzad said, "Don't be angry, brother. The man does seem to have a legitimate excuse."

"He has no excuse," said Salman, his voice hoarse with fury. "He's ill-bred and can't recognize merit when he sees it. But I'll show him what happens when he underestimates me."

He rushed off. Behzad stood following him with his eyes until he vanished from sight. He could think of a thousand things that Salman's threat might mean, knowing how shrewd and devious the man was, and how no considerations of trust, conscience, or fellow feeling could deter him from his purposes.

As for Salman, he went directly to al-Ma'mun's residence and asked to see him alone. "I'm at the service of the Commander of the Faithful," he said, "and I'm gratified that my efforts on his behalf were not in vain. God has blessed us by giving him long life and the caliphate that he deserves!"

Expecting that this speech was the preamble to some new piece of intelligence, al-Ma'mun played along, saying, "I'm grateful to my Khurasani uncles, who deserve the credit for my being in this position."

Salman swallowed, cleared his throat, and gave every impression of being reluctant to proceed with his speech.

"Speak up," said al-Ma'mun. "Don't be afraid."

"I know I'm risking my life by saying this," said Salman. "I'll say it anyway, hoping, as I do, that the Commander of the Faithful will enjoy a long and prosperous reign. But let what I say remain a secret."

Looking interested, al-Ma'mun said, "No need to enjoin me to secrecy; our cause was built on secrets. Don't be afraid: out with it!"

"Your vizier Ibn Sahl would have you believe that he's restored authority to you, but all the while he's kept it for himself."

Suspecting that Salman was actually acting on Ibn Sahl's behalf, al-Ma'mun said, "A man like him deserves to enjoy some authority after all he's done for us."

"I see that my master is keeping his thoughts to himself. That's his choice. But I'm telling you that Ibn Sahl has been seeking power for himself, not for its own sake, but as part of his plan to transfer the succession from the 'Abbasids to the 'Alids, and thus to the Persians. That's why he insisted on having 'Ali al-Rida appointed as your successor."

Al-Ma'mun, who had suspected something of the sort, acknowledged to himself that Ibn Sahl had certainly made great efforts to achieve that end, and that he himself may have complied because he needed help to defeat his brother. "But," he said, "I nominated 'Ali al-Rida by my own choice. None of the 'Abbasids are worthy to be caliph."

"But how do you know that the 'Alids are? And even if we concede that it was your choice, how can you be sure that Ibn Sahl will wait patiently for you to live out your reign? Forgive me for speaking so freely, but I trust that the Commander of the Faithful will keep what I've said a secret. All I'm asking is that he treat that man with caution, for the sake of his own life first of all, and then for the sake of his dynasty. And if it seems to him that I'm using this as a means of advancement, then I ask him to pardon me."

Many thoughts were running through al-Ma'mun's mind. He bowed his head as if in contemplation, but did not divulge whatever it was that he was thinking. All he said was: "What do you suggest I do?"

Encouraged by this display of interest, Salman said, "If the Commander of the Faithful entrusts the matter to me, I can resolve the problem with a mouthful of honey or a drink of water."

Taken aback at the man's boldness, al-Ma'mun thought to himself, "A man so quick to betray others is a danger to his friends as well as his enemies. After working so hard for Ibn Sahl, he's ready to poison him. Something must have made him change his mind, and whatever it was could make him turn against others as well." All the same, al-Ma'mun could see that the man was offering him a way to get rid of Ibn Sahl. He thought for a moment, then said, "We'll look into it." Salman contented himself with this reply, knowing, as he did, that the Caliph would never accept such an offer outright, for reasons familiar enough to persons of Salman's character.

After dismissing Salman, al-Ma'mun thought over what he had said. He still suspected that Salman might be an agent of Ibn Sahl's sent to sound him out. He accordingly decided to ferret out Ibn Sahl's position without arousing his suspicions.

That evening, Ibn Sahl, whose spies had informed him of Salman's visit to al-Ma'mun earlier that day, came to see al-Ma'mun in the evening, as was their custom. Ibn Sahl imagined that Salman had come to pursue the matter of Buran. It never occurred to him that Salman would go so far as to denounce him and his scheme, since doing so would redound against the whole community of Persians.

After making sure they were alone, al-Ma'mun brought the conversation around to Salman and then said, "I've heard that that man accomplished great things in Baghdad."

"Yes, Sire," said Ibn Sahl. "He put all his cunning and guile at the service of our cause. But he's very ambitious."

"There's no harm, then, in giving him a position."

"I offered him one," said Ibn Sahl with a smile, "but he had the effrontery to demand something more—something I think the Commander of the Faithful would be surprised to hear about."

"Which was?"

"He wants my niece Buran, and when I told him she was engaged he got angry, as if he were worthier of her than the Commander of the Faithful." Al-Ma'mun, as it happened, had asked Buran's father for her in secret.

Thus apprised of the reason for the rift, al-Ma'mun realized that Salman had revealed the Persians' secret only as a means to avenge himself on Ibn Sahl. He was also aware that the vizier knew of Salman's visit earlier that day. To dispel Ibn Sahl's suspicions, he shook his head as if in contemptuous dismissal of Salman and, feigning surprise at what he had heard, changed the subject. Ibn Sahl left persuaded that he had turned the Caliph against Salman.

Chapter 73

The Wages of Treachery

From that day forward, al-Ma'mun kept a close watch on Ibn Sahl hoping to confirm what he had heard about him. One day, 'Ali al-Rida, his heir apparent, came to see him. Al-Ma'mun welcomed him and, after they had been speaking for a while, 'Ali said, "I've come to tell you about something that Ibn Sahl has been keeping from you."

"What's that?"

"When your relatives in Baghdad found out that you had named me as your successor, they resented it, saying that you must be bewitched or insane. They then appointed Ibrahim Ibn al-Mahdi in your place, and revoked their oaths to you on the grounds that the caliphate would come to me."

All of this was news to al-Ma'mun. "I had no idea," he said.

"That's because Ibn Sahl intercepts the couriers and keeps certain messages from you to safeguard his own interests."

Al-Ma'mun thanked 'Ali for his loyalty and honesty, then said, "I do recall Ibn Sahl telling me that the people of Baghdad had appointed Ibrahim to rule them, but not as caliph."

"Ibn Sahl lied to you. Now there's a war going on between Ibrahim and your governor al-Hasan Ibn Sahl. The people resent the power he and his brother have, and they resent me, and my nomination as heir apparent."

"Who else knows about this?"

'Ali told him who his sources were, and al-Ma'mun had them summoned. He offered them immunity from retaliation by Ibn Sahl in the form of a document he wrote out in his own hand. Thus assured, they told him that Ibrahim had received oaths of allegiance as caliph. The people of Baghdad, they said, called Ibrahim "the Sunni caliph," and accused al-Ma'mun of being a Shi'ite on account of the honor he had done 'Ali al-Rida.[109] After taking all this in, al-Ma'mun thanked them and let them go. He also thanked 'Ali, who took his leave as well. Left alone, al-Ma'mun thought the matter over and decided to do away with Ibn Sahl. He also had misgivings about keeping 'Ali al-Rida as his heir apparent. So long as he remained alive, al-Ma'mun's own position would be awkward.

Learning of what had transpired between 'Ali al-Rida and al-Ma'mun, Salman realized that the time was ripe. He met secretly with al-Ma'mun, who needed to give him only the subtlest of hints. Salman left the meeting ready to embark on a new round of plots and schemes.

In 202 AH (818 AD), al-Ma'mun departed for Baghdad. During a stopover in Sarakhs, a group of men acting on Salman's orders attacked and killed Ibn Sahl in a bathhouse. Al-Ma'mun put the assassins on trial and had them executed. Shortly after al-Ma'mun's arrival in Baghdad, the news broke that 'Ali al-Rida had died after eating poisoned grapes. Many believed that al-Ma'mun was responsible,[110] though the real poisoner was Salman.

Al-Ma'mun's cause was thereby saved, and the caliphate remained 'Abbasid. But he remained fearful that Salman would turn against him, too, and so had him assassinated. Salman thus paid for his treachery with his life, or, as Behzad put it: "Every traitor is himself betrayed."

As for Behzad himself, he saw no more of Salman after they parted with Ibn Sahl. When he learned that both Ibn Sahl and 'Ali al-Rida had been killed, he lamented the failure of his efforts to restore sovereignty to the Persians. Even so, he found consolation in having successfully avenged his grandfather and his father-in-law. He lived happily together with his wife, no one knowing that he was the grandson of Abu Muslim and she the daughter of Ja'far the Barmaki. Later he inquired after Salman and learned that al-Ma'mun, fearful of being betrayed, had had him murdered. "Such are the wages of treachery," he thought to himself, "and the fruits of deceit."

As for al-Ma'mun, after reaching Baghdad he married Buran, as a gesture of reconciliation toward her father, al-Hasan Ibn Sahl, who had no trouble guessing what had happened to his brother. The marriage was celebrated with a pomp and circumstance undimmed in the annals of history.[111]

The End

109 Ibn al-Athir, VI.

110 Ibn al-Athir, VI; al-Fakhri; *Book of Songs*, IX; Ibn Khallikan.

111 *History of Islamic Civilization*, V.

The Caliph's Heirs

Afterword

Michael Cooperson

In Ramadan 2000, Iranian television broadcast a series called *The Rule of Love*, a historical drama about the life and times of 'Ali al-Rida.[112] Al-Rida, who died in 818 AD, is one of the imams (roughly, religious guides) revered by Shi'ite Muslims. He was supposed to be the hero of the series. But his career hardly lends itself to drama: the imam was a pious scholar who preferred to keep his distance from the rough-and-tumble of politics. To make the series exciting, and to show what a bad lot al-Rida's contemporaries were, writer and director Mehdi Fakhimzadeh gives big roles to the villains: first al-Amin, the sixth caliph of the 'Abbasid dynasty, and then his half-brother and successor, the Caliph al-Ma'mun. For the most part, *The Rule of Love* tells the same story about these two that we find in the old Arabic chronicles. In 809 AD, the Caliph Harun al-Rashid died, leaving his empire divided between his two sons, al-Amin and al-Ma'mun. The brothers quarreled and went to war. After several dramatic battles, al-Ma'mun emerged victorious. Then, having broken with his own 'Abbasid family, he nominated al-Rida—who belonged to a different branch of the Prophet's family—to succeed him as caliph.[113]

Though it accepts and builds on this account of events, *The Rule of Love* has its own story to tell. According to the modern Shi'ite point of view, neither al-Amin nor al-Ma'mun had any business occupying the throne at all. Only al-Rida, who was a direct descendant of the Prophet, had the right to lead the Muslim community. The series accordingly does its best to make the two 'Abbasid caliphs as unappealing as possible. Al-Amin, played with

112 *Velayat-e 'Eshgh*, written and directed by Mehdi Fakhimzadeh (Tehran: Sorush Media Productions, 2000). I thank Pari Iranmanesh for bringing this work to my attention.

113 For a more detailed account see Michael Cooperson, *Al Ma'mun* (Oxford: One World Books, 2005).

manic energy by Rambod Javan, spends his screen time issuing absurd commands, beating his servants, or shrieking in infantile frustration. His rival al-Ma'mun, played with engaging wiliness by Mohammad Sadeghi, seems at first to be a thoughtful, high-minded ruler who means what he says when he asks al-Rida to succeed him as caliph. But then, as the Shi'ite view of history requires, he turns out to be a scheming monster who poisons al-Rida when the imam's superior virtue threatens to undermine his authority.

During Ramadan 2006, Arab viewers gathered to watch a Jordanian-produced mini-series about the same characters and events. Titled *The Sons of Rashid: al-Amin and al-Ma'mun*, the series was acclaimed—and attacked—for breaking new ground in the way it represented historical figures.[114] If the series has a hero, it is al-Ma'mun, played with fresh-faced earnestness by Iyad Nassar. The series depicts him as a sincere seeker of truth and portrays his most dangerous rivals, the literalist Hadith-scholars, as self-righteous zealots. But it seems less interested in glorifying al-Ma'mun than in representing different points of view as sympathetically as possible. Many Arab historical series represent non-Arabs as sinister and dangerous, but in *The Sons of Rashid* al-Ma'mun complains of the prejudice he suffers because his mother is Persian. His brother al-Amin, played with self-absorbed poutiness by Mundhir Rayahina, is openly homosexual, and the series even suggests that he should never have been forced to marry and father a child. Most strikingly, the series portrays al-Ma'mun as misguided in his attempts to force philosophic reason down the throats of the Hadith-scholars. Some viewers were impressed: *The Sons of Rashid* won first prize for historical drama at the twelfth Cairo Radio and Television Festival in 2006.[115] But others were indignant. Shi'ite scholars, for example, remonstrated with the producers for showing al-Rida on screen: in the Iranian series, the imam's head is obscured by a halo.[116] Meanwhile, a family claiming descent from the 'Abbasid caliphs protested the depiction of their ancestors as wine-drinking, music-loving hedonists.[117]

---

114 *Abna' al-Rashid: al-Amin wa'l-Ma'mun* directed by Shawqi al-Majiri, from a script by Ghassan Zakariyya and Ghazi al-Diba (Amman: Arab Telemedia Group, 2006). I thank Awad Awad for telling me about this series and Abdulkareem Said Ramadan for bringing me a copy of it.

115 http://www.aawsat.com/details.asp?section=54&article=393635&issueno=10224

116 http://www.diwanalarab.com/spip.php?article6478

117 http://www.bawazir.com/Abbasid-caliphate/abbasids-objection-mbc.htm. I thank Elizabeth Buckner for this reference.

Both *The Rule of Love* and *The Sons of Rashid* claim to be based on pre-modern sources: that is, on books like the *History of Prophets and Kings* by al-Tabari, a massive Arabic work that claims to cover human affairs from the Creation down to the lifetime of the author, who died in 923 AD.[118] The Iranian series even lists the major chronicles of the period in the credits. For some audiences, such trappings of authenticity are convincing enough: Iranian and Arab viewers alike have reassured me, in all seriousness, that the series in their particular language happens to be historically accurate. To be sure, both productions do draw on the historical tradition, which does indeed say that al-Amin loved his male slave Kawthar, and that al-Ma'mun was a bookworm and a rationalist. But enormous liberties—whether for practical or ideological reasons—are taken by both productions. Given the nature of visual narrative, it is hard to see how it could be otherwise.[119] And, even if one had no access to the original Arabic sources, one has only to compare the two series' treatments of the same characters and incidents to realize that they cannot both be right about what really happened.

Despite their wildly different takes on their subject, the two productions nevertheless have one thing in common: their faithfulness to a tradition of historical representation pioneered by the Lebanese journalist, historian, and novelist Jurji Zaidan (1861-1914). Zaidan, the son of a Beiruti restaurateur, hoped at first to be a doctor and enrolled at the Syrian Protestant College (later the American University of Beirut). After he took part in protests against the dismissal of an advocate of Darwinism, classes came to a standstill and he decided to emigrate to Egypt. He also traveled to the Sudan and England before settling in Cairo, where he founded the influential journal *al-Hilal* (*The Crescent*). His name is indelibly associated with the Arab literary renaissance (*nahda*) of the nineteenth and early

118 This work is the major literary source for early Islamic history. It has been translated into English as *The History of al-Tabari*, in 38 volumes (Albany: SUNY, 1985-1999). Volume 31, *The War Between Brothers*, translated and annotated by Michael Fishbein (Albany: SUNY, 1992), deals with the period Zaidan describes in *The Caliph's Heirs*.

119 See, for example, Rosenstone, Robert, *Visions of the Past. The Challenge of Film to Our Idea of History* (Cambridge: Harvard, 1995); Natalie Zemon Davis, *Slaves on Screen: Film and Historical Vision* (Cambridge: Harvard, 2000); and the Review of Davis by Rosenstone, "Does a filmic writing of history exist?" in *History and Theory, Theme Issue* 41 (2002): 134-44 (I thank Mohsen Ashtiany for this reference). I have dealt at length with the Iranian series and its relationship to the sources in a forthcoming article: "Al-Ma'mūn and 'Alī al-RiÃā (Emam Reza) on Iranian Television," in *The Rhetoric of Biography: Narrating Lives in Persianate Societies*, ed. Louise Marlow (Washington, DC: Center for Hellenic Studies, 2011).

twentieth centuries.[120] In 1891, he published the first of his historical novels. Eventually he published twenty-two of them, including *al-Amin wa al-Ma'mun* (1907), translated here as *The Caliph's Heirs*. Together, the novels cover 'the history of the Arabs' from ancient Arabia down to the Ottoman period.[121] Continuously reprinted, they have probably done more than any other single source to create the modern Arab sense of what the past was like. Translated into such languages as Persian, Ottoman Turkish, Hindi, and Uzbek, they have also influenced—if not helped create—enduring images of Arab and Islamic history in non-Arab nations such as Iran.[122]

Zaidan's enormous influence does not of course mean that he got the history right. Arguably, he did not even try to get it right, at least not in his novels. History proper was the subject of a separate work, *The History of Islamic Civilization*.[123] Therefore, one should not read *The Caliph's Heirs*, or any other Zaidan novel, in the hope of discovering what really happened. But the novels do tell us something about what Zaidan and other historians of his day *thought* the past was like. Moreover, their power as novels, especially for readers who already know something about the periods he is writing about, has much to do with their manipulation of the scenes, events, and figures supplied by the Arabic sources. For that reason, it is worth looking briefly at what modern historians have to say about the period Zaidan writes about in this novel.

From a distance, the early 'Abbasid period—from the founding of Baghdad in 762 to the coming of the Buyids in 945 AD (among other possible dates)—deserves the commonly applied label of 'the golden age.'[124] The empire extended, at least theoretically, from Ifriqiya (now Libya) in the west to Sind (now Pakistan) in the east. The capital, Baghdad, traded with the world, welcoming Greek philosophy, Persian cuisine, Indian mathematics, Chinese paper, and many other things besides. There was no

120 On Zaidan's career see *The Autobiography of Jurji Zaidan*, edited and translated by Thomas Philipp (Washington, DC: Three Continents, 1990); and Thomas Philipp, *Gurgi Zaidan: His Life and Thought* (Wiesbaden: Steiner, 1979); Wiebke Walther, "Zaydan, Djurdji," in *The Encyclopaedia of Islam, Second Edition*, ed. P. Bearman et al., 11: 476.

121 See further Thomas Philipp, "Approaches to history in the work of Jurji Zaydan," *Journal of Asian and African Studies* 9 (1973): 63-85.

122 On Iran see Kamran Rastegar, "Literary Modernity between Arabic and Persian Prose: Jurji Zaydan's *Riwayat* in Persian Translation," in *Comparative Critical Studies* 4 (2007): 359-378.

123 *Tarikh al-tamaddun al-islami*, 5 vols. (Cairo: Hilal, 1901-1906). Volume 4 has been translated as *Umayyads and 'Abbásids* by D. S. Margoliouth (Leiden: Brill, 1907).

124 On the period in general, see Amira Bennison, *The Great Caliphs* (New Haven: Yale, 2010).

generally accepted authority to tell people what to think, and a hundred controversies bloomed. In the Arabic writing of the period, it is often possible to see what "bliss in that dawn it was to be alive." But it is equally possible to find the people of the age, indifferent to the role later generations would assign them, bemoaning the sufferings visited on them as the result of disasters both natural and manmade. Even Baghdad, the "rock of the caliphate," as one writer called it, was not spared. The most harrowing of its many ordeals—according, at any rate, to the tenth-century chronicler al-Mas'udi—was the civil war between al-Amin and al-Ma'mun.[125]

In 809, the Caliph al-Rashid, once famous in the West as the hero of the *Thousand and One Nights*, died while on campaign against rebels in the east. With him on the campaign was his son al-Ma'mun, who assumed governance of Khurasan, the great eastern province of the empire. A second son, al-Amin, had remained behind in Baghdad, and it was he who succeeded his father as caliph. The relationship between the brothers quickly deteriorated. Al-Ma'mun began calling himself 'imam' or 'rightly guided and rightly guiding leader.' He also began winning the local Iranian and Turkic princes of the region to his side and with their help recruited an army of his own. Amin, for his part, broke the succession agreement by naming his infant son as his heir apparent.

At least, so the sources tell us. One modern historian, Tayeb El-Hibri, has argued that the Arabic chronicles were revised after the civil war to put the blame for it on al-Amin rather than al-Ma'mun.[126] And, as El-Hibri has also argued, the historians often seem to be less concerned with literal truth than with telling a good story to illustrate a point.[127] Did Zubayda, al-Amin's mother, pressure al-Rashid to make her son his heir against his better judgment? Was al-Ma'mun really a philosopher-king in the making, passed over because his mother was a Persian and not an Arab? Did al-Amin really spend fortunes on boats shaped like various animals, and set fire to the tax records just for fun? Or did historians put these stories together to make sense of events that seemed larger than life? Whatever the case, Zaidan had no choice but to use the material the sources provided him. He seems to have

---

125 For more detail on these chroniclers, and references to their works, see Michael Cooperson, "Baghdad in Rhetoric and Narrative," *Muqarnas* 13 (1996): 99-113.

126 Tayeb El-Hibri, "Harun Al-Rashid and the Mecca protocol of 802: A plan for division or succession?" *International Journal of Middle Eastern Studies,* 24 (1992): 461-480.

127 Tayeb El-Hibri, *Reinterpreting Islamic Historiography. Harun al-Rashid and the Narrative of the 'Abbasid caliphate* (Cambridge, 1999).

taken it more or less at face value, though his respect for the sources did not prevent him from making up a good many stories of his own.

In his own effort to make sense of the civil war, Zaidan seized on an element that is present, though not conspicuous, in the chronicles. Whatever else it may have been, the civil war was a war between Baghdad and Khurasan. For many observers, Baghdad was Arab and Muslim, while Khurasan was non-Arab and only tenuously Muslim. For Zaidan, as for many historians, the civil war was thus a national conflict between Arabs and Persians. At the same time, it was a religious conflict, since the Arabs were Sunnis and the Persians Shi'ites. This way of looking at things is not entirely wrong, but it suffers from one major drawback: the labels it relies on meant something quite different in the ninth century than they do today. The people of Khurasan, for example, were not Persians in the modern sense. Many were of Iranian and Turkic descent, many were descendants of the Arabs who had settled there in Umayyad times, and some were of mixed ancestry. There is no reason to assume that any great number of them were Persians in the strict sense, that is, natives of Fars, the southwestern province of what is today Iran. In the ninth century, someone from Fars was a Persian and someone from Khurasan was a Khurasani. Both might be 'ajam, that is, people who spoke Arabic badly, or not at all. But they did not necessarily imagine themselves as belonging to a single people.

Equally problematic is the term 'Shi'ite.' Zaidan assumed that Persian nationalism and Shi'ite sectarianism went hand in hand, since both were opposed to the dominant Sunni Arab authority. As the historian Patricia Crone has recently argued, this view is not entirely mistaken, provided one understands that both Sunnism and Shi'ism were still works in progress, and differed in important ways from their modern descendants.[128] Al-Ma'mun, for example, was technically a Shi'ite, though no Shi'ite today would recognize him as such. As far as we can tell, he agreed with other Shi'ites that the leader of the Muslim community must be a member of the Prophet's family. But he also happened to think that the best qualified branch of the family was the 'Abbasid branch—that is, his own family—and that he himself was the rightly guided imam of the age.[129] This idea

---

128 Patricia Crone, *God's Rule: Government and Islam. Six Centuries of Medieval Islamic Political Thought* (New York: Columbia, 2005), 84-86.

129 See Patricia Crone and Martin Hinds, *God's Caliph: Religious authority in the first centuries of Islam* (Cambridge, 1986); Albert Arazi and 'Amikam El'ad, "'L'Epître à l'armée': al-Ma'mun et la seconde da'wa," *Studia Islamica* 66 (1987): 27-70 and 67 (1988): 29-73.

has no modern advocates, whether in Zaidan's time or in ours; and so it is hardly surprising to find it passed over in the novel. Even so, it is arguably central to understanding why al-Ma'mun acted as he did.

Whatever the role played by ethnic and religious identifications, it is clear enough that the civil war was a struggle between the center and the provinces—or, to be exact, the center and one extremely large and powerful province. But if there were political and economic reasons for the split, Zaidan is unconcerned with them. For him, the fight was about Persians seeking revenge on Arabs. To his credit, he makes the Persian side seem sympathetic: Behzad, the hero, is not only a fanatical Persian nationalist but also an honorable man with a genuine grievance. Unfortunately, such broad-mindedness is no longer the norm. In scholarly as well as popular Arabic writing, the decline of the 'Abbasids is often 'explained' as the work of malicious Persians. And in modern Iraqi parlance, Sunnis often denounce their fellow Iraqi Shi'ite using derogatory terms for Persians, including 'Magians,' that is, Zoroastrians.[130]

For all these reasons, *The Caliph's Heirs* can hardly be taken as a reliable source of information on the early 'Abbasid age. But for anyone familiar with the period, one of the great pleasures of the novel lies in Zaidan's reworking of the sources at his disposal. Only a true connoisseur of Arabic literature could have taken the scene, invented by medieval storytellers, of the meeting between al-Rashid and 'Abbada, the mother of his deposed vizier, and used it as the model for two entirely invented confrontations between 'Abbada and al-Rashid's widow Zubayda. Only a gifted novelist could have contrived the scene where al-Ma'mun's young daughter Zaynab confronts her uncle, the drunken and feckless al-Amin, and makes him feel ashamed of himself. And only a clever storyteller could have taken a circumstance that frustrates all students of this period—the fact that half the men alive at the time seem to be named al-Fadl—and exploited it to construct a Delphic prediction about the end of the war.

Admittedly, Zaidan's techniques of historical reconstruction are not entirely original. Many of them come from the work of Walter Scott (d. 1832), the inventor of the modern historical novel.[131] Like Scott, Zaidan chose what he considered to be pivotal moments in the history

---

130 Hassan Hussein, "Shu'ūbiyyah and Iranians in Contemporary Arabic Literature," paper delivered at the conference of the International Society for Iranian Studies, May 28, 2010.

131 For an illuminating discussion of Scott see Georg Lukács, *The Historical Novel*, tr. Hannah Mitchell and Stanley Mitchell (Lincoln University of Nebraska Press, 1983), 19-88. I thank Stuart Semmel for drawing this argument to my attention.

of a nation, in his case the Arabs. He then created characters to embody the forces he believed to have been at work during those moments. In *The Caliph's Heirs*, Behzad and Fatima represent the resurgence of Persian nationalism that Zaidan somewhat anachronistically believed to have been at work in the early ninth century. But Zaidan, like Scott, did not believe that history consisted only in the doings of the high and mighty. Rather, he realized that history might be equally if not better represented by looking at the lives of ordinary people. Since, however, the sources tell us little about peasants, tradesmen, and the like, it was necessary to create such people, which Zaidan unrepentantly did. His creations include many women characters; and if some are rather too helpless for modern taste, many—including Zaynab, 'Abbada, and Fatima in *The Caliph's Heirs*—are not. The novels also feature—or at least mention—people of many ethnicities and religions. *The Caliph's Heirs*, for instance, gives us a Christian tavern keeper, a Sabean sorceror, and a host of Persians. This variety reflects historical reality: ninth-century Baghdad, where the novel is set, was home to speakers of Aramaic and Persian as well as Arabic; to Jews (both Karaite and Rabbinite), Christians (both Nestorian and Jacobite), Zoroastrians, and Sabeans as well as Muslims; and to Iranians, Turks, Slavs, Greeks, East Africans, and Berbers as well as Arabs.[132] Modern Arabic historical drama tends to ignore this diversity. Zaidan, however, reveled in it.

Like Scott, finally, Zaidan strove to create an atmosphere of documentary authenticity. His detailed descriptions of buildings and costumes are often taken directly from the chronicles. His achievement in this respect is all the more impressive given the relatively few published sources at his disposal. When he is able to work in a fragment of popular culture— the cry of the Baghdad fish-mongers, for example, or a catalog of weapons used by gangsters—his delight is palpable. Admittedly, today's readers are unlikely to be taken in: with their romantic effusions, Zaidan's characters clearly belong to the nineteenth century rather than the ninth. But even in the mid-twentieth century, Zaidan could still hold his readers spellbound. In *Mashalla Khan at the Court of Harun al-Rashid*, the Persian comic novelist Iraj Pezeshkzad tells the story of a bank clerk so enamored of Zaidan's

---

132 For an exploration of this diversity, albeit at an earlier period, see Michael G. Morony, *Iraq after the Muslim conquest* (Princeton, 1984).

novels that he actually travels back in time to the court of the 'Abbasid caliph.[133]

In some ways, Zaidan's novels are easy to translate. In his time, traditional Arabic writing had come to seem top-heavy with wordplay and allusion. Arab writers, complained the Egyptian novelist Muhammad Husayn Haykal in 1914, did not care what they said, only how they said it. Breaking with tradition, Haykal, Zaidan, and other pioneers of the so-called *nahda* or 'Arabic cultural revival' made a point of writing in a plain, unadorned style. A century later, the *nahda* style in turn seems a bit musty: twenty-first century Arabic writing, especially journalism, is so heavily influenced by English that Zaidan's purely Arabic turns of phrase have become almost archaic. But his language still flows. In his autobiography, he tells us that the first stories he heard were those told by storytellers performing in the streets of Beirut. This is easy to believe: no matter what the scene he sets himself to depict, some memory of the spoken voice seems to guide his pen.

Even so, there are difficulties. The modern standard Arabic that Zaidan helped create has the advantage of being equally comprehensible to all educated speakers, no matter their native dialect. But it has the corresponding disadvantage of being a contrived language that no one speaks except on special occasions. As the language of formal communication, it draws on a rich tradition of figurative expressions and rhetorical devices whose equivalents belong to a different register in English. Translated literally, it can come across as stilted and unnatural. This is a real problem for translators of contemporary Arabic literature, but it is less of an issue here: a century-old novel sounds quite plausible when recast into a formal register of English. Ideally, perhaps, one might have tried putting the whole novel into the style of Walter Scott; but that would be a parlor trick rather than a translation.

If formality makes narrative hard to translate, it makes dialogue almost impossible. I have let the characters sound as formal in English as they do in Arabic, though I have tried at least to make their speech proceed in natural-seeming rhythms. One problem is nevertheless insuperable: since they all use the same formal register, all Zaidan's characters sound alike. The bandit chief speaks in the same measured tones as the Caliph's physician, and the captain of a riverboat uses the same vocabulary as a highborn lady.

---

133 Iraj-e Pezeshkzad, *Mashallah Khan dar Bargah-e Harun al-Rashid* (Los Angeles: Nashr-e Kitab, 1996).

Admittedly, it is not easy to see how Zaidan could have done any better. The sources rarely tell us how ninth-century people really spoke, and even when they do, the expressions quoted often make little sense to modern readers. The only obvious way for Zaidan to have differentiated the speech of different characters would have been to resort to dialect. Unfortunately, written dialect is just as annoying to read in Arabic as it is in English. The result, in any case, is that Zaidan's characters sound more or less the same; and there is not much a translator can do about that.

A number of points must be made regarding transliteration, Arabic names, and titles. This series follows a simplified version of the transliteration system used by scholars writing in English. It shows *hamza* and *'ayn* but not long vowels or emphatic consonants. The *hamza*, indicated by an apostrophe, is a glottal stop, the sound in the middle of 'uh oh!'. The *'ayn*, indicated by a reverse apostrophe, is like the vowel sound 'ahh,' but made deep in the throat; it can be produced by saying 'aah!' while pressing one's chin down to one's chest. The long vowels and emphatic consonants are equally important to the proper pronunciation of Arabic, but the effort necessary to indicate them seemed unwarranted in a work intended for non-specialists. There are two divergences from this system. A character named Harsh is here called Harch, since Harsh, being an English word in its own right, seemed a misleading and distracting choice. And Jurji Zaidan's name is so spelt even though the standard system would require him to be Zaydan.

Many of the names in this book consist of two or more parts. A common prefix is al-, meaning 'the.' Al-Amin means 'the trustworthy one,' and al-Ma'mun means 'the trusted one.' By convention, al- is spelled with a lower-case a except at the beginning of a sentence. Ibn means 'son of' and Umm 'mother of.' Because they are meaningful, these elements cannot be dropped: Umm Ja'far, for example, is quite a different person than Ja'far. A few of the characters have more than one name. I have generally used only one, though I have retained the variant name if it is meaningful in context. 'Abbada, for example, is occasionally called Umm al-Rashid, 'mother of al-Rashid.' One scene requires her to use this name and no other, so I have retained it there. One character, finally, goes by two distinct names because he is a double agent. In his case I have had to use both names, just as in the original.

Another problem is that of titles. I have tried to treat the word 'caliph,' which refers to the ruler of the 'Abbasid empire, like 'king' in English: capitalized when it refers to a particular person and not capitalized when it refers to the office (as in 'The colonists rebelled against King George' versus 'They no longer wanted a king'). I have treated comparable titles similarly. I have left one title, Malfan, untranslated, since its meaning ('teacher') would not be used as a title in English. The series editors of the Zaidan Foundation have made every effort to make the text clear and consistent, for which I am most grateful; any remaining errors and infelicities are my responsibility.

It is a pleasure to thank George Zaidan for his sponsorship of this series and his tireless attention to every detail of the translation. I am grateful, as so often, to William Granara, this time for proposing that I undertake this volume. I thank Rahim Shayegan for his help with Sasanian references, Joseph Lowry for explaining a legal term, and Yona Sabar, along with several members of Middle East Medievalists, for help with Syriac.

The Caliph's Heirs

Study Guide

Michael Cooperson

1. Who is a caliph?

A caliph is a leader or ruler. In the 630s and 640s AD, many parts of North Africa and Southwest Asia were conquered and came under the control of the Arabs. The Arabs brought a new religion, Islam. ('Islam' means 'submission to God' and those who accept Islam are called 'Muslims.') The head of the Muslim community, and thus the titular ruler of the territories conquered by the Arabs, was called the caliph.

The English word 'caliph' comes from an Arabic word that means 'representative' or 'successor.' Many historians think that the title originally meant 'representative of God' but was later understood to mean 'successor of the Prophet Muhammad.' (Muhammad, who died in 632 AD, was the prophet who brought the religion of Islam to the Arabs.) The caliphs were responsible for collecting taxes, enforcing the law, and defending Muslims against their enemies.

The first person to hold the title of caliph was Muhammad's friend Abu Bakr, who ruled from 632 to 644 AD. The last caliph was Sultan Abdulmecid II (pronounced "Abdulmajid the Second") who ruled the Ottoman Empire from 1922 to 1924.

2. Who is the caliph in this story?

The first caliph in this story is Harun al-Rashid, whose name means "Aaron the Righteous." He ruled from 786 to 809 AD. During his reign, Muslims controlled a territory that extended from Spain to northern India. Al-Rashid's capital, Baghdad, was a famously wealthy city that attracted physicians, philosophers, astronomers, translators, and men of religion, as well as singers, musicians, and entertainers of all kinds. Later generations remembered al-Rashid's reign as a golden age.

3. Who are 'the Caliph's heirs'?

Al-Rashid had two sons, al-Ma'mun and al-Amin. Al-Ma'mun was six months older than al-Amin. Normally, the older son might be expected to become caliph after his father's death. But al-Ma'mun's mother was a slave. Al-Amin's mother, on the other hand, was a member of the ruling family. For this reason, it seems, al-Rashid chose al-Amin as his successor. But he appointed al-Ma'mun as governor of Khurasan, a large province in the eastern part of the empire. He also named him successor to al-Amin.

In 809 AD, al-Rashid died. As expected, al-Amin became caliph, while al-Ma'mun became governor of Khurasan. Soon, however, the two brothers quarreled. It is not entirely clear who was at fault. But the disagreement between them soon lead to a civil war, with both sides claiming to be supporting the rightful leader of the Muslim community.

4. Who is the author of this book?

Jurji Zaidan was born in Beirut, Lebanon, in 1861. His family was poor and Jurji had to work to support himself and so he only received a rudimentary primary education at school. But he was an avid reader and was able on his own to prepare for and pass the entrance exam to the Syrian Protestant College which later became the American University of Beirut. When one of his professors was dismissed for teaching the theories of Darwin, Zaidan joined a protest strike and, when classes were suspended, decided to leave the College and move to Cairo, Egypt, where he began a career as a journalist, novelist, and historian.

Zaidan is considered a major figure in the nineteenth-century revival of Arabic literary and intellectual life. This revival, called the *nahda* (which means something like 'rise' or 'rebirth' in Arabic), aimed at creating a new sense of identity and common purpose among Arabs. During Zaidan's lifetime, most Arabs were subjects of the Ottoman Empire. Like members of other ethnic groups, however, they had begun to think of themselves as belonging to a distinct people. Many, therefore, wanted to break free of the Ottoman Empire and live in a nation (or nations) of their own.

Zaidan, like many other Arab Christian thinkers of his time and since, promoted a secular brand of Arab nationalism. For him, an Arab was anyone who spoke Arabic. He recognized the importance of Islamic civilization, but he did not define its accomplishments only in religious terms. And he gave Arab history and the Arabic language an identity that was related to but distinct from Islamic history and civilization.

Zaidan died in 1914. Ten years later, the Ottoman Empire had collapsed, and a number of new Arab territories came into being. But these territories were still not free: they were dominated, and in some cases occupied, by European powers. In the course of the twentieth century, all of them achieved independence. To one extent or another, all of them subscribe to an ideology of Arab nationalism that owes a great deal to Zaidan and other *nahda* thinkers.

As we now know, Zaidan's understanding of Arab identity and Islamic history is only one of many ways in which we might think about the past. Even so, his definitions have come to seem natural to many people all over the world.

5. Why did Zaidan write this book?

Zaidan believed that it was important for Arabs to understand their history. But in the late nineteenth century, there were few books of history for them to read. In earlier times, authors had written many chronicles (lists of events arranged by year) in Arabic. But most of these were still in manuscript: that is, they existed only in the form of a few handwritten copies, not as printed books that anyone could buy. Also, the chronicles were difficult to read. Many of the events being described no longer made sense, and the Arabic language they used was unfamiliar to most readers.

To address these problems, Zaidan did two things. First, he used the chronicles to write his own five-volume history of what he called 'Islamic civilization.' Second, he wrote a series of twenty-two novels covering the whole span of Arab and Islamic history. Both the history and the novels are written in a fresh, clear style that attracted readers who would not have been able to read the old Arabic chronicles. Although Zaidan's novels are full of romantic adventures, they were meant not simply to entertain his readers but also and especially to make the study of history more enjoyable.

By inventing imaginary characters—a device he seems to have picked up from the historical novelist Walter Scott (d. 1832)—Zaidan allowed himself to address a broad range of issues. In particular, he was able to give a prominent place to women. Women do appear in the chronicles, but they play a decidedly secondary role. In Zaidan's novels, the women are as important and as active as the men. In *The Caliph's Heirs*, a bereaved widow named 'Abbada, a governess named Dananir, and a girl named Zaynab all play major roles in the action.

Zaidan's novels were very successful and remain popular to this day. They are still in print in Arabic, and they have been translated into many other languages, including Persian, Ottoman Turkish, and Uzbek. Today, many Arabs and Muslims imagine their own history in terms borrowed directly or indirectly from Zaidan. Even people who have never read him are exposed to his ideas through movies and television, which often follow his example by representing the past in a colorful, romantic manner.

6. What did Zaidan believe about the Caliph al-Rashid and his heirs?

Zaidan believed that the war between al-Amin and al-Ma'mun was a war between Arabs and Persians. The Persians, he thought, resented being conquered by the Arabs. They wanted to overthrow their Arab rulers and bring back their own empire, which had ruled the region in ancient times. The 'Abbasid dynasty, which came to power in 750 AD owed its ascendancy to a Persian strategist named Abu Muslim, who was nevertheless executed by the Caliph al-Mansur. During the reign of al-Rashid, another Persian, a man named Ja'far, of the Barmakid family, became the caliph's vizier or chief adviser. According to the story Zaidan tells in another novel, Ja'far became a threat to al-Rashid, who had him executed. In *The Caliph's Heirs*, the Persians seek revenge for Abu Muslim and Ja'far. This time, their plan is to bring about a civil war between al-Amin and al-Ma'mun, and to help al-Ma'mun, whose mother was a Persian, defeat his brother.

For the Persians in the story, the struggle for national independence goes hand in hand with commitment to Shi'ite Islam. Shi'ite Muslims believe that the leadership of the Muslim community after the Prophet's death should have fallen not to Abu Bakr but to 'Ali ibn Abi Talib, the Prophet's cousin and son-in-law. They also believe that certain descendants of 'Ali have a special God-given ability to tell other Muslims what is right. These men, called imams ("guides" or "leaders" in Arabic), should have been chosen to lead the community. Unfortunately, say Shi'ites, most Muslims made the mistake of appointing caliphs instead. Many Shi'ites have therefore rebelled against the caliphs. Because of the connection between Shi'ism and rebellion, Zaidan thought it made sense for all his Persian characters to be Shi'ites.

7. Did Zaidan get the history right?

In all his novels, Zaidan uses the events of history to set the stage. In *The Caliph's Heirs*, al-Amin, al-Ma'mun, and their viziers, are real characters. But most of the other characters, all of the dialogue, and almost all of the incidents in the story are the products of the author's imagination. In some cases, Zaidan mentions an incident or detail of daily life and then adds a reference to one of the chronicles or to his own history of Islamic civilization. Even then, however, we cannot be certain that the detail is true. All we can say is that the chroniclers *thought* it was true, which is a different thing.

As for *why* things happened, Zaidan's idea that the events of the civil war come down to a fight between two ethnic groups is too simple to be entirely true. Modern historians might accept the idea that ethnicity played some role in the conflict between the Caliph's heirs. But they would argue that economic and other social factors must have played a role too. Also, they would point out that ethnic identifications change over time. What Zaidan understood by 'Arab' and 'Persian' in the year 1900 was quite different from what people meant by those terms in the year 800 AD. Similarly, the idea of national liberation is a modern one. There is evidence that some Iranians (the modern term for the ethnic group that includes Persians) in the age of al-Rashid resented Arab rule and wanted to bring back their ancient empire. But Zaidan's characters speak entirely in the language of nineteenth-century nationalist struggle—that is, in the language of the author himself.

The same holds true for what Zaidan says about religion. Today, Shi'ism is the official religion of Iran, where most speakers of Persian live. In Zaidan's time, too, many Persian speakers were Shi'ites. Like many other historians of the time, Zaidan assumed that this particular connection between ethnicity and religion was absolute and eternal. But the reality is different. Not all Persians are Shi'ites, nor are all Shi'ites Persians, whether now or in the past. Also, there are many kinds of Shi'ites, and not all of them fought against the caliphs. Thus the novel should not be taken as a reliable guide to political and religious conflict during the period it describes. For more detail on these points, see the translator's Afterword.

Other questions to keep in mind when reading *The Caliph's Heirs*

1. Many readers of the novel would have known how the story turns out: that is, who won the battle between al-Amin and al-Ma'mun. But the novel still manages to create suspense. How?

2. Like the novels of Charles Dickens, *The Caliph's Heirs* originally appeared in separate episodes printed in a newspaper. How does Zaidan keep the action moving forward across episodes? Can you find places where he slips up—that is, forgets to explain something, or has characters do something inconsistent?

3. Many of the characters in *The Caliph's Heirs* are identified as Persians or as members of minority religions. How does Zaidan treat these characters? What about characters who are *not* identified as belonging to a religious or ethnic group?

4. Zaidan's novels are based on the idea that a specific national group, the Arabs, have participated in something called Islamic civilization. Does this idea make sense? How does the novel support it? In what ways does it undermine it?

5. Like the press in many countries during Zaidan's time, the Arabic press helped readers create an image of themselves as citizens; as members of national, ethnic, or religious groups; and as men and women with specific gender roles. In what ways might *The Caliph's Heirs* have helped shape its readers?

OTHER RESOURCES

Bennison, Amira. *The Great Caliphs*. New Haven: Yale, 2010.

Cooperson, Michael. *Al Ma'mun* (Oxford: One World Books, 2005).

Crone, Patricia. *God's Rule: Government and Islam. Six Centuries of Medieval Islamic Political Thought*. New York: Columbia, 2005.

Thomas, Philipp. *Gurji Zaidan. His Life and Thought*. Wiesbaden, Germany: Steiner Verlag, 1979.

Philipp, Thomas. *Jurji Zaidan's Secular Analysis of History and Language as Foundations of Arab Nationalism.* (forthcoming).

Zaidan, Jurji, *The Autobiography of Jurji Zaidan* edited and translated by Thomas Philip, Washington DC: Three Continents Press, 1990.

Zaidan, Jurji. *The Caliph's Sister; Harun al-Rashid and the Fall of the Persians* translated into English by Issa J. Boulatta and published by The Zaidan Foundation as part of this series.

CPSIA information can be obtained at www.ICGtesting.com
Printed in the USA
LVOW11s1518210815

450813LV00003B/79/P